D1596295

OUT AND IN

A mystery-thriller

PAT DUNLAP EVANS

PUBLISHER'S NOTES

Copyright © 2016 Pat Dunlap Evans.

Cover redesign May 4, 2023 by Pam Boyd Roberts

Minor text revisions, May 27, 2023.

Cover Photo: © Svetography / Shutterstock

ISBN: 978-0-9968822-2-4 (Print Paperback)

ISBN: 978-0-9968822-3-1 (Kindle))

ISBN: 978-0-9968822-5-5 (E-Pub)

DEDICATION

For my children, grandchildren, great-grandchildren, and those yet to come. Thanks for being my family.

Chapter One

ALONE IN MY CELL

The worst part about being in jail is you can't leave. That may sound silly, but I've had claustrophobia since childhood. Being locked inside anything sends waves of panic through my soul.

I pace and try to focus. At least my cell has a high window where I can stare at the sky and watch for clouds and birds. That's the only reason I have not yet gone loony. But my neck is getting sore from the strain. I refuse to lie down on that steel bed.

I'm waiting for Ryan to get me out on bail. How I wound up in jail astonishes me. This morning, Detective David Reed of the Dallas Police Department showed up at my house with a search warrant, and asked me to come downtown to answer a few questions.

"What about?" I asked blindly.

"Well, you heard about the murder of Luca Scarlatti."

"It's all over the morning news on TV."

"You are a person of interest."

"A person of interest? I don't know anything about Luca's murder. I only heard about it this morning."

"Mrs. Donovan, I can cuff you. Or you can walk to my car on your own two feet. Which would you prefer?"

I shouted down the hall to my twin sons, who staggered out to see what the ruckus was about. Both looked hungover.

"Boys, call Ryan Ingles. Tell him I need an attorney. Now."

"Mrs. Donovan, you have the right to have your attorney present. I'll let you make a call as soon as we get downtown."

"Am I under arrest?"

"Not yet, but we have a search warrant and want to analyze a few things," Detective Reed replied.

Two other police officers then went inside and headed straight for my bedroom.

"Where are they going?"

"Ma'am, we have a search warrant."

"Then search the house. I'm fine with that. But why do I have to come with you?"

"Mrs. Donovan, if you prefer I arrest you, I will do so. But I'd rather we handle this the easy way. Less paperwork."

After a suffocating, anxiety-producing ride downtown in the back seat of the detective's car, I was led into a stark green interview room with a gray metal table, four metal chairs, and a gigantic mirror that I presumed from seeing so many crime shows was actually where the district attorney and whoever else peered at me—a person of interest.

I paced and paced. It seemed like an hour before Detective Reed returned. He motioned me to a seat and then sat across from me. I could smell stale coffee and a breakfast taco on his breath.

"Mrs. Donovan, your fingerprints are all over the gun that shot the Maestro."

"My gun shot Luca? Impossible. It's in the trunk of my car."

"Not anymore. It's in our lab. It was found at the scene."

"Then someone stole it. And how do you have my fingerprints?"

"We took them off your cello."

"You dusted my cello?" I was appalled. "That's a very expensive instrument. I hope it's not ruined."

"I'm sure they took good care. And our search proved that some of your clothes tested positive for GSR."

"You went through my laundry?"

"Part of the job."

"What's GSR stand for?"

"Gunshot residue."

"Well, of course. I shot my gun Saturday morning. I bought it recently because of the threats. You know…about Cole and the missing Odyssey funds. One wild-eyed man showed up at our house several weeks ago. I felt very sorry for him, but I can't get his money back. I don't have any myself. Not anymore."

"You've got enough to buy an expensive weapon."

"Yes, for protection. I'm alone now."

"Poor little you."

"Yes, poor little me. I bought a gun but I didn't know how to shoot the thing. So I've been taking lessons at Dallas Gun Club. They'll tell you."

"We spoke to them. They said you left about noon on Saturday. But I want to know where you were at ten o'clock Saturday night."

"I've told you. I was at home. I practiced my cello and watched the news."

"Your twins…let's see, Avery and Shawn, right?"

"Yes."

"Were they home too?"

"For dinner. Ask them."

"We did. Avery said the two left your house about eight-thirty to go partying on Lower Greenville. They didn't get home until after midnight. Can anyone else verify that you were at home?"

"Maybe a neighbor. The elderly man who lives behind us complains when I play my cello late."

"We'll ask him. You can bet on that. Tell me again about Saturday night."

"I played my cello and watched the news. There was a story

about a restaurant that burned in Addison. Channel 8. Sally and Jonas. You know, the pretty blonde and handsome Hispanic guy?"

"Channel 8 replays the same newscast at midnight. You could have seen it then."

"I was sound asleep by midnight. Besides, why would I come home and watch the news if I had killed somebody?"

"Maybe to see if there was any news about the Maestro's murder."

"I was making a joke. I didn't kill anybody."

"Mrs. Donovan, I want to believe you, but you need to give me every detail."

"There aren't any details. After the news, I put my cello away. Then I took a bath and crawled into bed. I was exhausted. I started a new job last week at Verano Highland Park Funeral Home. My best friend Lena Verano hired me. I have to work now."

"Welcome to reality."

"This doesn't feel much like it."

"Witty gal."

I didn't answer that one, just sighed in exasperation.

"Back to Saturday night. Did you call anybody? Send e-mails or do a little Facebook?"

"No. I don't like Facebook."

"So, tell me everything you did on Saturday."

"Again? Like I said, I took a gun class Saturday morning. We practiced until noon, and then I left for a League meeting at Rebecca Claridge's house. She'll tell you, anybody there will tell you. Call Doreen Ingles or Tina LeBlanc. Call Keith Warren at the Metroplex Opera office. He brought a baritone to the meeting… can't recall his name. He was from Italy. One of Luca's pals."

"Is a baritone the high voice or the deep voice?"

"Deeper than tenor, higher than bass."

"You must know a lot about opera."

"Your question was pretty basic."

"Pardon my ignorance. I'm just a lowly public servant."

"Sorry, I'm just frustrated."

"So, Keith Warren and a baritone were at the League meeting?"

"Yes, Keith gave us an overview of rehearsals, and then the baritone sang for us. The meeting ended about five. I picked up dinner on the way home."

"What kind of dinner?"

"Chinese food. I paid with a credit card. Call Howard Wang's. They'll tell you."

"Now, what would your having Chinese food tell me?"

"That I ordered a lot of things, which means I had to lug in a big sack of three different soups, three egg rolls, a combo *lo mein*, General Tso's chicken, and Lake Ting Tung shrimp, not to mention rosy-fried bananas, three Diet Cokes, and my purse. So that meant, I left my gun bag in the trunk."

"You're implying that someone broke into your trunk?"

"They must have. How else could my gun have killed Luca?"

"That's what I can't figure. Moreover, Mrs. Donovan, I can't understand why one of your fancy hairpins was found at the scene."

I reached to see if my hairpin was in its usual place. It was. "My hairpin? Like this one?"

"Not exactly. It was fancier."

"You're saying one of my hairpins was found in Luca's condo?"

"That's right."

"But I've never been to Luca's condo. I have about twenty hairpins, most at home, a few in my purse. Here's another one, see? And there was a hairpin in my gun bag. When I went to shoot, the earmuffs didn't fit over my up-do, so I had to take my hair down and pull it back in a George Washington."

"A George Washington?"

I let down my hair and pulled it back. "A low ponytail. See? Like this."

"Very pretty. So, you're saying someone stole your gun bag, and there was a hairpin inside that someone later stabbed into the Maestro's leg?"

"Stabbed Luca's leg? What do you mean?"

"Your hairpin was stuck in the Maestro's thigh. Our lab is analyzing the pin."

"I don't understand. I've never been to Luca's house, much less put a hairpin—"

"Funny how the evidence says you were there. Your new gun killed Luca Scarlatti. Your hairpin was found in his leg."

"You've got to be kidding me."

"Nope. I'm a serious kind of guy. That's why, Marie Harris Donovan, I have no choice but to place you under arrest for the murder of Luca Scarlatti."

"But you can't. I didn't kill him."

"Mrs. Donovan, you have the right to remain silent. Anything you say may be used against you in a court of law. You have the right to consult an attorney before speaking to the police, and to have an attorney present during questioning, now or in the future. Do you understand? If you cannot afford an attorney, one will be appointed for you."

"I cannot believe this. Call Ryan Ingles."

"That's a high-priced pair of tassel-toe shoes for poor little you."

I tried to control my angry, frightened tears. "He's a friend. Ryan and Cole played college football together."

Detective Reed punched an intercom button. "Ginger! Mrs. Donovan is lawyering up. Get that hunk Ryan Ingles in here. And get another box of Kleenex. We're out again."

"Yes, Boss," Ginger sighed back through the speaker.

"Mrs. Donovan, I realize you've had a hard time, what with your husband's suicide. But you're not the only one. My wife and I lost twenty-five thousand in Odyssey."

"I had nothing to do with Odyssey. That was Cole's doing."

"Pretty Mrs. Quarterback doesn't know a thing. But somehow, you've still got that big house in Highland Park, don't you?"

I blew my nose again. "It's for sale."

"How about you send me twenty-five-K when you find a

buyer? If your husband hadn't flown off that high-rise, I would have arrested the bastard, just to give him a piece of my mind."

"Detective Reed, Cole screwed all of us. You, me, our friends, people we didn't even know. You've got to believe me. I did not know a thing about Odyssey."

"Mrs. Donovan, I've been a detective a long time, and there's only one thing I trust. Evidence. Ballistics prove that your gun killed the Maestro. Your fingerprints are all over the gun. Clothes you wore had GSR on them. Your flowery gold hairpin was stuck in the Maestro's leg, and I'll bet our forensics group will have more to say about what was on that pin besides his DNA."

"But why would I want to kill Luca?"

"A whole lot of people say you and the Maestro had a big tiff about opera finances and his sexual advances. So, the means, motive, and opportunity add up to Y.O.U."

"But this is ridiculous. No one will believe you."

"I don't think there's a jury pool in Dallas that wasn't impacted by Odyssey. Your chances are not great to squeak out of this one."

"I refuse to say another word until Ryan Ingles gets here."

"Stay mum if you want, but I'll bet Terrance Nichols will start salivating as soon as he hears about your arrest."

"Terrance Nichols is a gossip and a liar. He and the *Dallas Daily Herald* are always being sued for libel."

"But everybody reads his column, 'Out and In.' Even my wife, and she's not in your artsy-fartsy crowd. Terrance will have your arrest posted in his 'Preview' online edition by 6:00 p.m. tonight. 'Course, you'll be in the slammer."

"You mean I have to stay in jail? But I have claustrophobia. I can't stand to be trapped."

"Poor little you. You're a guest of Dallas County tonight. In Texas, you only have to see a judge within forty-eight hours." He poked the intercom button again. "Ginger! Take Mrs. Donovan to Booking. She can talk to her high-dollar attorney after we've taken her prints and pretty picture."

Chapter Two

MURDERERS' ROW

Arrested for murder? Luca was a terrible man, truly lascivious, but if I were going to kill anyone, I'd have shot my dearly departed husband long before he wound up dead on Cedar Springs Road. Cole and I…well, it's a long story.

I can see why prisoners pace. There's nothing to do but wait. Movement helps calm the panic. Good thing I'm not in the main holding cell down the hall with the prostitutes, drunks, and burglars. From my position, I can hear different accents spewing ethnic insults. Now and then a fight breaks out with high-pitched oomphs and yips. Somebody hollers for a guard who hollers back louder. Then I hear bars and doors clang, and automatic locks thump. All settles down for a while.

It's already past four. Where is Ryan? Hopefully not in court.

The female guard saunters by. I wave and smile, not a happy smile but what Terrance Nichols would describe as a "wan" smile in one of his columns. I'll bet I'm his lead story tomorrow. Poor Luca must have been the blood and guts for today's "Out and In."

I didn't get a chance to read it. I got arrested instead. Maybe the guard can bring me a copy. Most people read "Out and In" for the lies, not for the facts. Terrance rather deftly teeters on a high wire between gossip, exposé, and hard news. Society marriages, divorces, romances, bankruptcies, and arts reviews.

Here comes the guard again. First time she saw me, she did a double take and asked, "What in the hell did you do?" When I told her, "I don't know. I've done nothing wrong," she smirked, "Everybody who winds up here says that."

I broke into sobs. She handed me a tissue through the bars. As I blew my nose, I noticed genuine concern in her hazel eyes. A comfort, so I told her about the claustrophobia.

She tried to cheer me up. "Take deep breaths, but be sure to blow out just as deeply. That will relax you. Your attorney will be here soon."

"I hope so. I'm worried about spending the night."

"At this late date, you're definitely in for the night."

"Oh, gosh." I started crying again, as panic rushed through my forearms.

The guard shushed me and handed me more tissues. "Now try not to worry. This is the safest area of Dallas County Jail."

"But I can't get out!" I screamed, grabbing the bars like an angry gorilla. Too many times when I was a little girl, my big brother Owen would slam me into a closet and cackle, while I panicked in the dark. Even today, elevators are torture. Airplanes suck the life out of me unless I'm in an aisle seat.

"Here, let's talk a bit to calm you down. Where's your husband in all this? You married?"

I told her my sad story until her eyes widened like everybody's did when I said my husband's name. I could have kept that to myself, but when people find out I was married to a pro quarterback who had won two Super Bowls, they perk up.

"But Cole Donovan's the one who…" The guard caught herself.

"Yes."

"I read about him in that gossip column. What's the name?"

"You mean 'Out and In'?"

She nodded her head. "I guess that reporter will have something juicy to say tomorrow."

"Thanks for reminding me."

"Sorry. Didn't mean to rub it in."

"I need something to take my mind off being in this cage. Can you get me a copy of today's 'Out and In'? I want to see what Terrance Nichols had to say about the Maestro's murder."

"I'll see if I can lay hands on one." Then she sauntered off with a shrug and an audible, "Huh," far less impressed about my marriage after she remembered more about Cole's misdeeds.

That's the way I feel about the great quarterback too. Tainted by affiliation.

Chapter Three

INTERVIEW ROOM "C"

"Marie, what in the hell?" Ryan Ingles all but shouted as he strode into an interview room later that first day, looking and sounding like the hero I so desperately needed.

I was thrilled he had come to my aid, but I hated for Ryan to see me like this, a physical, emotional wreck. I was overwhelmed with embarrassment, having to ask for help from a man I'd seen over the past ten years at every opera performance and fundraising event. Not to mention our college football days in Austin, when Cole and Ryan played on the same team, and I cheered on the same squad as Ryan's then girlfriend Doreen, my nemesis and the main reason we weren't close back then or years later as adults. Doreen is simply a bitch.

"Marie, this arrest is absurd. I'll try to get you out on bail first thing tomorrow morning. Hopefully the judge didn't lose a bundle in Odyssey."

Odyssey again. No one lets up. Tears started running, and I couldn't stop the river.

Ryan handed me a hanky from his breast pocket. "Sorry, Marie, I know this is terrible for you, especially after Cole… Doreen sent a bouquet for his service. Hopefully, you saw it. We were there too."

"Lena Verano hid me and the boys behind curtains. There were all sorts of threats. Still are."

Ryan extended his big hands and took mine. I felt kindness beneath his coarse masculinity but I also felt awful to be so needy. Especially since I've never even invited Ryan and Doreen to dinner. This goes back.

Years before, Ryan was senior middle linebacker on the same championship team Cole quarterbacked as a sophomore. That next spring, Ryan was drafted by the Atlanta Falcons, but he got hurt in training camp. A knee, or so we heard.

Cole played two more years in college, then six years with the Portland Explorers. After we returned to Dallas, we ran into Ryan and Doreen at opera events. Cole even sold Ryan on Odyssey.

That's why Cole insisted, "We've got to have 'Diver' over. He's invested a chunk."

Diver was the team's nickname for Ryan's thick prescription face mask he had worn on field, coupled with his diving pursuits of quarterbacks. But you might say I fumbled Cole's dinner pass. I've always had a chemical reaction to Doreen, one of those instant dislikes when you simply hate everything about someone. Her hair, her bug eyes, her incessant cackle.

I've always avoided Doreen like cancer. Like the night Cole died. He and I were dressed to the nines as we walked the red carpet to dinner before "La Traviata." Then Cole spotted Ryan and Doreen. She was draped in a heavy gold-beaded thing that had such a low neckline, you could see her ugly nipples. When Cole aimed their direction to say hello, I plastered on a fake smile and motioned "just a moment," before I rushed over to greet Rebecca and Barry Claridge like they were my best friends.

When Cole caught up, he leaned to whisper, "Where did you go? We've got to invite Diver and…"

❧

RYAN PATTED MY SHOULDER. I HAD FADED AWAY LIKE I DO lately, especially since Cole died.

I took a breath and looked up. Something was different about Ryan today, something I couldn't put my finger on until I noticed his eyes. Then it registered. Usually shaded behind thick glasses, his irises were sea-foam aqua.

I blushed and looked away, trying to refocus. "Detective Reed seems hell bent to convict me…says he lost big in Odyssey. Told me to send him 'twenty-five-K' after my house sells."

"That's blatant bias. What else did he say?"

"Ballistics tests proved that my gun shot Luca. I don't know how that could have happened. Last I knew, my gun was in the trunk of my car."

"Who else had car keys?"

"My sons, but they had no idea my gun was in the trunk."

"Did you ask them?"

"I haven't talked to my boys. I'm trapped in here." I kind of lost it then.

"Marie, calm down. I need answers. Why was your gun in the trunk?"

"I went to my gun class. I shot practice rounds until my wrists hurt. Afterwards, I put my gun bag in the trunk."

"Anything else in the bag?"

"Ear muffs. I had to take down my hair to wear them, so one of my hairpins was in the gun bag too."

"Did you tell Detective Reed that?"

"Yes, but he kept saying my fingerprints are on the gun. Of course they were. It's my gun. He also said there was GSR—that's what he called it—on the clothes I wore to the gun club. But all this can be explained."

"Except for the hairpin. Somebody break in to your garage?"

"Not that I know. Maybe there are fingerprints."

"I've got a guy who handles investigations…" Ryan's eyes twinkled with devilment. "Gosh, Marie, you know him. Think of the most gung-ho player at U.T. Insane over a win. Furious about a loss. Had to pump iron the day after and made everybody else work out too."

I had no clue. The guys were the guys, while we girls were treated with amused disregard. Just wave hi and move on. Not much connection.

Ryan's eyes widened with glee. "Remember the right-side linebacker my senior year called, 'Nasty Man?'"

Immediately, I could hear Cole's voice telling me an off-color tale. The stories always began, "You won't believe what Nasty Man did today."

I shook my head to clear the cobwebs. "You mean Billy Bob Hughes?"

"Good ol' Nasty Man. He's a licensed private investigator. Computer guru too. Rather, he hires that out."

Suddenly, I was overwhelmed. "Ryan, how much will this cost? Hopefully, the house will sell soon, but I'm living on my home equity line of credit until it sells."

"Don't worry about fees. Take all the time you need."

"I will pay you, Ryan. I don't need Doreen telling Tina or anyone else in D'Posse that I am your *pro bono* case."

"Doreen won't tell a soul because I won't tell Doreen anything. You've got to trust me, Marie."

When his eyes centered on mine, I took a breath to calm down. "I've heard you're the best. Doreen always jokes when somebody at a League meeting suggests we dip into the opera's accounts to pay for our fundraisers. She says, 'Don't worry. Ryan will get us off.'"

"You know Doreen. The mouth."

I could tell he was embarrassed. "I guess I should also tell you that Doreen told police about my wrestling match with Luca at the September wine dinner. No telling what she'll tell Terrance."

"That guy will print anything. But if it's a lie, we'll sue."

"Well, it's not a lie. Luca and I really got into a tussle. The letch took me outside on the patio to 'discuss important things,' he said, but then he tried to maul me."

"I heard about this. Right there at the party?"

"Grabbed me, tried to kiss me, put his knee in my...well, I managed to push him away. He threatened to tell the board I was the one who came on to him. Can you imagine? Doreen must have overheard. I didn't even realize she was nearby, but she zoomed over after Luca stormed off."

When Ryan leaned to get something from his briefcase, his face revealed dismay. "I'm sorry, Marie. I didn't hear about Doreen being involved, but I'll tell her to put a sock in it. She loves to gossip."

I tried to make Ryan feel better. "Sometimes Doreen just bubbles over." Then I wondered why I was being her eager cheerleader.

Ryan shook his head. "Bubbly in college…heck, you cheered with her. But now, well, there's gossip with Tina LeBlanc or the constant postings on Facebook. Sometimes, I want to say, shut the… Sorry. I shouldn't dump that on you."

Oh, dear. More about Doreen. I wanted out of jail, out of this situation. "Ryan, no matter what anyone says, I did not kill Luca."

"Of course you didn't."

"How do I get out of jail? Isn't there bail or a bond hearing or something? That's how it goes on TV."

"This isn't TV. Unfortunately it's too late for a bond hearing today, but I'll get things in motion for first thing tomorrow."

"You mean, I have to stay the night?"

"Capital murder case. They've got forty-eight hours to hold you. Sorry."

I started to cry again. Ryan handed me the Kleenex box. While I wept, I made a bigger mess of my mascara and must have looked a sight.

Thankfully, Ryan got on his mobile and spoke with his associate. Something about a preliminary hearing. In spite of my desperation, I wondered—just because we knew each other long ago, was Ryan the right guy to be my attorney?

When he ended the call, he noticed my inquiring eyes.

I made up a lie. "Sorry to keep looking at you that way, but I don't think I've ever seen your eyes without glasses."

"Laser surgery. I can see great now, except I have to use readers for fine print."

"I guess Cole can't call you 'Diver' anymore." I quickly realized my flub, since Cole was dead and couldn't call Ryan anything anymore. "Your eyes are very blue."

"Doreen says my eyes remind her I need to clean the pool. Guess our collegiate passion has turned into reality."

"Life happens. Things were so passionate back in college. When we won, the joy was ecstasy. When we lost, we wallowed in misery."

Ryan's low chuckle brought crinkles around his eyes. "Win or lose, we found some reason to get drunk and screw."

"Things went downhill in the pros. Drugs. Affairs."

"I still wish I'd had the chance. Doreen has never recovered."

"You were the one who got hurt."

He held up his hand and wiggled his fingers. "Right. But no Super Bowl ring."

I shook my head. "Ryan, I know that injury cost you, but it may have been for the best. Look at you. You went to law school, and now you're a prominent attorney. Not some football player relying on past glory to sell worthless investments."

"Come on, Marie. Any guy would like to have a Super Bowl ring. Hell, Cole won two."

"We were lucky. Portland had a great team. Still, by the time Cole injured his shoulder, I was glad to be done with the NFL."

Ryan smiled sardonically. "'Football is Family,' right?"

"Those ads make me choke. Life with the Explorers was an endless stream of drugs, booze, and sex, but Cole was the only one having any." In spite of myself, I laughed.

Ryan took a moment to think. "Doreen always said you

avoided us because we didn't make the pros. I know that's not true. Cole wouldn't have done that."

"Doreen and I…well, it goes back to college. She was senior captain. I was a sophomore. Two years age difference in college was a social chasm."

"Doreen was crushed when I got hurt. She had moved to Atlanta for training camp. Got us an apartment, but then she had to pack up all by herself and drive us back to Dallas. She put me through S.M.U. law school though."

"Doreen would have seen things differently if you hadn't gotten hurt. Explorers' wives were always calling each other to find out where in the hell our husbands were."

"That bad?"

"Our only choices were to outlast the football days, get divorced, or have affairs ourselves. I know plenty of wives who did. But when you've got children, things are not easy."

"Cole shaped up, didn't he? I never heard anything about him running around after you guys came back to Dallas."

"You might say Odyssey was his other woman."

Ryan's eyes hardened. "Marie, I'd better tell you. I lost three 'mil' and it hurt like hell. We're not zillionaires like you and Cole."

"If it's any consolation, my zillions have vanished. I have no clue how much your services cost, but I will pay you, just as soon as I get out from under the house."

"Don't worry about that now."

I looked at him with as much earnestness as I could muster. "People think I know where the money is. If I did, would I be in here?" I waved at the stark walls that penned us in.

Ryan took my hands again. "Knowing Cole, he saw Odyssey as a clever play. From what I've heard, he started out legit until the market tanked. Then I guess he robbed Metroplex Opera to pay off Odyssey investors, until he couldn't keep up."

"Do you think I can get a fair trial?"

"Their case is circumstantial. Damaging, but circumstantial. We've got to explain some things. Our first step is a preliminary hearing, where the judge will either dismiss the case or, hopefully, release you on bond. But for now, tell me everything you know about Luca Scarlatti and anybody who had dealings with him. You, Cole, anybody you know, even Doreen and me, and don't skip even one detail."

Chapter Four

OUT AND IN

with Terrance Nichols

"Palpable Disbelief"

My fingers tremble as I write this column. The Dallas arts community has suffered a second horrifying loss this fall after the body of Metroplex Opera Maestro Luca Scarlatti was found about noon yesterday in a bloodied bed at his Uptown condo.

I'm told that after Maestro Scarlatti failed to show for rehearsal this morning, Keith Warren, Metroplex Opera executive director, went to Scarlatti's condo, saw his dark cherry Maserati Gran Tourismo still in the garage and contacted police after there was no answer to Warren's repeated knocks.

Because this is a widely read column, I will refrain from gore. Yet, confidential sources at the scene whispered to me that the murder was something out of "Lucia di Lammermoor." White satin sheets, white plush carpet and white velvet headboard were awash in the essence of our dear Maestro.

An autopsy, ballistics, and toxicology tests are in the works. Forensic technicians tell me that real-life investigations take far longer than the stuff of CSI shows, so stay tuned for later results.

For those of you who do not know, Luca Scarlatti was artistic director and principal conductor of Metroplex Opera for the past six years. He came to us from the heart and soul of opera, La Scala, Italy, the oldest son of a large, wealthy, and influential family. A more extensive biography will appear in Sunday's edition.

Maestro Scarlatti was not only our opera's leader but also a dear friend. Most longtime readers are aware of my romantic inclinations, so it will be no surprise that I immediately developed a crush on the debonair bachelor from the time he first alighted the podium in his Brunello Cucinelli tails.

Alas he professed to prefer the ladies. But we remained close until the day he died.

As such, I supported Scarlatti when the Metroplex Opera board threatened to cancel his contract over a financial kerfuffle with former NFL quarterback, financier, and the Opera's chief financial officer, Cole Donovan. I also supported Scarlatti when New York critics described our company as the "mere shadow of mediocrity."

I also defended our dear Maestro when rumors flew of wild sexual dalliances, although most would not begrudge a dashing bachelor the occasional roll in the hay. Still, reports circulated that several of his paramours wore wedding bands, and the Maestro reportedly aimed his baton at Donovan's stunning wife Marie.

Our arts community has had its share of recent tragedies, what with Cole Donovan's apparent suicide last fall. If you are not aware, Mr. Donovan's Odyssey Investments evolved into a Ponzi scheme that foundered before his demise.

His widow, a former collegiate cheerleader and amateur cellist, is president of the Opera's fundraising arm, the League. I was unable to reach Mrs. Donovan at her home for comment. However, I was able to speak with Rebecca Claridge, founder and perennial chair of the Opera's board and a past president of the League.

I minimize when I say Mrs. Claridge was distraught.

"I spoke with Luca the evening before he died. My son Barry had an important tenor role in the production, which unfortunately will not open Friday night as planned. In fact, our performances are postponed indefinitely," Mrs. Claridge said.

I also attempted to reach president-elect of the League, Doreen Ingles, but I must wait until I interview her and other members of the executive board to include their remarks.

Until I am able to detail more, let us at least give a standing ovation to Maestro Luca Scarlatti's lively body of work and extend our city's deepest sympathies to his family.

Plans for a memorial service are on hold, pending the arrival of a family representative from Italy. For now, the Maestro rests at intermission in Verano Highland Park Funeral Home.

And I suspect that my role as crime reporter has just begun.

Chapter Five
VISITING HOURS

You were unable to reach me, Terrance? That's because I'm in jail. As usual, your column was a sanctimonious bit of self-aggrandizing, but the majority of your readers will not realize that.

They could not know that during Luca Scarlatti's "financial kerfuffle" with Cole, he and I kept Luca's fingers out of the Opera's till. And, you just had to mention that I was a cheerleader twenty-five years ago, as if that matters now, not to mention your use of the term "amateur" before "cellist." No, I've never played in a professional orchestra, but I am a darn good cellist. At least my instructors have told me so.

I dread to see what you will post in tonight's "Preview" edition about my arrest. Luckily, the print issue of "Out and In" won't hit the streets until tomorrow, hopefully after I'm out on bail.

Oh, dear. You will probably be in the front row at my bond hearing. What a thought.

❧

"Marie Harris Donovan?" I was startled when the male guard announced that I had a visitor. Ryan had alerted my sons about my arrest, but he had told them to stay home to avoid the media frenzy. He also had instructed the jail guards to let no media inside for interviews. Evidently there was quite a gaggle of reporters trying to get in. So, who was this visitor?

When I walked into the visiting room, I heard, "Well, hello, Jailbird" in that throaty voice that could only be my friend of many years and employer of one week, Lena Verano.

Growing up, I only had Owen, my older brother, but if I had a sister, she would be Lena. We met at a League meeting fifteen years ago. I felt such immediate chemistry, I knew I had made a friend. That does not happen often, but when it does, it is a treasure.

At that time, we were both new to the world of big money arts fundraising and had no idea what we were getting into. First off, we both came from middle-class backgrounds, not the moneyed family names etched on the walls of Claridge Performance Hall. Actually, Lena might have been considered lower class. She was born in Brooklyn but was one generational boat ride from an Italian-Jewish sheep farm, where her grandfather once hid in a cave to escape the Nazis.

Maybe it was the contrast between Lena and the other rather crude personas around us in the Dallas County Jail, but when I saw her, I remembered again how attractive she has made herself to be, in an East Coast-y way. Dark, stylish bob, arched black eyebrows, lips lined precisely. Dressed stylishly for winter in a burgundy Versace wool suit and steel gray Prada boots, even if the outside temperature was supposed to push seventy degrees today.

As I sat across the table, I gave her a fake glare. "Only you could get away with calling me 'Jailbird.'"

Lena laughed. "What I do for good friends...you would not believe the screening I had to endure to get into this toilet bowl. I just hope I get my purse back."

Lena's brash accent attracted the attention of a passing guard, whom I noticed was my same female guard, still on duty. I gave her a smile as she walked by, then whispered to Lena. "She got me a copy of Terrance's column."

"I saw it. Poor guy had to jump into 'crime news' mode."

"My God, he wrote that Luca 'aimed his baton' at me. And I loved how Terrance mentioned I was once a cheerleader, just before he added that I'm an 'amateur' cellist."

"That stuff sells newspapers. With the amount of advertising I place in the *Dallas Daily Herald*, I'll deal with Terrance if he plays too rough."

"I'm just happy that the guards are being nice."

"Good. I was worried some Butch would give you grief...you being a society darling and all that."

The guard angled her head to listen in. I spoke a bit more loudly so she would overhear. "I can't believe the police are blaming me for this."

Lena picked up on my tone. "I know in my soul you did not kill Luca. You couldn't squash a mosquito."

Satisfied and smiling, the guard moved toward another inmate.

I whispered, "Doreen told the police about the wine dinner, when Luca came on to me."

"Someone needs to find a roll of duct tape."

"Ryan said he'd take care of Doreen."

"Ryan Ingles is defending you?"

"Yes, thank heavens. I don't know how much bail is going to cost, but I've got enough home equity credit to keep me afloat...at least I think so. My bail hearing isn't until tomorrow."

"I've still got plenty, not to worry. Even after your hunk of a husband, God bless his soul, lost my two million. Even after I spent way too much on Luca's Maserati. I should have seen that coming."

Lena's eyes got weepy. Luca had given her the romantic rush last season. In spite of my warnings, she saw him for nine months and even bought him a car for his birthday. But she caught him with someone else. I still don't know whom. She refuses to say. Says it's too embarrassing.

Before he died, Luca made the rounds of every League member, even the anorexic Tina LeBlanc, who was last year's

League president. Rumors had it that, to impress Luca, Tina had two of her lower ribs removed so she would look even thinner. Now the only shapely thing about Tina is a very large nose, which she sticks into my business, using her position as past president to tell me what to do. *Sometimes I wonder why I'm even in the League...*

"We're both drifting off," Lena interrupted.

"It's hard to stay in the moment."

She scoffed. "The oddest things have filtered through my mind lately too."

I had to laugh at our absurd situation. Here I was, accused of murder, while Lena was grieving the death of the man I was accused of killing.

Suddenly, she threw back her head and hooted in her deep voice. "I cannot believe we are in this ridiculous dungeon."

"You? I can't believe that I was home playing my cello while someone butchered Luca and made it look like I did it."

"Ryan Ingles will get you off. Isn't that what Doreen brags about at every League meeting?"

"I hate to think my life rests in Doreen's hands. Do you think she'll come to my bail hearing?"

"Doreen and entire D'Posse? Can't you see our dear bipolar Sienna Gordon walking in wearing some outrageous costume, arm in arm with the Barbie realtor in boots, Krissy Langley, or the ever-anal retentive Penny Borden?"

We started giggling, so my guard friend peered our way. Lena lowered her voice "We'd better change the subject. For all we know, this guard may be a spy."

"I'm so nervous, I can't think of anything else to talk about."

"Well, I have something new to discuss beyond murder, guns, and prison. I am actually dating someone."

"A new boyfriend? Who?"

"He asked me to keep things confidential, but I wanted you to know I'm doing better now—after the whole Luca situation."

"Lena, you and I shouldn't keep secrets. Tell me."

Her eyes flashed a hint of devilment. "As soon as I can. Promise."

For a moment, Lena's intrigue made me forget where I was until reality returned with the announcement, "Attention. Visiting hours are now over."

I felt the panic of claustrophobia zinging to my toes. "Lena, I don't know how I'll make it through the night."

"Just like you've always made it. As my trainer says, 'When water and fire wage war, the water will be the victor.'"

"What in the world does that mean?"

"Stay fluid. Watch for opportunities. You and I do that every day. I circulate in arts society because every single one of those Opera buffs is a potential customer of Verano Highland Park Funeral Home. Cole milked the same crowd for investments. You've groomed the snobs for social connections."

"And friendships. After all, I met you."

"Yes, and we've met a lot of crazies too."

I smiled at that one. "Thank you for coming, Lena."

"If they'd let me hug you, I would. Just breathe easy. You'll be fine." She blew me a kiss, then off she went in her confident stride, calling to a guard, "Where in the hell did you people put my purse?"

Chapter Six

INMATE DRESSING ROOM

I don't think I slept the entire night in that horrid cell. I kept fighting waves of panic. Gnashing over the mess I was in. Wondering why me, why now, why wouldn't God let up. Okay, so I'm not the most religious person. I shouldn't expect God to intervene now on my behalf.

"Maybe for my sons' sake?" I asked. Then I cried in anguish, maudlin with memories.

This entire mess began when I fell in love at age ten. I remember the moment distinctly. My first week at school on a sunny, warm day. I was on a merry-go-round with my best friend Donna Boyd. As we slowly whirled, I saw a tall boy gliding across the sport court. He stopped and posed as if someone had asked him to hold for a photo. His blond hair glowed in the sunlight. He was summer-tan, leanly muscular. I can still see his starched madras shirt tucked neatly into his belted khaki pants.

As the merry-go-round kept spinning, I called to Donna, "Do you know that cute boy over there?"

Her face wrinkled in dismay. "That's Cole Donovan. They say he's a thug. Skips class. Gets detentions."

Why would Donna say such a thing about this amazing boy

with whom I was immediately, incoherently, and insatiably in love? With every turn of the merry-go-round, I strained to watch him stride like a young lion. When he broke into a run, he moved with grace, like the pro athlete he was to become.

From that day on, through the fifth grade, on to middle school, high school, and college, I was inexplicably in love with Cole. Even when I found out that my best friend Donna went to the movies with Cole in the seventh grade. Even when Donna invited him to the eighth grade Sadie Hawkins dance.

I guess Donna got over her aversion to thugs.

When my cheerleading friend Rosemary whispered, "They're going steady," I suffered in silence. In fact, I thought my true love was lost forever, until the two broke up suddenly our sophomore year in high school.

Donna never told me why. I didn't know if she truly loved Cole or simply wanted him. Even as a sophomore, he was the number-one high school quarterback in the state of Texas, ranked number-two in the nation.

You can imagine my amazement when, three months after Donna and Cole broke up, he called me for a date. I absolutely trembled but said the fastest "yes" a girl ever uttered. And I did not ask Donna if it was okay.

As Cole's arrival approached, a deep fear ached in my gut. Call it panic or a premonition, but suddenly I wanted to cancel the date and go back to just being "Marie," not Cole Donovan's girlfriend. But before I could stop the future, the doorbell rang. I bolted to the living room to keep Daddy from saying anything, doing anything, embarrassing me.

Daddy drank, you see.

When I opened the door, my heart melted. Cole was the most handsome boy I've ever seen. Hollywood handsome.

Oh, and he was cocky. "Hi, Gorgeous. Ready to go?"

At NorthPark Center, we saw *Out of Africa*. We both sat like sticks during the first half until Robert Redford washed Meryl

Streep's hair by the river. Silently, Cole reached and held my hand —the first time a boy had done that.

I didn't really know what to do…were you supposed to move your hand around? I gave him a shy smile. Then our handholding turned into a sort of finger intercourse with passionate movements that sent tingles through my sixteen-year-old body.

After the show, Cole slowly drove us home and parked in front of next door so my parents couldn't see. At first, we listened to a Foreigner cassette until Cole abruptly leaned and kissed me. That was my first kiss ever so I didn't know if I should I open my lips, do something with my tongue, hold him, or what? Didn't matter. After that clumsy kiss, Cole and I were together for thirty-four years.

I still question how a young girl could fall so intensely in love with someone who was so wrong for her and later spend decades trying to make the wrong thing right. But my valiant efforts came to a startling halt when my husband sailed off a twenty-fifth-floor terrace, ricocheted off a parked car and landed in a heap on Cedar Springs Road, only to be hit by a stretch white limo.

When the police came to tell me the news at 3:00 a.m., Lena was already at my house. As a funeral director, it's her business to know when someone famous has died. I suspect that she pays someone in the medical examiner's office to give her tips.

The following morning, Terrance Nichols' "Out and In" column was a damning tribute to Cole: "A Sad Goodbye to an Adonis." I still have a copy.

Right below the column was a half-page ad for Metroplex Opera that pictured a man lying dead as a disdainful crowd jeered at him. The headline screamed, "Life Imitates Opera."

A knife through my gut would have felt better.

Rebecca Claridge sent a note of apology. "For the good of the budget, we must continue our current ad campaign, in spite of our sensitivities to the concept's similarity to Cole's tragic plight. Please know that the deepest sympathies of Metroplex Opera are with you and your sons. My heart breaks when I think of your loss and troubles."

She signed the note, "Rebecca," a far more informal byline than her usual, "Rebecca Claridge, Chairman of the Board."

Chapter Seven

OUT AND IN

with Terrance Nichols

"A Stunner—Out on Bail"

J ust call me Dominick Dunne, the brilliant court reporter who served long and well at *Vanity Fair*. Due to the horrid events of late, your society columnist is now a crime reporter.

Here we go: Investigative news or bust:

Metroplex Opera League President Marie Donovan was released on $1 million bond yesterday after passionate arguments for leniency by her white-collar defense attorney Ryan Ingles.

As you may know, Donovan was arrested for the alleged capital murder of Metroplex Opera Maestro Luca Scarlatti, whose brutally maimed body was found in his Uptown apartment last Thursday.

Mrs. Donovan is widow to the now notorious financier, Cole Donovan, also a former quarterback for the Portland Explorers.

When Mrs. Donovan entered the courtroom, an audible gasp issued from the packed gallery that included society notables Rebecca Claridge and her tenor son Barry; Doreen Ingles, wife of Mrs. Donovan's defense attorney Ryan Ingles; Tina LeBlanc, wife of notable Dallas neurosurgeon Georges LeBlanc; and Lena Verano of the funeral home of the same name.

Also in attendance were well-dressed and coiffed members of

the League's board, including Sienna Gordon, Krissy Langley, and Penelope Bordon.

For a woman who had spent the night in the clinker, Mrs. Donovan elevated the adjective "stunning" to poetry in an emerald-green, two-piece suit with a white silk blouse. Her up-do was complemented by an audible tinkle from her signature cherry blossom hairpin. Smiling cautiously, she appeared delighted to see her arts friends, whom she greeted with a modest—if not chagrined—nod.

Next came what is called the "probable cause portion" of the hearing. During this segment, Ryan Ingles ardently rebutted the prosecution's circumstantial evidence—eloquently presented by District Attorney Clark Timberlake—about Mrs. Donovan's gun being the murder weapon, and her hairpin being tested for DNA and toxic substances after it was discovered rammed in the Maestro's thigh.

The robust Judge Gerald Victor presided over the hearing as if Moses from the mountain, quickly announcing, "There is enough probable cause to bind this defendant over. I see that the defendant has not waived her right to appear before a grand jury."

"No, Your Honor. My client is innocent and will be pleased to testify before a grand jury. We will pursue all avenues to prevent this miscarriage of justice from going forward," Ingles said.

"Mr. Timberlake, looks like you'll need a grand jury to indict."

"Piece of cake, Your Honor," Timberlake replied.

In the bail portion of the hearing, Timberlake presented a succinct overview of the charges and insisted that Donovan was emotionally unstable and a flight risk.

In contrast, Donovan's voice was soft as she responded, "Yes, your Honor," to Judge Victor's first booming question. "Mrs. Donovan, do you understand that you cannot leave Dallas County? And do you realize that you must appear for all court appearances or be incarcerated?"

""Yes, Your Honor," Mrs. Donovan all but whispered.

"Will you agree to wear a GPS tracking bracelet?"

Mrs. Donovan sighed a bit before her repeated "yes" answers, although her tone revealed hints of exasperation.

"I've read in defendant's motion that you have two sons. Are they living in your home?"

At that point Ingles seized an opportunity to paint the portrait of a distraught widow. Standing behind the table he spoke loudly. "Your Honor, the accused is a recently widowed mother of two who has enormous responsibilities at home. She has a new full-time job and numerous volunteer commitments. With this unexpected, unwarranted arrest, she's missing out on much-needed income from her job at Verano Highland Park Funeral Home. And she's had no time to hire someone to care for her sons and handle the cooking, shopping, cleaning and so forth."

At that point, Timberlake objected. "Your Honor, her sons are twenty-two years old. They can take care of themselves."

Ingles leapt to reply. "The twins have experienced tremendous losses. Their father's death. Financial ruin. And now their mother is accused of murder, with evidence so tenuous I doubt any grand jury will indict. I urge you to show sympathy for her sons, the innocent victims of this tragedy."

"Luca Scarlatti was an innocent victim. We should reserve our sympathy for him," Timberlake said caustically.

Judge Victor appeared a bit weary of lawyers. "Enough, Counselors. Mrs. Donovan, do you own any other guns?"

"No, Your Honor," she answered somewhat sarcastically. "This was my first. I only bought it for protection."

"Mrs. Donovan, do you understand the limitations of wearing a GPS tracking device? You cannot take it off until I say so. You must protect the device in the shower. You will not be able to take a bath or go swimming. Electronics don't work underwater."

"Yes, your Honor," she murmured with a disappointed sigh.

A few high-pitched moans from the mostly female gallery conveyed sympathy about not being able to take a long, hot bath.

At this point, Timberlake made one last ditch effort—fire in his eyes. "Your Honor, I implore you. Although the accused plays the role of frail victim, she has the financial means to leave Dallas County, if not flee the country."

"Your Honor, my client understands the penalties for violating the court's orders. As you've said yourself, the accused are innocent until proven guilty. I should think the district attorney would acknowledge that fact."

Not to be out done, Timberlake argued, "Your Honor, Mrs. Donovan took a concealed handgun class the day Maestro Scarlatti was murdered. Several of her arts colleagues have told me they fear retribution from her because they gave information to the police."

"My client purchased a gun because she has received threats, but she bears no animosity for her arts colleagues, one of whom happens to be my wife. If I trust Mrs. Donovan with my wife's life, I assure Your Honor that you can trust Mrs. Donovan as well," Ingles countered.

I must say, that was a strong rebuttal.

Judge Victor's eyes seared through the slits of his weary lids. "Other than the passionate opinions already expressed, does the district attorney have any solid evidence as to why Mrs. Donovan should not be released on bail?"

Timberlake weakly replied, "I reiterate, Your Honor. She remains a flight risk."

Ingles aimed a Hail Mary. "Your Honor, I have known this defendant for twenty-five years. I'll bet my bar card she would never flee."

One could tell from the glint in the renowned defense attorney's cobalt eyes that this case meant far more to him than an ordinary white-collar case. After all, Ingles and Cole Donovan were teammates on a Univ. of Texas championship team of yore.

"Given Mrs. Donovan's lack of criminal history and her status as a widow and single parent, I will grant bail in this case. However, because this is a capital murder case, bond is set at $1 million dollars. Bailiff, please take the defendant to the Custodian of the Court to make arrangements to be released."

Mrs. Donovan looked to her attorney with confused relief in

her golden eyes. Sources told me that she used the equity loan on her $5.4 million manse to pay the 10 percent required on a $1 million bond.

$100,000. Ka-ching.

In spite of myriad lawsuits pending against her husband's estate, and Mrs. Donovan's claims that she is penniless, she cannot lose her house because of the Texas Homestead Act. A nice deal, being that many of her husband's investors lost their shirts.

The question remains whether a grand jury will decide a "true" or "no-bill" indictment. But after hearing Clark Timberlake's *le motif essentiel*, and the evidence to bind over Mrs. Donovan on a capital murder charge, my radar is astounded to see that the D.A. may have the right gal. Scarlatti made many enemies, male and female. Numerous spurned opera stars and paramours among the lot. Surely, Timberlake and the DPD have explored all other suspects before charging Mrs. Donovan.

My heart aches that such a lovely and admired member of our city's arts society remains the one clear suspect.

Chapter Eight

EXECUTIVE POSSE

F ab job as a crime reporter, Terrance. Be sure to influence the Dallas County jury pool before I ever get to trial. Immediately, I called Ryan's office, hoping he could silence your torrent of innuendos. But Ryan was in court, probably representing a criminal who actually did something wrong.

As I picked up the *Daily Herald* to reread Terrance's slander, I got a text from Rebecca. "Attendance Mandatory: Emergency Meeting, 11 a.m., Executive Board, Claridge Performance Hall."

The audacity of that woman. So much for my having a day to recover after being in court. Not to mention that I'm now wearing a GPS ankle bracelet that I cannot remove for fear of being put back in "the clinker," as Terrance termed it.

He got one thing right. I was released on bond for a mere hundred thousand dollars drawn on my home equity line of credit.

Lena has said repeatedly that she'll help me out financially, but Mother always told me, never a borrower or lender be. That's why I keep writing HELOC checks, although that's more borrowing.

After I got dressed, I dashed to Claridge Performance Hall, built twenty years ago at a cost of one-hundred million. Rebecca's late husband contributed the first twenty-million to kick off the campaign; hence the ornate palace bears his name.

As the old saying goes, "He who gets there first with the most..."

At the time, the Italianate building was designed to be the world's best opera house by a famous Italian architect and a top Viennese acoustician. That's how the wealthy do things in Dallas —over the top—with millions spilling like pocket change from area CEOs and the old-Dallas moneyed set. To this day, Claridge Performance Hall is home only to the Metroplex Opera, while the Dallas Symphony plays across the arts district at the graceful Meyerson Symphony Center, designed by I.M. Pei.

As I opened the wide glass doors to the Opera's executive offices, I readied a smile to greet Keith Warren, that is, if I saw him, but I saw no one. The entire office appeared empty as I signed the "Visitors" notepad at the front desk and walked past it to the conference suite. Once there, I was not so much greeted as I was glared at by the likes of Keith and members of the League Executive Board, my pals Doreen Ingles, Tina LeBlanc, Sienna Gordon, Penelope Borden, and Krissy Langley.

Tina and Doreen are inseparable social climbers who administer a Facebook page called "D'Posse" that I see from time to time. That's where they and other members post photos of themselves, preening in expensive gowns, gripping wine glasses or dancing with their husbands. If you make D'Posse, you are on the ladder to the top of Dallas society, at least to Doreen and Tina.

Sienna, Penelope, and Krissy are all on D'Posse page, even though Sienna wears elaborate wigs and gaudy period costumes to each performance, as if she had a role in the opera. I understand this is a tradition in some circles, but donning a bloodstained gown and wielding a knife are a bit off-putting. I think Sienna just needs attention.

Krissy, a middle-aged Barbie look-alike, is a former court reporter whose trial-attorney husband comes from oil money. That keeps Krissy in Botox injections and Neiman's boots. She is one of those women who pulls on boots at the first whiff of cool weather, and heaven help you if you are not wearing boots when she sees you. "Don't you have boots?" she'll actually ask, as if wearing pumps or flats is a *fashionista faux pas*.

The only one with some smarts is Penelope—Penny for short —who was a Wall Street banker before marrying a millionaire on her third try. Penny seems to hold herself above the League's many "wives of," like me. She may expect to be the new Rebecca someday, although Rebecca will have to die first.

Ever since Cole's demise and the revelation of his misdeeds, I haven't been tagged on the D'Posse page anymore. And from the glares I received when I sat across from them, I won't be on D'Posse again.

Thankfully, this group's silence was broken when Rebecca strode in as if she owned the place, accompanied by her wisp of a son Barry. Rebecca founded Metroplex Opera more than thirty years ago and has reigned as chairman ever since, a position no one dares challenge. Yet, in spite of my disdain for her domineering ways, I've always thought of her as a handsome woman, even at her age, which I guess is about sixty-five. She's as tall as I am, but big-boned, and she could lose a good forty. Still, as she sat at head of the table in her deep purple suit, a passionate color that accented her aluminum hair and blueberry eyes, you could see the beauty she once was.

"I'm glad you all could attend," she said brusquely.

Barry sat beside her like an obedient cat, slim, coyly arching his fingers through his stringy salt and pepper hair.

"It's good to see you after what I've been through lately," I said as cheerily as I could, although I caught a note of sarcasm in my voice that I could not erase with even my best cheerleader smile.

Rebecca placed her hands on the huge table between us, her gaze searching. Her voice was hushed but urgent. "I've called this meeting of the League Executive Board because we must protect Metroplex Opera. I'm going to suspend the rules so that we can talk honestly and openly."

I glanced at Barry, who was not a member of the board.

Rebecca caught my implied question. "Pay no attention to my son. He's sworn to secrecy."

A flicker in Barry's eyes revealed his dismay, but he merely adjusted his bright pink tie.

"Marie, we are in this together, and I know I can count on everyone's confidence."

I nodded as though I trusted these people, although I certainly did not. "What did you want to discuss, Rebecca?"

"The murder charge against you impacts the League's ability to raise funds that Metroplex Opera must have to survive this season after Cole…well, you know what happened. Heaven help us if our League president will be convicted."

"Ryan Ingles is confident I will be exonerated."

Rebecca's eyes pierced. "Regardless, as chairman, I must ask you to take a leave of absence from your position as president."

"But Rebecca, I did nothing…innocent until proven guilty."

"I hope that's true. But in the meantime, Doreen Ingles…"

Doreen took a deep breath, as though a crown was about to be placed on her nervously bobbing head.

"Doreen, as president-elect, you will serve as interim president." Rebecca tapped the table twice with a fingernail as gavel.

That decision made me furious, but what could I say?

"Now that is settled, we deserve to know what evidence the police have. We must prepare for damage control."

"Rebecca, the police case is totally circumstantial. There's no proof I was ever in Luca's condo. Other than that, my attorney told me not to talk to anyone, not even trusted friends and associates."

"Surely Ryan did not mean us. After all he works closely with Keith and me on the board. And Doreen is his wife, for goodness sakes. We are all friends with a common cause. Save Metroplex Opera. As for Barry, he would never tell a soul, or I'll kill him."

"Not a soul," Barry murmured with a feeble grin as he batted his red-tinged eyes. Clearly, the mousy man had been crying earlier, probably grieving over the great Maestro Luca.

Because of Barry's mother's influence, he frequently appears in minor tenor roles for Metroplex Opera productions but, whenever he solos, his nerves set in and his voice turns shrill. I've always felt sorry for him, especially when Rebecca makes him solo at every after party and major fundraiser.

Rebecca interjected, "I've heard that you and Luca had an argument. Fisticuffs and so forth. What was that about?"

"I suppose I can say this much, since Doreen has told the police. At the September wine dinner, Luca wanted to talk privately. I should have known better, but I met him alone on the terrace. Turned out Luca had nothing to talk about. He had an erect… Well, many of you know how Luca could be."

Barry nodded, but Rebecca patted his leg to still him.

"Luca grabbed me, said something in Italian and tried to kiss me. I was so shocked, I didn't know what to do. I pushed back as he groped me and I screamed for help."

"Marie, I cannot believe Luca would have tried to harm you."

"You must be aware that he went after every diva who came to perform and practically insisted they have sex with him."

Barry laughed a squeaky giggle. "The divas called it, 'partly rape.' They don't get the part unless they go to bed with Luca."

Rebecca sighed in frustration. "Let's not speak ill of the dead. We have no concrete evidence about Luca's sexual exploits with the diva darlings of our world."

I ventured, "But he didn't just have affairs with divas. We all have friends—League members—that Luca has exploited."

Rebecca's eyes pretended shock. "Someone I know? Whom?"

My eyes swept the room as D'Posse averted their heavily mascaraed lashes and shifted in their silk skirts and hosiery.

"I refuse to name names but I will discuss what I've heard with my lawyer. No matter what anyone says, Luca grappled me on the terrace and, in spite of my resistance, he tried to push my head toward his…well, his groin area. Each time I tried to pull away, he pulled harder. Eventually, I wriggled to face him…then bit him, not sure where. My mouth tasted only tuxedo. He laughed, and I felt his knee climb into my crotch."

Rebecca gasped and D'Posse twittered.

"My apologies for this lewdness but you will hear worse in court. When I screamed, people who were smoking by the rail turned to see what was going on, so Luca glared and said, 'Another time, *mia signora.*' Then he slid away."

Rebecca scoffed like a prosecutor. "Others saw this event?"

"Yes. Two people in this room. Doreen and Tina. They each came over. I told them what happened but Doreen laughed things off. Said, 'Everybody knows Luca has problems.'"

Barry nodded silently, so Rebecca tapped the table again.

I was floored that the biddy was feigning ignorance. "Rebecca, you must be aware of Luca's proclivities. After all, you are chairman."

"And that's why we're here. To help you."

"Sure you are." I stood then, unable to remain the genteel lady I had intended to be. "Now I see why Ryan told me I should not talk to anyone. But I will say this, and I'll keep saying it until I'm dead. I did not kill Luca Scarlatti."

Rebecca waved the air, as if to dismiss my hysteria. "Marie, sit down. There's no need to be defensive. In fact, I defended you when I spoke with Luca's family in Italy yesterday. His mother is alive, although his father has passed. His sisters and brothers—all eight of them—are devastated. Who can blame them? Their oldest brother came to Dallas as our Maestro but was killed by a gun owned by the president of our League. I told them I'd get to the bottom of this. If you have anything revelatory to say, do so now. I promise, it will not leave this room."

I was exasperated to the point of screaming, but I stared into Rebecca's eyes as sincerely as I could muster. "You saw me last Saturday. Did I look like a woman with murder on her agenda?"

"Since I've never been involved with such a tawdry act, I wouldn't know."

"Neither have I, Rebecca. But I don't think murderers go to opera League meetings, then buy Chinese food, head home to their sons, do the dishes, play the cello, watch the news, and take a hot bath on the way to committing a murder a few hours later."

Barry stared at the table as he blurted out, "If this were an opera, our dear Luca would get up to sing. He'd tell us who really killed him."

"Barry, Dear, this isn't an opera, and luckily dead men can't sing," Rebecca murmured.

I blurted out, "Perhaps that should be the Opera's next ad campaign. 'Hear Dead Men Sing.'" I hadn't meant to sound snarly, but I could not help myself.

Barry sniffed. "Marie, you are not the only one Luca mistreated. If it will help, I'll share my side of the story with the press. I saw Terrance Nichols in the lobby as we came in."

Rebecca gripped Barry's arm. "Now, none of that. Our dear Luca is gone, and that is probably for the…" Her eyes drifted away.

I wanted to ask why Rebecca thought Luca's death was "probably for the better," but Penny Borden interrupted.

"Marie, please understand what we are facing. With the missing thirty-million from Cole's dealings, Metroplex Opera finances now depend on upcoming League fundraisers, like the ball and the wine tasting. If our president is convicted of murder, you can understand how that ripple-effect would negatively impact our bottom line."

"We may not make it through the season," Keith murmured.

"None of you seem to care that I'm being falsely charged. You're merely interested in damage control."

Doreen gave me one of her glares. "I cannot believe you would say such a thing. My husband is defending you and, in spite of our…well, differences, I don't want him to lose a case. The publicity would ruin his reputation."

"What about my reputation, Doreen? You've already slandered

me to the police, and if I see one untrue statement posted on your pretentious D'Posse page, I will file suit."

With that, Doreen collapsed in sniffles.

Condolences flowed. "Oh, poor Doreen." "Oh, our dear Maestro." The entire board gathered by Doreen, hugged, sniffled, and blew—even Keith and Barry—while I wondered if God was laughing at poor, accused me, surrounded by a bunch of snobs who were definitely not on my side, except for one insipid eunuch who might have something to tell me. His "side of the story."

I'd have to tell Ryan about Barry's insinuations.

Then I remembered again. My gun had killed Luca, my hairpin was in his leg, and tests revealed some sort of nerve agent on my pin. Who did that? One of these twits? God, how did I get into this mess?

As Rebecca and Keith whispered and D'Posse endlessly consoled themselves with tears, tissues, and hugs, wouldn't you know it, but I heard a knock on the conference room door just as my friend Lena bolted in, her dark eyes wide.

"I know, I know, I shouldn't barge in like I own the place, but I dropped by your house and your sons said you were here."

Suddenly, I was enveloped in Len's full body hug. "Lena, thank you, but…" I gestured around the conference room.

She paid no attention and instead locked onto my eyes. "Sweetie, I've been in the dead-body business a long time, and I know people who can make things happen all over the world. So, if this thing goes south, I'll have you on a sunny island in Bali before they can slap on the leg chains. Charter jet. New ID. You and the twins will have new lives in a heartbeat."

My eyes frantically angled around the conference room to see if anyone was listening. Then I plastered on a smile. "Lena, you know Rebecca and her son Barry? And Keith and the executive board?"

Lena's face instantly turned from concerned friend to funeral home owner, poised, in charge, conciliatory. "Of course. Ladies…

and gentlemen. I hope you will forgive my rather blatant intrusion. All I can say is, funeral directors are humans too."

"Of course," Rebecca murmured from the far end, although she clearly did not mean it.

"I cannot imagine why the police would target our dear Marie."

Barry shrugged with a sarcastic laugh. "Maybe because her gun killed Luca?"

Rebecca touched Barry's knee to silence him, then motioned with a curled finger for him to follow her to the door. I could see she suddenly wanted out of this room as much as I had never wanted to be in it.

Doreen tried to stop them. "Rebecca, now that I'm president, I want to see what I can do for you. For the Opera."

Keith interrupted. "Ladies, our staff is in chaos. We've got a production to postpone, and donors with questions. There's a full board and staff meeting in the other suite that we now must attend."

Rebecca spoke sternly. "Doreen, as I've said before, you are *interim* president of the League. Tina, please give her the guidance from your past experiences. And if the rest of you want to save the Opera, follow us to our next meeting. The more brains the better, except of course, we don't need yours, Marie."

And with that, the group filed out, leaving me and Lena to watch them waggle across the lobby to the other suite.

Through the glass doors I could see that darn Terrance Nichols who was stopping each one as they filed past, mouthing questions I couldn't hear. No telling what he heard. "Lena, he's interviewing everybody."

"Not to worry, I'll squash that. Terry and I are headed to lunch. I'll go tell him I'm here and ask what they told him."

"Terry? You two are pals?"

"He wanted an interview, so I thought it would be a good way to get your story in the public eye, not the versions D'Posse might tell him."

"Lena, he will twist anything you say."

"But didn't you notice this morning's column? I fed Terry that line about the other suspects…what did it say? 'Numerous spurned opera stars and paramours among the lot.' That was my line."

"Lena, he said I was the one clear suspect."

"Well, at least he mentioned Luca's many enemies."

"Did you tell him that Doreen and Tina apparently had affairs with Luca? Heck, four women who just left this room have been rumored to be his lovers."

She looked away. "We all got the big rush. Even you."

"Lena, please, watch what you say to Terrance."

She seemed a bit exasperated but gave me a hug and rushed out to the lobby to greet Terrance.

When she came back to the conference room, I told her, "I'm not talking to that man. Nor will I come out until he leaves."

"Not to worry. The huff-and-puff set gave him 'no comment' at Rebecca's insistence. You are safe for now. And I'll make sure that continues, I promise."

She gave me another of her sisterly hugs and I felt comforted, that is, until my mobile phone interrupted us.

My caller ID announced, "Wireless Caller, Ingles, Doreen." She must have been calling from the very next suite.

Lena's eyes lit up. "Let Doreen and D'Posse stew."

"I will never give those women another thing to gossip about."

"Ryan must have been some dumb linebacker to pick a blabbermouth like Doreen."

I lowered my voice so Terrance couldn't hear. "Doreen was probably a mistake of the loins. Just like mine with Cole. And yours with Luca."

Her black eyes lost their sheen. My comment may have hurt Lena's feelings, but her calling Ryan a dumb linebacker hit a nerve. My husband's teammate was now my only hope.

Chapter Nine

MY SIDE OF THE STORY

Luca deserved it. All of it. The shock, the horror. He was a user. Took everything, gave nothing except a few choice roles to his tenor lovers and diva darlings. How sad that so many like me had made love to a user like Luca Scarlatti.

I shouldn't blame them. Sex and *amour* get so mixed up.

God, what have I done? Each time I realize what happened, I run for the Oxycontin. I've been taking way too many of those little pink pills lately. Makes me a bit agitated.

I pray they won't suspect me. How could anyone connect the dots? Someone would have to talk. Break a promise.

The killer could have been any of us. There was a long line.

I have to admit, killing Luca was a thrill. The absolute vindication of ending a villain's life. But the gore! Blood in thick streams running over his "whitey white" sheets. That's what he used to call them when he tempted me.

"I've put on clean whitey-whites for you."

I could not resist.

Watching his eyes go from shock to paralysis was a joy. He would never rape again. To make sure, I kept a piece. Again, I couldn't resist.

Oh, the planning that went into the dastardly deed. Night after night, wondering, "Suppose this," or "What-if that."

Operas are littered with themes of murder and death. I cannot be insane to have dreamed up such a plan. Murder is the stuff of life, and life imitates opera, right?

In the end, Luca Scarlatti had to be stopped. Dallas and the opera world would be enhanced by his absence. So, I did what I had to do.

Chapter Ten

TEA AND SYMPATHY

A s if my life did not have enough troubles, Rebecca's son Barry called for what he termed, "tea and sympathy." When I demurred that I was not supposed to speak with anyone about my case, he persisted.

"This is a matter of urgency for me and my mother."

I knew Ryan would not want me to go, but I couldn't get hold of him for a firm yes or no. Court again. And Barry was so insistent, I thought I might discover something. Point the finger another direction for this horrid murder. Even if I would still be on the hook for my husband's Ponzi scheme, financial hell seemed the lesser of evils.

Barry did not recognize me when we met in the back of the Sports Grill at Dallas Country Club. I had worn my hair down for our afternoon meeting, something I rarely do in public, but I thought my altered look might deter inquisitive eyes.

As the waiter poured our iced teas, Barry's eyes searched the almost empty room for anyone who might overhear. "I must ask if you are wearing a wire," he whispered.

"A wire?"

"Yes, a recording device."

I stretched my ankle to reveal the tracking device. "Other than this, the only wire I'm wearing is in my brassiere. How about you?"

Barry's thin lips parted in a toothy smile. "Mother won't let me wear a brassiere."

We both tittered at that one, and I relaxed a bit. I've always liked Barry. He's someone I can joke with at parties, when I get weary of the snobs. I whispered, "Ryan said that in Texas only one party must know that a conversation is being recorded. So I must ask you the same. Are you recording me?"

"I am offended, Marie. I've known you for years and have always admired your grace and style."

"Thank you, Barry, but being graceful and stylish got me into the situation I am in. Please answer the question."

"Marie, I absolutely promise, on the health of my dear mother, that I am not recording you. She will never hear a word of this conversation. In fact, Mother is why I'm here."

"What does Rebecca want you to accomplish for her today?"

Barry's eyes furtively checked the room. In a high-pitched whisper, he confided. "There was much more to Luca than met the eye. Because of Mother, I cannot tell you all, but there were some backstage financial dealings that got sticky."

"What dealings, and what does that have to do with me?"

"Again, I cannot say."

"Barry, if you have any solid evidence…"

"I cannot divulge a thing. You simply have to trust me."

"Why should I trust you? Your mother seems hell bent to convict me."

"Marie, opera is my world, but I've never been able to break through. You remember that one-man show at Theater in the Round? Mother made it a benefit, so the entire opera board and League had to show up, millionaire husbands in tow, each paying grand dues to the Grande Dame. Problem is, I absolutely panic in a solo. From the moment the pianist chimed the introductory chord to 'Dalla sua pace,' I could not find my voice. I wanted to disappear. Just go poof and vanish."

"But there's always room for fill voices in opera. You don't have to be a Carnegie Hall soloist. You can sing in the chorus."

"Oh, but Mother wants the big time, even though artistic directors want a handsome Placido Domingo or the next Pavarotti. That's why her prominence has given me a life I could not have on my own. I only get parts because of her."

"Barry, have you ever thought about leaving Dallas? Try a new city. Get out from Rebecca's 'influence,' as you call it."

"How would I live? Mother's home is my sanctuary. But thanks to Cole's Ponzi scheme, we've lost a lot of liquidity."

"I don't understand."

"To put it bluntly, we are house poor. No cash flow."

"I'm in the same boat."

We were quiet for a moment, each a bit sorry for the other. Then Barry cleared his throat and narrowed his gray eyes. "I think Mother knows a lot more than she lets on about Luca's murder."

"Are you saying, Rebecca knows who killed Luca?"

Barry's eyes were so full of chagrin I felt his pain. "Yes."

I tried to absorb his meaning. "Do *you* know who killed him?"

"I won't say more."

"You must tell Ryan or the D.A."

"I am not about to speak to Ryan or the D.A. You may not discuss what I've said, per our confidentiality agreement. Don't worry. I have everything covered. I know what I must do."

He patted my hand and left me to wonder what "he must do."

I watched as he zigzagged between tables and out the door. To hell with my affection for Barry and promise of confidentiality. I will tell Ryan everything Barry said.

I refuse to spend one more night in jail.

Chapter Eleven

GRAND JURY

Even though I told Ryan what Barry had said, and even though Ryan called the D.A.'s office and also put his investigator Billy Bob on it, none of this new, intriguing evidence put the brakes on the grand jury schedule. You cannot stop a federal freight train.

According to Texas law, I'm not allowed to tell you what transpired during my grand jury appearance because anyone who appears must swear to complete secrecy or else be fined five hundred dollars and spend thirty days in jail. My two days in the Dallas County clinker convinced me that I never want to go back, so I will never say in complete detail what went on inside that fluorescent room at the Frank Crowley Courts Building. But I can say how I felt, how I looked, and what Ryan counseled me to do beforehand.

First, he told me to dress conservatively. The grand jury in Texas is made up of twelve people chosen in a secret process with no input from the prosecution or defense lawyers.

"And I'd better let you know, your lawyer cannot go inside the grand jury room with you," he told me, averting his eyes a bit, probably because he knew what was next.

"What, no lawyer to represent me?" This scared the world out of me. I thought I might throw up.

He took a moment to reply, then centered his thickly fringed blue eyes on mine. "Marie, I will be outside. If you need me, you can ask to speak to counsel. But it's far better for you to just 'be Marie' than to ask for help from your lawyer."

"Just be Marie?" That startled me, because it was almost the same thing I told myself so long ago, right before I went out with Cole that first time.

"Be yourself. The grand jury process is investigative, evidentiary in scope, not adversarial. The prosecutor will save his showboating for the jury trial. But he will present his evidence, which we agree is damaging. He'll ask you every question he can dream up. Just answer truthfully. If you interrupt the proceedings too often to speak to your attorney, the jury might think you have something to hide. Just tell them what you've told me. Including the stuff about Barry."

"Can Lena come along? The boys? Be there in the stands?"

"Not Lena, not your family."

"This is all too much."

"Just be totally truthful. The jury will see your sincerity."

"They might see the spoiled society widow of a Super Bowl winner turned Ponzi thief. The only difference between me and Bernie Madoff's wife is a pair of Super Bowl trophies, except my sons are still alive, and I've still got my house."

"You can win them over. This is not the time to argue. The grand jury is not there to decide your guilt, but to say whether the prosecution has cause to bring you to trial. If the jury says 'true,' I will do everything in my power to get an acquittal at trial."

❧

RYAN HAD ORDERED A CAR TO PICK ME UP AT 7:00 A.M., SO I showered and washed my hair the night before. I slept in spurts, waking in hormonal sweats, until I got up at five to patch myself together. When I looked in the mirror, I saw taupe skin and dark shadows. My God, I had turned into the ghost of my mother. When a wave of nausea hit, I threw up in the toilet. My hair was down, so it dangled in the bowl, which meant I had to wash my hair again.

That put me a half-hour behind.

Ryan had said, "Never be late for an appearance before a grand jury. They can assume you are not appearing. And since you're out on bail, they can rescind it. You will forfeit your one-hundred-thousand dollars and go back to the slammer."

Remembering those words made me so agitated I threw up again. But this time, I held my hair out of the toilet.

Rushing now, I went to my closet and grabbed my navy two-piece suit and an off-white blouse with a big collar. Under that, I tied a paisley scarf with swirls of red, blue, and gold. A bit military, but the gold matched my eyes. My driver's license says my eyes are hazel, but my irises are almost totally golden with flecks. I wore only gold studs in my ears and Mother's watch for luck. I'm not very religious, but I said a quick prayer to Mother, asking her to do what she could to help from wherever she was.

Ryan had told me to wear low heels but omit my cherry blossom hairpin. "All eyes and ears will be on you, and I don't need for you to jingle."

As if that was not enough to make me gag again, I pinned my hair in a prim *chignon*, applied a whole lot of makeup so I would not look dead, and promised myself in the mirror that when all this was over and the house sold, I would take myself to an exotic spa in a foreign land. Maybe Lena would come with me. A girls' getaway.

As I headed out, I peeked in the boys' suite and tiptoed to kiss them goodbye. They were still sound asleep. I don't think they had a clue how serious this event was.

Although they are legally adults, Mom's grand jury appearance was probably some sort of traffic ticket in their minds. Yes, Cole and I had spoiled them, but I wanted them to enjoy life. We had the means that everybody in America would love to have, that I dreamed of having when I was a girl. Although the marital aspect of my life did not work out as I had hoped, having two handsome sons and the money to raise them without denial was a delight and a privilege. But I should have been more disciplined. Neither Cole nor I taught them how to make it on their own.

As I shut the door to their suite, I decided to hire some sort of life coach. Maybe a male counselor could help them learn what Cole and I failed to teach.

The doorbell rang. Through the peephole, I saw the driver's hat. A sharp pain of dread shot through my gut. I did three of Lena's deep breathing exercises she always brags about—she has a trainer of some sort. The exercises actually worked—I'd have to tell her—so I kept the bile down.

When the driver opened the car door, I was relieved to see Ryan in the backseat. I had not expected him to ride with me.

We did not talk much on the way. He patted my hand and whispered, "You'll do fine."

At the courthouse, we walked through a high, arched entryway that looks out at the Dallas skyline.

Ryan pointed to his tall green office building, rising across the way. "Just remember, my office looks down on this place."

Tears welled. I sniffed to try to stop them. "Thank you, Ryan. For all you've done."

He held up a hand. "No tears. Be calm. Tell the truth. The jurors will fall in love with your sincerity."

When we found my assigned courtroom, he hugged me. He was still a big lunk but gentle in his touch. I felt myself melt into his embrace, where I lingered a bit too long. I enjoyed the comfort and scent of a male for the first time in years. I think he enjoyed our hug too.

Neither of us let go until a voice called out. "Marie Harris Donovan. You are ordered to appear."

Ryan disengaged, then gave me a reassuring nod. His eyes sparkled with deep empathy. "Just be Marie."

That phrase again. I did three more Lena breaths, put on a modest smile, and walked as confidently as I could into the room.

As I've said, legally, I can't tell you what actually happened at my grand jury appearance, but I can say what usually happens, and I can tell you how I felt. I don't think I've been this nervous, even during tryouts for cheerleader or before my first cello solo with the university orchestra. But luckily, I got to sit and listen before I had to speak.

The prosecution presented its case in a series of facts, like a report. All the stuff about my gun and the hairpin, test results about a nerve agent that paralyzed Luca.

Then I, the accused, answered all sorts of questions. I answered honestly and earnestly. I told them everything I knew, although I couldn't explain how or why my gun and hairpin wound up connected to Luca's murder, because I've never been in Luca's condo. And I said so repeatedly, until I wondered if I was protesting too much.

The prosecution also presented facts from the defense side, sort of in this style, "The accused says she had no motive to kill the Maestro, but the prosecution has a number of depositions from eye witnesses who contradict her statements."

Those are probably Doreen and Tina.

Next, the prosecution presented lengthy background about my role as president of the League and Cole's role on the Metroplex Opera board. Clearly, the prosecution was trying to set up a financial motive, not just the stuff about Luca accosting me.

Next, the D.A. asked even more questions about the League and the Metroplex Opera board. I can tell you what I told him, because this information is not secret.

"The two organizations have symbiotic relationships."

"How so, Mrs. Donovan?"

"The League holds high-dollar fundraisers but is not required to give the proceeds to Metroplex Opera, although we always do. The organizations were set up as separate entities. In that way, the

League can raise funds without oversight or interference from the Opera staff or the board."

Next, the prosecution made a big deal out of my serving on the League board at the same time Cole was on the Opera board. He chaired the Opera's finance committee and also invested Opera funds in Odyssey.

"This was not the normal role of an opera board CFO, was it, Mrs. Donovan?"

"No, but Rebecca Claridge and the board gave him that power."

"Wasn't that over the objections of the Opera's Executive Director Keith Warren and Comptroller Duane Thomas? Didn't they say that was like having the fox guarding the henhouse?"

I answered, "I don't know. I wasn't at that meeting."

I squirmed a bit over that one because Cole told me much later that Keith and Duane were furious about the deal. To change the subject, I added, "I do know that Metroplex Opera was flush with money earned from Cole's successful investments." My voice echoed with pride. Can't stop cheering for Cole, I guess.

"Until the opera's operating funds vanished, right?"

"I have no knowledge of Cole's financial dealings," I said in my well-coached line. I wanted to add that I've always hoped the FBI would find hidden accounts and pay back investors. But Ryan had urged me not to suggest there might be hidden accounts, for fear the grand jury members might think I know more than I do.

Clark Timberlake must have read my mind. "Several witnesses have testified that Mrs. Donovan has as much knowledge as her husband about the Opera's funds and perhaps knows where Mr. Donovan stashed the missing millions. But, as we've heard, Mrs. Donovan pleads ignorance about her husband's financial dealings."

That was a real zinger. I didn't reply.

Next, the prosecution included a few points on my behalf like, "The accused says one witness, Barry Claridge, has key evidence about Maestro Scarlatti's murder, however Mr. Claridge has rebutted Mrs. Donovan's testimony in his deposition and in subsequent interviews."

That's not exactly what the D.A. said, but I will say that Barry Claridge is a lying Momma's Boy, and I will hold his feet to the fire.

Throughout the proceedings, several jury members asked questions. I somewhat enjoyed speaking openly to real people, instead of answering zingers from an antagonistic district attorney who is clearly after my scalp.

After those questions, I was dismissed.

All in all, the grand jury process was not painless, but it was not as horrific as I had expected. Certainly not worth my pre-hearing nausea. I simply did my best to provide an explanation for every question, and I flatly denied things that were not true. Not once did I feel the need to consult Ryan.

When I walked out, I felt vindicated and relieved, hoping the truth would convince the jury that the D.A. had it all wrong. Then Terrance Nichols would have to present my side of the story instead of his tainted drivel.

Chapter Twelve

OUT AND IN

with Terrance Nichols

"Stunningly True"

Who said arts columnists are hacks? Once again, I am a crime reporter. Yesterday, the grand jury of Dallas County entered a True Bill of Indictment, which reads, "Marie Harris Donovan, on or about the first day of February…unlawfully did then and there, knowingly and intentionally, cause the death of Luca Scarlatti…by first injecting Luca Scarlatti with a paralytic nerve agent and then shooting Luca Scarlatti with a firearm, a deadly weapon."

Boom. And with that, Marie Donovan, vivacious arts supporter, stunning beauty and suspended president of the Metroplex Opera League, was indicted for capital murder.

I hate to say, but I expected this result. If you will recall a recent column, I stated that the lovely Mrs. Donovan appeared to be the sole suspect. In addition to the damaging hard evidence against her, information has surfaced that she had a terrible argument—some say it was a downright brawl—with Maestro Scarlatti at a Metroplex Opera wine dinner last fall. Although grand jury evidence is sealed, rumors have made their way into my voice-messages and e-mail regarding tense disagreements between

Cole Donovan, Scarlatti, and Opera CEO Rebecca Claridge over Scarlatti's request to write checks on the Opera's $30 million in operating funds.

The Maestro purportedly wanted to pay vendors and suppliers directly and more promptly, he told a number of League members with whom I am in close contact. One is Doreen Ingles, wife of Donovan's defense attorney Ryan Ingles. Mrs. Ingles is serving as interim League president during Mrs. Donovan's suspension.

Mrs. Ingles told me, and I quote, "The president of the League serves as a voting member on the Metroplex Opera board. In that capacity, Marie Donovan consistently refused to approve Luca's requests for check-writing privileges."

Mrs. Ingles would not go so far as to say, but many others have insinuated to me that Mrs. Donovan's nay vote was at the urging of her late husband, who persuaded the Opera to deny the measure.

In Cole Donovan's role as CFO of the Opera's operating fund, he reportedly kept the $30 million operating budget humming a happy tune, churning investment profits that went into a separate Opera foundation, until the "Tosca" opener last November. At a black-tie *soiree* afterward, key members of the Opera staff whispered that several checks for sets, costumes, and performers had bounced.

Reporter that I am, I felt obligated to ask Mr. Donovan if the Opera had financial difficulties.

"Some sort of glitch. I just need to move money around," Mr. Donovan answered. Then off he dashed in his Gucci tux, apparently to take care of the financial snag.

But the feds now say that Mr. Donovan allegedly used the bulk of the Opera's $30 million operating funds to shore up his failed Odyssey Investments. Instead of going to the Opera's executive offices to move the money, Mr. Donovan allegedly made a run for his Uptown penthouse one floor above his Odyssey Investments.

Not long after, Cole Donovan sadly became well-dressed road

kill, with his fly metaphorically unzipped after the world learned he had cooked Odyssey's books.

Months later, after Maestro Scarlatti's murder, questions arose about his wife's role in Opera finances. According to Mrs. Ingles and Rebecca Claridge, Cole Donovan had hands-on oversight, along with Metroplex Opera general director Keith Warren and comptroller Duane Thomas.

So, what did Mrs. Donovan really know? Was she aware that Cole Donovan had stewed the Opera's books so well, both Keith Warren and Duane Thomas had assumed all was flush? Until checks bounced.

This begs the question, did Mrs. Donovan also dip into the till of the Opera's $30 million *à titre d'* her husband? Some in the arts community murmur that the Donovans *allegedly* plotted her rise to the position of League president so that she and her husband *allegedly* could siphon funds through the Opera board.

Note my use of "allegedly," for fear of lawsuits.

Admittedly, these and other rumors may be fueled by a combination of well-heeled paranoia and gossip. But when the indictment came over the wire yesterday afternoon, this hack's radar went boing-boing. Perhaps the engaging smile and demure demeanor of Marie Harris Donovan is an enigma.

Time to dig up more facts.

The date for Mrs. Donovan's arraignment has been set for June 13. At that time, we shall hear her official plea.

The Dallas temps should be hot enough by then to make any cheerleader sweat.

Chapter Thirteen

CHANGE OF VENUE

Terrance's column about my grand jury indictment was the first time I'd heard about it. I was so furious, I called Ryan's office. He could see me that afternoon, his secretary said. But just as soon as I dressed, the doorbell rang.

I cannot describe the size of the knot in my stomach when I saw Doreen, Tina, Sienna, Krissy, and Penny through the peephole. What was it with these women? Why did D'Posse think they could simply show up at my house, especially now?

"Who is it, Mom?" Shawn called from down the hall.

"Nobody," I whispered in the direction of the boys' suite. I had hoped to ignore the intruders, but the doorbell rang more urgently.

By that time, both twins were hollering in their unconsciously male way, "Mom, did you hear? Someone's at the door."

Gads. Anybody in the neighborhood could hear them yelling, even the old guy who lives in back, so I opened the front door.

Doreen's brown bob was a blur as she stormed to my family room and sat, eyes wild. Tina, Sienna, Krissy, and Penny were not far behind. As I watched Tina skitter past, I wondered how anyone could be so thin and still be vertical? The woman was a walking set of very well-dressed bones, tailored by Nieman's.

Sienna swished by wearing one of her wild, heroine maxis, complete with a filmy gold head scarf and jewelry fit for Nefertiti. Krissy looked like she was ready for the League fashion show in a tan, leopard-collared long coat over tan wool pants, leopard leather boots, and an off-white satin blouse, open to reveal her beige push-up bra. Meanwhile, Penny fittingly wore a subdued navy jacket over black pants, still the banker, at least in her manner of dress.

Doreen blurted, "Ryan is going to kill me. I just read Terrance's column. I cannot believe what he wrote. Ryan told me not to say anything, but Terrance called and asked me simple things about the League and its relationship to the Opera board. Just straight facts that all of us know. I did not say that you and Cole plotted anything or stole anything. Terrance dreamed that up. All I did was describe the board policy…how things go for any League president as an ex officio, voting member. I even used myself as an example since I am president now."

"Interim president, Doreen. Until I am proven innocent."

"That's going to take a while, since you've been indicted for murder," Penny said with such sarcasm, I wanted to slap her.

"Ladies, this is my home. I can have you removed."

Penny perched on a sofa arm. "Oh, chill out, Marie. I apologize if I insulted you. But you know the facts as well as we do. This is some serious shit we are dealing with. All of us."

"Marie and I have had problems ever since we cochaired that decorations committee," Sienna chimed in. She mentions that every time we meet because Sienna was later drummed off the committee for being a screamer.

Doreen interrupted. "Let's stay on the subject. Some arts boards do not allow *ex officio* members to vote, but the Metroplex Opera board does. That's all I told Terrance, except we all know you voted 'nay' when Luca demanded to write checks. I told Terrance that I would have voted nay too. I knew Luca as well as anybody. After all, we were very close for a time…even while he and Tina…"

Doreen got up, went to my kitchen, and opened a cupboard as

if she owned the place. She fumbled for a glass and got some water.

Tina chased after and retrieved glasses for each of us. "Doreen, don't go into all that. All you need to do is explain to Marie that you did not say what Terrance wrote."

"Tina, what do you mean by 'go into all that'? You mean your collective love affairs with Luca?"

"Love affairs?" Krissy's Botoxed eyes were as big as the knobs on my cabinet doors.

"Don't play innocent, Krissy. These two allude to their affairs all the time...their 'close friendships' with Luca. That's code for 'lover.' Doreen and Tina both had affairs with Luca at one time or another. Apparently, it's a badge of prestige. Did you ever join in, Penny? How about you, Sienna...or our very perfect Barbie Doll Krissy? Ever jump in the sack with Luca and the gang?"

"Marie, you've always been jealous of me," Krissy said.

"Jealous of what, Krissy? Your boots?"

Sienna put her hands on her hips. "Marie, why do you always attack? This is just like the decorations committee..."

"Attack, Sienna? You four just marched into my home, insulted me, and then insisted you are not the liars I know you are. So, when I talk straight about Doreen and Tina's relationships with Luca, you act as if I've offended them."

Doreen slammed her glass down so hard, it cracked into pieces and fell to the floor. "Damn it, Marie. I came here to tell you something. Terrance twisted what I said and left things out that I did say. Please tell all of this to Ryan ... thanks to you, we're not even living together right now. I'm staying at Tina's." She burst into sobs and shudders while Penny, Krissy, and Sienna comforted her.

Tina grabbed a roll of paper towels and set to work clearing up Doreen's spill. As she dabbed, she murmured toward the floor, as though speaking in a whisper would make the truth vanish. "Marie, all of you. Hush. We must keep this between us. You must promise not to mention our relationships with Luca to anyone.

Just say, 'no comment.' You know how Luca was. So handsome. Forceful. Charming when he wanted. He took advantage of me long ago, then Doreen. Luckily, we warned Penny, Krissy, and Sienna, but Tina and I still share the scars. Rape of the body. Rape of the heart. Rape of the spirit. After Luca tried to rape you, Marie, I didn't blame you when you killed him. The son of a bitch deserved it. We'll cover for you best we can, but Doreen and I must try to repair our marriages. Our husbands' reputations…"

I grabbed Tina's towels to get her to stop this drivel. "I did not kill Luca. You and D'Posse must stop spreading lies. I swear on high heaven that my lawyer will silence you. Even if one of you is married to him."

Did that register? Doreen got that look I've seen before, as if her eyes were magnets with which she could ensnare me. Her pupils locked onto mine in a desperate effort to control. She paid no attention to what I had just said to Tina, but determinedly babbled more sob-drenched rationalizations, until I thought she would never stop.

To get her attention, I clapped my hands three times, the ready, set, go cheerleader signal from our college days.

Startled, Doreen shook her head as if coming out of a trance.

Then I absolutely roared in best cheerleader fashion. "Doreen, shut the fuck up. All of you, get the hell out of my home."

You should have seen D'Posse's collective jaws drop when that thundered out. God it felt good to expel my pent-up rage.

Penny glared. "Well, I never…" Then she pivoted to the front door. "Ladies, we are out of here. I will not put up with a filthy mouth. I don't care who her crooked husband was."

Sienna followed, her maxi swishing, "I told you gals about her. I worked with her on that decorations committee…"

"Seriously, Marie. You should see a shrink. It's jealousy, pure and simple. Jealous of me, jealous of all of us," Krissy said.

Darn, I should have held my temper. Truly, that was so unlike me to swear like a football player. No telling what D'Posse would post on their Facebook page later. And at the next League meeting, when I will be allowed to sit in but not speak, thirty collective glares would stare my way. That's fine, since most of them don't speak, anyway, except Lena.

∾

After Doreen's white BMW Seven-Series sedan blazed away, I noticed my phone blinking with a message. It was Ryan, detailing what Terrance already had told all of Dallas, only Ryan did it in an earnest way.

"Marie, I'm so sorry that Terrance beat me to the punch. The grand jury's ruling was delivered after we left yesterday evening, instead of this morning when I had expected. I'm also sorry to say that the grand jury did what the prosecution wanted. The D.A. has a lot of evidence, and a lot of leeway in presenting it. That means, yes, you've been indicted, but this does not mean you will be convicted. You must believe me. Call me after you get this. I want to see you as soon as possible."

In a shocked trance, I drove to Ryan's office in Bank of America Plaza, the tall one with the green argon lighting at night. The midweek traffic downtown was terrible, so I went around the block several times before I figured out where to enter the underground parking. Then I took an elevator to the main level, where I mistakenly got on the "Odd Elevators 51-69," which meant I could not go to the sixty-second floor. But I didn't know that, so I rode with several office workers to the top. When I didn't get off, one of them helped me figure out my mistake. Then I rode back down, got off, and took an escalator to the ground floor, where I found the "Even Elevators 58-70." That elevator zoomed up like lightning.

Once I got to Ryan's office, he took me on another confusing elevator ride to the City Club on the sixty-ninth floor. To avoid prying eyes, he requested a private conference room.

By that time, I needed something to calm my jitters, so I ordered a Bloody Mary.

Ryan ordered an iced tea. "I've got a preliminary hearing late this afternoon."

"Sorry to ruin your day," I sighed. I did not want to tell him about Doreen's visit with D'Posse unless I had to. Ryan had enough problems. "Our boy Terrance Nichols targeted me again."

"Tell me, was there anything in his column that was an absolute lie? He is entitled to his opinions, based on the facts, and I saw that my dear wife Doreen provided some of those. But anything Terrance says to support his insinuations must be factually true."

"The rat as much said I'm a murderer...even a thief!" I shouted too loudly. Maybe my Bloody Mary wasn't the best idea.

Ryan put a finger to his lips and motioned toward the glass walls. Just beyond were tables of executives and attorneys in expensive suits. Who knew what they could hear through the glass.

Ryan kept his voice low. "Terrance is a cagey writer. Everything he said was insinuation. But if he keeps it up, I'll file libel charges and ask for a change of venue. Not that I want a trial out of town."

An out of town trial? Weeks living out of a suitcase and worrying about Shawn and Avery partying at home?

Ryan seemed as depressed about the idea as I was. As he stared off to the surrounding skyline, I wondered if he was simply going through the motions and acting like he was on my side. What if he believed Doreen? And what about Barry Claridge's revelations? Had Billy Bob actually checked further into those, or was Ryan so busy with his higher-paying, white-collar criminals that he had done nothing in my defense?

When he turned my way, I guess he saw my doubt. He cupped my hand in his. "Marie, I know you are not a murderer." His eyes misted as he gazed out again at the amazing view of Dallas, where buildings competed to be the newest, the highest, the brightest. "We two go back, don't we? So long ago. Time has just vanished."

I was startled by the depth of his emotions. My case was personally affecting him, not just me. "Terrance's column brought out the worst in me. This morning, Doreen and D'Posse came over and I completely lost it. In fact, I told them all to fuck off."

He laughed. "Good for you! I am blown away by Doreen's involvement in this mess, everything from what Billy Bob has uncovered about her affairs with Luca, to Terrance's accusations. Believe me, I've ordered Doreen not to say another word."

"Good," was all I could manage. Poor Ryan. I guess he already knew about Doreen's affair, but did he ever wonder if she might have killed Luca? Or Tina? Although the idea may seem preposterous, I decided to put the bug in his ear. "I hate to mention this, truly, but if you look at possible suspects, Doreen and Tina might be two."

"Actually, we are looking into that possibility, not just those two, but all of Luca's paramours. Billy Bob is developing quite a long list. Seems they like to spill dirt on each other."

"Never underestimate the power of a woman scorned."

"Sadly, that's what the D.A. says about you."

I didn't like that remark, and my eyes told Ryan so.

"Sorry. But you've got to face the facts, Marie."

"Has Billy Bob found out more about Barry Claridge?"

Ryan nodded. "Barry gave Billy Bob a 'no comment.' We will have to subpoena him."

"Momma's Boy, always protecting Rebecca's world."

"Right."

We each thought for a moment, until I suddenly remembered. "Terrance's column reminded me of something I had forgotten. Two months before Cole died, Luca and Rebecca came to see Cole one night at his penthouse. He told me later that Rebecca blatantly ordered Cole to allow Luca check-writing privileges on all Metroplex Opera accounts."

Ryan perked up. "Go on."

"Cole was shocked that Rebecca was so insistent about this. You're on the Opera's board, so you are well aware that artistic directors should not have access to the Opera's purse strings."

"Right. That's to keep the Maestro from blowing money on extravagant productions."

"Rebecca was furious when Cole told her no. She threatened to take away Cole's authority to invest the Opera's funds."

The lights went on in Ryan's swimming-pool eyes. "It's not just Doreen and Tina blabbing to Terrance. Rebecca could be the source of his gossip."

"That imperious biddy."

"What else did Cole say about this meeting?"

"Rebecca told Cole that Luca would resign if the board didn't give him access to the Opera's accounts."

"Was Barry at this meeting with his mother and Cole?"

"No. Why?"

"Just wondered if Barry was another dot. I'll tell Billy Bob."

"Tell him to get busy. My life depends on what he can find."

"It's obvious that someone set you up. After Cole's Ponzi scheme was exposed, you became the perfect target."

"I was thinking back to the League meeting at Rebecca's that Saturday. Keith Warren was there, along with that Italian baritone."

"Why would Keith be out to get you?"

"The Opera lost big money in Odyssey."

"But that wasn't your fault."

"For all I know, he may think I've spent it."

"Let's see what Billy Bob discovers. After all, he found out that my wife of twenty-four years was screwing the Maestro—this at the same time he was screwing Doreen's buddy Tina."

I didn't know what to say, so I sort of sighed in sympathy.

"This morning, I had a talk with Tina's hotshot neurosurgeon husband. I don't know what he'll decide, but Doreen is about to find herself in divorce court."

"Oh, Ryan. I hate to hear that. Marriage is tough sometimes, but you have a family together. Even Cole and I kept things together for sake of our boys."

He twisted off his wedding ring and held it as though it were an eyepiece to the future. "What I used to interpret as Doreen's cheery prattle has turned into sordid scum about who was screwing whom. No wonder my wife wasn't 'interested' in me anymore. She had her Maestro lover. For all I know, they made it a threesome."

My laugh sounded bitter. "I'm with you. This morning, I also accused D'Posse of having group sex."

Ryan's eyes had angry sparks. "That Luca really got around."

"He was beyond pushy. I can see how women got into trouble. This morning Tina screamed at me that she felt raped. 'Rape of the body. Rape of the heart. Rape of the spirit.'"

"That's a laugh. Screw around and then claim rape?"

"Tina was very upset. She and Doreen were at the League meeting that Saturday. Had access to my car, my gun bag."

"You left it unlocked?"

"No, but my keys were in my purse. I left it in Rebecca's living room when I went to the ladies' room. For all I know, someone took my keys for a bit. But they were back in my purse by the time I left for home."

"More for Billy Bob to explore. I'll have him interrogate D'Posse. They'll have to testify at trial. Which brings up a point I've meant to discuss with you: my associate Colleen Ballard will handle parts of your trial. She's primarily a tax attorney but she does darn good criminal work when I need her to. You see, I can't interrogate my own wife."

I was disappointed but muttered, "Oh, I understand."

"Gads. What you don't know about someone you've shared a bed with since college."

"Don't feel alone. Cole and I were in the same, estranged boat."

"Even so, Cole and I, you and Doreen, well, we were on the same team. That should count for something. I'm telling you, Marie, I refuse to be married to a woman who would cover her sordid tracks by crucifying a long-time friend."

Maybe it was the Bloody Mary I'd downed, but suddenly I

became overwhelmed and burst into tears at the strain. Did I have the strength to get through a trial?

Ryan urgently handed me napkins. I think he would have come around to hug me, except for the gawkers through the glass.

When I looked up, Ryan's eyes spilled tears too.

That startled me. Maybe he was emotional about divorcing Doreen, but he seemed to really care about my horrid situation— even willing to investigate his own wife.

I wasn't used to having a man display such concern.

Good old Diver, going full tilt to take down our opponents. Wouldn't Cole get a laugh out that?

Chapter Fourteen

MY TROUBLED SONS

This is what astounds me. I'm going on trial for murder, but my daily life is like any single mother's. Full of the tribulations of dealing with family life and my two troubled sons.

They're twenty-two, going on sixteen, identical in looks except for the color and shape of their eyes. Shawn's are light golden, almond-shaped, like my eyes. Avery inherited his father's Labrador Retriever eyes. Big, wet and brownish with electric glints. Although handsome, my boys were problems I would wish for no single mother: A pair of party-hardy males, post-grad but unemployed and still living at home.

When I arrived, a police car was angled across the entrance to my driveway. I had to park on the street but wondered whether to go inside. What could the police arrest me for now? Should I call Ryan? But then I worried there might be a problem with the boys, whose car was parked in front of the police car. I rushed inside.

Both were seated like chastised choirboys around the kitchen island with a stack of tickets in front of them.

"What in the world?"

A pot-bellied stereotype of a small-town cop in his late fifties strutted around, emanating aromas of tacos and cigarettes with each huff. As soon as he saw me, he ripped another ticket from his booklet and slammed the filmy paper on the stack. "You the mother of this pair? This is for your sons' failure to follow police instructions."

Mother taught me long ago that the best thing I can do in any tense situation is plaster on a smile. I introduced myself in a sugary voice. "Sir, is there anything I can do to help?" I realized that was conniving, but I dared not indicate I wanted to start trouble.

"Ma'am, you and your husband might teach these two respect for authority. But for now, I am impounding their car. The tow truck will be here in a bit. That will clip their wings."

"But we need the car for job interviews," Avery whined. He was the oldest by thirty minutes and had assumed the "alpha" brother role ever since he found out his half-hour seniority.

"Yeah, Mom, we need the car for jobs," Shawn chimed in.

"How long until we can get their car out of impoundment?"

"As soon as every citation is paid. This sheet has the details. You can retrieve the car from Jordan Towing in Plano."

"Lovely," I said with as much sarcasm as I could inject without sounding snarly.

"All told, this stack of tickets should set you back about fifteen hundred. Not including costs for defensive driving classes."

"Again?" I glared at the boys.

"Avery was doing sixty in a thirty. I was just along for the ride," Shawn said.

The officer jumped in. "But you were the one who flipped me off, young man."

"Shawn? That's not like you at all."

"It wasn't the finger. I gave him the Seinfeld wave."

"Besides, the Supreme Court ruled that we can flip him off, and he can't arrest us," Avery said.

"That's not why I stopped you two. But flipping me off didn't help your case."

"It was 'the wave,'" Shawn insisted as he demonstrated.

"That wasn't what you did, young man."

"Officer, I apologize for my boys' behavior."

"Well, if these were my sons, I'd have a good, long talk, right before I took my belt to their fuzzy pink hides. I suggest you ask your husband to do the honors when he gets home."

My face fell and the boys averted their gaze.

The wheels turned in the officer's freckled head. "Single-mom?"

"The boys' father died last fall."

The officer's neurons slowly ignited. He glanced at his citations. "Donovan. Is this Cole Donovan's house?"

"It's my house, until it sells."

"You were married to that snake? Hell of a quarterback but not much of a fund manager. I rolled my IRA into Odyssey."

"I am sorry, sir."

"No wonder your sons act like a bunch of Highland Park brats. They *are* Highland Park brats. I'll bet my IRA paid for your swimming pool out there." He motioned to the backyard.

That irritated me. It was fine if he stopped the boys for driving too fast and flipping him off, but he had no right to insult me because I have a pool. "Sir, are you finished with the citations? If so, I would like for you to leave now."

He sauntered around my island and peered at my blender, my coffee maker, my wine refrigerator, as if he might find something suspicious to write another ticket about. "Tell me, does it make you squirm to see little people like me who've lost everything?"

I wagged my finger. "The boys and I knew nothing of Cole's financial dealings. You are not the only one who has lost everything."

"You've got this mansion. But I have to start all over."

"Again, sir, I regret your financial losses. Now, please gather your materials and leave, or I will call my attorney Ryan Ingles."

The officer puffed his chest to go another round, but luckily the roar of a truck engine emanated from the driveway.

"I'll take care of this tow truck, but I'm not through with you. I've got one more citation. Petty larceny. That's because you probably think my IRA is petty, but your husband stole it."

"I had nothing to do with my husband's investments."

"The charge may not stick, but you'll have to appear. Tell that to Ryan Ingles." With that, he pounded out to the front.

I slammed and locked the door behind him. Then I called Ryan's mobile, which went to voicemail. Rather than leave a message, I hung up. I worried Ryan might think I was too needy.

"That cop can't do that, can he Mom?" Avery said.

I sat on a stool next to my two sons, each the spitting image of their father. "The officer can issue the tickets, and you will pay me for your fines when you get jobs. But you must understand that you are adults. Even if you have to work at a convenience store, you must be self-sufficient. Stop partying. Apply for jobs, do yard work or clean the pool. I expect you to be productive members of this household."

Shawn batted his brown puppy eyes. "You sound like Benjamin Braddock's mother."

"More like the Wicked Witch of the West," Avery said.

"For centuries, children have had similar complaints about their mothers. But successful children have heeded their mother's teachings. I suggest you start now."

Other than that, I could think of no new words. In some sort of preposterous desperation, I wished Cole were alive to help me with this problem, although the man rarely, if ever, disciplined the boys. Cole was simply not there. When the twins were young, Cole had football practice and then drinks after with the guys, or he was out of town at an away game, an off-season golf tournament, a TV appearance. And then there was the Monday day-off drinking and bonding binge with the team, or the six weeks of training camp in Bend, Oregon, or trips to Vegas in the off-season to gamble, whatever excuse Cole used to be with "the guys," always the guys, but that really was an excuse to drink and screw around with groupies.

Shawn noticed my futile drift and gave me a hug. "Don't worry, Mom. We're just late bloomers."

He smiled, and I could see my eyes shining back.

Even the hotheaded Avery gave me a pat. "Yeah, but we're damn good looking and smart as hell. We'll make you proud someday."

When I looked into Avery's eyes, Cole's competitive spirit twinkled back at me.

❧

As I went back to my bedroom to take off my clothes, I thought to myself, how different my sons were, their personalities ingrained so early. I remembered a home game when Shawn and Avery were about six. We sat twenty rows up, mid-field. Shawn was wearing an Explorers' coonskin cap that day. He watched intensely as the players came on field, led by the Sacagawea-costumed cheerleaders and the Corps of Discovery mascots.

When halftime came, Shawn doffed his coonskin cap and shouted, "Here comes Clark and Lewis!"

The crowd around us laughed, but Shawn misunderstood their chuckles as derision. He sat glumly while Avery chided, "Louis and Clark, you dumb shit."

I tried to get Shawn to understand the crowd was not making fun, but he would not be cheered. He was the kind of boy who saw defeat where there was victory. Gloom instead of joy.

I've always felt for him and remain his strongest ally because, in contrast Avery and Cole, Shawn inherited my reticence.

❧

Bam, bam, bam, the officer was at the front door again. I grabbed a robe and ran down the hall.

Avery whispered, "Mom, should I get it?"

I motioned for him to hush. "He has no warrant, and I don't think he has enough cause to kick in the door."

Instead, the policeman put the paperwork through the mail

slot. "Order to Appear," my citation read. So again, I called Ryan but got his voice mail and hung up.

After the officer left, I went back to my bedroom and played Brahms in the nude until my fingers were sore. Then I had a drink from Cole's built-in bar and took a long, hot bath, even though I'm not supposed to take a bath with this horrid GPS tracker on my ankle. Nevertheless, I jury-rigged a cover for it, using waterproof tape and plastic wrap. Then I got into the dry tub, propped my ankle above the tub rim and turned on the water. As the water warmed me, flashes from Cole's and my six years in the pros started whirling in.

Chapter Fifteen
BOOTLEG!

T he first two years, Cole did not play a down in the regular
season game. The starting quarterback was an eight-year
veteran named Randy Kilpatrick, a.k.a., "Dandy Randy." He was a
slick looking guy with a voice destined to become a sports
announcer. In fact, he's still doing color on NBC, last I saw.

The longer Cole spent on the bench, the more frustrated he
became. "I'm calling my agent. Dallas might like a hometown boy
as quarterback."

But Cole's agent found no takers. After all, Cole was an
unproven commodity in the NFL, where the crème de la crème
rose to the top of the QB ladder. Cole either had to wait for
Dandy Randy to retire, or become a free agent at the end of Cole's
three-year contract.

While Cole soothed his ego with drinks, I waited for my
husband to come home. I was not alone. At that time, the NFL
was a cesspool of immature-male behavior. Things may have
changed since our days in the pros. I know the NFL now has all
kinds of ads about "Football is Family." But in our day, most
Explorers fell into six distinct categories: Drinkers, Dopers,
Philanderers, Abusers, The Pussy-Whipped, and Religious Nuts.

Cole belonged in the first four categories, often coming home at 3:00 a.m. to encounter a very angry me.

Yes, I was furious. By the time he arrived in a stupor, with some other woman's lipstick and makeup smeared on his shirt, I was in a rage. Like an idiot, I thought I could push or slap Cole, and he would somehow wake up and smell the roses. And I was foolish enough to think he wouldn't slap me back.

One time I called him a loser and that infuriated him. That was his excuse, anyway. I can still feel where he slammed his fist into my back, a blow so hard, I lost my breath, collapsed on the bed, and sobbed for hours.

A good little victim, wasn't I? Every time I see on the news that some football player has cold-cocked his wife in an elevator, I remember the why of it. Football is a warlike culture, where men rule and women are irrelevant.

Then again, every time I have whined to myself about Cole's behavior, I also tried to remember the many wild highs between the horrid lows. Some moments were wondrously joyous or tender.

By the time I was fully pregnant with the twins, Cole finally got his chance. Dandy Randy had hurt his knee so badly he was out for the season, if not his career. The Explorers' second string, running-style quarterback, Gene Hendrickson—nicknamed "Gene the Dream, the Sex Machine"—proved to be a misfit and was traded to Minnesota for a passing quarterback. But the new guy severely cut three fingers on his passing hand while carving his Thanksgiving turkey, so Cole got the starting call. A Monday night game against the Cowboys.

I was watching TV at my friend Monica's house, along with some other Explorers wives.

One announcer barked to his buddies, "All-American Cole Donovan has the start tonight, but he's been at third string for two years, and if he can't cut it tonight, the Explorers will have to bring in more proven talent at QB."

With the other wives around, it was hard to sit quietly with

announcers demeaning your husband. But after we got the ball—
and this was something you could not plan for, or even hope for if
your life depended on it—Cole dropped back, faked a handoff to a
running back, then turned the opposite direction and ran ninety-
three yards to a touchdown. Effortlessly, just like that gorgeous boy
I first saw on the playground so long ago.

The announcers screamed, "Bootleg!"

The wives screamed, jumped up and down and hugged me.

After Cole crossed the goal line, one commentator said, "Boys,
I guess Cole Donovan just made the team."

We wives screamed, "Damn right!"

Way later that night, several of us drove to meet the players at
the airport. We were so excited at the team's big win. Not only did
Cole run for that touchdown but he passed for three more. We
killed the Cowboys, 31 to 14.

When Cole saw me at the airport, he gave me a big grin. Then
he picked me up, twin-pregnant, and we spun in a circle to the
clicking, flashing media.

After we got home, I headed to the shower, but Cole stopped
me. "I know you can't get in and out of the tub very well, so I'll
help." He guided me into warm bubbles and gently washed every
inch of my body. "Here, Baby," he said as he stretched out a big
towel. "Gotta take care of our little mother." Then he dried me.
Led me to the bed. And made the most tender love to me, far
different from our usual, physical sex. This was an expression of
care and love. And I returned my love in passionate release.

When Cole rolled onto his back, he whispered, "I love you so
much, Marie. I don't show it like I should." That was something he
said so rarely, so I stored that murmured love forever in my
memories.

With Cole now at the helm, the Explorers won their division
championship during the same December the twins were born.
And Cole catapulted to NFL fame. Endorsements. Ads. Groupies.
Always the groupies.

The *Portland Oregonian* newspaper put the twins' photo on the front page and called my sons "Cole's Lucky Charms." They wore the cutest terrycloth outfits that my friend Monica had custom made, blue and gold with the Explorers emblem on their tiny chests.

Even though the article misspelled my name as "Mary," I felt Cole and I finally were on the same team.

Okay, so I was wrong about that. But for a moment, I felt I had the brass ring.

Chapter Sixteen

OFFICE OF RYAN INGLES, PC

The redheaded receptionist greeted me with a snotty, "May I help you?" Perhaps I had interrupted her Facebook surfing. What is it with people? Can't they do their jobs without chatting with their friends on social media?

In spite of her attitude, I gave the receptionist a smile so she might remember me. "Marie Donovan. I'm here to see Ryan Ingles." I smiled again. I'm good at that, if nothing else.

The receptionist's eyes did not yield one spark of recognition or concern, which amazed me. Right beside me on a magazine rack, the *Dallas Daily Herald*'s front page displayed my horrid mug shot. There I stood, hair down and stringy, mascara smeared, no lipstick, and my eyes full of fear, bewilderment, and pain. Beneath me, the headline screamed "Not Guilty?" in a question mark.

Yes, I had entered a plea of not guilty at my official arraignment. Only I had not stated it as a question. I had said it firmly, with authenticity, as Ryan coached me to do. I so wanted to please him. He's my only hope.

"One moment, ma'am…" the receptionist murmured. Then she urgently messaged someone far more important than I.

Fuming, I went to the publications rack, grabbed the *Daily*

Herald and held it in front of her. She took a while to notice, but when she did, she jumped.

"Yes, Mrs. Donovan. Mr. Ingles' assistant Stacie Veller will be right out."

"Thank you," I said with another of my best fake smiles.

When the office's interior glass door swished open, Ryan's aqua eyes sparkled as he peeked out. "Marie? Ready for more fun?"

The receptionist jumped. "Oh, Mr. Ingles. I thought Stacie would come to get her."

"Not to worry. My client is not only the prettiest woman who has been wrongly charged with murder, she is also a very good friend." Ryan extended a hand to help me up.

Thanks to his strong, warm hands, I felt vindicated, even if Ryan's comment was pure flattery. Part of me wanted to snub the receptionist, but I didn't want to appear arrogant to Ryan.

As he motioned me to his office down the hall, I suddenly dreaded today's "team meeting," as Ryan calls these sessions wherein he asks the same questions over and over. I feel buffeted and battered by the time each meeting is done. That's because I can't find anything new to say.

Ryan interrupted my angst. "I'm trying to decide whether to put you on the witness stand. As the defendant, you don't have to testify against yourself but, if your testimony would help your case, you should."

I nodded silently but that was my greatest fear. I've seen too many cross-examinations on TV and in films where the defendant breaks down and starts screaming, "Yes, I did it. I killed the bastard."

Ryan could see my doubts. "We'll see how things progress."

The firm's conference room is larger than most people's living rooms, with a view to the West where, on days when the Metroplex haze is not overpowering, you can see the shimmering image of Fort Worth's skyline thirty miles away. As I took my seat, I was surprised to see Billy Bob Hughes there in person. He greeted me with, "Hellooooooo, Baby," although I doubt he truly remembered me from the old days, just the fact that I was Cole's girlfriend.

In college, Billy Bob played strong-side linebacker. He was a walking block of muscles with pedestal thighs and monumental shoulders. His jowly face was flushed with freckles and his chin could stop a truck. As he fumbled in his briefcase for a pen, I felt a bit sad that the former linebacker now looked a bit old. Bald, big tummy, blotched skin. And from his whiskey voice, I suspected too much Scotch, cigarettes, or both.

Cole always called Billy Bob "Nasty Man," a nickname for his ribald antics. I could just hear Cole's voice, "You should have seen what 'Nasty Man' did today. After practice, he strutted around the locker room with a toothbrush stuck up his butt hole. He went to every freshman and asked, 'Hey, Fish. Did you take my toothbrush?' When they said, 'Oh, no, Sir,' Billy Bob would turn around, shoot 'em the moon and they'd see the toothbrush up his ass." Then Cole would laugh in a guttural trill, while his eyes shone with glee.

༺

I FELT A TAP ON MY SHOULDER. WHEN I LOOKED UP, RYAN'S puzzled eyes urged me back to reality. The memories never leave me.

"So…Marie, have you remembered anything new that we should know?"

Ryan had closed his door for privacy, but his legal assistant Stacie Veller was there to take notes. Ryan assured me she would keep everything confidential but I felt uncomfortable, as though something I might say or do—even a gesture—would make my legal team think I killed that slime ball Luca Scarlatti.

I shrugged. "Nothing new to share. I told you about my meeting with Barry Claridge. Maybe I shouldn't have met him privately like that, but I made sure he wasn't taping me."

Ryan's frown told me he did not approve. "Yes, and I told the D.A. about Barry, but then Barry denied having said a word."

"I guess I should have recorded him. But he did say, and I can almost hear his high tenor, 'To put it bluntly, Marie, we are house poor. And I think Mother knows more than she lets on about Luca's murder.' When I asked if Rebecca knows who killed Luca, Barry said, 'Yes.'"

"Unfortunately, the D.A. said that your conversation was a case of 'she said, he said.' We can't use it unless Barry decides to tell the truth."

"But there was something odd about what Barry said at the end…that comment, 'he knew what he must do.' His eyes got a distant, determined look, as though I wasn't there anymore. Like he had rehearsed this same line many times."

Ryan looked dismayed. "But if he won't tell anybody, we're stuck with you being the only one to say it. Marie, I need more to go on. So tell me anything else you can remember."

"Well, I've told you about the emergency meeting that Rebecca called the day after I got out on bail. With D'Posse gathered, along with Keith Warren and Barry, Rebecca pressured me to admit I did it. She said I must save Metroplex Opera. Then Lena Verano barged in and promised to fly me to Bali, which was unfortunate, what with D'Posse around. Then everybody left in a huff for the meeting across the hall. I saw Terrance in the lobby trying to interview each of them as they walked by. I've told you all this."

"Tell me again what Rebecca said about Luca."

"She murmured to Barry, something like, 'Perhaps things were for the best.' I can't remember her exact words, but Barry nodded. His eyes were red from crying. But Barry was the only one at the meeting who didn't seem to think I was guilty. He wasn't glaring or accusing. And that was the first time he said that he wanted to share 'his side of the story,' but Rebecca stopped him. She just kept pressing me to admit I had killed Luca. And D'Posse piled on. If

Lena had not barged in, I might have buckled under pressure just to get rid of them all."

Billy Bob perked up. "Everybody but Barry accused you?"

"Yes. I had a room full of people expecting me to confess. Rebecca may make a big deal out of Lena's promise to help me leave the country. You know how Lena is. So loud. And before I could shush her, she said something like, 'I've been in the dead-body business a long time and know people all over the world who can make things happen. If this thing goes south, I'll have you on an island in Bali before they can slap on the leg chains.'"

"Oh, thank you, Lena," Ryan said.

"I can explain all this to Rebecca if you want me to."

Ryan scoffed. "Don't explain anything to her. Or Barry. You must maintain zero contact with witnesses. Especially D'Posse and…my so-called wife." Ryan's face flushed. He got up and paced by the wall. "Billy Bob, you got anything to pull us out of this jam?"

Billy Bob spoke in a hushed tone. "Actually, I've been busting to tell you guys something, but I wanted to make sure everyone is on the same page in terms of confidences."

"Nasty Man, you know Stacie is bound by law."

"I know Stacie's cool, but actually, I'm worried about our lovely defendant and her pal Lena."

"Who, me?"

Ryan cleared his throat. "Marie…let's put the cards on the table. You and Lena are best friends, right?"

"Like sisters."

Ryan pulled a chair nearer, sat facing me. "If your life depended on it, can you keep a secret from Lena?"

I glanced at Stacie, the only other woman in the room. She paused in her note taking and gave me a sympathetic look. She understood how difficult it was for girlfriends to keep secrets.

I asked Billy Bob, "Is this something that will come out anyway during the trial?"

"More than likely, right Diver?"

Ryan looked as if he was about to jump down my throat if I
did not agree to secrecy.

"I can do it," I said with a firm nod.

I saw a faint smile on Stacie's lips. She was on my side.

"Okay, then swear her in, Diver. 'Cause I've got a lead."

I didn't realize that Ryan would actually pull out a *Bible*, but
darn if he didn't. He put my hand on it, then gave me a deeply
serious look that made me catch my breath. "Do you, Marie
Harris Donovan, solemnly swear never to tell another soul what
you are about to hear, that is, until after it becomes evidence at
trial?"

Ryan's deeply serious tone sent shivers through my soul. I
jittered, "I do. Truly."

"Marie, I am counting on you. This may be our only play."
Then he nodded to Billy Bob. "Nasty Man, Spill."

Billy Bob scooted his chair like gathering in a huddle. "Well,
after hearing what Barry Claridge told Marie, that his mother
knew who did it and 'he would do what he must do,' I snooped
around. There's a gay bar in the Oak Lawn area called the Round
Up Saloon, and I'm told that every gay goes there now and again."

I got excited. "The Embalming BoyZ from the funeral home
took me there my first day on the job." I was referring to the three
guys who did the embalming, body prep, dressing, makeup and
hair for our "clients." Their macabre jokes usually sent me laughing
to tears.

Billy Bob seemed amazed. "Well, I guess *everybody* does go to
the Round Up, even Marie." He grinned and nodded at his joke.
"So, I yakked it up at the bar with a few patrons and subtly
mentioned the Maestro getting killed. One guy perked up, so I
asked, 'You know Luca Scarlatti?' But the guy held up a napkin
with the Round Up's slogan."

"What happens at the Round Up, stays at the Round Up," I
said.

Everybody laughed, shocked that I would know the slogan,

but the Embalming BoyZ had made a big deal out of teaching it to me.

"That may be the slogan, but money loosens lips. I slipped the guy a bill, and suddenly he was my best friend. Said, 'I know one of Luca's boyfriends.'"

I was stunned. "Luca's boyfriends? You mean Luca was gay?"

"From what these guys said, Luca was a bi-. I had to part with several more bills, but I heard the same story from a number of fellows who hang there. And here's the biggie. Turns out your tea and sympathy pal Barry and the Maestro had a lengthy fling that eventually headed south."

"Barry and Luca?" I was shocked.

"Was it common knowledge in the gay community that Luca was bisexual?" Ryan asked.

"Indeed. But the Maestro didn't come out because of his family in Italy. He also screwed a lot of prominent arts mavens... well, we've heard that already. So, Luca 'took care' of Barry in order to keep his family and lady friends happy."

Ryan slammed a hand on the *Bible*. "When you say, 'took care,' you mean Luca paid Barry hush money?"

Billy Bob handed Ryan a list. "That's what the guys said. Here's names and numbers. It may take a few more dollars to get them to testify though."

"Legal Ethics 304.b, Nasty Man. You know I can't bribe witnesses to testify."

Billy Bob pulled the list back. "I'll put the bribes on my tab."

Ryan got up and paced around the conference table with new determination. "Stacie, make a copy of Billy Bob's list so we can issue subpoenas."

I was so excited, I must have glowed. Luca's affair with Barry now made him Suspect #1. Or his mother. Or both. "This should get me off, don't you think?"

"Marie, this is great news from a legal perspective, but we still have physical evidence to overcome. Your gun killed Luca. And your hairpin was found in his thigh with a nerve agent on it. We have to prove someone else put those things there."

"Anybody at Rebecca's that Saturday afternoon could have taken my car keys. For all I know, Barry may have been around. I didn't see him, but Rebecca's house is a castle. Maybe Barry slipped in to our meeting room when I went to the bathroom."

"You didn't see Barry at all that day?"

"I wish I had, then this would make sense. But if he set me up, why would he suggest to meet privately? Why would he tell me that his mother knew who killed Luca?"

Billy Bob's bushy eyebrows rose in a high arch. "He might have been baiting, to see what you knew."

"Stacie, hold those subpoenas. Billy Bob, set up private interviews with your witnesses. You can pay them for their time, but make it clear you will not pay them to testify. I want to verify what they will say on the stand, without hundred-dollar bills luring them to talk."

Chapter Seventeen

D'POSSE DUET

If I had wings, I would have flown home. We now have witnesses who can point a finger at Barry, Rebecca, or both. I couldn't wait to tell my boys. Call my brother Owen. Even maybe call Dad. Well, probably not Dad.

I pulled off the Tollway then turned south on Preston to Beverly, then into the drive of my increasingly mortgaged home. Thank heavens Cole paid cash when we bought it. Under the Texas Homestead Law, creditors cannot take it, that is, unless I miss a payment on my home equity line of credit. Cole got the HELOC when we renovated the pool and patio. He thought it was smarter to pay with a HELOC so we could deduct the interest. He requested two million in credit, and the renovations took about a half-million of that. After Cole died, I've used another half-million.

Sums like that astound me. I grew up a middle-class girl from Richardson, Texas, but funny how life becomes costlier when you are accused of murder. I've spent about a hundred thousand for estate lawyers to argue with insurance companies that refused to pay me a death benefit, since Cole's death was ruled a suicide. My estate lawyers have had to defend me in ongoing lawsuits, and IRS attempts to seize or freeze any money or property. Other than my salary, I have no way to function other than siphoning money from my home's equity.

On top of that, I have spent a hundred thousand for bail. Fifty-thousand dollars in retainer for Ryan, with another fifty thousand due next month. Plus the maddening expenses for the boys' college loans, traffic tickets, getting their car out of hock, and, have I mentioned, they have not managed to find jobs. Yet.

When I turned into my driveway, I noticed two cars parked by the curb. Might be media. Might be Cole's investors. Might be detectives. So I opened the garage door, drove in, then closed it immediately, checking the rearview to make sure no one followed me inside.

Call me paranoid, but I am learning.

When I walked through the kitchen, I heard loud music from Avery's side of the boys' suite. I banged on his door, "Your mother is home, please turn it down."

Avery breathed "Ugh," but at least the music softened. I almost wish it hadn't, because as soon as I could hear something other than Avery's rap, I heard an annoying tapping at my glass patio door. Who in the world was in my backyard? The gates have combination locks on them. Maybe the pool guy? He knows the combination.

When I opened the blinds, I saw Doreen Ingles urgently bobbing, and a head beyond hers was Tina LeBlanc. D'Posse, minus their bitchy cohorts. I was amazed that these two kept showing up at my home.

I swung open the patio door and almost hollered, "How dare you? I'm calling the police." But I didn't say it. I held my temper and glared in silence.

Doreen tittered. "We climbed the back fence. I hope you don't mind, but there's news media out front. We walked around to your neighbor's, that older fellow in back, and asked him if we could climb the vines on his fence."

"And he let you?"

"Yes. He says he peeks over when you are out by the pool."

"Oh, Lord. What has my life come to?"

"May we come in?" Tina asked after she tiptoed in.

"I can't seem to keep you two out."

"Marie, no need to be harsh."

I refused to mask my dismay. Ever since my entrée into the world of opera fundraising, I've had some sort of chemical reaction to this pair. First, Tina passed me over as chair of the Diamond Ball, the glitzy gala held at the Ritz Carlton. Who in the world would say no to a well-heeled, capable volunteer like me, who could financially support a ball that would garner a half-million in profits and make Tina's presidency a success? But Tina crooned that I probably did not have the time, what with my boys.

"Diamond Ball chair is almost a full-time job, Marie."

That was her lame excuse. Tina simply did not want me to succeed at anything, especially leading the Diamond Ball. Visibility in that position would set me up to become League president. In short, she intercepted me.

Still, I got the job a year later when Sherrie Donald was president. My event had the theme "Madame Butterfly" and made a record five hundred and fifty-thousand dollars. The following year, the League board elected me president, and when Doreen Ingles asked if she could chair the Diamond Ball, I gave her the job. I didn't like Doreen, but Ryan was on the board and had the bucks to back the event.

You would think Doreen would have been grateful, but now that she is interim president, she treats me like I have the Ebola virus.

Her pettiness reminds me of college days. When Doreen was cheer captain, she became so overbearing, I quit the team to focus on my cello. Maybe I should quit the League too. Being an arts maven has not proved rewarding, especially when one has to associate with D'Posse. Thank heavens the entire entourage did not show today.

With dread, I showed the pair to the living room.

Tina greeted me with a tense smile. "It was important that we speak to you in person. For all we know, your phones are bugged."

The pair nervously fluttered their eyes to one another.

"First off, do not climb my back fence again. Use the front door. I don't care who sees you. Secondly, you are welcome to say what you came to say, but I am aware you are prosecution witnesses."

"Marie, we only told the police the facts. The truth."

"Doreen, I hope you will tell the truth. You of all people know that nothing happened the night Luca attacked me. I pushed him away. You saw me. I didn't later plot to kill him. But someone who knew about that fight has set me up. You two were at the League meeting the day Luca was killed. For all I know, you could have stolen my car keys and gotten my gun and my hairpin."

Doreen exploded, "Here you go again with the accusations!"

Tina looked aghast. "Now, Marie. You cannot be talking about me or Doreen. Why would we do such a thing?"

"Marie, I know you cannot talk to us. But can you listen?" Doreen asked, tears brimming in her cockroach brown eyes.

I shrugged, but curiosity took hold. "You're here. I'm all ears."

She took a breath to settle her emotions. "We have information you might want to share with your attorney. My husband, need I remind you?"

"I'm well aware that Ryan is your husband. He also happens to be the best criminal attorney in Dallas. And I am paying for his services. Fifty-thousand so far, and another fifty thousand due next week. That ought to keep you in Prada."

"Now, Marie, no need to be so...competitive," Tina bubbled.

"That's a pot calling the kettle, Tina. As for you, Doreen, why don't you tell your husband yourself?"

"Ryan and I are not speaking...ever since he took your case. I didn't want him to take it. The publicity. What if he loses? Our reputation will be ruined. Hell, it's already ruined."

Tina giggled in embarrassment. "Doreen is trying to say that she and Ryan are having troubles, but she cares very much about

Metroplex Opera and the League. If we give you information to take to Ryan, it might help remove the stain."

"The stain?"

"The Metroplex Opera's reputation has been disgraced by this mess. The *New York Times* even wrote about us. The headline was, 'Tosca does Dallas.' Don't you care what you've done?"

"Tina, I haven't done anything. And I have more important things to worry about than the Opera's reputation."

Doreen's eyes grew angry. "Of course you do. First, your husband committed suicide after his phony Ponzi scheme cost Ryan and me three-million dollars, money we could not afford to lose, thanks to Ryan's knee injury that ended NFL football for us. And now you're on trial for murdering our famous Maestro. Every day in Terrance's column, our reputations are smeared by reports of Luca being blasted by your gun and stabbed with your poisoned hairpin. Surely, even you can see that this case isn't all about you. It's about the Opera. Dallas. Ryan and me. We're in this together."

Tina chimed in. "Has Ryan discovered anything?"

"I can't say. You know that."

Doreen stamped her foot. "I demand you tell us."

"Why? Because you two had motive to kill Luca?"

Tina started trembling. "Are you accusing us of murder?"

"For all I know, you two planned the whole thing. Tina, you were furious at Luca for using you."

Doreen fumed. "Ryan would never point the finger at me, his very own wife."

"You resented Cole's success. Ryan didn't get a ring."

Tina took a mighty breath to puff up her anorexic self, then positively screeched in the most piercing soprano I may ever have heard. "Doreen, tell her what we came to say."

Doreen jumped in shock, then fumed as she regained focus, and her eyes became bullet holes. "Marie, you must tell Ryan these two things. At the Opera board meeting today, Keith Warren took me aside and told me privately that Rebecca had cancelled her pledge. That's a half-million dollars. Keith said she had lost too much in Odyssey. Keith also told me that on the Friday before Luca died, the comptroller caught Luca trying to wire money from an Opera account. Keith threatened to tell the board."

"Evidently, Keith didn't do that, because Ryan would already know."

"Keith asked me to get Ryan's opinion, off the record. But Keith didn't know that Ryan and I are not speaking. And you're trying to blame us for Luca's death."

Tina stretched out her bony arms to hug Doreen. "We'll get through this. Like always. Luca deserved what he got. And no court will convict you or me. There's absolutely no evidence."

"Thanks to whoever killed Luca, there's plenty of evidence pointed right at me. That's why I cannot support your unholy little posse. But I will give Ryan your messages."

Doreen was sobbing by then. As much as I dislike her, I felt a bit sorry for her and said what I could say truthfully. "Doreen, I regret that this horrific situation has taken a toll on your marriage to Ryan."

As she dissolved deeper in anguish, I felt even worse because I had developed a reliance on Ryan that probably glowed through any mention of his name. And I was thrilled that Billy Bob had found a possible break in the case. I didn't tell the pair about that, but I did say, "With this new evidence, Ryan might be able to get the D.A. to investigate further."

Tina tittered sarcastically. "Well, I guess we'll have to rely on Ryan to clear all our names."

"As it stands, I'm the only one charged with murder. If you find out more about this case, you must tell Ryan immediately."

Tina's expression turned dark. "We've told you what we know, at great risk to ourselves. Because of you, we have to testify in a public murder trial. Admit to being raped. And possibly be under suspicion ourselves."

"Raped? I thought you both had consensual love affairs with Luca. I don't call that rape."

"Rape of our friendship!" Tina shrieked in that soprano again.

Doreen stopped sobbing long enough to say, "Marie, he screwed us both at the same time. We found out when we ran into each other at his condo. I opened the door and there was Tina with her key in hand. Luca just laughed at us. Suggested a threesome."

"How absolutely tawdry."

Tina raised her bony fist as though she might slug me. "We will be the victors, not the victims." Then she backed away and shuffled the weeping Doreen through the patio door.

As I unlocked the side gates to usher them out, I murmured, "If you're worried about your reputations, try mine, that is, if you can Rotor Rooter it out of the toilet." Then I smiled one of my best grins.

The two slammed the gate as they left. I banged my patio door shut in rebuttal and went to the kitchen for a Bloody Mary. My brain needed relief. Between sips, I called Ryan and left an urgent voicemail. He needed to know about Rebecca's cancelled pledge but, more importantly, Luca's attempt to steal money. I also wanted Billy Bob to take a closer look at Tina LeBlanc and Doreen. Find out what those two might be hiding.

Ryan may not be able to hinge my defense solely on the homosexual alliance of Luca and Barry Claridge, or on Rebecca's financial losses and dealings with Luca. If those leads don't pan out, Ryan may need to finger his own wife, and I don't mean in a romantic way.

Chapter Eighteen

MY SIDE OF THE STORY

When I realized Luca was untrue to me, I felt filthy. Oh, I knew he had affairs with others before me, and he supposedly hit on the ever-glamorous Marie, but once we began our affair, it turned into a passion bordering on obsession, at least on my side of the mattress. The man was a maestro in and out of bed. Call me a fool, but I was one, day or night. Whenever he needed sexual release, I ran to him.

But as time went on, Luca started complaining that he needed more time to edit the score for the next production, so I tried to be a good partner and back off. But I didn't hear from him for a week or two. By the end of those days, I knew he was dumping me.

I became so desperate for his touch, I could think of nothing else. So, I went to his condo and parked at the curb. His car was in its usual slot. I sat a while. Didn't know what I was waiting for. Maybe Luca would come down, go somewhere and I could follow. Accidentally bump into him at a café or shop.

"So good to see you," I would say. I've pulled that one before, a bit of accidentally on purpose stalking. So, I waited for him to appear.

What I did not expect was for someone else I knew to pull

into Luca's second parking slot. Then head up in the elevator while I watched from the curb.

I followed.

Outside Luca's door, I listened. Voices, arguments. Then Luca's visitor started crying.

Through the door crack I heard Luca croon in Italian, "*A te, o cara*," Arturo's aria from "I Puritani."

> *To you, oh dear one, love at times*
> *leads me furtively and in tears;*
> *now it guides me to your side*
> *in joy and exultation.*
> *At the radiance of such a beautiful hour*
> *if I remember my torment,*
> *it redoubles my happiness,*
> *and I cherish my heart's beating.*

Luca's sweet voice calmed his lover's anguish. Things went quiet until I heard footsteps shuffling from the living room toward Luca's bedroom. So, I shifted around the corner hallway, where I listened at a hallway door to the master bedroom.

Inside, the sounds of sex grew. Shouts of "harder, harder" and "don't stop" and then Luca's, "Ream me," followed by a series of anguished "uhhhh, uhhhh, uhhhh's" as he released on his always-white sheets.

And then rills of laughter. The two laughing deeply at their mutual, insatiable lust.

I was jittery in shock. Should I use the key Luca gave me? Just march in and catch the two entwined. I wanted the world to know what a scumbag he was. But too many would say, "You should have known better." I felt desperately alone, my nerves stunned. So, I tiptoed silently. Took the elevator down, walked in a daze to my car. Headed to a place where I would not see people from society. A place where people would not talk.

Inside, I sat in a dark corner, nursed my wounds with a drink, when who of all people walked in. I tried to hide, but he saw me.

He came over. "You look like you got hit by a train."

"Love hurts."

"Who's the lucky guy? Or should I say, 'gal'?"

"You know my orientation. Or should."

"One never knows. You're here. That says something."

"The Round Up is a good place to hide. The code, you know." I pointed to the napkin.

"Comes with every drink. 'What happens at the Round Up, stays at the Round Up.'"

We both smiled at that one.

"Relax. You're not the type of person I'm concerned about."

"Promise?"

He nodded. "I am a man of honor, upon request."

We chatted for a while and, after another drink and some back and forth chatter, I felt I could trust him. We had chemistry.

Slowly, my story flew out. I didn't mean to offer so many details, but the alcohol eased my inhibitions. Besides, this new friend knew far more about Luca than I did. He even knew about my affair with Luca, in fact, all of Luca's affairs. Males. Females. I wondered how he got Luca to spill so many beans.

"I'm sorry you fell for him but don't feel alone." His eyes were dewy with earnest regret. Maybe the martini had loosened his filter, but he confessed. He and Luca too, several years ago. "I never told a soul until now. As you said, love hurts."

"Luca has a way…you think you are his obsession. But then you realize he has played you like a cello. And you die inside when you know your spirit has been raped."

"One inventive lover," my new friend said.

"How do sex and love get so mixed up?"

"I don't know how the guy gets away with it. He's a public figure. You'd think someone would have shot the salacious son of a bitch by now."

"I considered it this afternoon," I said.

"Truly?"

"Oh, a mere fantasy. But I do have a key."

"Me, too. No telling how many there are. Pretty risky, if you ask me. But that's Luca. He thrives on dare."

"I could have killed him today—and his newest lover—then planted the gun in the lover's hand."

"But it's your gun, right?"

I laughed. "Details. I think I need a better plan."

"Let it go. Pretend you don't care. Luca cannot stand to be ignored."

"But I do care. It would be so easy to let him have it."

His eyes sparkled. "I've often fantasized that, if I could get away with it, I would love to settle the score. And that has nothing to do with opera."

I caught a glimpse of my new friend's attraction for me, or what quickly became our booze-fueled murder plotting. I had to laugh. "And here I thought you were the last person I wanted to see walk into this gin joint."

He took my hand. His touch was warm and firm. "As Bogart said in *Casablanca*, 'I think this is the beginning of a beautiful friendship.'"

We laughed again, then told more of our stories. Before the evening was through, we had begun the plan.

Chapter Nineteen

OUT AND IN

with Terrance Nichols

"Trial of the Century, Day One"

Checking in as pool reporter for the trial of Marie Harris Donovan, I arrived at 6:00 a.m. to get the front row seat for a 9:00 a.m. court date and, by golly, I had to stand in line. The courthouse should sell tickets. A swarm of courtroom flies want a bite of this juicy trial.

If you tout it, they will come. After four months of media coverage about Mrs. Donovan's astonishing arrest, bail hearing, indictment, arraignment, endless pre-trial motions, and a *voir dire* that lasted two weeks, the lovely lady went on trial Monday morning for murdering Maestro Luca Scarlatti of Metroplex Opera.

Judge Lillian Gillis presided. If you haven't met Judge Gillis, the woman is a wee mouse in personal appearance, but when she opens her mouth, she roars.

District Attorney Clark Timberlake's opening statement began with the undeniable evidence. Even Mrs. Donovan's attorney agrees that her gun killed Scarlatti. And her signature hairpin was found jabbed into his thigh, allegedly delivering a debilitating dose of nerve agent.

Timberlake paced with the determination of a bloodhound. With each pivot, his grey summer jacket and blue paisley tie wafted askance, as if there were a breeze in the still courtroom. I was so glad that I took shorthand in J-school. From my notes and a kindly court reporter's edits, I give you his opening statement:

"Members of the jury, a one-to-six punch killed the opera's beloved Maestro. Repeated ballistics tests prove that six bullets—count 'em—from Mrs. Donovan's gun penetrated Maestro Scarlatti's head and torso. Even the defense acknowledges these facts. There was gunshot residue on Mrs. Donovan's clothing. Add to that forensic evidence that her signature hair ornament, a gold, tinkly cherry-blossom hairpin, was found coated with a poisonous nerve agent and then rammed into the deceased's thigh. DNA tests show that trace evidence on the hairpin's decorative elements came from Mrs. Donovan. To add insult to the gruesome murder scene, Maestro Scarlatti's body was mutilated. I will spare you the details until later.

"As for motive, you will hear first-hand about a knockdown argument between Mrs. Donovan and Maestro Scarlatti at a black-tie affair, only a few weeks prior to his death. The defendant claims that he attacked her, although multiple witnesses say that she assaulted him.

"Opportunity is even easier to prove in this case. Not one person can vouch for Mrs. Donovan's whereabouts the Saturday night of Scarlatti's murder. Not her sons. Not one neighbor. Not even her best friend. As a result, we have the means, motive, and opportunity. There is absolutely no doubt. And you, the jury, will see with your own eyes, hear with your own ears, and pronounce with your own voices. 'Guilty as charged.'"

In an earlier decision, Judge Gillis denied the use of television cameras. As a result, we print hacks are pool reporters for all Dallas news teams. You probably saw my first reports splayed on last night's TV broadcasts, but what you did not see is what I perceived from my perch.

Fear.

In my decades covering arts and society news, I have never seen Marie Donovan so drawn. Clearly, the months of accusations, her husband's suicide, her financial ruin, and her social fall from grace have taken toll.

To her right, criminal defense attorney Ryan Ingles was first chair. His associate Colleen Ballard patiently took notes to Mrs. Donovan's left. Unlike Mrs. Donovan, the six-foot-four Ingles appeared energized, as if ready to play linebacker again at University of Texas, where he was an All-American his senior year and drafted by the Atlanta Falcons. Only a knee injury kept Ingles from NFL greatness.

He looked dashing in a milk-chocolate suit with faint windowpanes of light rust and a burnt orange tie. Just the right touch of collegiate verve.

Mrs. Donovan had donned an antique gold two-piece suit (Vera Wang, I was told) and a lovely Galliano floral scarf. All eyes locked on her as she entered, but her eyes held fast to her two strikingly handsome sons, Avery and Shawn, seated in a reserved row. Her older brother Owen Harris from Silicon Valley and her father Warren Harris from Sun City, Calif., were also in attendance, each dressed in their courtroom best.

One noticeable absence to Mrs. Donovan's accessories: although her brunette locks were swept in a customary *chignon*, her cherry blossom hairpin was missing. Allegedly one of the murderer's weapons, the hairpin may have been declared *verböten* by Ingles, so as not to remind the jury of the one found speared into the deceased's thigh. Still, I missed Mrs. Donovan's signature tinkle.

Her striking face was adorned with little makeup, albeit a bit of pastel on her full lips. Perhaps that was a ploy to make her appear the victim of this firestorm. Defense attorneys often employ stylists and cosmetologists to present the accused in the best light. Although pale, Mrs. Donovan's beauty still shone through. You cannot deny classic cheekbones. In fact, she reminded me of Ava Gardner in her forties. Still beautiful. In fact, more beautiful.

Clark Timberlake named several notables to his list of witnesses beyond the expected slate of detectives and county medical examiners. Ingles' wife Doreen and her sidekick Tina LeBlanc have been subpoenaed, as well as the grand dame of Dallas arts, Rebecca Claridge, her tenor son Barry, and surprisingly Mrs. Donovan's friend and employer, Lena Verano.

Mrs. Donovan gasped when she realized that Timberlake had put Verano on his witness list.

Ingles quickly rose to object. "Your Honor, I had no prior knowledge of this witness."

Before the dear mousy judge could roar, Timberlake explained that he added Verano at the last moment. "Your Honor, my office will courier the revised list to Mr. Ingles' office immediately after court today."

Ingles huffily withdrew his objection.

My legal advisors say that objections during opening statements are rare, as both attorneys want to avoid irritating the judge, the jurors, and the opposition.

Clearly, Timberlake pulled a fast one with his late addition of Verano, but Ingles' objection was a solid hit. Judging by the jury's expressions, I think Timberlake lost a point with his secretive move.

Ingles' opening statement is tomorrow.

I will be in line by 5:00 a.m. Show up with coffee and croissants, and you will have my undying affection.

Chapter Twenty

LIKE A SISTAH?

A computer printout of Terrance's preview edition of "Out and In" greeted me on the kitchen island when I got home after a post-trial meeting at Ryan's office. Owen had downloaded the drivel as soon as it appeared online.

Ava Gardner? That's what my father always said, "You're a budding Ava Gardner." That is, when the man was sober. Trouble was, at my age, I didn't know who Ava Gardner was. From Daddy's late-night rants, when he came in my room and seethed at me, I thought the woman must be a whore.

Terrance was right about one thing. When I heard Lena's name on the prosecution's witness list, I inhaled so loudly, it echoed around the courtroom. If Ryan had not cautioned me against contacting Lena, I would have let my dear "Sistah" have a few coarse words. I also would have posted a reply online about there being no stylist or cosmetologist on Ryan's legal team. For gosh sakes, if I had all that help, would I look as bad as I evidently did?

"Dear Terrance, I looked afraid because I am scared to death."

But I refrained, especially since Lena is dating the man, if you can believe her ongoing poor choice of mates. I'm beginning to wonder if Lena has a moth-to-flame disorder.

Her first husband was a wife-beater whom she escaped within

an inch of her life, according to Lena's dramatic tales of his irrational anger disorder. And her second husband, well, he can't be blamed for dying, although Lena called their marriage, "a difficult relationship." I understood what that meant without knowing all the details.

Lena has never dwelled on either relationship, probably avoiding pain, although I've certainly have spewed my guts to her about Cole. That's why I want to be supportive. After all, she is my number-one supporter. Actually, my only close friend. And I have done my best to advise her. Even last year at one of our weekly lunches. This was months before Cole died. Lena told me she had a thing for Luca.

"Lena, he hits on everyone. Watch out."

"Even you?" she had asked.

"Not yet. Probably too scared of my husband. But I know from all the League scuttlebutt: Luca has screwed every diva that performs here. Or they don't perform here."

"Not to mention certain members of D'Posse," Lena sneered.

"Which begs the question, if you know this, why do you want to go to bed with a man who screws all the women in the League and Opera company?"

"You gorgeous married women are great at telling us singles how much fun we have being alone. Try doing without sex or companionship for five years."

"You are an attractive, stylish woman. You just need the right guy. If you think my marriage is an endless sea of romance, Cole and I have not made love in forever."

"All right," she said in a huff. "I just wanted a little…satisfaction."

"Buy a vibrator," I whispered over the pepper shaker. We both laughed at that one.

"I already have a vibrator. And I have to tell you…" Lena giggled. "I have an old-fashioned defibrillator at the funeral home. They replaced it with a new-fangled one, but one night when I was at the office, I got so horny, I thought I might see what that old defibrillator would do. But I was afraid I'd shock myself to death."

I laughed at her fantasy. "I am shocked. Shocked!"

"Desperation drives women to danger."

"During the football years, Cole and had some wild times. Once during training camp in Bend, Oregon, we had sex in the end zone of the practice field. Cole told all the guys the next day, and the whole team got collective erections in the showers."

Lena hooted. "You see? You've had adventure. Why can't I live on the edge and roll the Maestro too?"

"Be careful what you ask for. I wanted Cole, and look what I got. Ignored."

Lena rolled her eyes. She thought I complained too much, and maybe I did.

Although I argued my best, she plunged ahead with Luca and later shared the graphic details. Luncheon after luncheon, I relived her raunchy exploits. Lena and I would laugh until we sputtered over her descriptions of their sexual activities.

"Luca's bedroom is all-white, floor to ceiling. White sheets, drapes, headboard, walls, carpet. And he loves lying spread-eagle while I give him a little blow. This week, I inserted the tiniest lubed vibrator into his…you know…and he screamed in absolute high C."

Evidently, Luca could not get enough. He wanted Lena with him night and morning, except when he was composing or arranging. Over last spring and summer, she saw him as often as possible, until suddenly the affair ended.

Over another lunch, she refused to say why.

"Did you catch him with someone? Was it Doreen? Or Tina?"

A tear rolled out and down. "Marie, you were right. I was wrong. I truly messed up. Please, ease my pain and don't ask questions."

"Playing the silent victim is not like you."

"I've told you all I want you to know. Please let it go. "

When she blew her nose on a tissue, her eyes had sunk beyond sadness. I've seen that vacant sorrow when someone feels despair beyond pain, and I felt terrible for her.

For months after, she avoided our weekly lunches. I called. I e-mailed. But she did not return my outreach. When we saw each other at League meetings or opera events, she was cordial but not the energized, animated friend she had been. Her eyes were dark with gloom, perhaps anger, surely depression. I understood her pain, but I felt a deep loss. During that time, I had no confidant.

That's why Cole's death was good for something. Immediately, Lena was back in my corner.

The night he died, he and I had driven to Claridge Performance Hall in separate cars. I went early to help D'Posse with their elaborate centerpieces for the pre-concert dinner. This was the season's opening night, and the red carpet was out. The League members arrived overdressed in gilded long gowns, beads, silks, sequins and chiffons. A grand occasion.

After the performance, I went to meet Cole upstairs for the after-party. He was entangled in a heated discussion with Terrance Nichols, Keith Warren, Duane Thomas and others I didn't know. I figured the topic was financial, so I did not join him. I found a circle of chatty League members and waited for Cole to say, "Let's go home."

Eventually, he did come my way, but he whispered, "I have to move some money around. Don't wait up." Uncharacteristically, he kissed me full on the lips, gave me a lingering look, then left in a rush.

I stayed to help dismantle the decorations, but I was so weary of the social climbers, I begged off when they gathered to gossip over champagne. Luca this, Luca that, who was screwing Luca and which diva got the next part.

When I arrived home, the boys were still out. I retrieved my cello and briefly played Elgar's concerto in E minor. As I swayed to the melancholy of the first movement, I did not hear the doorbell that Lena later insisted she rang repeatedly. But eventually, as my bow poised above the next note, I heard ding-a-ding.

"Probably the old guy out back coming to complain," I whispered to myself. But when I opened the door in a huff, there stood Lena, distraught.

"Marie, I'm sorry to bother you at this hour."

"What in the world? Did Luca do something to hurt you?"

"May I come in?" Her nervous formality was uncharacteristic.

"Of course," I said broadly, hoping my friend wanted to confide in me again. Tell me what Luca did that made her so very deeply sad.

Instead, she went to the living room and spied my cello. "I heard you playing, through the door."

"I hope I didn't sound like a cat in heat. That's what my neighbor says."

As Lena sat, her fingers toyed with her green satin pajama pants.

"I looked for you at the after party," I said.

"I had some business. That's what I need to tell you. I have some very bad news."

"What happened?"

She got up and paced. Her fingers swept through her hair. She looked askance. "Marie, I don't know how to tell you this. I can't believe it myself. It's like some drama you see on TV. Not real."

Suddenly I got the feeling this was about *my* life, not hers. "Lena, this isn't about the boys…"

"Not the boys." She took a breath and let out a long "argh," as if she wanted to make the terrible thing disappear. Then she waved her hands to clear the air.

"Lena, for God's sake, what happened?"

She sat next to me and took my hands. Donned her funeral director's persona—suddenly calm and composed—and looked me squarely in the eyes. "Marie, I got a call from the medical examiner's office. I have an inside contact there. He tells me when…Marie, no one else knows this yet, and I hate to tell you, truly I do. But Cole is dead."

All I could think to say was, "What do you mean?"

"I promise you. This is true. Cole is dead."

"But what happened? Where is he?"

"He's in the morgue."

"What morgue?"

"Dallas County."

"Oh, no! What happened?"

Lena exhaled one of the deepest sighs I've ever heard. "Cole's body landed on Cedar Springs Road. He fell from his penthouse balcony. And then a limo hit him."

"Don't joke with me." I got up and went for my coat. To hell with the fact I was in my nightgown and slippers. I went to the kitchen and got my car keys. "There's a mix up, that's all. Cole went to move some money around. He's at the penthouse. Let's go."

Lena wheeled me to face her. "Marie, listen to me. The police say he must have jumped."

I could tell she meant what she was saying, but this could not be true. Cole would never jump.

"They found his body on the street. A limo hit him."

I screamed, "Lena, stop saying that. I just need to go to the penthouse." I tried to head out to the garage.

Lena is shorter by five inches but a whole lot stronger from her daily training exercises. She managed to angle me toward a kitchen stool and sat me down with a steady push. Her eyes revealed nothing short of determined control. "Marie, Cole is dead. I'm so very, very sorry."

After that, the only thing I remember were my far-away screams of "no" that went on too long. Lena told me later that I had fainted.

I woke up on the kitchen floor with a squad of paramedics hovering.

"There, now, feel better?" one asked.

I nodded, but very slowly remembered what Lena had said and started screaming again. One guy called on a radio, and then another paramedic gave me a shot that made me feel the most mellow I've ever felt in my life. Although I was aware Cole was dead, the medicine did not allow me to feel the depth of the shock or the pain. I was almost happy. I tried to stand but was too wobbly, so they carried me to the bedroom.

Lena spread the covers over me. As the EMS techs left, she told them, "Not to worry. I'll stay the night."

"The boys," was all I could murmur.

"You sleep. I'll take care of everything."

I don't remember another thing until a flicker of light hit my eyes about noon. When I awoke, I had a feeling that something was terribly wrong. Then the recollection hit. Something about Cole. Lena said Cole was dead. No! This could not be.

I bolted to the boys' rooms. They were still asleep. I didn't want to wake them because I wasn't sure what they knew, or even what I knew. Was this true? In the kitchen, I unfurled the newspaper that Cole usually brought in, and there was Terrance Nichols' column with Cole's photo and a headline in huge letters: "A Sad Goodbye to an Adonis."

My knees buckled. I heard a terrible, internal thud as my head hit the tile. Lena screamed for Avery and Shawn, and the boys picked me up and put me in bed again.

Shawn slid in with Avery on the other side, and we three cried deeply and hugged for a long time. That was the closest physically I had been to the boys in many years. We clung to one another and bawled, calling, "Why, oh why? Dad's dead. Dad's gone. I can't believe it."

When I turned to face them, I felt as if something I had done caused this horror. Although my love for Cole had vanished, he was the father of my children, my first love, and my husband for more than twenty years. Now he was gone. "I'm so sorry, boys. I'll do everything I can to protect you. We are still a family. We have each other."

Lena sat and patted us. "Aunt Lena will handle everything. The media is stationed outside. I even caught one climbing the fence. So, I hired a security guard. He's outside, so don't be scared when you see him. I've closed every drape and blind, and taped sheets over the back windows. I will not let the fuckers take one photo of you in your sorrow."

"Lena, I need to see Cole. I need to be sure."

"The M.E.'s office says they have to do an autopsy first, but I will take you to see him as soon as my staff fixes him up."

"An autopsy?"

"Standard procedure."

꙰

THERE I GO AGAIN, RELIVING MEMORIES THAT STILL haunt me.

Maybe I keep looking back because Lena left a slew of apologetic messages today on my landline, mobile and e-mail. The message on my cellphone was the longest, and I saved it to play again.

"Marie, I am so sorry. I got the subpoena early this morning, along with a list of 'Witness Do's and Don'ts.' Number Four says, 'You may not have any verbal contact with other witnesses or the defendant during the trial.' So, I'm breaking the law by even leaving this friggin' message, but I wanted you to know I am on your side. I have not told Terry a thing, I promise. Mum is the word until this is over. Clark Timberlake's office set up a conference with me tonight. I think I got subpoenaed because of what I said at Rebecca's emergency meeting. That stuff about flying you to Bali. I was just blowing steam, but not really. I will charter a jet and fly you and the boys out in caskets if you need me to. But I won't tell anybody that. You can count on me, Marie. Please don't be angry. I love you like a sister."

That last word made me smile, since Lena pronounced it "sistah." Hearing her urgency comforted me.

Just then, my brother hollered from the family room, "Marie, that you? The news is on."

He and Dad are staying with us during the trial, so I joined

Owen on the leather sectional. The boys occupied the reclining chairs. No partying tonight. In fact, no partying during the trial. At dinner last night, Owen delivered an edict in his "Uncle" tone, and I was relieved that someone, a male voice, was taking charge.

Having him and Dad here makes me miss Mother even more, but I do feel comfort in having family with me, albeit four males, including my sons.

I sat next to Owen and avoided Dad. He has admitted to being an alcoholic but seems sober. No rages like he used to subject me to at night. The guy even quit smoking. Regardless, I don't want to hug him or be close. I guess humans pull back from rage.

On the TV, news anchors Tyler and Chris, both blond and beautiful, sensationalized my trial with colorful photos of Cole in his Explorers uniform; close up shots of his two Super Bowl rings, which my sons now wear; Cole and I, dressed formally for operas; me and the boys when they were young—not sure where they got that photo; then a video of me, Ryan, Dad, Owen and the boys heading into court with a "No comment" wave from Ryan.

After the report, which stated mostly the damning facts, the broadcast ran more video of us after trial. We stopped in front of the courthouse, while cameras aimed their lenses, and reporters held microphones with black foam. I saw myself squint in the lights. I could see the fear Terrance wrote about. A pall clouded my cheeks. Shadows sank my eyes. My lips had no color. I reminded myself to put on a better face tomorrow.

Luckily, Ryan's broad shoulders blocked my face as he spoke. "Tomorrow we will have our say. After the jury sees how weak the prosecution's case is, we will erase all doubts of Marie Donovan's innocence."

On the couch, Dad scratched his head. "I feel like this is a scene from a movie, but it's real. This is about our family."

"Sorry, Dad. I didn't mean to drag you and Owen through it."

Owen's dark eyes narrowed. "Marie, don't apologize. This is misdirected justice. The prosecution is trying to hang you for what

Cole did with Odyssey. You're the only one who is still alive to target, since the snake took the coward's way out."

"Owen, the boys."

"I'm sorry, guys. I know you love and miss your Dad. He was a magnificent athlete, but I think he lost his way."

"That's all we need, Uncle Owen. More of your fucking advice." Avery threw a magazine at the TV and stormed to his room. A door slammed.

Shawn shrugged. "Avery shouldn't have said that, Uncle Owen. But Dad was our Dad." Then Shawn followed Owen to the kitchen, where the two retrieved beers and another slice of delivery pizza.

I would have gone to soothe Avery but I needed soothing myself. I had hoped to calm my nerves with a bit of cello, but wardrobe selection awaited. And there was no stylist to help.

"We leave here at 7:00 a.m. sharp," I called to everyone. I didn't hear a word back, so I knocked on Avery's door.

"Goddamn it, Mom," Avery hollered, punctuated with another thud of something thrown.

My son was acting like a brat, but I understood his fury. We were prisoners. Just like the night Cole died, we could not leave our home without being assaulted by media, who camped on the street in vans. We were the lead story at five-thirty, six, and ten. We were on the front page in the daily.

Tomorrow is Ryan's opening statement. He will present his list of witnesses, and I'm sure Clark Timberlake has busily investigated why Ryan listed three patrons from a gay bar.

Ryan said that Billy Bob has solid details about Luca paying off Barry. We don't know how that relates to Luca's death, but that will at least cast a shadow on Barry. And Rebecca. She's on our witness list too. Ryan plans to hit hard about money when he cross-examines them both. If he cannot get a breakthrough on cross, he will call them back to the stand when he presents our defense.

And then there's Ryan's irritating wife and her anorexic pal,

Tina. Ryan promised he would leave no stone unturned, "Even if that means my own wife confesses to the murder."

I will have to choke down a protein bar in the morning and pack one in my purse. Ryan urged me to keep up my strength. And to wear a bit more makeup.

"Not flashy. I want you to look wrongfully accused, not scared."

We also decided I should wear one of my hairpins for luck. There are many ways to explain that piece of evidence, so I will decorate my *chignon*, tinkle when I walk in, and give Terrance more to snipe about. What does Lena see in that twit?

Chapter Twenty-One

OUT AND IN

with Terrance Nichols

"Trial of the Century, Day Two"

First, let me thank the generous gang who showed up so early with lattes and croissants. I had no idea the power of my pen. You were deliciously kind.

On "Day Two" of the capital murder trial of socialite Marie Donovan, her counsel Ryan Ingles delivered a powerful and passionate defense of his lovely, albeit *allegedly* murderous client. A former collegiate and NFL middle linebacker, Ingles' vigilant stance reflected the athlete he remains, ready to block, tackle, intercept, dive—anything to prevent the opposition from scoring.

From my trusty recorder and transcribed notes:

"The prosecution's evidence is circumstantial. Not one person has testified that Mrs. Donovan was anywhere near Luca Scarlatti's condo on the night of his murder. Not one security camera, either in his condo hallway or on the surrounding grounds, shows Marie Donovan enter or leave. Not one traffic camera on either end of Beverly Drive, the street where Mrs. Donovan resides, shows her car venturing out. Even her security company's records show that the home was armed between 10:00 p.m. and 2:00 a.m., when her twin sons returned. Not one neighbor can say that Mrs. Donovan was not home that evening. In fact, one neighbor swears that his cat screeched after hearing her cello, which Mrs. Donovan often plays during the ten o'clock news.

"There is an explanation for every ounce of the prosecution's hard evidence, including the facts that Mrs. Donovan's gun killed Maestro Scarlatti, and one of her decorative hairpins was found at the scene. The defense acknowledges these facts to be true, but we vehemently assert that her gun and hairpin were taken without her knowledge and later used to kill Scarlatti.

"In short, the defendant has been set up. But who would do such a thing?"

Ingles stopped and slowly swept a pointed finger across the courtroom audience. "I can safely guarantee that it is one of the witnesses you will hear during this trial."

A collective gasp issued from the packed gallery as jury members craned to see who looked the guiltiest. The scene was reminiscent of the old TV series "The Mentalist," where psychic detective Patrick Jayne deciphers "who did it," simply by the way the culprit's eyes flicked.

Ingles hammered on, so I'll summarize his remarks: Mrs. Donovan was an easy target. Since the discovery of her late husband's financial misdeeds and his subsequent death, which was declared a suicide, Mrs. Donovan has received a staggering number of death threats by mail, telephone, e-mail, and even in person. As we speak, the FBI is poring over fingerprints, phone records, and IP addresses from the e-mailed threats, and the Feds promised to share the results of their findings.

"A thorough investigation has not been completed. But, members of the jury, even if we cannot tie FBI discoveries to this case, I remind you that your verdict must be decided solely on the facts presented and the witnesses' testimony. Please erase from your memories any news reports, opinions, or prejudices, and consider each bit of evidence. Because I did so before I took this case.

"Those who know me also know that I don't like to lose. I believe this to be true: Marie Harris Donovan did not kill Luca

Scarlatti." Again, Ingles gestured for effect. His palm painted a wide swath between himself and the packed gallery. "Someone else did, and he or she is probably in this courtroom."

Timberlake objected. "Your Honor, enough dramatic rhetoric."

Judge Lillian Gillis banged her gavel to silence the commotion. "Mr. Timberlake, in opening statements, a bit of rhetoric is permitted. Even expected."

Mrs. Donovan's lovely lips issued the first faint smile I have seen since these proceedings began. Indeed, she looked optimistic. In addition, I noted the reappearance of her golden cherry blossoms in their customary perch atop her classic brunette *chignon*.

Ingles concluded his remarks. "Members of the jury, we assume the worst when a grand jury indicts a defendant for capital murder. I agree that many defendants—yes, some I have defended —would not be on trial were they not shamefully guilty. Although I've done my best to defend them, I felt a bit slimy in the process."

That statement brought a twitter from the gallery as Ingles plied them with his brawny charm.

He continued, "But I am honored to represent Marie Donovan. If you assume this defendant is guilty before hearing all the evidence, you are violating her rights. That is why she will testify in her own defense so that you, the jury, can see her sincerity for yourselves. When you hear what my client has to say, you will believe her, as I do. Marie Donovan was framed."

With that, Mrs. Donovan whispered worriedly to Ingles' second-chair Colleen Ballard, who gave Mrs. Donovan a comforting pat.

In addition to Ingles' opening statement, he presented a long list of witnesses, including Rebecca Claridge, her son and operatic tenor Barry, Tina LeBlanc, wife of the famed neurosurgeon Georges LeBlanc, and even Ingles' wife Doreen.

District Attorney Clark Timberlake complained, "Your Honor,

many of these are already on my witness list. Are we going to question everyone twice?"

Ingles responded, "If the D.A.'s witnesses tell the truth, and the prosecutor's office doesn't prevent the truth from surfacing, most of my questions will be answered on first cross. But I reserve the right to call each witness for direct questioning."

Timberlake sighed an anguished, "Your Honor...this trial might go on forever."

Ingles interjected. "Judge Gillis, I've stood before your court many times. If there's one thing I know, you want the truth. Not just a high-profile notch in the D.A.'s belt."

From the looks on many jurors' faces, Timberlake lost a point on that round as well.

Curiously, Ingles' witness list includes the names of three men I have met socially, although they are not involved in Big D's arts society. This was a surprise.

More of my "Dominick Dunne" investigative work is required. For now I must file this piece for our online "Preview" edition, then make a few calls before I shower and crash.

I feel the need for protein tomorrow. May I hope for breakfast tacos? Chorizo, Cotija, brown eggs, and black bean. Oh, and a chile-mocha latte too.

Chapter Twenty-Two

TEAM MEETING

After the trial, Ryan, Colleen and I went to dinner and relaxed before heading back to his office, where Stacie printed out Terrance's "Preview" edition. As she read it aloud, we tittered over his commentary.

I was pleased to hear Terrance praise Ryan's opening statement. In fact, Ryan had made me so confidant in court, I glanced around the gallery and gave Rebecca, Barry, and D'Posse a smile that said, "See? I'm not guilty."

None of them smiled back, although Barry gave me a sinister grin, one you might get before someone stabs you in the back. I don't know what to make of that little man. He says one thing, does another. And we're still waiting for him to "do what he must do."

As Terrance noted, I was taken aback by Ryan's announcement that I would testify. "That means the D.A. can cross-examine me, right? He can say horrible things, dredge up gossip about me, and try to make me look like a murderer."

Ryan gently patted my shoulder. "But you are not a murderer, and that truth will shine through. Besides, I don't think this trial will get to a point where I'll have to put you on the stand. Billy Bob has been interrogating the three, shall we call them, 'gentlemen' from the Round Up. Some major tidbits have come to light."

I turned to Billy Bob with big question marks.

His wide green eyes were moist with emotion. "I think we've got something, Marie."

"Tell me, please…"

He paced by the windows. "Ryan won't let me tell you for fear you'll spill the beans."

"But I wouldn't say a word. All along, I have not said a word, even to Lena. She left me a long voice mail yesterday, apologized, said she's on my side, but I didn't call her back. Just texted, "Mum's the word.'"

Ryan took my hands in his, and our eyes connected with a spark that made us both shy away. "Legally, we have to tread carefully. We've subpoenaed three fellows to appear, so the prosecution knows something is up. Even Terrance Nichols mentioned our witnesses. And we'll eventually have to provide the D.A. with transcripts of our depositions, but we won't do that today. That's why I have to keep everything between Billy Bob and myself."

I looked to Colleen for help, but she shrugged. I was chagrined that Ryan did not trust me after my prior swearing on the *Bible*. I was also concerned about going on the stand without knowing all facts. I didn't want to endure whatever mud the prosecution would throw—and there is some from my past that I don't want anybody to hear, not my sons, father, brother, or the damn D'Posse.

Long ago during the football days, I had an affair with my cello instructor Eric Lebeau, a Canadian with the amazing gift of teaching me how to love my musical instrument. Our affair was interrupted when Cole injured his shoulder, and he and I moved back to Dallas. I only told two people about Eric, my Explorers buddy Monica and Lena, but who else might know? I trust Lena, but Monica was not exactly tight lipped. She screwed around a lot.

Ryan could see that I was waffling about testifying, so he swiveled my chair with his linebacker's strength. Then he took my shoulders and looked at me the way people do when they are trying to break through. "If I put you on the stand, I need you to be there for me. You have far more strength and power than you realize."

As his thickly lashed eyes searched mine, I felt a charge, call it lightning, call it trust, call it faith. I don't know what happened but the synapse ran from his pupils into mine, then down into my heart, where it tingled into my arms, legs, fingertips, and toes. I caught my breath and managed to say, "Okay" in a voice that sounded more like a teen girl's than a grown woman's.

"Uh-Oh," Billy Bob said.

Ryan's pupils narrowed as he slowly withdrew into attorney mode. He shook his head like recovering from a hit. "Good girl."

Colleen Ballard sighed and fanned herself with some papers.

I felt the flush of a blush and excused myself for the bathroom. In the mirror, my face was still ignited. I told myself, "I am just needy. And he is needy. I must contain this. Suppress this." I took a deep breath and exhaled. Straightened my hair, smoothed my makeup. And told myself in the mirror, "Marie, you have more strength and power than you realize."

When I returned, Ryan and Billy Bob were reviewing transcripts of the depositions by the three Round Up witnesses. Ryan abruptly turned the pages so I could not see.

He didn't look at me. Just kept to the next business at hand.

Billy Bob said, "Back in the game?"

"Yes. Let's win one for the Gipper."

He gave me a high-five. "Atta girl."

Chapter Twenty-Three

ON THE HOME FRONT

A s I've remarked before, when you're a woman on trial for murder, you still have to take care of your home and family. At first, I mistakenly assumed that the boys, Owen and my father would take up the slack. But after stacks of pizza boxes piled up in the kitchen and living room, I figured I'd find even more this evening if I did not put a stop to it.

After the team meeting, I drove to the grocery and filled my cart with anything I could find that was somewhat healthy and could be eaten without my having to cook it, or the males having to order it. And perhaps they might even dispose of the packages and wash any dinnerware when done.

When I arrived home with the car loaded, my family members were engrossed in a doubles tennis match on ESPN between four short, hairy guys from an obscure Baltic nation. I grabbed the remote, turned off the TV, then asked the males in my sweetest voice to unload the car and put everything away.

"Awww, Mom. That was the final set," Avery moaned.

"I don't care. No more pizza delivery. I have bought fairly healthy food for you to eat. Fix it yourselves, dispose of the containers, then wash whatever you've used. I am exhausted. I want a Bloody Mary and a hot bath."

Dad looked startled at my anger, while Owen's fake grin communicated a signal to the other males that the woman of the house was about to lose it, and all males present had better hop to her aid quickly.

"Boys, let's get those groceries in."

"Thank you, dear brother. Before you head out, I want my sons to hear this. I've been thinking about your situations. After this trial, I am going to hire a life coach help you set goals. As Owen said, there will be no more partying, no more lounging about, feeling sorry for yourselves. It is time for you to be self-supporting adults."

There was stunned silence to that announcement.

"And when I am exonerated and this house sells, you boys will have to find your own place to live."

"That makes it easy then," Avery said.

"What do you mean by that?"

"Well, you're never going to get off."

"What are you saying?"

"They've got the evidence. Your gun killed the guy. You can't deny that."

"But I didn't pull the trigger, Avery Harris Donovan. And if you think I did, you can get yourself another place to wallow in your young-adult male rage."

Owen stepped in to temper the argument. He took my side and we faced the boys together. "Boys, your mother did not commit murder."

"But the jury's going to believe the police, not her." Avery got up and stormed to the kitchen, where he grabbed another beer, which might have been why he was so testy. Just like his father, Avery downed a few too many.

"No more alcohol," I shouted.

Dad went to calm him. "Avery, put the beer aside. Booze is bad news—about ruined my life, and you need to take a look at yours. We will get through this mess. Even if things go wrong, you two can live with me in California if you want. This house will be put in your names. You can sell it and you'll be able to manage on the proceeds."

I was astounded by my father's comments. That fucker had planned things out. As I rotted in jail, the boys would get the house and, when it sold, he wanted them to bring the money and live with him in California.

I glared at Dad and the boys. "I will never sign over this house. Before you lock me in the slammer, keep this in mind. Ryan Ingles has solid evidence that will come out during trial. After I am free, you boys will indeed see a counselor who will teach you the life lessons you apparently did not learn from your crooked, lying, philandering, boozing father, not to mention mine."

The stunned looks said it all.

"I am on trial for my life, you self-absorbed jerks. Now get the fucking groceries out of the car and put everything away. If I find one goddamn pizza box or one fucking plastic dish, metal can, or plastic bag out of place anywhere in this house, you boys, you men, all of you, will be staying in a hotel on your own tabs."

With that, I went into my suite and slammed the door, trembling with anger, exhausted, afraid, and very alone. The only one on my side appeared to be my brother Owen. Even my father doubted me.

In spite of his alcoholism gene, I thought maybe a cocktail might help my disposition, so I made myself a drink.

"Your precious built-in icemaker came through tonight," I murmured to Cole's spirit as I taped my waterproof cover over my GPS tracker, then bathed in a torrent of hot, jetted water. Then the tears came as I collapsed in dismay.

What a mess. All through the football years, I had felt alienated, ignored, alone. Then on we went to the "real life" I had hoped for, but I found it even emptier than life in the NFL. Now Cole was gone, but I was blamed for his theft of people's savings and financial dreams. And I'm fighting for my life in a murder trial, thanks to a detective who lost money in Cole's scheme. I can't even call my best friend because she's testifying for the defense. How unfair can life be?

Needless to say, I melted into self-pity that ended only after the water turned cold. Chagrined that I had lost it, I dressed and went to the living room. I heard music on low from the boys' suite and I heard a TV in the guest wing. There was a new trash bag in the compactor, and all signs of whatever the males had devoured for dinner were disposed of properly. The island was shining spotless.

Maybe I should be a screaming bitch more often. I got out grocery store chicken salad, a box of roasted pepper soup, and some crackers. I even made a second drink. I'll have a bit of a bad head tomorrow but my trial does not start until ten.

I sat at the island and re-read Terrance's "Out and In."

Owen shuffled in, wearing his robe. "Are we human?"

"Yes. I'm sorry I was so rude in front of you, but the boys… well, as you can tell from their attitudes, Cole didn't give them much direction. Avery has immense anger. Shawn is depressed. Cole was like a fraternity brother to our boys, an entertainment system he turned on and off. He wasn't a good guide to living as a responsible male."

"But you tried."

"I don't know. Looking back, I think I somewhat abdicated my role as parent because I was so unhappily married. Besides, boys heed the call of dominant males."

"That may be true, except I listened to our Mom. Even though she died when we were young, her lessons have guided me."

"I still miss her, even though it's been years."

"Me too. But we still have Dad."

"Well, not really." I took my drink to the living room.

Owen shuffled behind. "You think he's still drinking?"

"I haven't smelled it on him."

"His rehab counselor was pretty good. I met her while I was out there. Did you?"

"Just once. She told me I was lucky, unlike so many other children of alcoholics."

"Maybe she was jealous."

"Of what?"

"Marie, look in the mirror. You are an absolutely beautiful and talented woman." Owen blushed when he said that.

I wasn't accustomed to his compliments. He had tormented me when I was young. When I was in sixth grade, he was in high school. By the time I got to high school, he was in engineering school and by the time I got to college, Owen was working for Intel in Silicon Valley.

"Sorry. I didn't mean to embarrass you. I'm just proud."

"Thank you. One never knows what your brother thinks."

"Dad always called you, 'my Ava Gardner.' That should have been a clue."

I laughed. "I had no clue who Ava Gardner was."

"Have you ever seen 'The Sun Also Rises'? Ava Gardner was amazing as Lady Brett Ashley. Such a bitch, with the power to make men grovel."

"I think Dad may have had a thing for Ava Gardner."

"All men have a thing for Ava Gardner. Those lips. Those eyebrows!"

That felt good, being brother and sister. Took us decades to find each other, but in middle age, we were no longer years apart. I noticed how horizontal lines now crinkled Owen's forehead, and deeper lines etched the corners of his hazel eyes. His dark hair had thinned, leaving a circle of scalp at the back.

Maybe it was the second drink but I felt the urge to tell him more. "That counselor at rehab… I wanted to tell her something about Dad, but I didn't have the courage."

Owen picked up the remote and turned on ESPN. Typical guy. A close moment with his sister then back to sports on TV.

I was not in a mood to be silenced. I slid closely beside him, then looked to see if Dad or the boys were near enough to hear. "Owen, you must promise never to tell. Not your wife, not your kids, and especially not Dad. He may not even remember this, what with the drinking, but late at night when I was young, he would come in, close the door, and then go into a rage at me."

Owen looked astounded. "I never heard anything like that."

"This was all done in a seething whisper. You and Mom couldn't hear. Still, it was a rage. He would say terrible things, abusive things. Tell me to stay away from boys. Stay away from Cole. I was not to let any boy get inside my panties. I was a whore in the making."

"Jesus. Did he ever do anything physical?"

"No, thank heavens. I smelled booze on his breath. Realized he was drunk. I pretended to be asleep."

"Did you ever tell Mom?"

"I was afraid to."

"You should have."

"I know that now."

"Gosh, Marie. I'm sorry."

"Did he ever do anything odd with you, Owen?"

He tiptoed to the hallway to make sure Dad wasn't listening. When he got back, Owen whispered, "There were a couple of nights I woke up and smelled cigarette smoke. I wondered what was going on. Then I saw his shadow in the corner. I called out, 'Dad, is that you?' But he didn't answer. I peered at him, straining to see until, finally, the tip of his cigarette lit up red. I hollered, 'I see your cigarette! I know that's you.' Then he went out the door. Not a word. I saw the light from the door open and close. And I can still smell that cigarette."

"Gosh Owen. I think our father was a bit weird."

"Most of the things Dad did were because of the booze."

I whispered back, "Maybe so, but that doesn't excuse him."

"You okay about it now?"

"No father should say the things Dad did to his little girl. That's why I don't sit close to him, in case you haven't noticed."

"From what he told me later, he and Mom weren't happy. But I didn't know. I mean, I was a kid with an alcoholic father and an unhappy marriage, but Dad was always there, and Mom was always there for us, so how could we know?"

"I wonder if any marriage is happy."

Owen took a sad breath. "Yeah, you got me there."

"You and Janis doing all right?"

"We're hanging in. I think marriage is more a test of tolerance than a test of passion."

"Maybe so. Cole and I were what you would call 'estranged.' We loved each other passionately when we were young. I always felt so comfortable being with Cole. Like we belonged together. But he wouldn't come home. I foolishly hoped he would let go of his compulsions and be a husband to me and a father to his family."

Owen patted my leg softly. "Marie, when your trial is over, follow up on your idea. Hire a counselor. The boys have shitty attitudes. Avery especially. He is Cole Donovan reborn. Shawn is more like you. He's got a soft heart. But maybe a counselor could help them with moral issues. And help you with your feelings about Dad. I've been to one, myself. And it helped."

I gave my brother a kiss on the cheek. He grinned. Probably thought he had solved my problems with his suggestions, but my problems seemed insurmountable.

After that, Owen settled back to watch more tennis.

Poor guy. When he arrived from Silicon Valley for my trial, he did not realize what he was getting into. Not just the possibility that his sister would be convicted of murder, but tales of an abusive father, two young men who desperately needed direction, and their mother who's lost her way.

Chapter Twenty-Four

MY LIFE ON TRIAL, DAY THREE

Another day on trial for my life. The arrogant District Attorney Clark Timberlake looked like his wife had stuffed and zipped him into a too-tight navy blue suit and militaristically striped tie.

As he huffed and puffed around the courtroom, he orchestrated what turned out to be a marathon session with testimony from the lying Detective Dave Reed, followed by Dallas County Medical Examiner Gerald Garrett, the ever-haughty Rebecca Claridge, and my pals from D'Posse, Doreen Ingles, and Tina LeBlanc. From the gallery, that face-lifted Krissy Langley, judgmental Penny Borden, and nutcase Sienna Gordon looked on with absolute glee, apparently convinced I would fry soon.

I was tempted to take Lena's offer of a casket ride in a charter jet to some exotic island.

Clark Timberlake even listed me as a witness, but Ryan announced that I was exercising my fifth-amendment rights. Darn if Judge Gillis didn't ask me to state that myself, which I did, although I felt slimy. Everyone knows that if you take the fifth, you're guilty. Even I felt like I had done it, what with the way D'Posse glared at me.

But then Ryan added that he intends to call me to testify when the defense presents its case. That will give the D.A. the chance to go for a kill on cross-examination. Ryan didn't say that part, but my brain feared it.

Once things got going, Clark Timberlake led Detective Reed through the litany of circumstantial evidence that I've come to accept as oh, gee: My gun killed Luca Scarlatti last November. In addition, gunshot residue was found on my clothing. And my hairpin delivered a dose of nerve agent to Luca's thigh.

No one has ever asked me, or explained to me how I got hold of a nerve agent, but that doesn't seem to matter. The D.A. simply says my hairpin delivered a paralytic toxin, and everybody thinks, "Marie keeps nerve agent in her garage, doesn't she?"

But on cross, Ryan really let the detective have it. "According to your taped interviews with Mrs. Donovan, you apparently hold a grudge for your losses in her husband's Odyssey Investments."

Clark Timberlake rose to shout, "Was that a question?"

"I'll rephrase. Detective Reed, did you lose twenty-five thousand dollars in Odyssey Investments?"

Clark Timberlake roared, "Objection. Relevance."

"Goes to prejudice against my client, Your Honor."

Judge Gillis overruled. "The witness will answer."

"Yes, I lost a good bit of money in the Ponzi scheme," Detective Reed murmured.

"Did you tell Mrs. Donovan that she should, and I quote, '...send you twenty-five-K after your house sells'?"

The detective squirmed. "I'm sworn to fulfill the duties of my office in a fair and impartial manner."

To which Ryan said with heavy sarcasm, "Of course you are, but you didn't answer the question."

Ryan's dismissive tone hung like a cloud. You could almost hear an audible, "Hmmmmm," as the gallery interpreted the detective's reply as a diversion. Ryan had sacked the QB with that comeback. But then he abruptly let the guy go. "Your Honor, I have no further questions at this time, but I reserve the right to call Detective Reed as a witness for the defense."

I asked Ryan later why he did that. He said, "I wanted our dear detective to sweat."

Clark Timberlake next questioned the effervescent Doreen, who was the queen of babble as she testified that she had seen Luca and me in a horrid tussle at the wine dinner.

Because Ryan could not ethically cross-examine his wife, Colleen Ballard took over. Dressed in a nondescript beige linen suit, she asked tough questions in a soft, sweet voice that did not sound offensive.

"Mrs. Ingles, you have testified that you saw Mrs. Donovan and Maestro Scarlatti arguing on the terrace. May I ask what brought you outside when the party was inside?"

Good question, wasn't it? I knew why Doreen was there. She was snooping.

Doreen lied. "I was concerned about the Opera. At that time, Marie was League president and I was president-elect. My role was to shadow her activities. So, when she and Luca went outside, I felt I should be present for any opera-related discussions. But Luca and Marie's 'discussion' turned into a wrestling match. I couldn't believe my eyes. Here we were at a formal event, but the two were actually fighting. Marie's a tall woman, as you can see, so she towered over Luca. He desperately tried to stop her attack, but she bit him on the arm and pushed him back. It was so embarrassing. I mean, Marie was fighting like some low class…"

Colleen interrupted. "Your Honor, could you instruct this witness to stick to the facts and not her opinions?"

Luckily Judge Gillis agreed and dutifully lectured Doreen, although she appeared unfazed. Her eyes were a Bambi stare. That's what always got me about Doreen. You can insult her. You can probably even hit her. But she will simply come back with the same wide-eyed, incessant prattle.

But Colleen got her with this one. "Perhaps there was another reason you followed them outside. Maestro Scarlatti was known for having a roving eye, especially for lovely members of the

League like yourself. Were you trying to find out if he and Marie were involved? Were you and he romantically involved?"

Clark Timberlake objected. "Not introduced during direct questioning."

Judge Gillis sighed. "Sustained."

Colleen demurred, "I understand, your Honor, but the defense reserves the right to call Mrs. Ingles during direct examination. I remind her that she will remain under oath to tell the entire truth about the extent of her relationship with Maestro Scarlatti."

Clark Timberlake jumped up. "The jury should be reminded that Mrs. Ingles is not on trial."

Judge Gillis glared. "Mr. Timberlake, it is my job to tell the jury their duty, thank you."

Doreen's eyes were saucers by the end of the questioning. As she left the box, she avoided my gaze and walked straight by Ryan without a nod. I was amazed that he would let Colleen go after his own wife. But after Doreen's affair, maybe he was angry enough to try for an embarrassing revelation.

When I turned to peek at Doreen in her seat, she was watching intently as Tina LeBlanc took the stand.

In Terrance Nichols' column later that night, he called Tina, "an impossibly thin and effervescent woman who twittered her corroboration of Mrs. Ingles' testimony."

In other words, Tina tried to make me look like a murderer. "By the time I got to the terrace, Marie was in a frenzy. She's so… you know, athletic from collegiate cheerleading and cello playing. She was shouting at Luca, hitting him, pushing him, and looked angry enough to kill."

"Your Honor…" Ryan said.

"Strike that last sentence. The witness is instructed to respond with facts, not opinions."

When Ryan rose to cross-examine, he spoke softly and sweetly. "Mrs. LeBlanc, according to others, you arrived on the scene a good five minutes after the alleged scuffle, so you cannot have any idea what had happened or why the tussle took place. Correct?"

Tina protested. "But your wife told me all about it."

Ryan objected. "Hearsay, Your Honor."

"Agreed. Strike the witness' remarks about the alleged fight. And, Mrs. LeBlanc, I ask you again, please answer the questions factually with what you, yourself saw and heard."

Then Ryan stuck a knife in the heart. "Mrs. LeBlanc, did you ever have a sexual relationship with Luca Scarlatti?"

Clark Timberlake jumped. "Objection! This topic was not introduced during direct questioning."

As his face flushed red from the many up and downs he had to execute in his too-tight pants, I felt a bit sorry for him because he looked like he might explode.

Although Judge Gillis sustained Clark Timberlake's objection, Ryan had made his point. In one of our team meetings, he said that our primary tactic was to expose the many salacious dealings between Luca and his paramours or colleagues.

"Clearly, someone got hurt enough to kill."

As Clark Timberlake announced his next witness, I thought the man might even bow. "I say this with tremendous respect—the people call Rebecca Claridge."

Although she was stylishly dressed in deep blue with a silver scarf to augment her hair and eyes, Rebecca looked a bit haggard. You might think that a petty remark, but her blue-blue eyes were surrounded by dark shadows that no makeup could hide.

Clark Timberlake's first questions provided background for the jury about Rebecca founding Metroplex Opera and the League forty years ago with money from her late-husband's oil dealings.

"Since founding the Opera, you've served as chairman of the Opera's board, president of the League several times, and you've taken several VP roles, correct?"

"Yes, and I also founded the Diamond Ball, which has raised millions for the Opera over the years," Rebecca said a bit huffily.

Then Clark Timberlake got into the Luca and Cole topics.

Rebecca testified there had been major disagreements between

Cole and Luca over his demands to control the operating accounts.

"In fact, both Mr. and Mrs. Donovan voted 'no' to the Maestro's requests for monetary control, although I thought he should be given banking authority at least. Our Opera has benefited from doing things differently from other companies. After all, Cole Donovan had authority to invest the Opera's funds. Why not allow the Maestro to pay vendors quickly and directly?" Rebecca said, gesturing to the courtroom as though they were her board.

"As we know now, Cole Donovan used the Opera's money to plug holes in his Ponzi scheme," the D.A. said.

Ryan objected, saying that was not a question. Then Clark Timberlake rephrased it, and Rebecca basically restated his exact remark, giving Ryan a glare.

By the time Ryan got his chance to cross-examine, I expected him to go for the jugular. Instead, he played Rebecca the same way Eric once taught me to warm up my cello, gently at first, letting the instrument become accustomed to my touch. I suppose this was Ryan's ploy to impress the jury with his deference for the old biddy. But he managed to ease an admission from her that Barry and Luca had been "very close," her words. And Rebecca's voice revealed an ever-so-slight intimation that she had meant more than buddies.

There was a collective inhalation from the gallery as they realized Rebecca's term meant Luca was gay or a bi-, but when Ryan pursued more about Barry and Luca's "closeness," Clark Timberlake objected that Barry had not been mentioned during direct questioning, so that topic was not allowed on cross examination.

With another sigh, Judge Gillis sustained the objection, but admonished, "Mr. Timberlake, we are after answers here. Your refusal to allow the defense any latitude will merely prolong this trial. And, I caution you, what goes around comes around."

I like Judge Gillis. She doesn't tolerate legal gymnastics from either side. And I suspect more wrangling will arise when Ryan cross-examines Barry, who is slated to appear tomorrow. I'll bet the prosecution will coach him tonight.

In Terrance's online column after I got home, the hack said, "Because mine is an opinion column, I will go out on a rope. Set the dial for a heavy duty load of dirty laundry about several witnesses' relationships with Maestro Scarlatti. Tomorrow's witness list includes Mrs. Donovan's friend and employer Lena Verano, who may share intriguing details about this high-class soap opera."

No telling what Lena has told Terrance. I would give anything to speak with her. I'm sure she's nervous, but she does a great job at putting a good face on sad situations.

I apparently have no poker face and again looked fearful on the evening TV news. I will try harder tomorrow.

As Mother always said, "Plaster on that sweet smile and make people forget why they were trying to ruin you."

Chapter Twenty-Five

MY LIFE ON TRIAL, DAY FOUR

Today was a better day. Lena testified, and I was proud of her for standing up for me. Dressed in black as though she were conducting a funeral for one of Dallas' elite, she was so vehement in her defense of me, the D.A. asked Judge Gillis to declare Lena a hostile witness.

Her black eyes flashed. "You can declare me hostile, you can declare me Jewish, or you can declare me Italian. I admit to being all of those things, and I'm proud to say so. You are trying to crucify my best friend for her husband's misdeeds. She is incapable of killing anyone. You need to stop this ridiculous trial and find the real killer."

Judge Gillis roared back. "Ms. Verano, we need factual answers, not lines from a 'Law and Order' rerun."

That brought a titter from the courtroom gallery.

"Your Honor, I apologize for my Brooklyn accent. Comes from a long line of Italian Jews who escaped Nazi persecution. For three years, my great-grandfather hid from Nazis inside a grotto near Fabriano. That's why it's in my genes to fight persecution each time I see it. I can even smell it." Lena inhaled dramatically and pointed at the prosecution and onlookers. "Persecution permeates this courtroom. These people are persecuting my friend like the Nazis persecuted my ancestor."

"Your Honor!" Clark Timberlake exploded.

"Ms. Verano. We appreciate your adamant defense of your friend but, if there's another outburst, I will be forced to hold you in contempt. Please answer 'yes' or 'no.' That's all. Otherwise, you will be handcuffed and led to jail. Is that clear?"

"Yes, Your Honor," Lena murmured with a sardonic smile.

As I smiled back, our eyes exchanged a moment of delight between the madness of this trial. And when I glanced at Ryan, his grin told me he was very proud of Lena too.

After her testimony, Clark Timberlake recalled Dave Reed. As the paunchy detective settled in his seat, Ryan's eyes expressed curiosity as to why Detective Reed had been recalled.

"Detective Reed, yesterday when defense counsel asked you about a remark you made to the defendant about her compensating your losses in Odyssey Investments, were you in fact being humorous?"

"Yes, sir. I was making a joke but it came off badly."

"Did you actually expect Mrs. Donovan to pay you for your losses after her house sells?"

"No, sir. And I apologize. That was a slip of the tongue. I am sworn to uphold the law, protect the citizens, and behave in an ethical manner. Even joking about my personal loss was a mistake."

When Ryan's athletic bulk rose to cross-examine, he looked as if he might spring at the witness. "Detective Reed, how much did you say you lost in Odyssey?"

"Twenty-five thousand dollars."

"Do you resent that loss?"

"Objection. Calls for speculation," the D.A. shouted.

Ryan replied, "Speculation? I think Detective Reed is capable of expressing how he felt after losing a large sum."

I was relieved when the judge told the detective to answer the question. The twerp should not get off with a glib apology.

Detective Reed adjusted his tie and a-hemmed. "Well, I suppose you could say that I resented the loss. The money came from my wife's inheritance."

"Your wife give you trouble for losing it?"

"A bit."

"Like maybe a whole lot of grief?"

The gallery tittered.

Detective Reed sighed. "You might say that."

"Enough to cause her to withdraw her marital affection?"

"Your Honor! Detective Reed's love life is not on trial here."

Clark Timberlake was positively huffing with that one.

"But Your Honor, if the detective's conjugal harmony was negatively impacted by his Odyssey losses, that might explain his monomaniacal pursuit of Marie Donovan as the sole perpetrator. The defense would like to emphasize that police did not pursue any other suspects during its cursory investigation of Scarlatti's death. If Detective Reed's wife won't make love to him because Cole Donovan squandered the wife's inheritance, Detective Reed might be rather prejudiced against Mrs. Donovan, if not downright revengeful over his losses."

"Objection overruled, Mr. Ingles, but please stop pontificating. Ask your questions of the witness."

"Yes, Your Honor. Detective Reed, did your wife withdraw her marital affection after you lost her inheritance in Odyssey?"

Detective Reed hesitated, but muttered, "We've been a bit distant lately."

"And, did you resent Cole Donovan for that loss?"

"Of course I did. The man was a thief."

"Did you also resent Mrs. Donovan, even though federal investigations have exonerated her from any connection to her husband's dealings with Odyssey investments?"

Detective Reed huffed and puffed, then murmured, "I suppose so. A bit, anyway. I mean, she still lives in a mansion."

That was what Ryan wanted. "Your Honor, I move to have this

case dismissed on the grounds of a singularly prejudiced investigation by this Dallas Police Department detective."

Judge Gillis rolled her eyes. "Good try, but detectives are entitled to resent financial losses. Now, if Detective Reed were prejudiced against your client for being female, you might have case."

Clark Timberlake announced in his suck-up voice. "Thank you, Your Honor. There *is* justice in this courtroom."

"Your Honor, I reserve the right to recall this witness for direct examination," Ryan said, his stern tone plying the jury.

When I glanced their way, which I was not supposed to do, I saw several jurors writing notes.

☙

AFTER THE JUDGE DISMISSED COURT, WE WENT BACK TO Ryan's office to discuss the best thing that happened that day: The D.A. did not call Barry Claridge as a witness.

"Our pal Clark Timberlake reviewed his copies of the depositions from Luca's pals from the Round Up and decided to keep Barry off the stand. But I'll nail him on direct. He's been subpoenaed and will testify, one way or another."

Billy Bob slapped Ryan on the back. "Hell of a day, Diver. You kept them running the wrong way."

"They messed up by recalling Detective Reed. And the prosecution's strategy will backfire after we recall each witness, even my wife and her buddy Tina. For all we know, those two might have dialed 'M' for murder. When Marie mentioned this to me, I laughed at the thought, but with the lies those two told today, I wonder. Trouble is, they could scream 'rape' in their defense. Apparently, that's their story after Luca stopped screwing them. 'Rape of the body. 'Rape of the spirit.'"

Everybody grew silent as Ryan stared out the window.

"I'm sorry, team. I shouldn't burden you with my marital strife. I've got to pursue all possible suspects."

Billy Bob chuckled. "We all go through hell on the highway to marital heaven, don't we, Marie?"

There was another uncomfortable pause when each remembered that my husband was already in heaven or hell.

Billy Bob apologized. "Oh, gee, Marie. Foot in mouth."

I waved him off. My mind swirled with so many thoughts, I could not add shock or insult to the mix. I just wanted to go home, relax, and play my cello.

Each person in Ryan's law office has "the law" or "investigation" as their identities. Cole had "quarterback" and "financier." I was the "quarterback's wife" for too long, and then "arts volunteer." But now I rely on music to keep myself centered. Although I've never played with an orchestra beyond college, the cello is one thing I do well, and I often play with passion and devotion. When the loneliness surrounds me, and it's just me and my music, that's when I play my best.

Chapter Twenty-Six
LIFE IMITATES ART

I feel like a heroine in a Puccini opera. As I take a hot bath in my own wonderful jetted tub, my mind replays each moment of today's trial chronologically, because real life indeed imitates art.

Morning testimony began in a boring fashion with far too many factoids from medical examiner Gerald Garrett, a thin-bearded man who already had described every gory detail about Luca's death on the first day of trial. But Clark Timberlake put Dr. Garrett back on the stand to detail the use of my hairpin and a nerve agent in Luca's murder.

The D.A. led with this question. "Dr. Garrett, when I first questioned you, some crucial test results were yet to be determined, isn't that right?"

"Yes, we knew the hairpin had a toxin on it, but we were still waiting for reports from the Centers for Disease Control and Prevention in Atlanta to determine what the exact compound was."

"And that compound was …?"

"The nerve agent Tabun," Dr. Garrett said with a smile and bit of glee in his voice. I guess having something intriguing like a nerve agent to talk about was far less boring than a plain old murder.

"How was Tabun used in relation to the murder of Luca Scarlatti?"

"Before the gunshots killed Mr. Scarlatti, Tabun was inserted into the deceased's thigh via a decorative hairpin."

"Dr. Garrett, how would someone, say a housewife, get hold of a nerve agent?"

Ryan immediately objected "Speculation."

Clark Timberlake rephrased. "How easy is it to purchase or manufacture Tabun?"

"Tabun is one of the easiest to manufacture. Third world countries often use it in their terrorism exploits."

"Would the required chemicals be readily available? In other words, could an ordinary housewife make Tabun herself?"

"Probably not. Then again, all she would have to do is cook up a solution that equals…" Then he referred to his notes to read a very long chemical compound I cannot remember.

Ryan leapt to my defense. "Your Honor, as you've requested, let's stick to facts. Dr. Garrett's insinuation that a homemaker like Marie Donovan could cook up a chemical compound like Tabun is simply a journey into fantasy land."

Judge Gillis overruled. "The chemical got into the decedent's leg somehow, and your client's hairpin was covered with the toxin, so I must allow the prosecution to pursue this."

I was disappointed in Judge Gillis for allowing that one. Now I'm a mad chemist who cooked up a nerve agent in my microwave?

Luckily, Clark Timberlake did not take this idea much further. "Dr. Garrett, how long after administration of Tabun would disability occur?"

"Generally, this poison would work more quickly if the agent is absorbed through the respiratory system than by other routes." Then Dr. Garrett went on a lengthy discussion about lungs, skin, and blood vessels, all of which was to say that the nerve agent paralyzed Luca, but did so slowly.

"And, the defendant's hairpin administered this nerve agent?"

"As medical examiner, our role is to determine cause of death, while our forensics investigators determine the exact murder weapon. But our lab tested for and found traces of the nerve agent on the hairpin, as well as on the decorative cherry blossoms."

Ryan rose to stop this litany of damaging remarks. "Your Honor, must we reiterate every bit of circumstantial evidence? Detective Reed already testified that the nerve agent was used to disable the deceased, but it did not kill him. The cause of death was from gunshots, so I cannot understand why the D.A. is dwelling on this adjunct evidence."

Judge Gillis shook her head. "Overruled, but Mr. Timberlake, please move this along. We've had enough chemistry lessons."

"Just one more question, Dr. Garrett. Would this nerve agent eventually have killed the deceased?"

"I can't speculate, but if enough Tabun had been inserted, it could have killed the victim."

Ryan leapt up. "Objection. The witness himself said, 'I can't speculate.'"

"Doesn't really matter, since Marie Donovan's gun killed the comatose Maestro," Clark Timberlake sneered.

"Enough, Mr. Timberlake. You are beating dead maestros," Judge Gillis said.

"Yes, Your Honor. We know Marie Donovan's gun was the murder weapon. But if I may, Dr. Garrett, where would an arts volunteer, mother, and funeral home assistant like my client find something like Tabun? Is this easily accessible?"

"We live in a global village called the World Wide Web."

Gads. This testimony again pointed the toxic hairpin at me. When I stole a glance, I could see the jury and gallery wriggling in excitement by the time the prosecution rested, and Ryan called our first witness, Rebecca Claridge.

He had promised he would not be gentle. But at first, Ryan metaphorically tiptoed around the matriarch, until a hint of sarcasm rose in his voice, and he pressed for details about her relationship with Luca. Was their association purely Metroplex

Opera business? Was it friendship? Did she know of any financial arrangements between her son and Scarlatti? Did she herself have any financial dealings with the Maestro?

Rebecca answered innocently to all, but it was clear that Ryan was insinuating something quite the opposite by the line of his questioning. Still, he did not badger her or even attempt to persuade her to change her answers. He simply asked if she had anything else to add.

Rebecca sweetly demurred, "No, but thank you for allowing me to tell my side of the story."

When Judge Gillis announced, "This witness is dismissed," the courtroom gallery sighed. They wanted more.

As did I. I was stunned that Ryan had treated Rebecca with kid gloves, making her testimony a non-event. Why had he even called the old biddy, if he wasn't going for the kill?

My questions were answered after Ryan called Barry Claridge, and he took the stand.

Ryan danced around Barry with polite, introductory questions but suddenly went straight for Barry's Adam's apple. "Mr. Claridge—Barry—did you and Luca Scarlatti have a sexual relationship?"

A loud gasp echoed through the courtroom. The judge's gavel attempted to silence the gallery, but the chatter and rustling in the seats echoed loudly.

Ryan asked sternly, "Barry, do you need me to repeat the question?"

"Yes," he whispered, followed by another collective shifting in the seats.

"Did you and Luca Scarlatti have a sexual relationship?"

Barry took a big breath, then exhaled, "Yes."

Another gasp. Judge Gillis gaveled again. "If the courtroom does not remain absolutely still, I will remove anyone who has not been subpoenaed. Now proceed, Counselor."

"Barry, did you blackmail Luca Scarlatti about your affair?"

"I refuse to answer," Barry murmured.

"Did Luca Scarlatti pay you to remain silent about your affair and the fact that he was bisexual?"

Barry furtively glanced to the gallery, where his mother sat with her azure eyes wide in teary dismay. Abruptly, her son shouted with a voice choked in emotion. "I'm sorry, Mother! Luca said the money might help us, since you lost so much in Odyssey."

Rebecca melted into her seat and stared at her lap while her protégés in D'Posse comforted her with murmurs, hankies, and pats.

Judge Gillis banged her gavel, but Ryan did not let up. He spoke sternly, like a father chastising his son. "Barry, did Luca Scarlatti suddenly stop making these payments?"

"Yes."

"Did you and Luca argue about this?"

"Yes. He told me that his family in Italy had cut him off. Something about his extravagances."

"Hearsay!" Clark Timberlake cried, desperate to stop Barry's revelations.

Judge Gillis shook her head. "Overruled, Mr. Timberlake, and do not interrupt again. The court wants to hear what this witness has to say. Mr. Claridge, you said that Maestro Scarlatti had cut off payments to you?"

"Yes, Your Honor, but Mother was desperate after Marie's husband took her to the cleaners. How could Mother honor her financial commitments, her pledges? I had to help, so I went to see Luca. Begged him to keep his agreement, but he just pooh-poohed me in that way he had…so damn heartless. I threatened to tell the Opera board about our affair, but he laughed. Said he would tell the board that I was an obsessed homosexual who had come on to him! That's what he always did. Twisted everything."

Ryan thundered back. "So Luca stopped paying you?"

"Yes. That's when I decided to hell with him. I'd tell the world." Then Barry stood and swept his fingers across the gallery as if placing them under a spell. "I want everyone in this courtroom to know. Luca Scarlatti, the great Italian Maestro, the about-town lover of every diva darling, tawny tenor and lovely League member, was a bisexual and a sex addict. He used me, used all of you, every one of you. Lena, Doreen, Tina, Krissy, Penny, Sienna, all you darlings from D'Posse. You and your Facebook hints about how 'close you were' to Luca. You think you knew Luca and loved him? I knew him best. I had licked his hairy balls, the fucker."

Gasps enveloped the courtroom.

As Judge Gillis gaveled, I wondered if this was the thing Barry had told me...the plan to "do what he had to do?"

In defiance of the judge's gavel, Barry refused to sit. In fact, he leapt out of the witness box and paced in front of it, ranting until a veritable specter appeared. The squeamish Barry had vanished, and in his place a raging bull stood, spewing a river of swearwords I cannot repeat. Then he began to physically deteriorate, gnashing, weeping, and shuddering until he ultimately collapsed on the floor in an appalling convulsion. Head to toe, his body shook, his mouth foamed, and his eyes rolled back in his head.

I was so shocked, I wondered if this was an act, but Barry convulsed until the judge shouted to the bailiff, "Call 911. Now."

From the gallery, Rebecca flew to her son's side. "Barry, my love, please tell me you did not do this terrible thing. Tell me you did not kill Luca to save me. To save us!"

At Judge Gillis' commands, a second bailiff rushed to do what he could, which was to put a rolled handkerchief between Barry's teeth, until an EMS crew arrived with bags of equipment and a gurney. An overweight blonde in men's slacks took instructions over a two-way radio, then gave Barry some sort of injection. After Barry went limp, the EMS team lifted Barry onto a gurney and rolled the comatose tenor out.

After Barry was gone, Clark Timberlake aided Rebecca to the exit, surrounded by crooning support from D'Posse.

I couldn't believe my ears as I overheard Penny say, "With all this on your shoulders, Rebecca, you must step down as board chair. As VP of finance, I'd be happy to take the helm."

That's Penny. Always looking for an opening.

After the courtroom doors closed, Judge Gillis gaveled three ardent times to still those remaining. "Mr. Ingles. I imagine that the defense has a motion?"

Ryan Ingles boomed, "Yes, Your Honor. The defense moves for a bench acquittal."

Clark Timberlake shouted, "Your Honor, there was no admission of guilt from this witness. As such, double jeopardy would then apply to the defendant."

The judge sighed in exasperation. "Because of Mr. Claridge's testimony, I am directing the district attorney's office and the Dallas Police Department to thoroughly investigate Barry Claridge's revelations. I also remind the defense that, due to the concrete evidence presented by the prosecution, this defendant may be tried again on the same charge. However, given Mr. Claridge's testimony, as well as the depositions Mr. Ingles submitted from three pertinent witnesses, who confirmed Mr. Claridge's revelations, this cause is dismissed. The defendant is free and her bond is released."

With another bang of the judge's gavel, I dissolved into a shuddering huddle of confused tears. What in the world had just happened?

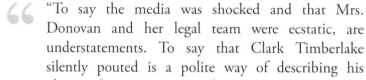

I saved this bit from Terrance's "Out and In" column:

> "To say the media was shocked and that Mrs. Donovan and her legal team were ecstatic, are understatements. To say that Clark Timberlake silently pouted is a polite way of describing his obvious disappointment and anger.
>
> "In a fury of shouts, hugs, and applause from Donovan's twin sons Avery and Shawn, and her brother Owen Harris and father Gregory Harris,

both of California, Mrs. Donovan was released. But not exonerated.

"This point must be clear: Although Barry Claridge has intimated in a convulsive rage that he allegedly had blackmailed Luca Scarlatti, or allegedly knows something about his murder, this unresolved case remains an open sore.

"I asked the district attorney if he will charge Barry Claridge, but Clark Timberlake replied, 'No comment.'

"And so, if not Barry Claridge, whom? I assume more suspects will surface as the D.A. and detectives do a more thorough investigation.

"After they do, who knows? Perhaps they'll find they had the right gal all along. Stay tuned."

❧

THAT'S TERRANCE. POINTING THE FINGER AT ME TO SELL HIS newspapers, in spite of Lena's efforts to silence him. However, Terrance did do a nice job of describing when Owen, the boys, and my father embraced me in a family hug. Billy Bob came to hug us too, as did Colleen Ballard. She and I had mascara streaming in black rivers, smeared by many tissues.

Before long, Lena made her way through the crowd and grabbed me, her sable eyes gleaming. "I can't believe Barry confessed...but I am so relieved for you."

Eventually, we made so much noise celebrating, the bailiffs shouted, "Clear the courtroom." Then we inched to the lobby in a joyous cluster, dodging camera flashes and harsh TV lights.

Billy Bob shouted, "The DPD should be investigated! It's corrupt to its core."

Terrance didn't include that part. He writes what he wants people to hear. Kind of like Donald Trump's 'alternative facts.'

I hope Lena eventually breaks up with Terrance, as it appears to be an unhealthy alliance. I am convinced she can do better than a gossip columnist, gay, straight, or otherwise.

At our press conference afterward, Ryan was so elated, you'd have thought he'd won a Super Bowl. He crowed, "Barry Claridge set up my client. How and why must be investigated. Otherwise, a shadow will linger over Marie Donovan's reputation. I charge the Dallas Police Department and Dallas County District Attorney with the duty to clear her name. She has endured their persecution with grace and dignity. I demand they launch a more thorough investigation to find the real killer, whether that is Barry Claridge or any of Luca Scarlatti's paramours who apparently had axes to grind. And I will turn over all evidence we've gathered to the D.A.'s office to help bring the true perpetrator to justice."

In the blare of lights, someone from NBC asked how I felt. I said with my best smile, "So relieved. I feel terrible that Luca was killed. I feel terrible about Odyssey and Cole…but I had nothing to do with any of it. Someone took my gun. Stole my hairpin. I don't know who. But I'm going home free, thanks to the efforts of Ryan Ingles and his amazing legal team."

With that, all of us got into a town car and sped to Ryan's sky-high offices where his sky-colored eyes gave me a jubilant twinkle.

"And now, my dear friend, you are free. Unless they've got a whole lot of evidence that you and Barry, or you and Rebecca colluded to kill Luca, you probably won't be retried. If Clark Timberlake even looks like he's gonna try, I'll take him down."

Then Ryan gave me a lawyerly hug that I melted into until he pulled away, as he should have, ever the honorable attorney and good friend.

When I looked at him again, the crinkles around his eyes had disappeared, and you could see the youthful Diver from days past, reveling at a winning game.

Before this moment, I had never thought Ryan was handsome. Funny how you see things differently from the perspective of middle age. Or maybe it was the perspective of a soprano being rescued by the handsome tenor in a Puccini opera.

Chapter Twenty-Seven

BACK TO NEW NORMAL

With the trial and ensuing chaos of interviews with reporters from all major networks, local news, and even the great Lester Holt's "Dateline" inquired about doing a two-hour show on my case, my emotions dance between joyous, exhausted, jittery, relieved, and waiting for the other shoe to drop.

I went back to work today at Verano Highland Park Funeral Home. Donned my dark-olive suit and off-white silk blouse, and smiled at the somber clients who waited for Lena to come in. My job is to get them coffee and make excuses for Lena, who texted me, "In bound," although that was an hour before she arrived.

At the office, Lena is the most organized, efficient woman I've ever met but sometimes I cannot figure out where she is. That's okay. She has a private life and a boyfriend. For all I know, she went shopping for more of her signature black suits after toying with Terrance.

When she eventually dashed in, she gave me a hug and a kiss. "So happy to have you back. Lunch later?" Then she went to her office where her phone line glowed immediately.

The Embalming BoyZ bounded by my desk and gave me hugs and high-fives all around.

"How do you feel, Gorgeous?"

"Amazed that I am free."

"We knew all along. You're a heartbreaker, not a killer."

Then off the BoyZ flew to the back to do whatever they do to bodies. And I was astounded that these gadfly men were the ones who had taken such good care of Cole.

≈

THE NIGHT BEFORE HIS FUNERAL SERVICE, LENA HAD MADE sure I got a chance to see Cole before the gawkers arrived. She came to pick us up in her midnight blue Cadillac town car. The twins rode in the back while I rode in front. Just like children, the boys played with the buttons that operated a small TV, CD player, computer, and the bar.

"Stay out of the booze," Lena called to the back, followed by another of her husky laughs.

"Yes ma'am," Shawn answered.

But in the rearview mirror, I saw Avery take a nip out of an airline-sized bottle of vodka. Then he tucked another bottle in his pocket for later. I decided not to say anything. At that time, I had little strength for parenting. My husband had just died.

Thank heavens for Lena. I relied on her for everything: the body transfer, Cole's best suit from home, the embalming, and whatever else, including the service, invitation list, a minister, security guards, and a reception at Highland Park Country Club after the service.

That was a Highland Park thing to do, and Cole always did the "Highland Park thing."

Lena was a country club member, so she made the arrangements. She said she had joined only to make connections. "I had to lie to get in, because they didn't take single females. So, I told them I had a husband, but he had Lou Gehrig's disease and wouldn't be playing much golf."

Depressed as I was, we both laughed at that one.

After she pressed a button that opened the funeral home's

rear garage, the row of hearses appeared like tanks lined up for battle. I braced myself with a sigh. Would this be gruesome? Lena had promised that her BoyZ could work miracles, but Cole had fallen off a high-rise, then bounced off a car onto the pavement, where he was hit by a limo. What damage would the boys and I see?

As Lena led us inside, she did her best to lighten the mood. "Not everyone has a pal who owns a funeral home. Stay put until I check on things."

She was gone about five minutes, a long time for us to wait in a hallway, but I really did not want to see Cole before Lena saw for herself that everything was okay.

Avery tapped the wall with his second empty vodka bottle. Shawn scolded him to stop, which was uncustomary. I was about to yield to frustration when I heard the door open.

Lena peeked out with a big smile and motioned us inside. "He looks great. So handsome."

Avery and Shawn exhaled sighs of dread, reminding me that this tragedy was not all mine. The boys had lost their hero. Mr. NFL quarterback and Super Bowl winner with two rings. But I don't think the boys knew much more about Cole than that, and probably had no clue that their parents' marriage had become a platonic, rote-shared duty.

As Lena brought us into a private viewing room with gold velvet drapes drawn across wide windows, and walls covered with brocade, I could see Cole's Roman nose jutting above the mahogany coffin's white satin lining.

Shawn gripped my arm tightly as we approached. There was his father in a navy Brioni suit, stiffly starched white shirt, and a blue and gold Hermés tie, a nice touch. Explorers' colors. But suddenly, Shawn cried "No!" and bolted for the door. I tried not to blame him, but then Avery cursed, "Goddamn it, Mom, we don't want to see Dad dead." He ran out too, leaving me with Lena.

I didn't know what to do. There I was with the task of saying goodbye to someone I had loved with illogical passion. "I wanted this to be a family thing. Was that foolish?"

"Not to worry. I'll take care of the boys. You say your goodbye."

That left me with the body that had been my lover. I had seen dead family members. My grandparents, my mother. I was better prepared than the boys. Maybe I should have prepared Avery and Shawn better. Maybe I should have done a lot of things differently. Focused less on my despair, my love affair, my volunteerism, my nighttime cello playing, my needs. Here I was, a woman with two sons, but I had no clue know how to raise them. I'd always hoped their father would jump in. Wasn't that his role? Or, was mine to play the stern headmistress to Cole's super hero?

As I stood beside his casket, Cole looked as if he might sit straight up and say, "What the fuck am I doing here?"

There was not one bruise that I could see, but Lena had told me the trauma was extensive internally and on his torso. Somehow, he had protected his beautiful face.

As I leaned to give him a kiss on his cold cheek, my mind flashed to a night long ago, the NFL Awards ceremony in Las Vegas.

I whispered to Cole, so Lena would not overhear. "You won 'Quarterback of the Year,' remember? We both were so proud. I wore that blue with gold satin gown, custom designed in Explorers' colors. You wore a matching royal blue bow tie and a gold paisley cummerbund. When we walked up the steps to the Bellagio Hotel in Las Vegas, the gawkers cheered.

Women shouted, 'Oh, who is she?'

Someone said, 'That's the quarterback's wife.'

"I smiled as glamorously as I could, my arm tucked inside yours. I felt like a film star at the Academy Awards. I had that thrill. That taste of celebrity you enjoyed, and I learned what that does to you. Fuels your pride. Fuels your arrogance. I was full of both as you and I passed by the fans, and I bowed a hello to them with my best cheerleader smile.

"You glanced at me and said, 'You look so beautiful in that dress.' Your eyes ignited with the passion we shared.

"Later that night in our suite, remember the glittery view of the Bellagio fountains? Remember how we made love? Husband and wife love, comfortable, full of laughter, then pleasure growing to urgency. You looked into my eyes with the lights aglow on your flushed cheeks. And you laughed as that shared joy crept into your eyes and mine.

"You've got me, Baby." That's what you said. And I know you felt love for me again. As I did for you. Afterward we slept in one another's arms the way we did when we were younger, fully entwined all the way to our toes.

"I didn't say it then, but I felt that there was hope. If we hung onto this marriage, maybe we could find each other on the other side of football, on the other side of Odyssey, on the other side of your addictions. That's what I always told myself, but your dependence on life's highs did not allow us ever to find a satisfied plateau.

"They say you jumped. They say you lost everybody's money. Hid money. Stole money. How selfish. The boys and I bear some of the guilt. Our demands, our expectations, our existence? I am truly sorry everything went so wrong.

"I don't know what I could have done to change things. Maybe if I had demanded accountability or details or counseling. Would that have turned things around?"

"The twins are destroyed. You were their hero. How dare you do this to them? To me? That's bitter, I know. But I am bitter, Cole. Angrier at myself. I sold myself cheaply. Maybe my father was right. I hate to even think that. Maybe Dad was right all along. Goddamn you, Cole!"

My voice echoed in the chamber as I sobbed deeply, remembering how much I loved him in my youth—a childish fury, teen rebellion, passionate first love. For reasons only God and Freud know, I loved Cole Donovan beyond reason.

I pressed my cheek to his chest until my tears streamed onto his beautiful suit. Better not ruin Lena's handiwork, so I pulled back. Dabbed at the tears with a tissue. Took a deep, shuddering breath.

Time to say goodbye forever.

"As Terrance said in his column, you were *my* Adonis. And now I must say goodbye to you, my beautiful thug. My beautiful Cole."

～

WILL I EVER BE ABLE TO BE A HAPPY PERSON? HERE I WAS, back at work and relieved to be free, but I was gnashing mentally over the pain of my past. I must focus. Focus on work. Focus on the future.

Between phone inquiries from clients, I re-read Terrance's more lengthy print edition of "Out and In." Longer, yes, but it still didn't mention the chaotic explosion of moans from Rebecca Claridge, after her son dissolved into lunacy, while I stood at Ryan's side and gazed at Barry's disintegration. Even with his wild insinuations, he did not confess anything. Although he did "what he must do," no one knows what he did. Still, it broke him.

Such a tragic act for Rebecca but a joyous dénouement for me.

Now back at my desk, I heard the rustle of hosiery as Lena rushed to meet a family that had been waiting. As she gestured them toward the conference room, she stopped at my desk to whisper that Barry had been admitted to the psyche ward at Methodist Hospital.

"Terry's been to see him and said that Barry is catatonic. In a stupor, unresponsive. If he doesn't come out of it, they'll probably stick him in a state mental hospital until he is competent to be interviewed."

My whispers grew louder as Lena headed toward the conference room. "As a mother, I feel Rebecca's pain."

Lena came back beside my desk. "Phooey. You cannot tell me that she and her son were not in cahoots. The woman at least knew Barry was blackmailing Luca. For all we know, she planned it herself."

"Yes, I know. Rebecca wanted Luca to hold the Opera's purse strings so he could pilfer funds and channel them to her. My God, they were as bad as Cole. She must have been as desperate. That's why I feel her pain. I know what despair feels like."

Lena strutted off again, fists clenched. "You and me, Sister."

Later that morning after Lena's clients left, she came by again. "Terry said he would write more tomorrow about your being innocent. I gave him a few more lines."

"Hopefully, he's better in bed than on paper."

She murmured under her breath, "Please keep it quiet about me and Terry. As the worm turns, things haven't headed in the right direction, if you get my drift."

"Do you think you should waste time on a relationship that can go nowhere?"

She pulled over a guest chair and sat. Her eyes were dewy. "I know Terry comes across as a pompous twit, but I've told you. He's playing a role...an arts snob who is snobbier than the snobs. When he came out publicly as gay, he was 'in' with the arts crowd. That's why he calls his column, 'Out and In.' But the real Terry is an earnest guy, somewhat broke, but we talk and laugh until we are sick. We are experimenting with kissing these days. Seeing if that brings anything up. He swears he's a bi-."

"Lena, I don't want your heart broken by another gay man."

"Luca lusted for women as much as men. He came after you!"

"He screwed anything that moved, even Barry."

"Barry's Mommy is the one they ought to investigate. He might have been her lure and muscle."

"That would be such a black mark on Metroplex Opera."

Lena stopped short, her eyes like bullet holes. "Marie, do you know what your problem is? You are too damn nice. Barry and Rebecca framed you. It's as plain as my Italian-Jewish nose."

I laughed. "I'm always nice to anybody who screws me."

"Well, it's good to have you back. A free woman." She paused for a bit, concerned. "You okay working so soon? Do you need some time off?"

"I would like a day to interview counselors about Shawn and Avery. I think they need direction. A life coach."

"Just let me know when. One of the BoyZ can cover for you."

As she went back to her office, I again counted my blessings to have this job. When Lena first offered it, I didn't ask how much salary. And when my first paycheck arrived, I did the math and realized she was paying me seventy-five thousand a year, essentially to be a greeter and a phone answerer.

When I protested that was too much, she crooned, "Not to worry. You're a write off."

Thanks to Lena, I've gotten by. But legal fees have sent me deeper into debt. The house—my son's only inheritance—remains unsold with a second mortgage now reaching astronomical heights.

My uptight real estate agent nervously told me, "I think we need an out-of-town buyer. Your house bears the stain of Cole's dealings."

Again with the "stain." Everybody's favorite word.

Adding insult to my joy about being released, Ryan's office faxed me a bill for another hundred-thousand dollars. "Due upon receipt." I'll have to write another check on the second mortgage and mail it to Ryan's office next week. I won't bother to drop by. With his drama about Doreen, he's got enough worries without my perpetual angst.

That's what I need: a one-stop shop for angst elimination. Every moment, I fear the FBI investors. People lost their savings, homes, college funds. They blame me, but I've always suspected that Cole hid a bundle somewhere. That would be like him. The man even cheated when playing "Go Fish" with our sons.

"If I ever admit to cheating, the boys won't play with me," he'd protest. Then he'd give me one of his amazing smiles.

A shrink would call him a sociopath. I call him a con man. Conned me. Conned the public. Conned the Opera.

Although the FBI has searched diligently, they haven't found a trace of any funds. But maybe I should see if Billy Bob can figure out Cole's secret play. If Billy Bob could investigate where might have hidden any money, I could pay back the losses. Maybe have enough left for my boys and me. And get rid of the friggin' stain.

Chapter Twenty-Eight

JUST LUNCH?

W hen I got home, I was thrilled to hear my landline announcing Ryan's caller ID. After my hello, there was a surprisingly soft allure to his voice. "Hi, Marie. I wanted to see if you are okay."

I felt my cheeks flush. "Much better, of course. Back at work, but I still wake up with night sweats, wondering when Detective Reed will arrive to take me back to the dungeon."

"That's a common problem with defendants who were wrongly accused. Guilt by association. By the time you get to trial, you wonder if you really did it."

I laughed. "Throughout the trial, I was afraid I would stand up and shout, "Yes! I killed Luca. Take me away."

"Thanks to Barry, you don't have to be afraid anymore."

"Hopefully."

There was a long pause. I took stupidly interjected. "You and Doreen patch things up?"

Again, another pause, then a wistful sigh. "No. The divorce is moving forward. Lots of wrangling over things I bought decades ago but she now wants."

My reply came out half-sincerely. "Oh, dear. I'm sorry."

"I'm sad that my marriage is ending, in fact, I'm horrified, what with telling our kids and breaking up our family. God. It's horrible, even though they are adults now, but there's a grandchild on the way. I hate to think about not spending holidays together. If nothing more, we were a family on special days, and it kills me to lose that."

"I understand what you mean."

"Then again, I do enjoy living without Doreen's constant talk-talk-talk. I guess I had tuned her out until the shock of her affair with Luca opened my ears…and my eyes."

"Doreen and I were never close, but I wish you both the best. As you've said, we go back a long way. I so appreciate your help."

"You are welcome." Again with the softened allure.

"By the way, the check is in the mail," I said, although I had no idea why I blurted that out. Maybe my defenses were on alert.

He paused. "That sounded like goodbye."

I took a moment to say what I truly felt. "Ryan, you have a lot going on. I feel like I shouldn't intrude on your personal life."

"Why would I call you if I felt you were intruding?"

When I heard that, my heart leapt, as the corny poets say. Ryan was exploring our potential, wasn't he? "I guess I'm out of practice. Not sure what to say."

Another pause, more wondering, then he chuckled nervously. "Marie, I miss our team meetings. Can't we at least have lunch and pretend we are working on a case?"

I was taken aback. I haven't had a date in decades. I took too long to reply, especially since I didn't want to say the fastest yes any woman ever uttered.

Ryan mistook my pause for rejection. "Maybe I'm overstepping. I didn't mean to make you uncomfortable."

"No, it's just…there's so much garbage swimming through my mind. I'm trying to think this through. Why not have lunch? We're friends. That's what TV ads say, right? 'It's Just Lunch.' In fact, I actually have an issue to talk over, investigative stuff, probably for Billy Bob."

"How about today?"

"Not today," I said, although I wanted to. Instead I said, "How's next Thursday?"

"I have to wait until next week?" He sighed.

"I have a lot of catching up to do. I've been on trial for murder."

"Right. I'll make a reservation for 11:45 a.m. at City Club."

"Good."

"Until next Thursday. And…thanks, Marie," he blustered.

I guess we're both out of practice. After he hung up, I was tempted to call back and say, "Let's do that lunch today." But I was determined to be the new Marie. Less eager to please.

Besides, I really needed to focus on the boys. I spent the morning reading Internet profiles and reviews of counselors with offices nearby. I chose a male named Theodore Lockett, who described himself as a "life coach." I set an appointment for the boys and made an appointment for myself right after. Then I called Owen.

"Atta girl, Marie. One step at a time."

"I'm a bit frightened by what I might discover."

"About your sons?"

"About myself."

Owen chuckled. "Well, there's that. But don't worry. The rest of us are even crazier."

I felt comfort in my brother's joke and wished he lived closer. With Mother gone and Dad being, well, not my favorite guy, family to me has always meant my boys. Perhaps this horrid trial has been good for something. Brought me a brother and maybe a new…well, at least a deeper friendship with Ryan. Opened my eyes to my sons' needs. And my needs to resolve some lingering angst.

Chapter Twenty-Nine

COUNSELING, SESSION I

G ads, the boys were furious when I announced they were going to see a counselor. I will omit their cusswords and the thuds of thrown objects I heard flying inside Avery's bedroom, but with a mother's determination, I decreed, "This is a requirement. Otherwise, pack up and move out."

"I'll move out," Avery spouted. But I am well aware that he's too broke, so, when our appointment loomed, both of my sons shuffled out to the car.

We met first in a family session at Dr. Lockett's Preston Road offices, stylishly appointed with polished limestone floors, off-white sofas, and accent pillows with Native American patterns.

A slight man about fifty, with garden-green eyes, worry lines, and a dimpled chin, he began simply. "How can I help you?"

The boys looked to me, so I plunged in. "I hope you can be a 'life coach' for the boys and help them find their way."

Dr. Lockett scoffed a bit, then asked, "Are you two lost?"

Avery and Shaun shrugged and smirked.

I was embarrassed by their childishness. "Dr. Lockett, my sons grew up in a culture of money and fame. Along the way, their father and I didn't do a very good job of teaching them how to set goals, achieve something on their own. The boys are drifting, in my opinion, anyway."

When I finished, Dr. Lockett peered dubiously over his readers, as though I had said something wrong.

I embellished, "I don't know whether I told you. Cole Donovan was their father."

Dr. Lockett examined our client information sheets. "Marie Donovan. Oh, now this makes sense. Someone I spoke with last week had some dealings…oh, I shouldn't say. Sorry. Let's see, you were on trial, my goodness, for murder."

"My case was dismissed." He looked at me dubiously, so I added, "I was framed, as they say in the movies. But one witness revealed he might have been involved."

Dr. Lockett's eyebrows raised into arches. "Well, the fellow didn't actually confess. At least, that's what I've been told."

I was exasperated with Dr. Lockett's lack of empathy. If my boys hadn't been with me, I would have walked out. But I wanted to make a good impression. Stand my ground. "Yes, what you've heard is correct. But I am a free woman. And my boys have had a lot of trauma over the past year. Their father's death. Financial distress. And then their mother was accused of murder. That's a lot for anyone to bear, but my boys have their father's physical strength, and I hope they have my desire to find the right direction."

Dr. Lockett wrote something in his notes, then asked the boys why they were there.

Avery grumbled, "Mom made us."

Again, I was exasperated, until Shawn spoke up. "Avery and I need to get jobs, but people think Dad was a thief and Mom was a murderer and a thief too."

"They say that to you?" I asked.

"Yeah, Mom. The minute I go to an interview, the manager sees my last name and asks the trick question," Avery said.

"The trick question?" Dr. Lockett asked.

"Yes. 'Any relation to Cole and Marie Donovan?' And then I

don't get the job because everybody thinks Dad stole their money and you know where it is."

"I'm sorry you've had so much trouble. I feel terrible."

The boys mumbled something like, "That's okay, Mom."

"Dr. Lockett, my husband's misdeeds seem to have made our family infamous."

"Not to mention your recent murder trial," Lockett murmured sarcastically.

"Yes, but I was framed." I said that with more bite. Darn this guy, he was not going to keep accusing me of murder.

"But you were not acquitted."

"As you keep reminding me. But I am determined to rectify any confusion about missing funds. I am meeting with my lawyer to see what we can do to trace them."

Avery perked up. "You are?"

"Yes. I knew your Dad better than anybody. I might be able to find a trail."

"Well, Mrs. Donovan, if you do find the money, what would you do with it?"

"Give it back, of course. It would be illegal to keep it."

"You'd give it all away while we stay broke?"

"Avery, the money belongs to your Dad's investors and the Opera. It's not yours or mine. And it is time for you to make your own way."

Dr. Lockett held up a hand to silence me. "Avery, Shawn, I'm starting to see what the issues are. You had it all, didn't ya? But suddenly the rug was pulled out from under you. That's tough."

The boys nodded. Shawn's face reddened and his eyes misted.

"That's why I hoped to get the boys on track with some fatherly male guidance."

Dr. Lockett gave me a withering look. "I'm not their father, Mrs. Donovan. I'm a therapist."

"Yes, I realize that. I was speaking in terms of a 'life coach.'"

"Some leftover football analogy?"

Again with the sarcasm. I so wanted to bolt, but I plastered on a smile and said as calmly as I could manage, "The term 'life coach' is on your Web site, so I would think you are familiar with it. In fact, here's a printout I brought with me. It says, "Dr. Lockett is a life coach who helps clients manage their reactions to disappointment, and he provides guidance to set goals for success.'"

Dr. Lockett's eyes shone in delight. "That, I can do."

I guess he had been playing a mind game by making me dodge his barbs and state in certain terms what my idea of 'life coach' meant. But I was mentally exhausted by that time and did not look forward to my own session afterward. "Shall I stay or leave now?"

"I'll visit with Avery and Shawn for a while. You and I can speak afterward."

"Good. Boys, I will be outside."

"Mrs. Donovan, you can begin this process now by not calling your sons 'boys.' They are fully mature adults."

"Of course," I said, feeling the sting of another barb. No telling what they said after I went to the waiting room and halfheartedly read *People* magazine. No telling what one's children think or say, or this shrink interpreted or remarked. Only the starlets in *People* want their dirty laundry revealed to the world. But something had to change. If the boys—rather, Shawn and Avery—could choose positive directions to aim, and I don't mean at the toilet, I would feel more hopeful about their lives.

As for myself, I had no clue what I wanted, other than stability and normalcy. No more photos of me in the paper. No more TV interviews. No more lies in Terrance Nichols' column. And a nice quiet lunch next Thursday with Ryan that perhaps might lead to, oh, who knew? I've missed having a man in my life. But Ryan Ingles?

Sooner than I expected, my sons walked out, so I went back in. Now that I was the client, Dr. Lockett was much less on the offensive. He even gave me a welcoming smile, which reaffirmed that his tough stance had been for my sons' sake.

"Now, Marie. Tell me your concerns. Free associate. Let things bubble out."

"I'm not the bubbly type," I said with an uneasy laugh.

"Tell me things you think to yourself. What you worry about."

"What was that old movie... *The Graduate*. I think I'm worried about my future."

"And...?"

Over the next fifty minutes, all sorts of things poured out. My angst about Cole, my disappointment in his love, or loss of it, my sadness, depression, even my desperate affair with Eric.

Dr. Lockett interrupted. "How old was this Eric?"

"Early forties."

"You were, what, mid-twenties? Did he remind you of anyone?"

"He was different from anyone I have ever known."

"How so?"

"He was French-Canadian, for starters. Which sounds cliché, since Frenchmen are notorious for being ardent lovers."

Lockett smiled. "Us Texans ain't bad."

I giggled. Things were loosening up. "Eric wasn't flirtatious when we met. He was professional, in a witty way. The best cello instructor in the Pacific Northwest, I'd been told. By the time I enrolled in his class, I had decided to stop being in the Run-Around Wives crowd. In the pros, those were the wives who got even with their philandering husbands by picking up men in bars. I always went out with my friend Monica. She was cute and blond and fooled around a lot, but I didn't want to be that kind of woman. My goal was to focus on my sons and my cello. But when I went to Eric's first class, he plopped on a desk and looked at me with a mesmerizing glint. I can still remember his introduction. 'I am sorry to be late, but I just returned from a sailing trip through the San Juan Islands, and I've got *mal de mer* and a horrid hangover.' That made me laugh like the girl I still was inside. Then he asked about my motives for taking his classes. I think he saw through me immediately, saw the vacuum that I desperately wanted to fill."

"Sounds like a Svengali," Dr. Lockett said.

"A bit. And looking back, I probably was one of many female students he had seduced. But he was oh, so articulate and passionate. I fell head over heels."

"Did he reciprocate emotionally?"

"He never said he loved me. But he taught me how to love. Love my music."

"Tell me more about that."

"At first, he wanted to know which pieces I loved to hear, not just the famous pieces I thought I should play. As Eric said, 'Always begin with love.'"

"Very nice thought."

"He had an exercise where you closed your eyes and felt your cello inch by inch. Then he took your hands and gently drew them over the strings, the hourglass body, the bridge, the scroll, the wood grain. And he would croon in his French accent, 'Do you feel the coolness? The richness of the varnish. The dedication of the craftsmen who made this instrument for you. For every part of your cello, there were human minds, hearts, and hands creating it. Each time you touch a part, you touch the master who made it for you. Can you feel their pride, their devotion coming through? Don't you imagine they want your instrument to sound the very best it can play?' Of course, I answered 'yes.' And then Eric said, 'That is your commitment. To honor the craftsmen who made your instrument.'"

Dr. Lockett was flabbergasted by my speech. "You remember every word. Like a movie."

"I can't say everything as well and not with the sexy accent."

He chuckled. "What happened between you and Eric?"

I exhaled in dismay. "Well, my marriage with Cole was empty. I thought there would never be an end to the football days, his drinking, philandering, gambling, golfing. So, after I completed that first term, I signed up for Eric's master's degree program, which meant three classes each week alone with him. I practiced every night. I think I must have gotten pretty good, because one day when I was playing, Eric's eyes widened. He came and sat in front of me. Said, 'Play that movement again.' It was the final movement of Elgar's E Minor, and by the end of my repeated effort, Eric's eyes had tears. He said, 'My dear, you are getting very good at this.' I burst into tears, relieved to hear I had achieved what I had worked so hard to do. Nobody had ever defined me that way, said, yes, you are a cellist. Then he hugged me, at first a fond teacher's hug, but then he pulled back and looked at me again, a look that said more. I drifted in a dream to him and kissed him, like some movie when the student swoons into the teacher's arms."

"Oh, dear. And you fell for it."

"Yes. I realize the student falling for the teacher was trite, but that's why clichés are clichés. This kind of stuff happens. We lunged at one another, clothes flying, and made love under a piano. Luckily, no one walked in."

Dr. Lockett's eyes twinkled. "Well, you've got my glasses steamed, Mrs. Donovan. I can't wait to hear what happened next."

"We saw each other for a year, always on the sly when Cole left town, which was often."

"Did Eric ever ask you to leave Cole?"

"No."

"Did you want to?"

"I fantasized about it. Pretended Eric and I would move to Quebec, where he would join an orchestra and I would give cello lessons. But in reality, Eric taught better than he played. He was third-chair violin with the Portland orchestra and taught music for his day job. He wasn't well off, financially. His apartment was spare. We spent most of our time there, since we couldn't go out. Someone might see the quarterback's wife."

"When did the affair end?"

"That fall. Cole hurt his shoulder midway into his sixth season...ended his career. Suddenly, he retired from the NFL. This was before today's zillion dollar contracts. We had money, but not enough to last forever, not the way Cole spent money. Luckily for us, he landed a finance job in Dallas with some former college buddies. And we moved home."

"What happened with Eric?"

"Everything was so chaotic with the move, I couldn't get away to see Eric. I left messages. But he never responded."

"Odd way for such a passionate affair to end."

"Knowing Eric, he simply disconnected. He once said, "Americans put too much emotional value on sex. All love ends.""

"Were you hurt by his detachment?"

"Yes, of course. But he was right. I had placed too much value on our relationship."

"And…?"

"I was crushed to be without Eric's attention and guidance, but I had two boys, rather, my sons to raise. After Cole and I moved to Dallas, he wanted me to climb the arts society ladder to help him with his career. We both volunteered with the Metroplex Opera, and he trolled various country clubs and churches for investors. But now I find 'society' so vacuous, I don't know if I want to continue volunteering."

"Don't throw the baby out with the bath water. Surely you've made good friends. And now that you are single, you might meet a new mate. Has it occurred to you to contact Eric?"

"No. My goal is not to be used anymore."

"Well, don't harden your heart. That doesn't seem to be who Marie Donovan is."

"You may know me better than I do."

Dr. Lockett smiled and ended my session with that. "I'll see you next week. Same time work well for you?"

I said yes, but worried that I had gone on too much about Eric. Still, I guess that part needed telling, although I had not yet mentioned my father. The next session for sure. The Dad issue has smoldered too many years.

❧

THE BOYS, MY SONS, WERE WAITING IN THE PARKING GARAGE, playing the car stereo too loudly. As I motioned for them to turn it down, I saw a silver-haired woman walking past the next lane of parked cars. I could have sworn it was Rebecca, but a yellow delivery van suddenly blocked my view. After the truck moved, the woman had disappeared behind a smoked glass doorway, so I could not be sure. Not sure, but I got a chill that said it was Rebecca.

Chapter Thirty

A TEAM AGAIN

Thursday finally came, and I timidly found my way to the City Club, although this time I managed to navigate the confusing elevators in Ryan's building. The attendant seated me in a private room Ryan had reserved, where a buffet luncheon steamed a cloud in stainless chafing dishes. Iced champagne nestled in buckets. Candles flamed. Florals effused. And a waiter stood at attention.

I felt rather silly seated alone at the huge conference table, until Ryan and, to my surprise, Billy Bob, and Colleen Ballard walked in, power suits buttoned. Although I was stunned to see my legal team, I was relieved that I had worn my burgundy silk two-piece suit and looked professional too.

The greetings were celebratory hugs all around, but I glanced at Ryan to see if there was more warmth to come, especially since I had thought this was to be his and my lunch, not a team meeting.

As we grouped around the curved end of the table, Colleen asked, "How does it feel to be a free woman?"

"Wonderful. But I wish a cloud wasn't still hanging over my universe."

Ryan shook his head. "Cloud? they're not going to drag you back to jail. Barry Claridge did it, guaranteed, and with Mommy's help. Everybody could see that. The DPD promises me they are thoroughly investigating both of them. And the police are no longer looking at you."

"But I heard Barry is catatonic."

Billy Bob exploded. "The twit's faking insanity. Otherwise, they'd charge him with first-degree murder and, in Texas, that'll lead to the death penalty."

"I feel sorry for Rebecca."

Ryan gave me a frown. "Don't be. She may have helped her son frame you."

"I know, but I can't help it. I'm a mother."

Colleen touched my hand. "I know what you mean. I would die if one of my boys wound up like Barry Claridge. What a mess he's made of his life and Rebecca's."

"That's what confuses me. When he met with me, he told me he was determined to protect his family's reputation. But then his breakdown ruined it."

Billy Bob jumped in. "Terrance Nichols' column made Rebecca look like a wounded mother, that is, until DPD uncovers her motives...again, if the damn detectives conduct a thorough investigation."

"Still, I feel Rebecca's pain. My boys...my sons are still struggling over this mess."

Ryan patted my arm but nervously pulled away, as though he had overstepped. "Shawn and Avery will move beyond this. As time goes on, they'll understand who caused your family's situation. Definitely not you."

"Now, let's have some of this expensive lunch and champagne that the firm bought to celebrate your victory," Colleen said.

We toasted with bubbly and dined on Coquille St. Jacques, rice pilaf, avocado and mint salad, and petit fours. A lovely luncheon that I should remember forever because it meant I was free. Still, all I could wonder was, why are all these people in this room with Ryan and me?

After the waiters cleared, Ryan asked, "Well, Marie, why did you want us to meet?"

That startled me, since he had suggested our meeting, but I picked up the ball best I could. "I want to find any money that Cole may have hidden from the Ponzi scheme, Odyssey, and Metroplex Opera. Knowing how 'clever' Cole was, I believe he tucked quite a bit away. That's why he ran to his penthouse."

"The FBI has all the records, right?"

"Yes, but I've been thinking. A good sum of money Cole pilfered passed through Opera accounts. As League president, I can request an audit. Maybe Billy Bob could spot something in the Opera's records that the FBI has not."

Billy Bob jumped up. "Everybody, quiet. Now." He grabbed his attaché case and pulled out some sort of wand scanner, which he pointed up, down, at every corner of the room, under the table, at the waiter's pockets. "I should have done this before we started talking. Luckily, the room's clean." Then he gave the waiter a twenty. "You, sir, are dismissed for a bit. We need to speak privately."

After the waiter left, Ryan asked in a lowered voice, "Marie, are you sole executor of Cole's estate?"

"Yes."

"Boss, are you calling the play?" Billy Bob asked with a sly grin.

Ryan asked him, "Do you think you can find a path into the Opera's system?"

That surprised me. "Ryan, I don't want your firm to get in trouble."

Ryan leaned in. "We can explore this option without getting anybody in hot water."

Billy Bob whispered softly so his voice would not carry through the surrounding glass walls. "Marie, an audit would give you what appears on paper. What a data investigator can see are electronic footprints. Hidden stuff between the lines. Every time a record is made, even if it's deleted later, there's a footprint. Cole may have made deposits that he later moved or erased, or he may have had accounts that won't appear on balance sheets. We might be able to track those."

"Let's go for it, Nasty," Ryan all but shouted.

"Diver, I'm not hacker enough for this job, but I've got a gal. She's a lot younger, smarter, better lookin', and a whole lot more, shall we say, devilish. For a price."

Ryan looked concerned. "Marie, what Billy Bob has proposed is illegal, that is, hacking into Metroplex Opera systems and accounts, so as an officer of the court, I am telling Billy Bob very clearly that I don't want him to do this. We will not break any laws."

"Trouble is, Boss, I'm stubborn as hell and sometimes I do these things in spite of what you say."

"What happens next is, B.B. Hughes Investigations has the audacity to send me a bill for 'computer services,' which my administrator pays and then sends my clients' invoices. In your case, Marie, I imagine this will cost you fifty Gs."

My vision blurred as I imagined myself writing another HELOC check. "Fifty thousand? Oh, dear."

Billy Bob thumped the table. "Bottom line…is it worth that much to clear your name from Cole's fraud?"

I could see he was eager to get started. "Could I get in trouble if anyone finds out?"

Ryan shook his head. "There will be no traceable connection. Just Billy Bob not following orders. He does that now and then."

The two men grinned, and I could see the football players still in them, eager to win.

I heaved another sigh. "Well, the house will sell eventually, and I'll be able to pay all this off, so there goes another fifty grand in debt. Billy Bob, you'd better find something before I run out of home equity credit."

A slight shake of Colleen's head told me she was disturbed by this, but Billy Bob high-fived her, and Ryan cocked an eyebrow as if to say, "Colleen, Baby, you're on the team."

"Let's regroup next week, but without the pricey buffet. And, Billy Bob, don't you dare break into the Opera's accounts. That's against the law."

"Right, Boss."

With that, the meeting ended with hugs, professional, friendly, fun. In the elevator that took us to the floor where we changed to other elevators and headed our differing directions, I tried to catch Ryan's eyes before the doors closed, but there were too many others crowding in. Ryan had said he missed me. I had hoped to find whether I could return his interest, that is if he and Doreen were officially through, whether he and I, oh, what, would we do, suddenly fall into bed?

I have read self-help articles about single people hooking up post-marriage for the wrong reasons. Did I even want another man in my life? A relationship with Ryan might merely be a temporary bridge to the past. Is that what I was clinging to?

More questions with no answers. Suddenly, I looked forward to seeing Dr. Lockett again.

Chapter Thirty-One

YOU CAN'T BLAME A MOTHER

Lena and I met for a long lunch a week later. Patrizio's was packed with the overdressed business crowd, so she got us a table in back, away from the noise. As we noodled through our Pasta Puttanesca, I confessed my surprising attraction for Ryan and my disappointment about the lunch date that turned into a team meeting.

"Here we go again, huh? Sometimes you think you only want companionship. Or sex. Then love rears its ugly head and you wonder, what am I getting into?"

I laughed. "Are you talking about you and Terrance or Ryan and me? He and I have not gotten to a date yet, much less sex."

"Let's just say, you were right about my mistake with Luca. When that romance went into the ditch, I was so embarrassed I wanted to crawl into one. And that almost cost you and me our friendship."

I took another bite, delaying. I didn't want to hit Lena over the head with my righteous curiosity but still, I was dying to know. "You never told me what happened between you and Luca."

"Let's just say it was ugly. Nobody likes to be that wrong."

"I won't say, 'I told you so.' Promise."

She squeezed my hand. "I'll tell you when I feel I can. In the meantime, you keep me posted on Ryan. He's a bit of lunk, but then, I seem to go for the slight type. Not sure where that yen comes from."

"You and Terrance getting serious?"

"He's seeing a counselor. Trying to get in touch with his male side. He says things like, 'I have all the feelings. It's just when I try to make love to a woman, all my feelings go down with my erection.' Needless to say, that's, well, not like Luca."

I shook my head. "That must be frustrating."

"Maybe it's better to change the subject. Did Ryan or Billy Bob mention anything about the Claridges?"

"Not really. I just wish Barry had confessed. As it is now, the police are investigating both Barry and Rebecca, but Barry's in the nut house and can't be questioned until he's declared competent."

Lena giggled. "In my fantasies, I imagined the real killers were Doreen and Tina."

"I pressed Ryan about that idea, but he always wondered how they could hold Luca down."

Lena glanced around to be sure no one could hear, then she whispered like a storyteller around a campfire. "I imagined them in a threesome. Scrawny Tina humping on his penis, while Doreen sits on his face."

I started laughing. My raunchy Lena was back, full of graphic sexual details.

"So then, Tina announces she's going to get a vibrator, but instead grabs the Tabun-laden pin and stabs him. Luca screams but can't move because Doreen's crotch is now arched over his neck. So, he kicks and thrusts, but the Tabun gets to him. Suddenly he's immobile, and that's when the two finish him off with your gun." Lena was laughing by that time. Almost gagging, she leaned nearer to whisper, so nobody could hear. "Although I would love to think that the dynamic duo from D'Posse were the real murderers, in my heart of hearts, I think Rebecca hired somebody to do the deed."

"But why would Rebecca have Luca killed?"

"Remember when Luca tried to wire a check on the Opera's account but Keith Warren caught him?"

"Yes."

"Did Keith see whose name was on the check?"

"I don't know."

"Get Ryan to find out. If Luca was wiring a check to Rebecca or Barry, that would expose them as blackmailers. And that's why she killed him. To keep Luca from spilling the beans."

❧

LENA'S COMMENTS GOT ME THINKING. I DECIDED TO PLAY sleuth before I spoke with Ryan. Every step Billy Bob takes costs me thousands, so if I could do some of the legwork, that might shorten his investigation.

First, I called Rebecca. Yes, I called the woman who had framed me. Surreptitiously, my call was to express sympathy for her sad situation with Barry. But I actually wanted to know if Barry was still nuts and if Rebecca was the woman I had seen in the parking garage. What that might prove, I was not sure.

When she answered, we stumbled for words. I expressed my sympathy. She murmured a weak apology. We were silent for a bit until she abruptly said, "Marie, it might be better if we meet in person. How about a cup of tea on Saturday at Maudee's?"

❧

AS A WISPY SERVER POURED OUR FIRST CUP OF TEA, I WAS amazed that Rebecca was not only sincere but conciliatory. She nervously balanced a floral-decorated cup of black boysenberry tea and looked me straight in the eyes for the first time since the trial. Her deep blue irises conveyed shadows of dread, mortification, and sorrow. "Marie, I appreciate your reaching out. It is I who should have called to express my regret about your ordeal. I am ashamed of my son's actions."

Before I said something bitingly sarcastic, I took a sip. The aroma was so rich, I drank quickly, then poured another cup from the large pot between us, taking a moment before I answered. "How is Barry doing? Any improvement?"

"I visit him every weekend. It's a long drive to Kerrville State Hospital, but I stay overnight with friends who have a ranch nearby. I visit Barry from one to five, then again Sunday morning before I drive home."

"Is he talking? Last I heard he was, well, the term someone used was 'catatonic.'"

"He speaks in short phrases and sometimes seems cogent, but whenever the guards are around, he gets nervous and starts talking about a man named Jacob. The psychiatrist told me he is a figure in Barry's delusions who tells him what to do."

"Oh, dear. I'm sorry to hear this."

"Evidently, Barry had a psychotic break. He has been diagnosed as paranoid schizophrenic with delusions of grandeur. He frequently hears what the doctors call command voices."

"Command voices?"

"Yes, 'friends' who tell him what to do. Jacob is one of them."

"Do any drugs help?"

Rebecca's eyes brimmed with tears. "He's on everything they can prescribe. One drug makes him salivate so badly, the poor guy wears a towel around his neck to catch the drool."

I patted her veined, but well-manicured hand. "As a mother, I understand how difficult that must be for you."

Rebecca sniveled into a tissue. "At least Barry gets to sing. He performs arias every Sunday after chapel. The volunteer organist is musician enough to accompany him, and the two have developed a following. Since Barry's nerves are calmed by the drugs, his voice rings clear and true, even in solo."

I saw this as my opening. "I'm so happy to hear that. Raising sons as a single woman is difficult, isn't it? You pull so hard for them. My twins have had adjustment problems, mostly related to

Cole's misdeeds with Odyssey. I've taken them to see a counselor, Theodore Lockett."

Rebecca's eyes grew wide. "On Preston Road?"

"Yes. Do you know him?"

She put down her teacup with an uncustomary clink. "Well, this is confidential, but I've seen Dr. Lockett myself. I needed emotional support after Barry's breakdown. And our finances are in ruin ever since Odyssey."

So, that *was* Rebecca I'd seen in the parking garage. Darn it, she and I are seeing the same therapist. What might she tell him? Even more, should I trust Dr. Lockett to keep my confidences?

Rebecca misinterpreted my bewildered state. "Odyssey is a sore subject that we might need to put aside."

"Please don't blame me, Rebecca. Truly, I did not know about Cole's dealings. Odyssey was Cole's other woman. He lived and breathed his fund. Didn't even leave his penthouse office until weekends. The boys...my sons and I rarely saw him."

"I'm sorry to hear that, Marie. A lovely woman such as you should not be lonely. There's time enough for that in the senior years. Certainly not much joy without adequate money, either."

"I've always wondered if Cole hid money somewhere."

Rebecca's berry eyes perked up. "Do you think the FBI might recover my investments?"

"I hope so. If it helps you feel better about giving Cole control over Opera funds, Ryan Ingles once said that Cole was only trying to win. That's the way ball players are. They'll do anything to win."

"I hope you can find the Opera's money, if not my own. That would redeem my reputation. I'm embarrassed to say, I might have to sell our dear Claridge House, although I don't want to diminish Barry's inheritance."

"Gosh, Rebecca, I'm upside down in my home too, and dealing with two errant sons and financial ruin. Let's try to support one another," I said with my best smile.

She offered her hand as if we were partners, but I could tell from the reignited spark in those piercing eyes, Rebecca saw me as a conduit for future dole. If she were involved in Luca's death, I could not tell from our conversation, but she no longer defended Barry as innocent.

I will tell Ryan that much, anyway. The new me has learned to keep friends and enemies close, even if I am pretending affection and affiliation. After all, if Rebecca thinks she needs me, that's a change for the better.

Chapter Thirty-Two

COUNSELING, SESSION II

Shawn and Avery went in to Dr. Lockett's office before me, and when they came out, Shawn was crying and Avery' flushed face looked more angry than sad. The two stormed by me and took the elevator before I could ask what had happened. Concerned, I asked Dr. Lockett when I went in.

Over his readers, his eyes revealed dismay. "I cannot discuss your sons' therapy. They are adults."

"I don't mean to pry. I'm just concerned, and I'm the one who's paying for these sessions."

"Let's just say, we've made progress. As you probably know, your sons are quite angry."

When I asked for more, Dr. Lockett put a finger to his lips.

I settled in my chair, determined to ask the boys later. See if I could lift their spirits.

Dr. Lockett must have read my mind. "Mrs. Donovan, don't question them. What they are going through is a process that has little to do with you. As you know, your husband was a champion but also a thief who was your sons' hero. That is all I will say. Now, tell me what you've been thinking about lately."

"Before I begin, I want you to know that I had tea last Saturday with Rebecca Claridge. Seems she and I share the same therapist, and I wanted to be sure this would not become a problem."

I waited to see if there was a reaction.

He glanced at his note pad. "I'm not sure what you expect me to say."

"I don't need Rebecca Claridge hearing my hopes and fears, or any details about my life or sons. After all, her son Barry set me up. And I'm not completely sure Rebecca's role in Luca's death was totally innocent."

He sat quietly, formulating his reply. "Confidentiality laws prevent me from discussing the case of any client with another, or with authorities, except to protect the patient or the public from serious harm. You signed the confidentiality agreement before our first session."

"Yes, I know."

"Marie, if you would prefer to speak to another counselor, I will be happy to refer you."

Darn him. He was not going to admit a thing or promise a thing. Should I trust him?

He probably could tell I was going to bolt, so he patted my arm. "Marie, I have many clients who know one another. I even run into clients at restaurants or the symphony. In therapy, people talk while I listen. Then I talk and they listen. We do so in trust. In order to help you, I need you to disclose your thoughts and feelings, and I assure you that you can trust me. Now, can I trust you?" He sat back and waited.

Should I run or stay? I closed my eyes and tried to get to that moment last week after the meeting at Ryan's office when I suddenly wanted to see Dr. Lockett again. I remembered what I had told myself. "I want to find out what I want."

"You haven't a clue?"

"Not really. And I'm pushing forty five." We both chuckled at that one.

"Life does not come with guidelines," he said.

"You're telling me." And then I went through my history of

smiling, doing my best to please. "Only lately have I become angry enough at people's unfairness to challenge them, but I blow my cool, immediately regret it and think I should apologize."

"Were your parents wealthy?"

"Not at all. Dad taught school. Mom was a homemaker. She died when I was a senior in college. Dad remarried after he retired."

"How did you feel about that?"

"What?"

"Your mother's death. Your father remarrying."

"Do we have to go into all that?"

"I think so."

I weepingly told him how shocked I was when Dad called to tell me Mother had died. How I had not known the seriousness of her illness. Non-Hodgkin Lymphoma. Mother had pretended to me that all was well.

"'The doctor said my blood was clear,' she used to tell me cheerily on our weekly phone calls. And she attended every concert that spring, driving back with Dad the next day. I can still see Mom with her colorful paisley scarf tied around her bald head. Her eyes were still bright, although shadows surrounded them. But only two months after my final concert, she died. I was in Austin when my father called. I remember screaming into the phone, 'She didn't make it? You mean, Mother died?' I can still hear my voice reverberating."

Dr. Lockett interrupted my litany. "That's why you don't have a close relationship with your Father?"

I scoffed. "He married a blonde my mother would hate."

"That's not what I asked."

"Okay, okay. You've got me. In fact, one of the reasons I wanted to see a counselor in the first place was about Dad."

"I'm waiting."

"Well, this was long ago, so I only remember it in shadows."

"Go on."

"My father would come into my room when I was a girl and,

well, I guess you would say he verbally abused me." I looked up to see if Dr. Lockett's expression had changed but he hid any surprise. No doubt, he has heard worse, so I went on, "He would smell of cigarettes and cocktails, at first murmuring something about how he wanted to kiss me goodnight. But he would lean over my bed and, instead of kissing me, he'd let loose in a raging whisper. Stuff like, 'You're a very bad girl, Marie. It's wrong for you to wear makeup and flirt. Boys only want one thing, and that's your little fuzzy pussy. But you must never let a boy touch you there. They only want to get in your panties and, if you let them, you'll always be a whore.' On and on. Horrible stuff like that. The only way I could get him to stop was to pretend I was asleep."

"Did your father ever…was there ever…"

"No. Just the harangue. Never ending."

"Some women have repressed hurtful memories. Too horrifying to recall. Have you ever awakened in a start, or suddenly had a moment of *déjà vu*, maybe you felt as though something terrible had happened and you felt tremendous guilt?"

"I think all of us do now and then."

"The next time that happens, close your eyes and try to visualize where you were and what was happening. Will you?"

"You think I was sexually abused, don't you?"

"You tell me."

"I know what my father did was not right. He was a fairly normal guy during the day—history teacher and all that—but get a few Scotches into him after work, and he became a maniac."

"Did he verbally abuse your mother or your brother?"

"Mother, yes. He'd go on about how she never took physics and that's why anything bad happened. Truly. As if taking physics would solve the world's problems. And my brother Owen told me that Dad would come into the room now and then and just stand there smoking. Owen was scared of the dark but could see a cigarette, but Dad wouldn't answer him."

"Just stand there? That's odd."

"Very. The booze made him weird."

"Has Owen forgiven your father? Have you?"

"Why should I?"

"You're an adult now. Perhaps you might understand more about his alcoholism."

"I've never had any major revelation. As a parent, I cannot imagine going into my sons' rooms to say filthy things to them. But as time has gone on, I understand that Dad had a mental illness."

Dr. Lockett wrote something. "Time's up for today. But you're doing well, Marie. Better than I expected."

"Then why don't I know what I want?"

He glinted at me with his green eyes. "We'll get there."

Chapter Thirty-Three

MY SIDE OF THE STORY

After the opera last fall, Cole was backstage with several vendors and the general director Keith Warren. Terrance Nichols was there too, notepad out, questions pointed.

"Are there improprieties in the Opera's accounts?"

In the backstage shadows, I pulled up a folding chair to listen. Most everybody was upstairs partying, even the cast and orchestra. I would eventually have to make an appearance, but first I wanted to hear what this discussion was about.

Cole patted Terrance on the arm. "No problem at all and Keith can confirm it."

Terrance pressed. "Mr. Warren, these vendors just told me that Opera checks have bounced."

Keith shuffled in his patent leather shoes. "Yes, checks have bounced, but my records show a full till. I think Cole might have the explanation."

"Mr. Donovan, does any of this have to do with Odyssey? I know the Opera has a ton invested. A bit risky, isn't it?"

"Odyssey is solid. So are the Opera's various accounts. But a deposit was slow to post. Infuriating. Embarrassing. The funds will be available Monday. Is that good enough for you?"

Cole was so defensive, I suspected he was lying. Terrance and the vendors shouted more questions.

"Are things stretched that thin? Why would one late deposit result in a bunch of bounced checks?"

In quarterback mode Cole barked, "Gentlemen, I apologize for the inconvenience. If it will make everybody happy, I'll skip the party upstairs and go to my office. I can move funds from Odyssey into the Opera accounts electronically so that all checks will clear as soon as you resubmit them. I will personally cover any service charges."

Then Cole bolted away in his suave tux, leaving Terrance to furiously scribble notes for his column, while the vendors and Keith murmured questions no one could answer.

Maybe it was the too-many wines I'd swilled on top of some Oxycontin, or maybe it was simply my incurable curiosity, but I followed Cole to the parking garage. We both had VIP spots. I gave Cole a wave as he sped out in his black Mercedes CL550, but he was driving so fast, I don't think he saw me. I tried to follow, but at his pace, I could not keep up. I knew where he was going anyway.

I tailgated another car into the garage and went up the service elevator. When I rang Cole's penthouse door, he saw me through the glass. Still good looking in spite of a thick gut, he mouthed, "What in the hell are you doing here? I'm working."

"We have to talk. It's urgent." In reality, I did not know why I had followed him, except I was afraid Odyssey was in trouble and a whole lot of my money was involved, including mine. I don't like to lose.

Cole gave me a withering look but let me in.

"Sorry to intrude, but I overheard you and Terrance. Seriously, is the problem with the Opera or Odyssey?"

Cole wiped his brow with the cuff of his starched white shirt, then loosened his silver bow tie. With a sigh, he unhooked his silver cummerbund and tossed it over a leather sofa. "Odyssey, the

Opera, Odyssey, the Opera. Jesus H. Christ, too many investors want to cash out."

"Makes me think I want my money back too."

He grinned. "I can write you a check. That good enough?"

"Will it clear?"

"Probably not." He laughed a big laugh. Kind of unhinged.

"Well, this is a fine mess," I murmured in jest, and yet my heart raced with disbelief turning to rage. That money was a good chunk.

"Yes. We, collectively, are in a big fucking mess."

"Can't you move money around?"

"There's no money to move. The Opera's broke, although Keith Warren doesn't know it. And Odyssey is broke too."

"You're serious? Jesus, Cole. What will you do?"

"If you must know, I came here to grab my passport, my Super Bowl trophies, and split, that is, until you showed up."

"What about your family?"

"If I don't split, it's the federal pen."

He gave me a penetrating glare and, with a snap of his fingers, told me his plan.

"I was thinking La Paz. I speak a bit of Spanish and have some cash tucked away in another location. If the cash runs out, there's always these two." He displayed two hunky Super Bowl rings. The diamonds and sapphires sparkled.

"I thought those would be for your sons."

"Best laid plans."

"What kind of plan is Mexico?"

"The only call I can make right now." He shook his head and went out on the terrace, where he stood, hands on the rail.

I went out with him. "Let's talk this over. Maybe we can work out a plan that makes sense for everybody. Turn yourself in. Throw yourself on the mercy. Fork over your hidden funds."

For a moment, he mulled that over. So, I headed inside to get him a Scotch, thinking that might calm him down. Then I rejoined him on the terrace, two upset, supposedly mature adults, with one huge problem to solve.

He took a sip. "Life isn't what I expected. Not even close."

"You might have been better off if you hadn't played pro."

"You think I would have made all that money if I'd been some nameless financial planner?" He gazed at the sparkling Crescent Hotel across the street and heaved a big sigh. "Dallas is such a pretty city at night. I've always been in love with the lights."

I put my hand on his back. "I love the lights too, Cole."

Until that moment, I hadn't planned on doing what happened next, but suddenly I felt detached, like watching a character on stage. "And I hope you see some pretty lights on the way down."

He turned and looked at me like I was crazy. I can still see the shock and question in his eyes.

That's when I got into position and pushed the fucker over. As if I could save him, he shouted my name all the way down. Twenty-five floors.

I leaned over and watched as he hit the dark green awning above the first level. A bounce from the taut, thick weave catapulted him onto a parked car, where he cartwheeled, landed in the road, and began a tuck and roll.

Wouldn't you know it, Cole was enough of an athlete that he made it alive. I was stunned to see his arm reach out to right himself. For a few seconds, fear shot through me that he might actually survive. But thankfully a white limo peeled around the corner without a care. Rolled the stuffing out of him. The driver probably thought Cole was simply a big bump in the road.

Call me vengeful for my financial losses, but I took care of the narcissist who was Cole Donovan.

I was scared to death until I got unexpected help from the press.

The next morning, Terrance Nichols proclaimed, "I regret, along with each of you, that Cole Donovan jumped."

Jumped? Nobody ever wondered otherwise.

Power of the pen.

Chapter Thirty-Four

HACKING AWAY

A very long three months passed until our next team meeting at Ryan's office, when we met Billy Bob's hacker Natalie, a tall African American woman about thirty-five, with auburn-streaked black hair and a deep alto voice. She wore a burgundy DKNY t-shirt over black jeans. Every time her head turned, two impossibly long, gold earrings twirled alongside her gracefully arched neck and shoulders.

After introducing Natalie, Billy Bob strutted around the glass-walled conference room like the linebacker he imagined he still was. "My gal found some amazing numbers in the Opera's accounts, rather, she injected a worm that did whatever worms do, then it wriggled out with numbers and dollar amounts in the multimillions that were transferred on several dates before Cole slammed into the blacktop."

I winced.

"Sorry, Marie, but those dates are important because Cole may have tucked money away right before Odyssey collapsed. Natalie wrote a computer algorithm, is that what you call it? Seriously, I have no clue how she does these things. Natalie, how about you help me out with this bit of our report?"

For a hacker, Natalie was no stereotype like a fat, blemished, long-haired male or a disturbed, sexually abused female I've seen in recent movies. Although Natalie's wardrobe was casual, she wore it with an element of class.

"Thank you, Billy Bob. In a nutshell, I write code that sets up processes to penetrate firewalls and system apps. It's not easy but, for some of us, it's a fascination that pays well. However, I want to make this clear. I don't steal or alter records. I simply provide information for a fee. That is, if the motives appear to be above board."

"That's what I told her. All we want to do is find out if Cole hid any money. Then Marie can claim it and turn it over to the IRS, especially since they have her accounts under surveillance," Billy Bob said.

"If there's any leftover, may I keep it?"

"If the accounts are solely in Cole's name, the IRS will freeze the funds. You might get something if all investors and taxes are paid," Ryan said.

Colleen Ballard chimed in. "Marie, you know that most of my legal practice focuses on tax law. I think you should turn this information over to the Feds now."

Ryan gave her a shake of his head. "Colleen, I'm not sure I want to tell them we hired a hacker. After all, the Opera did not give us permission to access their records."

Colleen frowned but kept quiet. Clearly, she didn't like some of Ryan's methods.

"Before we go spilling the beans to the FBI, let's get back to Natalie's algorithm. The big story is, she traced activity between the Opera's operating fund and five numbered accounts, located at a branch of the Mehfooz Bank in the Seychelles Islands."

Ryan slammed his hand so hard I thought the table's inch-thick glass might break. "I knew it. Cole threw a 'hail Mary.' Where in the hell are the Seychelles?"

"East of Africa in the Indian Ocean. About nine-hundred miles from mainland Africa."

"Good heavens. Why there?"

After a pause while Natalie Googled on her laptop, she said in a low voice, "This…fascinating stuff, actually. The Republic of Seychelles was one of the holdouts to the United States' 2010 Foreign Account Tax Compliance Act, called FATCA. This law requires foreign financial firms to identify every American account holder with assets of more than fifty thousand dollars, and to report details of their account activity to the IRS or face significant penalties. Needless to say, FATCA—which sounds an awful lot like "Fat Cat"—is not very popular with foreign banks, tax-haven governments, and Americans who live abroad."

Colleen jumped in. "Yes, before FATCA, the wealthy simply ignored IRS reporting laws. U.S. taxpayers are supposed to pay taxes on all income earned worldwide, and they also must report foreign financial accounts if the value exceeds ten thousand dollars at any time during the calendar year. But with anonymously numbered accounts, how could the IRS trace anything? That's why the Feds dreamed up FATCA, to force banks to do the reporting."

Ryan seemed confused. "Does this mean that offshore banks can't hold numbered, anonymous accounts for Americans?"

"Depends on the bank and location. Even with cooperative nations, FATCA is hard to enforce. Under this law, willful failure by a U.S. taxpayer to report holdings in a foreign account can result in a fine based on the account's value. Depending on the institution, that fine might be thirty percent of the account's balance at the time of the violation," Natalie said.

Billy Bob looked pissed. "Yikes, thirty percent? Even if we latch onto this money, we'll have to dole out thirty percent to the goddamn Feds?"

Colleen grinned her evil lawyer grin. "Cole died. There is no 'willful misconduct' on Marie's part. She is simply claiming his estate. All this is spelled out in something called the Offshore Voluntary Disclosure Program that gives Americans a way to get off the hot seat by reporting accounts not previously reported and pay a reduced percentage. When we acknowledge these accounts, the IRS will take a certain flat fee. And we can negotiate that."

"Death, divorce, and taxes," Ryan puffed.

Colleen peered at her laptop. "Seychelles is part of the African Union. I'll bet it's rife with corruption."

Ryan leaned over her shoulder to see the map. "My God, it's in those waters where the Somalians raid ships. 'Captain Phillips' territory. Why would Cole choose a place like that?"

"Tax havens like Switzerland, the Cayman Islands, and Costa Rica immediately started reporting to the IRS, so Cole chose a very good location. Seychelles has been very slow to cooperate with FATCA regs, and many banks there are based in the Middle East," Colleen said.

"Diver, can't Natalie simply move these funds electronically? Now they see them, now they don't?"

Natalie glared. "Billy Bob, I did what you asked: find tracks leading to numbered accounts. I don't steal, even if the bank is out in the Indian Ocean. You guys can decide what to do next."

Ryan punched the intercom in the center of the table. "Stacie, please find which airline flies to Seychelles in the Indian Ocean. Also, ask if we need any shots, if there's a waiting period, if we need visas...all that. There will be five of us. I'll get you everybody's passports."

"Five passports for what?" Billy Bob asked.

"You, me, Colleen, Natalie, and Marie. We're going to the Seychelles. I hope your passports are current."

My mind flashed to Cole, who always kept our passports up-to-date. "Never know when we might need to leave the country," he would say with a grin. Now I know what he meant. He probably planned to flee the country the night he died.

"Marie, you'll need Cole's death certificates and current letters testamentary showing you as executor."

I nodded and made more notes although, in the back of my mind, I was dreading a very long flight in a crammed airliner over the Indian Ocean. But I plastered on a smile and bravely said, "Yes. Death certificates and current letters testamentary, signed, sealed."

Billy Bob looked a bit worried too. "What if these five accounts turn out to be in the Opera's name?"

"Game over," Ryan said.

Colleen shook her head. "Boss, even if the accounts are in the name of Metroplex Opera, Cole was the board's CFO at the time he opened them and would be the only authorized signer. Marie, as his executor, could still claim those funds, although the money would be wired to the Opera."

"Don't forget, I'm still president of the League," I said.

"The Opera and League are two separate entities, but we'll keep that idea in the playbook. Be sure to bring cards with your title on them." Ryan hit the intercom again. "Stacie, please clear my calendar as soon as possible. Then give these people a list to to-dos."

I glanced at Colleen. From her bewildered look, she was as stunned as I that we were flying off to some corrupt island.

Ryan noticed. "Come on, team. Get cracking. Pack a bag, do whatever Stacie tells you to do, and get all documents ready. We are bound for the Seychelles, wherever in the hell that is."

Chapter Thirty-Five

SEYCHELLES VIA ABU DHABI

S pring rains pummeled the roof of our town car as it pulled up to curbside check-in. As I tipped the driver to lug my bag, I worried that the rain might be another omen. For starters, our trip had been delayed for several months, since two judges would not grant continuances on Ryan's most important cases.

While I waited, I saw him only at Opera board meetings. Just a hello and a light hug. No meaningful glances or invitations to lunch. Part of me was disappointed that Ryan had backed off.

Except for occasional updates from Stacie about our trip, time dragged through the fall opera season and the depressing holidays, with my sons missing their father. Even if Cole was a jerk, he was actually home on Christmas Day, although he was terribly hung over. For reasons that defied marital logic, Cole always went out with "the guys" on Christmas Eve. He and his buddies probably had to give their girlfriends their presents.

My only break from New Year's boredom was the Metroplex Opera ball in March. In the Chantilly ballroom of the Anatole Hotel, I sat under a crystal chandelier at Lena's table. She hosted a number of area funeral home owners. Sounds intimidating, but these people were quite pleasant. Even funny. I guess funeral home owners have to maintain two faces. As do columnists. Lena had included Terrance Nichols on her guest list.

His longish hair was pulled into a ponytail to reveal a single diamond earring above his Ralph Lauren tux that Lena probably bought him. His royal blue satin cummerbund and bow tie matched the royal blue in Lena's gown. A nice touch that Lena surely orchestrated.

I was amazed, but Terrance turned out to be a fun guy. His brown eyes twinkled as he danced with every lady from our table, even me. I still don't trust him, so I made sure to dance only the fast songs with him. No telling what he might write about my body, once he copped a feel. He can ruin me in a heartbeat with his rumors and lies.

As he danced with Lena, I could see her eyes glimmer in either passion or excitement, which I couldn't tell, but I felt like an intruder watching them. Clearly, they were in love or lust.

She insists they have not had intercourse in a heterosexual way, but the pair manage to achieve what Lena calls, "mutual orgasms." Unlike her hilarious stories about antics with Luca, she has refused to give me graphic details. I can picture this, but I don't want to.

She did whisper, "Sex with Terry involves a number of inventive Chinese products. You can get anything on the Internet." Then she laughed that delightful way that makes me feel life will be okay.

Between dances and table-hopping to pay my dues to the many notables at the ball, such as Rebecca and other board members, I missed seeing Ryan. He was out of town on a case, so I had no way to bump into him, accidentally-on-purpose or otherwise.

I wasn't the only one without an escort. Doreen and Tina had escorted one another because Tina's husband had an emergency surgery to perform. To my dismay, the entire D'Posse sat at a table right next to ours. In a long ivory formal gown, complete with a three-foot train, no less, Doreen spent most of the evening glaring at me, although she had nothing to glare about.

In my most recent session, Dr. Lockett said that Ryan's distant behavior was for the best. "Time heals. Ryan is in the middle of a divorce. Until he is officially single, I think you should hold back. The Marie Donovan I know would prefer to do things properly, like a good Richardson girl, in spite of what Daddy told you."

Dr. Lockett was right.

Other than the ball, I've focused on preparing for this scary trip, anxious to resolve Cole's mess. Weary of living under a cloud. I spent days jumping bureaucratic hoops to update the letters testamentary showing me as Cole's executor. But I had to update them again, as they are good only for sixty days. I also packed some old Opera letterhead listing "Cole Donovan, CFO," and I packed my now-outdated League business cards, showing me as president, although my tenure is over.

To hell with Doreen.

❧

AFTER ALL THAT EFFORT AND DELAY, THE TOWN CAR PICKED me up for the airport. No matter if God or Cole Donovan's spirit were trying to rain us out, my pricey legal team and I were headed to the Seychelles, where we would try to claim Cole's accounts. Pay back investors. And free me, hopefully.

On the Boeing 777 Ryan sat next to Billy Bob and Natalie, while I sat on the aisle next to Colleen. This was a business trip, I reminded myself and did my best to mask my disappointment. The first leg was from Dallas to Atlanta and, after an hour layover, we flew overnight to Abu Dhabi, where we checked into Emirates Palace, a gorgeous hotel right on the sea.

As we gathered in the lobby, I told Natalie, "When this offshore banking mess is over, I want to come back to this hotel for a spa getaway."

Billy Bob overheard and gave me one of his investigator frowns. He motioned for Colleen and Ryan to lean in to hear his whispered advice, then slyly pointed to cameras he had spotted. "I know we are here only for a layover nap, but I gotta warn you. The United Arab Emirates is a terrorist target. Because of this, major hotels in Abu Dhabi, as well as Dubai, have extensive video surveillance in the lobby, the elevators, the pool. For all I know, maybe even your rooms. Check the ceilings for cameras before you strip. And don't say a word aloud about the purpose of our trip."

Colleen frowned. "Why does the UAE care about us?"

"They don't. But this hotel hires security services that review and transliterate every video recording. No telling who gets hold of those reports, besides this hotel. Keep things on the QT. We are not in the good ol' U.S.A., and all eyes may be on you."

So much for a long bath in my lovely room with an expansive view of the Persian Gulf. I couldn't enjoy it for fear someone was peering at me. Besides, our flight for Seychelles was supposed to take off in just six hours, so it was a bit extravagant to stay at an expensive hotel for a nap. But Ryan had urged us to get at least a few hours of sleep in a real bed.

I did my best. Hung two towels over the shower's glass door so that no one could spy on me. Dried off and dressed in the shower too. Lay down on the bed fully clothed. I think I even drifted off, at least the flutter of sleep came, but the alarm rang far too soon.

I met everyone downstairs, and we took a limo back to the airport. Then off we flew to Mahé Island and the city of Victoria.

On our jam-packed flight, Ryan and Billy Bob sat on the left, while we three women sat on the right. Again, that meant I barely saw Ryan during the four-hour final leg. At least Stacie had booked an aisle for me due to my claustrophobia.

"You're paying for it, so you should be comfortable."

Stacie didn't realize her big joke. Here I was, making seventy-five thousand, but paying for my wealthy legal team's airfare, food, and hotels. I should have studied the law instead of the cello.

By the time we landed on Mahé Island, we had been at our journey a good thirty hours. At the baggage area, a rumpled and disheveled Ryan announced, "I don't want to see any of you until another day has passed. I want a hot shower, quiet, and sleep."

❧

LITTLE DID RYAN KNOW, BUT WE HAD LANDED IN THE middle of preparations for Seychelles' biggest event of the year. Carnival. I had wondered why our flight was so packed, and the airport so crowded for such a small island nation. But we quickly learned from our limo driver that people from all over the world travel to celebrate Seychelles newest annual event, designed to bring in visitors and the dollars they spend.

Our limo had a difficult time winding though the crowded streets of Victoria but, as soon as our driver headed west across the island, we got to our hotel in a half hour. Stacie had booked us at the Four Seasons on the southwestern tip.

Once there, we weary travelers shuffled to our villas. If the others were like me, they bathed and crashed.

I awoke in shock that afternoon with a call from Colleen. "Meet us at the pool. Wear your swim suit."

Swim suit? I thought we were on a clandestine trip to claim money that my dear husband may have stashed in an offshore account. Luckily, the resort's gift shop had my size in a dark cherry halter-top tankini. I also found a filmy white crochet maxi cover-up. I pulled my hair into a low pony and topped things off with a wide straw hat with a rainbow band.

I have to admit, Ryan and Billy Bob did double takes when I walked to the pair's lounge chairs. The two men looked a bit silly gawking at me as they tried to hide their hairy, overweight midsections with fruity, umbrella-topped drinks.

As I arranged myself in a chaise and took another secretive glance, Ryan seemed in better shape than Billy Bob. In fact, Ryan looked darn good for forty-seven years, so I was the one who kept gawking.

My chaise was beside Colleen's. Her beige suit matched her pasty skin, to which she applied coat after coat of suntan lotion. She and I did our best to chat, but we had run out of things to say after being on a plane for thirty hours. I guess the guys were in the same conversational boat, because they scooted their chairs nearer to ours.

Just then, Natalie sauntered our way between cramped rows of lounge chairs, and I noticed Billy Bob doing a major rubberneck at Natalie's deep purple one-piece suit. Her dark skin shimmered with each advance of her lovely thighs.

"Whew," Billy Bob whistled under his breath.

I glanced in Ryan's direction. Had he noticed?

He had. "Billy Bob, are you sure your relationship with Natalie is purely business?"

Billy Bob blushed and tapped his breast. "I'm a bit old for this stuff, but I'm telling ya, my heart is a flutter."

"Nasty, is it your heart or a different body part?"

Natalie was embarrassed. "Did I just walk into a high school physiology class?"

Luckily, a server interrupted to get our drink orders. He spoke English, but it was thickly accented.

After he left, Natalie delivered one of her many Googled factoids. "English is one of three official languages here. Mahé Island is a bit like New Orleans, culturally. The locals call themselves 'Seychellois Creole' because Seychelles has been a British and French territory. Now what's left is a mixed race of African, French, English, and European cultures, while New Orleans' Creoles stem from African, French, Spanish, Native American, and European cultures."

"Do you know everything there is to know about everything?" Ryan asked.

"A walking, talking Wikipedia," Billy Bob smirked.

After the server brought more drinks, Ryan's eyes shifted into lawyer mode. "Although I said we wouldn't work today, I didn't have anything to do after my nap. Since Billy Bob and I had talked over a plan on the plane, I thought we could at least go over it."

Billy Bob gave Ryan the hush sign, then silently motioned us all to stand. While we stood bewildered, he lugged each lounge chair to a far corner of the pool area, away from curious eyes and ears. Then he scanned each chair with his electronic wand for a possible bug.

Natalie smirked. "I feel like I'm in a James Bond movie."

"Call me paranoid, but we're in international territory. I can guarantee that eyes and ears are upon you."

In a low voice, Ryan outlined the plan. He, Colleen and I would go to the Mehfooz Bank the next day and present our documents. "We will play it like we actually know these accounts are in Cole's name. We're not fishing. We're saying, 'Here's the documentation. The money rightfully belongs to Cole's widow.'"

"Boss, there's another thing Natalie researched last night. In Seychelles, Mehfooz is primarily a trade bank. That means Cole may have provided organizational papers for some sort of trade enterprise. Might have been for Odyssey Investments or a shell trading company."

Ryan didn't like that. "If the five accounts say, 'Cole Donovan' or 'Metroplex Opera,' we're okay to claim them in Cole's name. But if the accounts say, 'Odyssey Investments,' we're screwed. We'd have to call IRS immediately. Regardless, we'll just present the numbers and see what flies."

Billy Bob whispered, "I'd give anything if Cole parked the dough at a Barclays or BMI bank, instead of this Mehfooz deal. It's the largest bank in Pakistan."

I was confused. "Pakistan? But we're in Seychelles."

Billy Bob nodded dismally. "Yes. All sorts of nations have branches here to handle offshore accounts and avoid IRS 'regs.' Natalie did more research online about doing business with Pakistanis. It looks like our business here might take a while."

"Basically, you cannot rush things. Pakistani companies are hierarchical. The highest-ranking person makes decisions, so you need to ask for the highest level manager. Don't expect an immediate answer. If you try to rush things, you will give offense and jeopardize your business relationship."

That made me nervous. "How long do we have to wait?"

Natalie summarized from her iPad. "Says here, most decisions require several layers of approval, so it may take multiple visits to accomplish even a simple task. Ryan, it's best if you take the lead. In Pakistan, relationships are to the person and not the company that they represent. If you change representatives, negotiations have to start all over."

"But I need Colleen along for the tax aspect. I don't know this stuff," Ryan said.

"Pakistanis don't want to do business with women, so you must introduce her up front as your law partner and co-representative to get that relationship established."

Colleen laughed. "Gads, I get enough good ol' boys in Dallas."

"The good thing is that Pakistanis strive for win-win outcomes. Profit is often a determining factor in closing a deal. Don't ever use high-pressure tactics, like a threat or ultimatum. Pakistanis can become highly emotional during negotiations. It is imperative you remain calm. If discussions become heated, a Pakistani might revert to Urdu, which is their national language."

"Good job, Natalie. You see, Boss? I told you she's gold."

Natalie rolled her eyes, a bit embarrassed. As Billy Bob fondly patted her shoulder, she relaxed into his touch and his hand slipped down and lightly massaged her back.

Guess there was more than business between these two.

Ryan looked over and gave me a wink.

Colleen fanned herself with her hat. "Oh, Lord. How did a happily married mother of two wind up on a tropical island with a bunch of middle-aged heart throbs?"

Chapter Thirty-Six

DOWN TO BUSINESS

A fter a team dinner and a very long bath, I fretted in a nervous ball on my luxurious pillow top bed. The thought of going to a foreign bank to claim ill-gotten funds that might be in the Opera's name or Odyssey's name, with no protection from U.S. laws, put me near the edge of panic. I desperately wanted to talk to Lena or Owen, but Billy Bob had ordered us not to use any phones for fear the FBI and IRS were tracking us.

"I'd buy some burner phones, but the Feds might be listening to the people you call. Don't call. Period."

As my sleepless night wore on, I felt more isolated, alienated. Were I at home, I would have played my cello to calm my nerves, but I had no cello.

I got up and tuned in the classical music channel on the hotel's TV, but it was not much help. I kept the music on anyway. Sat on the end of my bed and air-played cello to the London Philharmonic's version of Elgar's Enigma Variations. But I caught a glimpse of my frowning self in the TV reflection and was upset at how anxious I appeared. More a distraught lunatic than a passionate musician.

Oh, dear. What to do? I wasn't at any stage of a relationship with Ryan that I could call him in the middle of the night, and besides, you never know whether a guy will understand a woman's wee-hours angst. I did not want to burst the bubble between us. Besides, Ryan was sharing a villa with Billy Bob.

That's why I called Natalie. She seemed like the worldly sort who would understand my nervousness. But when she said hello, her breath was heavy, and I could hear rustling in the background. A male voice whispered, "Damn it."

In the most Creole accent I could muster, I blurted, "So solly, wrong number, apology," but my voice sounded more Chinese laundry than Seychellois.

"Shit," I hollered after I hung up. I should have known. Billy Bob and Natalie's body language earlier said it all.

With no one else to call, I paced in my villa, then opened the drapes to the balcony and looked out. A setting moon glimmered in a huge orb just above the horizon of the Indian Ocean. I ventured out, glancing to see if anyone else was out too. Even a wave from a stranger could ease my sense of loneliness, but I was the only one outside, that I could tell. I leaned on the rail and let the coastal breezes and rhythmic rush of the waves soothe me. And watched the moon slip into the silver sea.

Above it, the sky's glorious diamonds brightened, giving me a sense of hope. Maybe we would find the money, clear my name from Cole's Ponzi debacle, clear my sons' names. I had wondered if we might need to leave Dallas, cut all ties, start anew, but the way I felt tonight, maybe I would not need to run.

The next morning as I dressed, I remembered that Natalie had instructed me to wear black—grieving widow and all that—but that color seemed so severe in this island climate. Instead, I chose a tan linen jacket over a brown skirt, with a pale ivory blouse and floral scarf. For luck, I put my hair up with my hairpin, donned modest stud earrings, and went to meet Ryan and Colleen for breakfast.

I was relieved that Natalie and Billy Bob were not there yet. I probably would have blushed or started speaking Chinese.

Colleen was in tax lawyer mode—yet another beige two-piece

suit, this time with a striped pink and white blouse. Ryan wore a lightweight navy pinstriped suit with an ivory shirt and checked tie, not flashy, but tasteful. I enjoyed knowing that he dressed well on his own, with no Doreen to match fabrics to her gowns.

As he sipped his coffee, he detailed our plan. "Marie, you are a grieving, wealthy widow. Colleen and I are your estate lawyers. Don't say a word. Just smile and nod. Let us do the talking."

"I'm so nervous about this."

"I understand, but if you play your role, Colleen and I will negotiate our way. Just don't mention a thing about the lost Opera funds, FBI investigations, Odyssey, your recent trial, or your current financial situation."

"In other words, don't tell them my life is a complete mess."

He laughed quietly.

Even the tense Colleen smiled. "Do you have all your papers?"

"Right here." I patted my folder.

Ryan slapped me on the back like I was his left linebacker. "Great. Now, let's tackle the world of Pakistani banking."

≈

OFF WE THREE WENT IN A WILD, WINDING CAB RIDE ACROSS Mahé Island to Victoria. The streets were packed with workers constructing booths, wheel-of-fortune games, floats, vendor tents, and Ferris wheels, all in preparation for Carnival.

Colleen was agitated. "Ryan, maybe you should call to see if this Mehfooz Bank is even open today, what with the festival."

"You heard Billy Bob's rule."

"Showing up without an appointment may be a bigger mistake."

"Nothing ventured...we'll see how things go."

Since Carnival traffic occupied the main roads, our driver wormed his taxi through narrow side streets and alleys, until we arrived at a storefront that could have been in any strip-center in the United States.

"Mehfooz Bank," the cabby said.

"This is the largest bank in Pakistan?" Colleen asked.

Ryan helped Colleen and me out of the cab. "Looks like we cannot judge a Pakistani bank by its cover."

The bank doors opened automatically, so Ryan stepped lightly inside and up to the counter. His body language was less the linebacker than an inquisitive businessman presenting his card.

"Hello. I am an attorney from the United States, and I represent my American client, Mrs. Cole Donovan. And this is my legal partner Colleen Ballard, who handles tax and revenue cases for our law firm in Dallas, Texas. We are here to claim funds from accounts established at Mehfooz Bank by Mr. Cole Donovan. You see, Mr. Donovan died in a tragic accident, and Mrs. Donovan is his sole beneficiary and executor of his estate."

The teller's darting black eyes made me even more nervous.

"One moment, sir." Then he quickly went to a room in back.

A minute later, another Pakistani male appeared. With olive skin and a dark beard above a navy blue banker's suit and striped tie, he looked like a Middle Eastern man trying to look Western. "I am Zaheer Masari, the bank manager. How may I be of service?"

Ryan repeated his speech. Then Mr. Masari signaled for us to follow him to a glass-walled conference room. As we gathered around an oval table made from exotic wood, Mr. Masari snapped his fingers. Within a heartbeat, an older, dark-haired woman in a blue floral sari arrived with small glasses of milky, aromatic tea.

She gestured for us to pick up a glass. "Doodh Patti Chai, please enjoy."

As Natalie had said, English is almost a second language in Pakistan. When Mr. Masari spoke, his English was almost perfect except for minor anomalies. "Now please, in this privacy, describe to me the business you wish to conduct with Mehfooz Bank."

A bit more slowly, Ryan recited his spiel. Then he bowed with humility and presented copies of his passport, business card, state bar card, Colleen's legal credentials, and all passports.

We sat silently while Mr. Masari surveyed the items, then motioned to Colleen. "This woman here. She is your legal partner?"

"Yes, sir."

Mr. Masari pointed at me. "This woman here is your client?"

"Yes, sir."

Ryan handed Mr. Masari my file folder. "These documents are for your consideration as well. A death certificate and letters testamentary from the state of Texas."

"Texas!"

"Yes, Texas."

Mr. Masari's dark eyes flashed. "Dallas Cowboys. Austin City Limits. Remember the Alamo!"

"In a nutshell," Ryan said with a chuckle.

"Nutshell? You have many nuts in Texas?"

"Yes, actually we do. Pecans everywhere. But the term 'nutshell' is a phrase that means 'to put things in very few words,'" Ryan said with his most charming smile.

Mr. Masari grinned. "I hear it is hot in Texas. Like Pakistan."

"Can be at times."

"Sometimes over a hundred degrees," Colleen said.

Mr. Masari held up a hand. "Only one representative."

Colleen nodded demurely and took a sip of her tea, but a flash in her eyes revealed her dismay at Mr. Masari's sexism. Like me, she probably hated being called "this woman here."

Ryan did his best to smooth things over. "I am the lead person for our delegation, but my partner Colleen Ballard is a board certified attorney in tax law. At one time, she worked for the IRS. Because of her expertise, she and I would be honored if you would please review all of our documents. We have records detailing our authority to claim all accounts held by Cole P. Donovan. These notarized copies are for you. We'll retain the originals."

Mr. Masari's eyes narrowed. "This is a busy time. As you can see, our nation is preparing our annual Carnival next weekend.

Mehfooz Bank is a major sponsor. You must stay long enough to see the parade. We have a float."

"Thank you. We didn't know about Carnival when we planned our trip, but I'm sure we will take in the sights during our stay."

"Yes. No sense flying all this way just to sit by the pool at the Four Seasons." And then Mr. Masari stood to dismiss us.

Billy Bob was right. There were eyes everywhere.

Ryan motioned that it was time for our exit. "Mr. Masari, we will await your call."

"I will review the documents," Mr. Masari said with a bow.

Ryan bowed back. We mere women nodded and tiptoed out.

That was that. We took a cab back to the hotel and waited. One day, two, but there was no call from Mr. Masari.

Over yogurt and mango on Thursday morning, Natalie said, "He probably had to contact his superiors, and they had to contact their superiors, all the way up the bureaucratic chain."

"No telling how many layers of authority are in this friggin' bank," Billy Bob mumbled.

Ryan fumed. "I'll give this Masari character until Friday afternoon. Then I'll have to get the U.S. Embassy involved."

Natalie blurted another of her facts to amaze us. "The U.S. Embassy for Seychelles is a thousand miles away in Port Louis, Mauritius. But they've got a virtual office set up to handle U.S. citizens' business via e-mail."

Billy Bob hooted. "No wonder our quarterback opened accounts here. Absolutely no physical presence of U.S. authorities to enforce FATCA regs."

That didn't sit well with Colleen. "For all we know, Mr. Masari has already moved the money back to Pakistan."

I felt a bit frantic. "Does this mean we won't be able to get anything back?"

"Not necessarily, but we will need to spend more time here than we planned. Don't worry, Marie. My firm will cover some of these expenses, that is, if I can get back any of the three million I invested in Odyssey. My accountant is tough as nails but I know how to get around her expense reports."

Colleen sighed quietly. "Now I know why my annual bonus wasn't all I expected."

"There will be an extra bonus this year. It's not every tax attorney who will back her boss at a murder trial, but you tackled my ex like a pro. And I'll depend on you to take a good run at the IRS, once we intercept what's in Cole's accounts."

Colleen puffed sarcastically. "No more football analogies, please, unless I get to play quarterback."

"Can't get football out of our blood, can we, Diver?"

Ryan's eyes glimmered like sunlight on aqua waves. "Guys… gals, I apologize for my corny football lingo. Let's take a break. Here we are at the start of some wild, tropical Carnival, but we're working ourselves into despair over a foot-dragging Pakistani banker. Natalie, since you are obviously the world's greatest sleuth, would you use that sweet iPad to find out how we can have a little fun on this corrupt island nation?"

Chapter Thirty-Seven

CARNIVAL, SEYCHELLES STYLE

Turns out the festival's second day on Saturday was the one we really wanted to see, according to Natalie's research. So after a team breakfast, we gathered in the lobby to head into town.

"Let's party!" Natalie sang out as she scampered in a multicolor blur to hail a cab, doing a mock disco and shaking her booty. When several Seychelles cabbies gave her a whistle, Natalie seemed to revel that her dark skin fit in with most locals.

"Gotta protect my stuff," Billy Bob mumbled as he huffed and puffed to catch up.

After a breezy ride across island, we got out a few blocks from the festival's main route, then made our way through the crowds.

The morning began with a wild and colorful parade. Men, women and children, with skin colors from dark to pale, dressed in astounding and outrageous costumes. One woman looked like a giant bouquet of calla lilies. Men in top hats and tuxes walked on ten-foot-high sticks. Showgirls in feather headdresses and sequined leotards joined forces with a muscular guy in the back of a pickup who wore nothing but a skimpy black Speedo. They were followed by a truckload of elementary-school boys in aqua and gold floral polo shirts, sporting baseball caps in chartreuse, red, and blue. Next, about ten dark-toned men strutted by in tribal headdresses, wearing wide wings made of purple, gold, and red feathers. But my favorites were the shy high school girls who wore gold, red, or purple satin sashes over their breasts. Their skirts were in matching fabrics, while tropical-print bandanas held back dark braids that revealed the beauty of their youth.

I silently hoped their lives would be full of love, laughter, and as little pain as the island gods would spare them.

To frighten the crowd, a group of men marched by dressed like monsters, while street bands, school bands, commercial floats, and club floats sailed by. We called hello to the float riders, and they proudly shouted back, "Welcome to Seychelles Islands." We did our best to catch the candies and trinkets people threw our way.

At the parade's end, the Mehfooz Bank float drove by, decorated with U.S. greenbacks enlarged to gigantic size. The riders were Arab women wearing myriad-colored saris. We did not see Mr. Masari, who might have thought himself too important to ride on a float.

By the time the parade ended, all of us except Colleen were tipsy, although it is illegal to drink on the streets of Seychelles. But local bars sold cocktails throughout the day, so we stopped for a round here and there, then watched the parade while strolling to the next bar for another round.

With that much alcohol in us, the desire for food grew urgent. We wandered across a booth that offered grilled fish and rice with a "cari" sauce, which turned out to be coconut milk and curry with lemongrass seasoning. It was delightful. For dessert, we devoured wonderfully short, plump bananas covered with a caramel sauce.

Walking the streets after our meal, we saw a booth that sold "roussette on a stick."

Natalie, of course, had the answer. "It's a bat. Bigger than U.S. bats. This bat eats fruit from the trees...not insects, so it's considered a delicacy."

Billy Bob grimaced. "This woman stays up all night surfing for tidbits like that one."

"Aha, that's where you spend the night," Ryan said.

Billy Bob blushed, confirming he had been the grumbling voice when I called that first, scary night.

I glanced at Ryan. He again winked at me.

Colleen put a stop to our titillation. "Okay, you drunken, swinging singles. I'm a married woman with children. This is a business trip, isn't it?"

"Colleen, lighten up. I know you'd rather be home with your husband and family, but how many times have I asked you to enjoy an all-expenses paid week on a tropical island with not much to do, other than put up with four drunken, middle-aged swinging singles?"

She seemed to give up after Ryan's comment, so we five aimlessly strolled the streets until we arrived at a nightclub called, "The Blind Rousette."

"Kismet. We've definitely got to go in there," Colleen laughed.

Inside, we ordered a round and listened to a band playing what Natalie told us was, "Seggae, a combination of 'Reggae' and 'Sega' from Mauritius."

"Good old Mauritius. Where the U.S. Embassy is of no use."

"Yes, Americans are out of luck if you get in trouble here, unless you've got a Lear jet in your pocket," Colleen said.

Natalie took the old Mae West line even further, "Is that a Lear Jet in your pocket, or are you just glad to see us?"

Those metaphoric images led to a groan from Billy Bob, but even the sophisticated Ryan blushed. "Oh, dear. Forgive me if I don't stand up."

As our jokes faded, we looked to the dance floor, where women in bright, tropical colors ground their hips and twirled, while the men shuffled, the soles of their shoes rarely leaving the floor.

I wanted to hear more about this music, so I shouted over the drums. "Natalie, what's the difference between Seggae and Reggae?"

She borrowed a smart phone from a guy sitting next to us.

"Says on Wikipedia, and I'm reading verbatim, "Reggae is a style of music with a strongly accented subsidiary beat, originating in Jamaica. Reggae evolved in the late 1960s from 'Ska' and other local variations on calypso, and rhythm and blues, and became widely known in the 1970s through the work of Bob Marley; its lyrics are much influenced by Rastafarian ideas.'"

"Whatever that means," Billy Bob shouted above the din.

Natalie started searching for "Rastafarian," so I stopped her. "Finish the description about 'Seggae.' I was a music major."

"Seggae comes from Mauritius and is a combination of Creole slave music called 'Sega,' which primarily uses percussion instruments—like drums and triangles—and Reggae, which has a wider variety of instruments, like guitar, horns, and so forth. They call the music 'Seggae,' but the dance people are doing here is locally called 'Sega dancing.'"

Suddenly, Colleen shouted, "Let's go try it," grabbing Natalie's hand. Off the two went to the dance floor, with Billy Bob soon following behind.

Since Natalie was African American, I expected she would be a natural talent at this dance, but she looked a bit awkward as she tried to swivel her hips. Through the crowd I saw Colleen, yes, beige Mommy Tax Lawyer Colleen, wowing the band. She swiveled her hips in a tribal grind, arched her back, thrust forward, then spun in a circle, while Billy Bob scooted around like the other males, then sort of chased Natalie, who couldn't get the hang of this Sega dance at all.

Too shy to try, Ryan and I applauded our team's gyrations until the next upbeat song began. Then we grew quiet. Neither of us knew what to do. He was my attorney, my husband's football buddy, my nemesis' ex-husband, and we had landed in this situation not by design, but by chance.

"Would you like another drink?" was all he could say.

I shook my head. "My gosh, we've been drinking all day."

Ryan gave me a look of desperation. "Marie, ya' a gotta help me out. I'm out of practice."

"You've said that before."

"I did?"

"When you asked me to lunch."

"Right." He turned away, embarrassed.

"And then you showed up with an entire staff."

He thought for a moment. "But we needed a team meeting."

"We did, but I expected you and I would have 'our' lunch first. We go way back but we don't know each other, not one-to-one."

"Right. Well, I guess you can say I panicked."

"Panicked?"

"Marie, you're the quarterback's wife."

"Cole is dead."

"There's a code. The guys. You never date another player's girl."

"The guys. Again with the guys." I was dismayed. Maybe Ryan was more football player than I had hoped, and my attraction to him was another of my mistakes. Maybe I should change my name to "Marie Needy."

He could see my chagrin.

"Marie, it's not about the guys. Doreen and I signed divorce papers last week. I'm kind of in shock."

"You are officially single?" My smile must have conveyed more glee than surprise.

"Right. And it cost me, but not as much as it would have, because she openly fooled around. I am now free. And the reason, well, not the total reason, but I went ahead with the divorce because—maybe I shouldn't say this, since I'm still your attorney, and there are ethical considerations—but I have always been attracted to you from afar. I do want to explore our potential, but in the background, always in my memories, I see you and Cole together after games or, more recently, walking the red carpet at the opera. You may not understand this, but Cole was my hero. Two Super Bowl rings. That was so amazing. And later he managed the Opera's finances so well, truly he did, before everything went south. I was sick when I found he'd lost all that money. And it was like a double-edged sword to my gut when he killed himself."

I was drunk enough to say it. "I don't think Cole killed himself. He would never jump. He would run. Leave me, take everything, and run like hell."

"Did the police find any evidence that he was murdered?"

"No. Just paint scraped off the balcony rail where he went over, so they called it a suicide."

"That building has video security, doesn't it?"

"Yes, but nobody rode the penthouse elevator except Cole."

"Do you want me to put Billy Bob on it?"

"What difference would it make? Cole has been dead for over a year. I've been a good girl and mourned him. Better than he deserved. It's time for me to start new." I looked into Ryan's big blue eyes, which glistened as they centered on me with boyish hope and desire. "And I think I'd like to start new with you."

He gently took my chin in his hands. I could smell the rum he had consumed, and I'm sure our collective breath smelled like bananas and curry too, but I didn't mind.

"Marie, I'm scared to death, but I think, oh, what? I think I am in some sort of infatuation. I haven't felt this way in so long, not since college, really."

He kissed me tentatively as his soft, full lips touched and explored, then coaxed me to accept his yearning. We held our kiss for so long we didn't realize the band had stopped playing, and Colleen, Billy Bob, and Natalie were standing around our table, just as embarrassed and shocked as Ryan and I were when we finally pulled away, unable to breathe, speak, or focus.

Colleen sighed, "Oh, dear. I really need to sober up." And off she went toward the front door.

Billy Bob called for the server. "Check, please. It's motel time."

Outside the club, we hailed a town car. Throughout the winding drive, we did our best to chat as if nothing had happened. But when we got to the Four Seasons, Ryan announced in his very serious attorney voice, "I'll show Marie to her villa. No telling who might be lurking on the pathways tonight."

I was embarrassed and mumbled, "Oh, I can make it fine."

Billy Bob winked. "See you in a bit, Boss."

"Nasty, don't give me any trouble or I'll put a hold on your next expense check."

"Why do you keep calling him 'Nasty'?" Natalie asked.

"His nickname in college. You may not want to know why."

Colleen had enough. "This married woman is headed for a hot bath and to sleep. You lovebirds go do whatever lovebirds do. I wish you all a pleasant goodnight."

The cocktails had lightened my head to the point I couldn't stop smiling all the way to my villa. When I opened the door, I wondered what was protocol? Was this really a date? Like Ryan, I was out of practice. When I turned to see, he was standing outside like a gentleman.

"Would you like to come in for a while?" I asked, not knowing what else to say.

"I would like to come inside you for a while."

I was shocked at his crudeness. "Ryan, I don't know. We… well, we've just begun."

He blushed in dismay. "I'm sorry. That sounded crass. I guess the drunken linebacker forgot he is now a grown up."

"I slip into football trash talk at times too. That was a good part of our youth, and it's hard to suppress it."

He nodded silently, still standing outside the door.

"Don't be silly, Ryan, come in. But tonight, I think we should just talk. In the football days, booze and sex were inseparable. But we're grownups now. We need to find more reasons to be together than you and Cole played on the same team long ago."

"You're right, Marie. When you are one thing for many years, then you have a second profession, you wind up with a split personality. Cole and I used our football identities to build new businesses. Now I need to learn how to be a middle-aged single attorney who is very interested in an absolutely gorgeous woman who used to be married to a guy I worshipped, and get over the shock that I can be with her myself. Figuratively, not biblically."

"As you always say, 'Right.'"

"I do say that a lot, don't I?"

"Right. But I kind of like it. Makes me feel like one of us knows what we're doing."

"Let's sit on the balcony. Gosh, you've got a better view than Billy Bob and I do, although he's never in our villa."

"I think I interrupted something the other night. Called Natalie late but heard a lot of heavy breathing and Billy Bob swearing."

"He's twenty years older than Natalie, but I guess she likes him. He was always the stud of the locker room, if you get my drift."

"TMI."

"Right."

"Did you see the moon the other night? I couldn't sleep, so I came out and saw this huge full moon, right before it disappeared into the sea."

He reached and held my hand. "Sorry I missed that, but I'll sit here all night if we can see that same moon again. There should be enough of the old man left."

Then we watched as the almost-full moon angled toward the sea until only the tip of the old man's head was visible. And then he was gone. In the sky, stars blinked like fireflies on velvet, as Ryan and I chatted comfortably, leaned across to kiss now and then, at first sweet, tender kisses, followed by longer, deeper kisses that eventually turned into a full, ardent press that stirred us to the point a decision had to be made.

Ryan made it for us, issuing a sigh that sounded more like a groan. "The responsible attorney has won over the crass football player. Although I would like to crawl into bed with you, I think we should table this until I have a deal with Masari. After that, I can safely say I am no longer your attorney."

"Right," I said. And I was not being sarcastic.

Tonight had been lovely, so wonderful to have a man hold me and kiss me longingly, but the timing was not right. Hopefully, Mr. Masari would relent on Monday. Then Ryan and I would have another reason to celebrate.

If we could solve the money puzzle, we could put more effort into clearing my name from the murder charge too. Maybe find out for sure if Barry killed Luca. Or Rebecca. Or both. Even at the height of romantic euphoria, I can't get that hope out of my mind.

Chapter Thirty-Eight

NERVES

All through our team's breakfast Monday morning, Ryan avoided my eyes. I wondered if he was having second thoughts. We had not spent time alone on Sunday because Colleen wanted to attend the children's parade at Carnival—something the guys had no interest in, nor did Natalie.

Colleen and I took a cab to Victoria and watched as hundreds of adorable children preened in vivid costumes, dressed as lotus blossoms or queens and kings, each masked, crowned, or feathered, along with accompanying bands, pets, and mothers. Such a joy to see the collective happiness this event gave to the families.

After the parade, we went shopping so Colleen could bring gifts to her kids. And I bought several things for my sons.

Sunday evening, the team regrouped for dinner. Conversation surrounded the trip to the bank the next day, so the mood was more somber than our festive Saturday night. After dinner everyone retired to separate quarters, except Billy Bob and Natalie probably paired up later.

Alone in my villa, I felt a bit rejected, now that Ryan played the attorney card. Yes, I had not wanted to have sex that first "date." But life is like that old song about wanting you to want me. Then again, I wondered if Ryan might be one of those guys who feared involvement. Maybe that's why he married Doreen. No involvement needed. The woman was a talking, walking, blabber machine.

I coached myself that time would tell, and did my best not to be Marie Needy. Still, I hoped Ryan wanted me as much as I suddenly wanted him, especially if we were stuck on this island much longer. The Carnival had been a nice diversion and Mahé is lovely with mountains, trees, beaches, and clear aqua waters, but I was tired of being alone in a hotel room. I was stuck, missing my sons, my cello, even missing my funeral home job, Lena, and the Embalming BoyZ who made the dead look alive. So, I perched on the end of the bed and played air cello to the TV. Only this time, I refused to look at myself in the reflection.

The next morning, Ryan helped Colleen into the back of the cab, and then me. As I slid inside, he tapped my shoulder and, when I looked to see what he wanted, his eyes expressed more than words could say.

Luckily Colleen could not see his eyes' ardent glow. After he gently closed the door, I felt a rush of excitement and issued an amazed sigh.

"You okay?" Colleen asked, her eyes concerned.

"A bit nervous." I did my best to sound sincere, although Colleen could not know what my nerves were for.

"Just think of this as a game," she said.

Ryan sat in front, and our cab zoomed off. From my back seat, I silently judged Ryan's interactions with the cabbie. He was friendly to him. Funny. Courteous. I liked that.

Ryan is still a big guy, six-feet-four, well over two-hundred and twenty pounds, although in his playing days he probably weighed two hundred and sixty. In that era, the guys took steroid shots. They are banned now, but the players often joked how the team doctor, an osteopath who supposedly was there to treat players with the latest advancements in physical therapy, lined up the guys at practice and gave them shots of what "Doc" said were supplements.

The players eventually figured out these were a mix of steroids, testosterone, "Andro," human growth hormone, stimulants, and who knew what else. Doc wouldn't say, and the players did what the coaches ordered.

Cole didn't though. "I told Doc I wasn't going to take that mother fuckin' joy juice. Makes my balls ache."

I giggled out loud in the cab, remembering.

Ryan turned to see why. "Marie, you ready for Act Three as the grieving widow?"

"Of course. Notice my somber dress?" I smiled the most alluring smile I could muster. I wanted Ryan to know how I felt, grieving widow and all.

He grinned and held my dilated gaze a bit too long.

Colleen sighed. "Come on, y'all. Give a girl a break."

"Not to worry, Colleen. As your employer, I want you to know that no attorney/client relationship has been breached, symbolically, or physically. And it won't be until after we get this deal signed, sealed, and delivered."

"Good. I don't want to find myself testifying in some sexual harassment lawsuit before the State Bar. Even if you are my boss, I refuse to lie for you."

I gave Colleen a demure look.

She again sighed. "Just cool it until this dang case is over and I can go home to my boring life. Please!"

Even the cabbie grinned as he wound through Victoria's streets, which were littered with debris from three days of Carnival. All around, men in blue jumpsuits sluggishly cleaned up the mess. I'll bet most had hangovers and wished they could spend the day in bed. Me, too.

When we pulled up to the bank, Ryan whispered, "Take a breath and exhale. You'll be fine."

That reminded me of Lena's deep breathing exercises she always coached me to use.

The same slight, dark teller glared at us when we walked in. Clearly, he did not expect us or want to see us. He escorted us to the conference room and shut the door. A polite knock brought the same aromatic tea, delivered by the same lovely woman, today in a mustard colored sari. Then we waited. An hour. Hour and a half.

Ryan paced. "This tricky bastard wants to keep the money, or a thick slice. But he'll have to deal with our Feds before I give in."

After a full two hours, Mr. Masari walked in. His frown conveyed his dismay. He was wearing a brown, Western-style suit that flattered his skin tone more than the ubiquitous dark blue he had worn during our first visit.

I thought I might compliment him. "Mr. Masari, you are very well-dressed today."

His eyes froze me with a glare. "Forgive my tardiness, but yesterday was family day at Carnival, and my wife and I have four children. Too many hours have gone into making costumes, and too much candy was eaten by children who refused to sleep. School began late. I myself just arrived."

Ryan gave him a smile. "We enjoyed your Carnival greatly."

"A lovely event and so well organized. The children's parade was delightful. I wish my kids could have seen it," Colleen said.

Masari glared, but Colleen merely smiled back.

"Mrs. Donovan, you were able to attend? Or are you still grieving your husband's death?"

I glanced at Ryan, who gave me a subtle signal that it was okay to answer. "Mr. Masari, I will always grieve my husband's death. But since my trip to your beautiful country coincided with your magnificent Carnival, I felt I should attend it, even if my spirits were a bit down."

"And, did you enjoy the Sega dances and cocktails at The Blind Rousette?"

I almost blurted, "How do you know that?"

Luckily, Ryan jumped in. "Mr. Masari, we are not here to discuss our social lives, which seem of greater interest to local gossips than our business dealings. Mrs. Donovan rightfully and legally claims the proceeds from her husband's accounts with Mehfooz Bank. You have our documentation. What is the delay? We cannot remain here indefinitely, but we will not leave until we have an answer."

"As an attorney you must know of the United States law called FATCA, under which Mehfooz Bank is required to report to your Internal Revenue Service details about any activity related to offshore accounts held by American individuals or organizations."

Colleen held up a hand, as if asking a teacher if she could speak. In spite of Mr. Masari's refusal to acknowledge her, Colleen stood, like the tax lawyer she is. "We understand that Seychelles has been slow to support this requirement. In fact, Mehfooz Bank has never reported the existence of Cole Donovan's accounts to the IRS. This in itself is a violation of FATCA. But our records list the account numbers, and we will provide those to the IRS, since we are law-abiding citizens. As a result and, according to U.S. tax laws, the IRS may penalize Mehfooz Bank a large percentage of the amount held in Cole Donovan's accounts for your bank's failure to report. If your branch fails to pay the penalties, our government has the power to freeze, or even seize all assets related to Mehfooz Bank operations in the United States. Is that something you want to be responsible for?"

"Only one representative!" Masari shouted, furious at this threat from a woman, no less. Then he said something in Urdu, clearly distressed.

Ryan rose to his full linebacker height, massive in comparison to the wiry Mr. Masari. "Mrs. Ballard is my legal partner. As I've discussed with you, she handles tax law for our office, while I focus on estate work and criminal law. I would appreciate your doing business with both of us, as she is far more proficient in U.S. tax situations than I am. I trust her implicitly."

Mr. Masari's eyes grew wide, apparently intimidated by Ryan's physical presence. "This is not the way we operate in Pakistan or Republic of Seychelles," Mr. Masari muttered.

"I understand, sir. We respect your national culture and business practices, but what Mrs. Ballard knows about the IRS may be of financial benefit to you."

Ryan sat again and was silent while Mr. Masari glared. The banker took a sip of chai, straightened his tie, took another sip, flipped through our documents, and eventually said in a measured tone, "Mr. Ingles, my superiors would like to discuss a proposal." Then he tossed a new folder of documents on the table.

As Natalie had instructed, Ryan leaned in but avoided making eye contact. Instead, he leafed through the folder. "We are listening."

"Mehfooz is an international bank, but the one hundred and fifteen islands in Republic of Seychelles are part of the African Union. As such we conduct business as Africa does. Likewise, in the United States, we conduct business as America does. And in Pakistan, as Pakistanis. You see our dilemma. I have discussed your situation with my superiors, and Mehfooz Bank would like to offer Mrs. Donovan ninety percent of the proceeds currently held in Mr. Donovan's accounts."

Colleen spoke up. "Mehfooz Bank keeps ten percent?"

"Yes. An administrative surcharge."

Ryan looked at Mr. Masari. "We are not privy to the most recent statements. May we ask, ten percent of what total?"

"I am not at liberty to discuss the total amount, as it rests in five different accounts."

"Will the IRS be notified?" Colleen asked.

"As I said, Mrs. Ballard, in Seychelles we do business as Afrikaners."

"I take it you will not report to the IRS," Ryan said.

"Mr. Ingles, ten percent of the total is far less than the higher penalty and interest Mrs. Donovan likely would pay the IRS for her husband's failure to report his accounts. Likewise, we would rather not pay penalties for accounts opened prior to Seychelles cooperation with FATCA. In fact, my superiors think United States is wrong to demand foreign banks pay penalties on accounts initiated outside your country. Because you became aware of accounts only after Mr. Donovan's death, my superiors view our proposal as a compromise. Mrs. Donovan will receive the funds, less the administrative fee. Please let me know if you accept our terms. The contract has the details."

Mr. Masari picked the contract from the folder and gave it to Ryan, who handed it to Colleen, who read it line by line over the next half hour with the best poker face I've seen.

After Colleen nodded in agreement, Ryan told Mr. Masari, "My partner agrees. We will provide Mrs. Donovan's U.S. bank account details for the transfer. When might we expect the proceeds?"

"I am sure your American bank will flag this transfer, and Mehfooz Bank will have to verify it as authentic. Because of this, the transfer will take three business days. In addition, Mrs. Donovan's bank will report this transaction to your IRS, but Mehfooz Bank will let your lady tax lawyer deal with them. Mehfooz Bank wants no part of IRS, since U.S. tax laws do not apply to Republic of Seychelles or to Pakistan."

Ryan and Colleen appeared totally calm, but my heart pounded in amazement. We had no idea how much was in Cole's accounts, or even what names the accounts had been in, but it appeared Colleen had Mr. Masari over a barrel. The only thing he wanted was to make sure that Mehfooz Bank's operations in the United States would not be jeopardized.

Ryan handed me the contract, which I signed with a quivering hand. Colleen had warned me that the IRS would impound the funds immediately upon receipt, but she promised she would press the Feds to pay off Odyssey investors as soon as possible. And let me have any leftovers, if any, after penalties and interest.

I doubted there would be much but I wanted to use whatever funds there were to clear my name. Hire Billy Bob to find who really killed Luca.

Ryan signed the contract as my lawyer, as did Colleen, although Mr. Masari had not prepared a line for her signature. She simply marked a line, signed her name above it, and with a sweet smile handed the papers to Mr. Masari. He refused to take the contract from her, so Ryan heaved in exasperation and handed him the papers. "Sir, we await the funds transfer. We will not leave the islands until Mrs. Donovan's bank certifies receipt. Until that time, you may contact us at the Four Seasons if you have questions."

With that, we left in silence and hailed a cab. As we rode back to the hotel, Ryan held a finger to his lips to keep Colleen and me from saying a word during the full half-hour ride. Our driver might be a plant for all we knew.

∽

AT THE HOTEL, WE HEADED STRAIGHT FOR THE POOLSIDE café, where Natalie and Billy Bob had arranged a supposedly secure circle of chairs. However, I had to laugh, since Mr. Masari seemed to know everything we had done during our trip, secure circle or not.

We drank two celebration rounds of tropical cocktails while Ryan took off his tie, unbuttoned his dress shirt and told and retold the story, every line.

Billy Bob issued a low hoot. "How much was in those accounts?"

Colleen whispered in a low voice. "We don't know, but I can't wait to see what names are on those transfers. If there was an account only in Cole's name, it would be an inheritance for Marie. That is, if the IRS will let it go. This is where good media relations might help. Maybe after we get home, your gossipy 'Out and In' buddy will write a good story."

"My friend Lena might pull some strings with Terrance, but I've had enough public relations mayhem for now." I stood and gave them each a high five. "Tonight we celebrate. On me. You four are worth it. You've helped me get my life back. And because you've found the gosh darn money, I might be able to afford your ridiculously high fees."

While everybody laughed, I took off my heels and strutted in my widow's suit to the end of the long swimming pool, where a diving board towered. As cheers, whistles, and catcalls escalated from the partiers around the pool, I determinedly climbed the high ladder, ignoring the rising hoots, claps, and jeers.

When I got to the top, I looked back down the café patio. There stood Ryan, Billy Bob, Natalie, and Colleen.

"Go, girl, go," they cheered and clapped from across the turquoise rectangle that stretched beneath me.

In my mind's eye, I was the teenager who used to wow them at the pool each summer, that long-legged girl who loved to swim and dive. Daddy's Ava Gardner.

I took a breath and strode out on the board. One, two, three, lift, jump, push, spring, soar. I sailed over the expanse in my very best swan dive. As I fell, I thought I would never reach the water's surface until the wallop, rush, and chill greeted me, and my ears almost exploded with the pressure. I had plunged too deeply, forgetting the technique for staying shallow upon entry. My suit jacket came off in the force, leaving me only in my blouse and skirt as I stretched toward the surface, terribly out of breath.

At the ladder, Ryan came to help me out. He seemed quite proud. Such a rewarding feeling to have a man's approval, not his dismissal or anger.

The pool crowd cheered and whistled. Everyone could see my bra through my soaked blouse, but I didn't care.

I could return home a free woman, maybe have enough money to investigate Luca's murder, maybe pay off my HELOC mortgage, see my sons, play my cello until my neighbor squawks, maybe teach cello or play with a chamber quartet. I think I'm good enough. Eric said so. Lena said so. And Cole is no longer here to scoff, which was like saying, "What you do doesn't matter. It's all about me."

Well, Cole, now it's about me. And you're dead.

Chapter Thirty-Nine

FOR REAL, OR A DREAM

Our team got quite snockered around the pool that afternoon, so tipsy in fact, we needed naps. Each of us headed to our separate villas to rest before dinner. It was wonderful to shower and sleep, which I did wet-haired and absolutely naked on top of my king-sized bed. To hell with security cameras. If Mr. Masari was watching, he could see that I had nothing to hide.

About six, Natalie woke me with a call. Time for our team dinner. We went to a lovely spot on the edge of the clear sea, where I lapped up lobster spaghetti in a whisky sauce, while Ryan and Natalie chomped on crispy, spicy prawns. Colleen tried another exotic curry dish and Billy Bob, well he's a beer and fried fish guy. Afterward, we headed downtown to "our place," The Blind Rousette, to celebrate even more.

The bar was far less crowded after the crush of Carnival. A six-member band, seemingly of every race and culture, played the now-familiar mix of Reggae and Sega music. Colleen sailed out to the floor, immediately a showstopper. The scattered crowd applauded and cheered, which spurred Colleen to more outrageous gyrations. For a Mommy, she had gotten in touch with her tribal mojo and put most Seychellois to shame.

Billy Bob was in a stupor from too many rum drinks, but he

dragged me out to dance, and I gave Sega a try. Like Natalie, my long legs got in the way. By the time the song finished, Ryan and whatever stray drunk were still there had come out to the floor, where they scooted in circles to the women's bumps and grinds. We laughed so hard, I almost felt sick. But we had memorable fun celebrating our big win.

When the lights came on, the band announced, "We don't care where you go, but you can't stay here."

We laughed loudly, since that announcement ends many evenings at American nightclubs, thousands of miles away.

∾

WE HAILED A TOWN CAR FOR THE RIDE BACK. ONCE ON THE road, our celebratory pitch mellowed into quiet, separate thoughts and memories.

To me, this felt like the days when the Explorers would celebrate after a big win. This was twenty years ago, mind you, but home games were the wives' days to shine. We dressed like movie stars. The Anglo women—far fewer of us on the team than in college—tried to look like Sharon Stone or Demi Moore, and dressed in brightly colored suit jackets with huge shoulder pads. The African-American gals, like my friend Diana, tried to look like Whitney Houston or Tina Turner, decked out in *faux* purple leather, furs and feathers.

After the game, the wives and girlfriends gathered in the Explorers' office lobby to wait for the players to come up the elevators from the locker rooms. If the team had lost, everybody was hush-hushed, and there were few smiles. You were scared that your guy might be benched or even traded. But if the team won, everybody was hugs and yeh-yehs. Winning was everything in the pros. This was your livelihood, not just a game.

When your guy walked out of the elevator, he didn't greet you directly, but silently sauntered your way, while he "Hey, Man'd" other players about the game. Afterward, the team headed to a party at The Heathman Hotel in downtown Portland. Throughout the evening, most of the guys drank way too much, and far too many did cocaine or marijuana in the bathroom, while the Religious Nuts prayed in a corner. But eventually all the guys gathered to talk about the game for hours.

Meanwhile the women talked in little cliques. Some of the older wives like Dandy Randy's wife Louise were kind of overbearing. "I've always told Randy, you quarterback the guys and I'll quarterback the wives," she once told me. I didn't like that, since my husband was a quarterback too.

As the parties wore on, everyone got drunker, higher, wilder. Blacks, Whites, Latinos, Samoans, everybody danced with everybody. Some got so drunk they passed out, especially the fabled Dandy Randy. I still can see him guzzling a fifth of vodka until his chair tipped backward and he slammed to the floor like a dead man. Party after party, Louise would organize the linemen to carry Dandy to their Lincoln Continental, and she'd drive him home. The team's big secret. All-Pro Dandy Randy was a drunk.

Cole and I were not far behind. In those days, I drank as much as I could and still walk. That was the culture. But I did not want to do drugs beyond booze. That's where Cole and I parted ways.

After he got to the pros, he started using cocaine and smoked marijuana to the point he went into a trance. When I pleaded with him to stop, he angrily called me a "cunt" and threw one of his trophies at me. Luckily, he was so loaded, he missed his target.

Why did I put up with it? The language, the drugs, the booze, the female groupies ready to take your guy, the male groupies hanging around your husband. If you had children, you stayed. Even then, you could find yourself suddenly replaced.

At one party our fourth year, Gary Hays, a defensive lineman whose nickname was "Bulldog," was dancing besides us with his wife Lilly. We four laughed and acted silly, trying out new dance moves. Lilly was known as, "Mrs. Bulldog."

But just two weeks later, news swept the team party that Lilly —mother of Gary's four children—had found out he was having an affair with a divorcée who had four children herself. That was a shock to hear, but even worse for me, Gary had brought his mistress to the party that night.

Someone even called her, "The New Mrs. Bulldog."

As Cole and I danced on the crowded floor, I looked around. Which one was she?

Suddenly my friend Monica tapped my shoulder. When I turned, she introduced us to a pretty blonde with a hardened look. Gary was beside her, smiling like this was nothing new.

I could not bring myself to smile a hello.

"Welcome to the Explorer family," Cole said in his charming, quarterback way.

Monica whispered to me, "Now you know her."

What did that mean? Was I supposed to add this woman to invitations for baby showers? Was I supposed to simply erase Lilly? I wondered if Cole had known all along. Even worse, I wondered if Cole had a mistress, some divorcée with four kids who had nailed my husband at The Goal Post bar. By the next team party, I could disappear just like Lilly.

≈

NIGHTMARE, NIGHTMARE, NIGHTMARE, HOW MY MIND succumbs to these memories. Luckily, the town car pulled into the hotel and interrupted my depressing thoughts. I reminded myself that those days were past. I was starting anew.

As Colleen headed to her villa and I toward mine, Ryan waited until Colleen was out of sight before he caught up. Natalie and Billy Bob didn't hide their affection and went arm in arm to her villa across the walkway from mine.

When you are in the tropics, something envelops you. Maybe it's the climate, the aqua water, the mystical mountains, the swaying palms, miles of sand, but you are freer to be the person you would like to be. No American class structure. No striving.

As Ryan and I waved goodnight to Billy Bob and Natalie, the

feeling was so natural, two couples accepting the joy of the others' love. That same amazing feeling overcame me as Ryan kissed me at my door. His mouth, his hands probed. Should we make love, his every touch asked, while my body pressed in a yes that abated only long enough for us to fumble for my keycard.

I had not been with a man in years. Sex with Cole had always been drivingly sexual. I loved him, hated him, needed him, wanted him, gave myself to him, but to no reward or sense of security, because the very next day, he refused to be my friend, my partner, protector, playmate. It unnerved me to succumb to this resurgent desire. Could I really let go?

Ryan may have sensed this. He stopped pressing when we got inside. "Would you like to sit on the balcony and watch what's left of our old man in the moon?"

That was so dear. There he stood, huge shoulders raised in a question, as his wide eyes searched for a way to make me feel secure—this, all the while his trousers protruded with an enormous erection that my eyes could not resist.

"I think what we should do is take a moment. You sit on the balcony, while I freshen up."

He sighed in relief, perhaps even nervousness. "Oh, thank you. I tried not to get a hard on, but I really couldn't help myself."

We both laughed.

While Ryan sat outside, I pinned up my hair and showered. Then I donned the only nightgown I had packed, a long, purple tank that was my favorite thing to sleep in. I hadn't brought anything sexy, so I dimmed the lights the way I like them and sat on the bed.

"Ryan?"

When he came through the balcony's sliding doors, he left the door open for the breeze. Then he showered and asked if he could use some of my toothpaste. He came out with a towel draped around his lower half, his erection a terry-clothed lump.

"May I come in?"

That sent me giggling at his collegiate humor.

"Couldn't resist." Then he shyly sat beside me for a while. "Well, here we are."

"What do you think we should do next?"

He reached for my hairpin. "Is this how you do it?"

My hair fell in streams.

"I had no idea your hair was so long and thick. Beautiful." His wide fingers smoothed my waves as he kissed me tenderly. And then his hands slid to my neck and breasts. As he lightly explored, the rolling sounds of the ocean enveloped us. His hands pressed more passionately, his tongue penetrated more deeply, and I felt swept to sea, buoyant and awash with a rush of emotions that felt all new, but even more passionate than my youthful days with Cole.

Ryan was tender. He was masculine. He was instinctive.

We were exhausted by the time we reached our peak. Ryan breathed heavily, while I curled inside his muscular arms and resisted the urge to fall into a deep, relieved sleep.

He whispered softly. "You are an inspiration."

"I feel jealous that Doreen had your attentions all these years."

"I hate to admit it, but sex with Doreen was somewhat mechanical. Collegiate screwing."

"Cole's and mine was very physical too, except now and then he would let go and love me. I still treasure those moments, although they didn't make it to the morning."

"I'm beginning to see that sex with Doreen didn't evolve beyond the basic fucking stage because our relationship never did. Here I am, forty-seven years old, and I've just made real, passionate love to a woman for the first time. I feel like I've awakened after a long, boring dream."

I kissed his neck lightly and wrapped myself in his arms. As we drifted to sleep, I dreamed I was floating on a warm ocean, bathed in the light of a huge silver moon.

Chapter Forty

BANG!

W ithin what seemed like a millisecond after falling asleep on Ryan's chest, I awoke to a loud bang, like a hotel door slamming shut. My mind was not alert enough to understand what was going on. I was startled, fearful, in shock.

Ryan shouted, "What in the hell?"

"I don't know!" I tried to turn on the light, but I knocked over the lamp instead. I got out of bed and tried to retrieve it.

Suddenly, I made out a human shadow by the dresser.

"Ryan, there's someone in our room...who are you? What are you doing?"

Something flashed from the shadow, followed instantaneously by a bang so loud my eardrums screamed. My God, someone was shooting at us. Frozen in terror, I worried that Ryan had been hit. "Ryan, are you okay? Were you hit?"

He didn't answer.

I started screaming his name, and my mind was telling me I needed to run. But I desperately wanted to see if Ryan was okay. In shock, I couldn't do anything but stand there and scream.

In slow motion came another flash and bang, this time breaking the glass in the framed picture above our bed. I heard glass tinkle.

Again I yelled, "Ryan, are you all right?" He didn't answer, so I finally summoned enough mobility to run out on the balcony, where I hollered at the top of my vocal range, "Help, help us, Villa 1464, we need help. Call police! Someone is shooting at us. Help! Villa 1464."

Then from inside, I heard Ryan cursing and the intruder howling as something crashed into something, followed by scuffling, grunting, swearing, a terrible thud, and a yell.

I ran inside, afraid I might be shot, but I had to help Ryan.

"Stop, you are hurting me," the intruder yelled in an Arabic accent.

"Good, you Mother Fucker. Marie, I've got him pinned. Get the gun. He dropped the darn thing somewhere."

In the dim light, I was looking for the gun, but suddenly there was another bang, and the brilliant overhead lights in our room came on. I jumped and screamed in terror, fearing another gunman, but soon realized that Billy Bob had burst through our door, wearing nothing but his boxer shorts. His graying chest huffed and puffed as he grabbed the intruder's gun and aimed it at him.

"Not one move, you stinkin' little weasel."

In the jarring hotel room light, I was aghast to recognize the man beneath Ryan. He was the young Mehfooz Bank teller.

"Don't shoot. Please. Mr. Masari made me do this. No one was injured. I could not see in the dark. Please let me go."

"You broke in here and tried to kill us. If I have anything to say about it, you're gonna fry in jail for a while."

Billy Bob suddenly started laughing. "We all might want to get some clothes on first. I gotta call the cops and hotel security."

Only then did I realize I was standing there buck naked, with Billy Bob grinning with a delighted gleam in his eyes.

Meanwhile, Ryan was still straddled *au natural* over the bank teller, and the view of Ryan's scrotum pressed against the teller's back seemed more a gross image from some gay porn film than the lovely memory I had in my mind of our glorious evening of sex.

About then, Natalie peeked around the doorway and burst into giggles. "Looks like a Pakistani hit man doesn't have a chance against two naked linebackers and a very underdressed cellist."

I grabbed my robe and wrapped up quickly.

Billy Bob patted my shoulder to soothe me. "Natalie won't say a word and neither will I. I don't want Terrance Nichols' next column to be about us having a five-some in a Seychelles hotel room with a Pakistani hit man," Billy Bob joked sarcastically.

I yanked a sheet off the bed and tossed it over Ryan's muscular derriere just before two hotel security guards bustled in, followed by two Seychelles policemen who did a lot of shouting.

"Foreigners must go to station. Bring papers for verification."

Billy Bob barked, "You people need to secure this scene. Arrest this dude. We won't leave until the evidence is preserved."

Ryan struggled up, clasping the sheet around his body. "Look, officers, this fellow broke into our room—not sure how he got a keycard...probably bribed somebody—and then the bastard tried to kill us. Luckily he was a lousy shot, even from ten feet away. You'll find bullets in that wall."

The police officers unholstered their guns and pointed them at Billy Bob and Ryan. "You foreigners come to station with us. Bring passports and identification. Now."

That quieted Billy Bob and Ryan. Quieted all of us, in fact.

Ryan and I took turns dressing in the bathroom, while Natalie and Billy Bob grabbed clothes from her villa. Then we rode in police cars, sirens screeching to the Victoria police station.

In a dingy gray interview room, a rotund Creole detective asked the same questions over and over, and Ryan and Billy Bob answered them over and over, until Ryan demanded an attorney.

"You make one call only," the detective said.

Luckily Colleen answered the phone in her hotel room.

"You wouldn't believe what happened while you were sleeping. I'll give you the details later, but for now, Marie and I, along with Natalie and Billy Bob, are being held in the Victoria police station because that snake Masari from Mehfooz Bank sent his puny teller to kill us. For all I know, the hit man wasn't even arrested. I want to file charges. I need you to get hold of the U.S. Embassy. Tell them this banana republic is trying to railroad us."

"Now, Mr. Ingles, I assure you there is no railway in Seychelles," the detective said after Ryan hung up the phone.

That would have been funny if the situation were different.

About ten minutes later, Colleen called the station back and told Ryan the Embassy wasn't open yet. She had sent an e-mail and would call them again after they opened.

For hours, we four sat in the dimly lit interrogation room, where I stared out a smudged window until I could see the night outside lift to the hint of dawn.

At 7:00 a.m., Colleen arrived in full attorney mode, beige linen suit and a determined jaw, but her face was flushed with excitement. "I am an attorney who represents Ryan Ingles and his party. According to his statement, as well as the hotel security guards I've interviewed at the Four Seasons, my clients have done nothing wrong except defend themselves from a murderous attack. I have contacted the U.S. Embassy in Mauritius. Unless you want to deal with an agent from the U.S. government within the next twenty-four hours, I suggest you release my clients now. In addition, we want to file charges against the man who shot at them. He was hired by Mehfooz Bank to murder my clients, so the bank would not have to release Mrs. Donovan's rightful funds."

"I know nothing of this, ma'am. I am not connected with Mehfooz Bank," the detective said.

"Well, I imagine our FBI and the IRS will be very interested to hear about this situation, since Mehfooz Bank has branches and financial operations in the United States. Our government can shut Mehfooz Bank down all across the U.S.A., and freeze all funds coming or going between the U.S.A. and Mehfooz Bank. And they can do it in the blink of an eye, if there is one ounce of impropriety in terms of handling the legal complaints of United States citizens."

To our relief, Colleen's threat sent the pudgy detective to his office, where I watched through his open door as he made several calls, murmured earnestly out of earshot, and shook his head in frustration. When he returned, his arched eyebrows revealed his agitation. "Ladies, Gentlemen, our apologies for your troubles in our beautiful Republic of Seychelles. We are honest people, but some foreign-owned businesses do not always follow our laws. You are free to go."

"Thank you, sir. We expect a thorough investigation into this matter, and charges filed against those who perpetrated this crime. Attempted murder of U.S. business travelers is not how Seychelles wants to be featured on international news, correct?" Colleen said.

The detective mumbled a "no" and apologetically walked us outside. He paid out of his own pocket for a cab.

On our way back to the hotel, a very angry Ryan decided to go on offense. "To hell with Mehfooz Bank. We weren't the bad guys here. In fact, we've righted a wrong."

From my villa, he called the Embassy, told them our story, and said we would scan and e-mail all documents. Needless to say, Ryan glossed over a few details about Natalie being a hacker.

"Our trip here was purely investigational," he told the Embassy. "The IRS had failed to locate any funds from Cole Donovan's dealings, but our outside investigator had a hunch there were offshore accounts. We took a chance and came to claim them. All assets will be surrendered to the IRS. Mrs. Donovan's sole desire is to reimburse her late husband's investors and the Metroplex Opera."

⁂

TWO DAYS LATER, A TEAM OF TWO FBI AGENTS AND TWO IRS agents met us at the hotel. In spite of the tropical weather, the men had worn their ubiquitous business suits and claustrophobic ties. Surely they would rather be in bathing suits, plunge into the waves, drink umbrella drinks, dance the Sega, and succumb to the island fever that had compelled Colleen to dance like a native Seychellois, pasty white skin and all.

In a hotel conference room, she and Ryan led the agents through our documents. Within the hour, the FBI-IRS team zoomed away in a cab to Mehfooz Bank.

We waited by the pool for them to return. Under wide red umbrellas, we nervously talked contingencies, everything from my not getting any money because it would all be paid to investors and the Opera, or my getting some money.

"No matter whether Mehfooz Bank or Seychelles honors FATCA, the FBI and IRS will try to squeeze as much as they can out of the bank and also Marie, penalty-wise. The long arm of the U.S. Federal Government…" Colleen trailed off.

"Either way, our names will soon be splattered in Terrance's column," I said.

As the wait became more tedious, we nursed our nerves with rum drinks and huge curried-chicken salads.

"We at least had a good time on this misadventure," Billy Bob said, his arm around Natalie.

Ryan glanced at me and winked.

Colleen sighed. "Home. I want to go home."

Later on that afternoon, we saw the lead FBI investigator stride over. He pulled up a chair and detailed in a cursory tone, "The situation has been resolved. Mehfooz Bank has released all funds to Mrs. Donovan's account. Of course, the IRS will impound them, but we congratulate you on a fine job of investigating and resolving this affair. Our office will be in touch."

With that, the agent left for whatever chartered jet awaited, while we five shook our heads in amazement, delight, and relief.

Billy Bob mimicked the agent's body language. "We congratulate you on a fine job of investigating and resolving this affair."

"In other words, we did their job for them. And now the IRS will count all of Marie's money and decide how much to keep," Natalie hooted.

"It's not my money. It belongs to Cole's investors."

Colleen's eyes glinted in the tropical sun. "The IRS will use tax 'regs' and the law to their advantage, but the agency is very exacting in their inquiries. If any leftover money was simply in Cole's name, you are the rightful heir. But don't count on getting it soon. The IRS loves keeping money in the Federal Reserve Bank."

Ryan suddenly gasped. "My gosh, Colleen, do you realize? This means you really can go home. I'll call Stacie to book flights. Until then, let's enjoy what time we have left in this tiny paradise before we return to our stressful American lives. Quite honestly, I think Americans could learn a thing or two about enjoying life island-style."

All afternoon, I tanned on a chaise beside Ryan. Now and then our fingers reached to touch, as if to say, "I am here, are you?" Between those moments, I baked in the glorious sun and thanked my stars for Ryan and this new chance at love and freedom.

Chapter Forty-One

OUT AND IN

with Terrance Nichols

"Joy Reigns"

Words cannot express my joy and amazement. Our city's beloved Metroplex Opera not only is solvent again but flush with a surplus, after $45 million was recouped from two offshore accounts, both held in the opera's name in the Republic of Seychelles, an island chain in the Indian Ocean, 900 miles off the coast of Africa.

As you may have read in yesterday's *Wall Street Journal*, the IRS has completed audits of five offshore accounts opened by Cole Donovan at the Pakistani-owned Mehfooz Bank in Victoria, capital city of the Seychelles.

Donovan served as the Opera's CFO until his suicide, almost two years ago.

From the *Journal's* investigative piece, as well as my phone interviews with key personas, these five accounts held sums approaching $3 billion, an astounding amount that includes millions Donovan invested from the Opera's operating fund.

Two years ago, the Opera had written off these funds as a loss, according to board chairman Rebecca Claridge.

"Except for the emergency donations we received from our

generous, ardent supporters, we almost lost our company. But my motion, which the board approved, for Cole Donovan to invest the Opera's funds turned out to be a wise and very lucrative decision for our beloved company. Cole was an investment *savant* and, in the long run, Metroplex Opera was the better for his financial leadership," Mrs. Claridge remarked.

According to Metroplex Opera General Director Keith Warren, "Not only do we have our $30 million operating fund back, but dividends and interest over the years amounted to another $15 million in our coffers. Cole Donovan was a genius. I only wish he were alive so I could thank him for his generosity."

The *Journal* article also reported that about $2.5 billion, held in three accounts under Odyssey Investments, had sufficient gains since Donovan's death to reimburse all of his investors.

This was the big surprise, as authorities had assumed Donovan and his wife Marie had lived large on the profits from his Ponzi scheme, leaving only her $5.4 million Highland Park manse. Indeed, Cole Donovan had dipped into Odyssey proceeds, but he also invested a good portion in obscure global stocks that exploded in value during recent bull markets.

IRS investigative chief Chester Colcannon told me by phone, "Even with such tremendous yields, Odyssey eventually would have imploded. Only because Mr. Donovan's hands were out of the till did the investments balloon during what turned out to be a multi-year, record-breaking surge."

Colcannon also remarked that funds in one personal account in Donovan's name, less IRS taxes, penalties and interest, would be returned to Donovan's estate.

His widow is executor. Mrs. Donovan refused calls for comment, but sources report she is greatly relieved.

Her attorney, Colleen Ballard of Ryan Ingles' firm, said in a prepared statement, "I want to thank the IRS for their diligent audit of Mr. Donovan's offshore accounts. As both the IRS and FBI joint investigations have concluded, Marie Donovan had no knowledge of her husband's dealings or of these secret accounts. I also want to thank the FBI and IRS for their protection during our journey to claim these funds, and for the relative speed with which the IRS audited the accounts and reimbursed Metroplex Opera, Odyssey investors, and Donovan's estate. Mrs. Donovan and her sons have endured a difficult financial period, and we are delighted to see them solvent again."

Ballard, a former IRS agent herself, apparently knew how to negotiate with the Feds.

And so, almost two years after the fall and death of Cole Donovan, we can safely say: What goes around, comes around.

On a personal note, I am relieved that this announcement removes suspicion from the lovely Marie Donovan. The Opera, our Dallas arts scene, and our community are the better for the ever-present tinkle of cherry blossoms dancing above her *chignon*.

Congratulations are also in order for another victory. Sources report that Mrs. Donovan, who is past-president of the League, the Opera's fundraising arm, anonymously auditioned this past summer and won the role as first-chair cellist with Metroplex Opera orchestra.

I look forward to her appearance at the season opener, Benjamin Britten's "A Midsummer Night's Dream."

According to the Opera's newly appointed Maestro, Ronald Garrison, "The cello is considered 'the voice' of the orchestra and sings out over other instruments. Mrs. Donovan will play an important role in leading the cello section."

I suspect that her signature gold cherry blossom hairpins will be kept mum until afterward in the Green Room.

One final and very important note to the future of the Dallas arts scene:

Rebecca Claridge, founder *emeritus* and perennial chair of our city's illustrious Metroplex Opera, confided to me yesterday that she will step down after the opening performance this fall.

"Life is like a Wagnerian opera. I am at a point that I must focus on my family and my health," Mrs. Claridge said in a long phone interview.

A new chairperson will be named after the next Opera board meeting in November. Sources whisper that former Texas football great Ryan Ingles will take the helm.

In a harrowing action-adventure, Ingles' law firm was responsible for discovering Mr. Donovan's offshore accounts. I'm told that *Texas Monthly* magazine will publish an extensive piece about Ingles and his investigative team this month.

Ingles' firm also defended Marie Donovan when she was prosecuted for the murder of Maestro Luca Scarlatti, whose killer has yet to be convicted.

Tenor Barry Claridge's breakdown as a witness during Mrs. Donovan's trial has put this case on hold. Mr. Claridge currently resides in Kerrville State Hospital, pending competency to stand trial.

Mrs. Claridge visits each weekend but admits that the frequent trips take their toll.

I extend my sympathy. No mother should be blamed for the sins of her son.

Chapter Forty-Two

KERRVILLE STATE HOSPITAL

Terrance has this way of pissing me off while praising me. First he quoted Rebecca, who called Cole a genius, and then he quoted Keith Warren, who thanked Cole for his generosity, as though secretly investing funds for private gain is a good thing to do.

But then, Terrance as much said I was wrongly prosecuted, called me lovely, and said that my presence graces the community. And, he gave me a promo for my orchestra debut.

When I read his column, I screamed, "I got it. I got it," but nobody was at home to hear.

I don't know who Terrance's sources were, but that morning's "Out and In" column was the first I'd heard that I'd landed the job. I won the title in an open blind audition that I discovered through the newspaper, of all places. Here I was, past president of the League, but I had no clue that Metroplex Opera posted auditions in the *Daily Herald's Guide* magazine. But there it was. "Open Auditions for the following positions: cello, base, violin."

Needless to say, I was absolutely the most nervous cellist on God's planet when I auditioned.

My weekly confidant Dr. Lockett taught me to meditate and focus on the one thing that gives me energy. That one thing? You might think my cello, as Eric once taught me. You might think Ryan. You might think my sons. But no. The one thing I focused on was Mother.

I remembered her pride when I played in college. Mother and Dad drove down for each performance and sat on the third row, cello side. By spring of my senior year, Mother was wearing a colorful scarf to hide the hair loss from her treatments, but her wide-set eyes shone with the joy and intensity only a mother can convey.

So, when my turn came to audition, I meditated on that pride in Mother's eyes. And let my soul become a part of the piece.

Thanks to blind auditions, no one can say I got the job because of my status in the League. In fact, if the committee knew who I was, they probably wouldn't have awarded me the position. But, since the 1970s, orchestra auditions in the United States have been conducted anonymously. Applicants play behind a screen. The committee hears you. They don't see you. Orchestras began this process as a way to eliminate gender or other biases.

❧

RONALD GARRISON WAS QUICK TO CALL THIS MORNING TO confirm.

"You must attend all rehearsals. No exceptions."

"Of course. I have played with an orchestra and understand the commitments."

"Well, that's been a while...college days. With your social duties, daytime job and so forth, I wanted to be sure you will not...well, flake out on me."

"Flake out on you?" My voice sounded harsh, but I wanted to be taken seriously, not as an opera groupie with a meaningless hobby.

"Apologies if my tone was pedantic. Your cello introduction in this upcoming production is very important. 'Over Hill and Dale' sets the tone for the first act, and I need you at performance level. That's all I meant."

"Maestro, I won't let you down."

"Good, then. I'll expect you tonight. Five-thirty warm up."

"I'll be there, over hill, over dale," I trilled rather foolishly.

But after I hung up, I thought, *Oh, no.* I would have to cancel dinner with Ryan. He had made reservations at Fearing's Restaurant and said he had something important to talk about.

I did too. I had to tell him about my trip last Sunday to see Barry Claridge in Kerrville.

☙

LENA HAD DREAMED UP THIS ASTONISHING IDEA. WHEN WE had lunch two weeks ago, she said that Rebecca Claridge mentioned at a League meeting that she needed help on a drive to visit Barry in Kerrville. It's a Hill Country town, four-and-a-half hours southwest of Dallas.

"Rebecca usually goes down on Saturdays, then spends the night. But she has a fundraiser next Saturday, so I volunteered the two of us to drive her down and back next Sunday. Okay?"

I was taken aback. "Lena, what's with your sudden benevolence? Barry set me up, or Rebecca did, or both, although we won't know until Barry gets better or Billy Bob finds out more."

"Call it your random act of kindness." She winked.

"What happened to your mantra, 'You're too nice'?"

"Marie, here's the deal. Nobody, I mean, not one of D'Posse twits, not even the babbling Doreen, bony Tina, wacko Sienna, Botoxed Krissy, or pompous Penny, no one, *nada* volunteered to help Rebecca after she asked at a board meeting. Every single one shifted in their chairs and lied about commitments. Quite honestly, I felt squeezed and volunteered us both, primarily to make the D'Posse twits look like the twits they are."

"Do it yourself and leave me out of it."

"Marie, I need you to go along as a buffer. I can't imagine being on a long road trip alone with Rebecca Claridge."

"Then you shouldn't have said yes. 'You're too nice,' remember?"

"Okay, call me a softy. Too many years in the funeral biz."

That's how and why the three of us left at 8:00 a.m. last Sunday and drove two hundred and eighty-eight miles, with a stop to pick up lunch at a German restaurant in Fredericksburg.

"Barry's favorite," Rebecca said.

With the car smelling like kraut and schnitzel, we drove about twenty miles to the neighboring town of Kerrville, where we pulled in for a 1:00 p.m. visit at Kerrville State Hospital, a set of four-story red brick buildings on a hill outside of town. We checked in at the gate, then lugged in the food and snacks for Barry.

This was my first time to visit a state-prison hospital, so I was very nervous, especially when I realized I would be locked inside. The horrors of my stay in Dallas County Jail returned. I murmured to the guard that I was a bit claustrophobic.

He smiled knowingly. "Don't worry. Anytime you want to leave, just tell the guard."

That really helped me relax, best I could.

We waited in a family visitation room that had blue farm-table furnishings, faded gray drapes, and a window that looked over a sunlit courtyard.

Rebecca set the table for the four of us and brought out sodas in plastic bottles. "No metal cans allowed. The inmates might use the metal tabs to commit…" And then she broke down in sobs to the point one of us had to do something.

Lena looked at me as if to say, "Hug her, how about it?"

I shook my head and mouthed, "You started this."

Lena reached and gave Rebecca a pat. "I'm sorry you have to go through this. Hopefully Barry will come out of his spell and tell us what we need to know about Luca's murder."

Rebecca slowly gathered her composure and thanked Lena, not revealing further emotion or glancing in my direction.

Moments later, a guard arrived with Barry in tow. He was dressed in prison pajamas with a towel around his neck. His salt-and-pepper hair was now long, pulled back in a ponytail. And he had grown a sparse gray beard, which was coated with spit. He didn't greet us and had to be escorted to a chair, where the guard sat him down.

Rebecca went to hug him, then wiped his face. "One of the medications has a very bad side effect of making him drool."

My flight instinct took over. "Oh," was about all I could muster.

Lena crooned a funeral director remark. "I'm very sorry for your difficult time."

"Barry, you remember Lena Verano and Marie Donovan, don't you? They helped me drive down. Say hello to your opera friends."

Barry glared at nothing but managed a mumbled, "Hullo." Then his eyes darted toward a corner as his head shook "no" to someone we could not see.

"We brought your favorite German food. Hungry?"

"Uh," came the reply and more drool.

"You two go ahead and enjoy your meals. I have to feed Barry. His medication disrupts his coordination."

I stabbed at my schnitzel while Rebecca fed Barry in small bites. The veal, kraut, and potatoes turned out to be delicious, but the grim surroundings and Barry's drooling ruined my appetite.

I shot Lena a look that said, "I hate you" for getting us into this situation.

She chatted to Barry and Rebecca in a nervous patter of opera news. "Marie landed the first-cello chair for 'Midsummer Night's Dream.'"

"Yes, we are proud of our dear Marie. First chair! Will you come to the Green Room and take a bow as guest artist?"

"Not sure, Rebecca. Maestro Ron is a tough cookie. All business. At least that's how he seems."

Rebecca shoveled another bite into Barry's drooling gateway. "I do wish Barry could sing in this production. He would make the perfect Oberon."

While Barry gnashed his schnitzel, I caught a glimmer that he understood what his mother had just said. I asked him directly, "Oberon is a counter-tenor part, isn't it?"

Barry's eyes perked up.

That told me he was in there. "Do you sing much here?"

He mumbled with his mouth full, so Rebecca chimed in. "Barry's meds make it hard for him to speak, but for some reason he can still sing like Mario Lanza. Barry's social worker tells me that he sings arias after Sunday morning chapel services, and he holds a recital each Wednesday for the hospital guards and volunteers."

Barry's eyes twinkled.

"That's wonderful. Gotta keep those pipes in tune," Lena said.

Again, Barry's eyes sparkled as he garbled a reply.

Rebecca shushed him. "Now, don't try to talk until the doctors get you off that terrible medication."

After Rebecca fed her son, she ate a few bites herself. When we were finished, she and Lena packed up the containers to take down the hall to the guard station.

"I need to stop at the potty too. Marie, will you please stay with Barry? I assure you, he's harmless."

I nodded yes, but I did not want to be alone with Barry. The guy was certifiable, and his drooling made me want to throw up. But I did my best to smile. That's me. My mother's daughter. Always with the smile. But the very moment Rebecca and Lena left, Barry jumped from his chair and went to close the door. That scared the devil out of me, especially when he walked straight over and sat beside me. I was so frightened, I couldn't speak.

"Marie, it's me. Don't be afraid. I'm really okay. And I am very sorry, truly, for the trouble my mother and I caused you. I beg you, please forgive us."

I was so stunned, I didn't respond.

"Marie, I'm not crazy. I just pretend to be."

"Barry, what in the world?"

"I don't take the meds when I can get away with it. They make me feel awful. And the drool is impossible. When Mother comes, I pretend I'm still nuts and take the meds so I'll drool."

"If you are okay, why don't you tell someone?"

"I have to save Mother. Save the estate."

"She's been reimbursed for her Odyssey losses. She should be flush with money."

"She told me that, but Marie, there's more. I faked my breakdown to protect Mother. You see…" He dashed to the door, opened it, and peeked out, then closed it and scampered near me again. "Marie, you must promise not to tell a soul."

I looked at his earnest, pleading gray eyes and wondered what he might know that could help my desire to be exonerated. "I'm not promising you anything. You and your mother put me in a terrible position."

"Marie, my secret will exonerate you forever. But I need you to keep this private for one year from today."

"One year?"

"Thereabouts."

"Why a year from today?"

Barry's tone grew hushed and full of sorrow. "Way last year, Mother was diagnosed with non-Hodgkin lymphoma. She hasn't told anyone but me. She's been living with it for a while, but she is terminal. Her doctors give her six months to a year."

I was shocked. "My goodness! My mother died from the same disease. This is ironic. I'm very sorry."

"That's why Mother stepped down. She has nursing help at home but will enter a facility when she cannot manage. I would give anything to be with her during her last days on this earth, but I can't let anyone know that I'm not mentally ill. After Mother dies, my so-called schizophrenia will improve. I'll be declared sane, but instead of being tried for Luca's murder, I'll suddenly remember with great angst and horror who actually killed him."

I was dumbfounded. What would Barry say next?

He leaned very near, to the point I could see a spark of regret and shame in his eyes, as he whispered, "Mother."

"Barry, you don't mean Rebecca. Are you certain of this?"

"Believe me, I know Mother. When she wants something, she can be vicious in her pursuit. She hated Luca with a passion, not only for using me. I loved him, you see. But he had stopped paying for my silence. His family in Italy had cut him off. That's why Luca wanted control of the Opera accounts...to skim. Mother threatened to tell the board, but Luca said he would expose us...tell everyone that we had been blackmailing him."

I had to smile at that one. "But you *were* blackmailing him."

"Admittedly. But Mother was furious that he had us in his slimy grasp. 'Compromised,' was what she called our situation."

"Are you saying Rebecca set things up to appear that I killed Luca? How in the world? No one will believe you."

"They will believe me when I show them the records. Luca's monthly payments kept Mother going for a while, but then he stopped. He was seeing Lena by that time. I went to see him, literally begged him to continue the payments. I even had sex with him, although I wouldn't call it making love. It was desperate, male fucking. Afterward, he promised to help if I kept our affair quiet. But then Luca twisted things."

"Ahhhh. Blackmail turned on the blackmailers."

"Exactly. And with Mother's status, she couldn't handle the fall. I recorded a conversation between her and Luca. Mother threatened to kill him."

"You are kidding."

"No. And I heard Mother leave the house the night Luca died."

"Barry, you should tell the police."

"If Mother is charged, her lawyers will take her for every penny."

"Your mother is dying, but you're thinking about your inheritance?"

"Blame Mother, not me. She's the one who killed Luca."

"Where in the world could Rebecca get hold of Tabun?"

"For all I know, she made it herself. Mother has a master's degree in chemistry. She and Dad met as lab partners in college. One of the first things I had to do as a little boy was recite the table of elements. The woman was a walking..."

Suddenly the door opened and a guard burst in. Barry reassumed his delusional stare as the guard barked, "This door must remain open at all times during visitation."

I blustered a lie. "One of the ladies must have closed it on the way to the restroom."

The guard looked from me to Barry. I'm not sure the guard believed me, but luckily Rebecca rushed in about then and distracted him.

She gave Barry a tender hug, a mother's goodbye. "No matter what you've done, you have your mother's love."

As we walked down the hall to leave, I wondered how Barry could be so calculating as to have his mother think he was crazy, all the while he thinks she killed Luca. Then again, he is the apple, she the tree. And if Rebecca really is Luca's murderer, she knows full well that Barry was lying.

Which begs the question, could Rebecca have done the deed alone? Did Barry help her? Both are putting on a charade. Just how much does each know about the other?

As a guard escorted Barry out of the room, the cunning little tenor caught my eye and winked. That was an image I could not get out of my mind the entire ride home.

I so wanted to tell Lena but, with Rebecca in the backseat, I couldn't say a word. So, we three played and replayed a CD of "The Three Tenors" most of the way home, singing along best we could.

Rebecca wept at every high note and blew sniffles into many tissues. "I'm so grateful for your help. I've lost so much, not having Barry to be with me. Being so alone."

As a mother, I did feel sorry for her. But here I was, riding along, singing arias with a woman who may have killed Luca Scarlatti in a blood fest. And then heaped the blame on me.

Lena kept giving me concerned glances, her black eyebrows arched, but as the car wound through the dark, unlit limestone hills and cedar-lined dales, I couldn't wait for this horrid trip to be over.

The moon had risen by the time we dropped Rebecca at her 1918 mansion on Lakeside Drive. Barry had wanted me to feel sorry for his lack of means, but Rebecca's home is worth three times my neoclassical two-story. Her mansion was one of those classics that would live on, owner after owner.

Considering Barry's comments about his mother's disease, I helped her out of the car and gave her a polite air-hug, refusing to melt into "too nice."

Terrance Nichols and *Texas Monthly* will crucify her soon enough, after Barry reveals his evidence.

Is it better to die with a false impression of one's greatness, or is it better to die with the full truth exposed? If there is an afterlife, both Luca and Cole know that answer. I hope each spirit has suffered anguish for their mistreatment of others. No one should treat another's love with such disregard.

Back in the car, Lena asked, "Something on your mind?"

"Yes, but I have to tell Ryan first. It's a legal thing."

She didn't like that and kept pestering, but I wouldn't budge.

"Well, since you won't talk to me, I've been dying to tell you something." Lena held up her left hand and, even in the dark, a diamond shone. As did her dark eyes.

"You and Terrance?"

She gave me a devilish smile. "Things are working out."

"I'm stunned...are you sure you want to commit to a gay man?"

She glared. "That was milk toast in terms of congratulations."

"You know my feelings about Terrance."

"He's my best friend."

"I thought I was your best friend."

"You are my best girlfriend. Besides, Terry considers himself bisexual, not gay. He's weary of the gay life, the promiscuity, and wants to settle down. Even have a family."

"Luca was bisexual, and you saw how that turned out. Can you trust Terry to remain on the *hetero* side just for you?"

"That's what marriage is about, isn't it? Commitment."

"My marriage proved that promises are not always kept."

"You and Cole were very young. My God, Terry and I are in our forties, a whole lot wiser. And he even wants kids."

"Can you still conceive?"

"I sincerely doubt it. We can buy a baby if my eggs won't hatch."

I was silent for a while, imagining Lena and Terrance handling 2:00 a.m. feedings. *She'd hire a nanny first.*

"Cat got your tongue?"

I lied. "Something about Barry."

"But he's delusional."

I didn't reply, just shook my head in silence.

We finished the trip and hugged murmured goodbyes, a bit miffed at each other. But for once, I was determined to be street smart. The only person I should tell was my lawyer.

෯

THAT'S THE STORY I HAD INTENDED TO TELL RYAN OVER dinner, that is, until Maestro Ron called. I dialed Ryan's office to cancel.

"Sounds like this is your big chance. I'm disappointed to miss our dinner, but I understand." Ryan's voice sounded wistful, as if my new job might negatively impact our relationship.

I don't blame him for that. He and I have seen one another constantly since our Seychelles adventures. From that wondrous first night—interrupted by a rather scary attempted murder—our relationship has deepened and matured, based on a friendship that goes both ways, nothing like my one-sided passion for Cole.

A long time has passed since I first fell for him at age ten. I now see that I was a needy, desperate girl.

Indeed, Dr. Lockett mused during one of my sessions, "Your father called you his 'young Ava Gardner' but then verbally abused you. Perhaps the frightened little girl inside latched onto his movie star ideal. Since you didn't know how to achieve success or fame, maybe you tried to find it all through Cole the quarterback."

Bingo.

Chapter Forty-Three

NOT IN MY FATHER'S SHADOW

The cliché about life being full of surprises, well, I'm on a roll. Both of my sons are now employed in the financial sector as associate brokers with an investment firm owned by a friend of Ryan's.

I am so very relieved.

Every morning, the two jump out of bed with purpose. Like their dad, they dress like *GQ* models, then drive off in their new, albeit five-year-old BMW Seven-series sedan that the two financed with down payments from their first paychecks. They are now part of the great American work force and in debt.

I love it. There is nothing that drives people to succeed more than paying off a loan.

My sons got their jobs with help from Ryan. I didn't ask. He volunteered.

"I'll show them around my offices, and give them my speech about honor, duty, country. Then we'll make some calls."

"I so appreciate your help. Without Cole… Oh, hell, the twins probably didn't learn any solid messages from him. Or from me."

"Cole had it easy, Marie. The guy was one hell of an athlete. Handsome as a movie star. Didn't have to hide behind horned rims like me. He took to the role of NFL star like a duck to water. If he hadn't gotten hurt…"

"We would have divorced. I could not take the football world."

"You always say that, but was it really that rough?"

"Maybe not for every football wife. But for me, I don't know which was worse: the insecurity of being a quarterback's wife, or the loneliness of being an obsessive fund manager's wife. If he had not died, I probably would have had another affair."

Ryan's eyes narrowed like he had just badgered a witness into submission. "Another affair?"

Oh, dear. I hadn't wanted to go into all this. What did Ryan need to know? We are adults. We each have past loves. I figured I'd tell him down the way, confess. Tell him my faults and hope he could see past them. Isn't that what love is? Warts and all?

Forced by my *faux pas*, I took a sip of wine for courage, then told Ryan the short versions about my foolish affair with Eric.

By the time I finished, his eyes were cold and angry. "I don't know what to say, Marie."

"Ryan, I was so down. My spirit was extinguished. Looking back, I think I needed to prove I was a desirable woman. That I interested a man, and I don't mean for sex. Eric talked to me. Listened to me. We had a friendship. Yes, I felt terrible that I had broken my marriage vows, but I needed to feel I existed. Maybe things have changed for pro football wives now, but in the Explorers' culture, the gladiators would simply toss us aside the moment a prettier princess appeared. That was a horrible way to feel."

Ryan thought for a bit after my confession. "Marie, I had one woman run around on me, and I'm not going to have another. Here you are, joining an orchestra. What if the oboe player turns out to be a 'good friend' who likes to talk and listen to you too?"

"Oboe players are nerds," I scoffed, trying to divert, but I could see Ryan wasn't buying my flippant approach. I took a moment to form my words. "You have nothing to worry about as long as you and I are involved." Then I leaned nearer. Looked him eyeball to eyeball. "A good while back, you asked me to trust you. Now, I'm asking you to trust me."

He pouted a bit. Probably recalled Doreen's antics with Luca. "Males don't want to be fucked over, any more than women want to be ignored."

"I hear you."

Because some concern lingered in his eyes, I decided to let him think. After we silently loaded the dishwasher, I gathered my things and kissed him lightly. "I'm heading home."

That took him by surprise. "I thought you'd spend the night."

"Too many people in the room with us tonight. When we can get back to just you and me, we'll make love again." I gave him an affectionate kiss and off I went.

I could not believe I did that, and so abruptly, but I was pleased that I'd asserted my independence. Ryan was still stewing about Doreen's infidelity. He needs time to adjust and answer questions about whether he can trust me, whether I am the woman he wants. In fact, we both need time. Although I feel love for him, we have not progressed to the expressed aloud, "I love you" stage. In a way, that is a relief, because I can retreat. Ryan can too. And each of us can step forward when we know better how we feel.

❧

I HAD AN APPOINTMENT WITH DR. LOCKETT THE WEEK AFTER the trip to see Barry. I didn't tell him what Barry had said, but I did tell him about my assertion with Ryan. When I finished, there wasn't much praise, however.

"Hmm…" was all Dr. Lockett mustered.

"Do you think I should have stayed the night with Ryan?"

Dr. Lockett peered over his notepad. "Do you?"

"I felt like Ryan wanted me to prove my loyalty with sex."

"Then you did the right thing by leaving."

"I don't know. He was wounded to hear about my affair."

"He was wounded by Doreen's affair."

I took a moment to digest what Dr. Lockett had said. "This wasn't about me, but Doreen."

"Feel better about your decision?"

"Yes, but I've missed being with him, and he hasn't called. Should I call him? I do have something important I need to tell him. Something about the Maestro's murder."

Dr. Lockett blurted, "Now, what's this? Please don't confess. I'll have to report that."

"Confess! I had nothing to do with killing the Maestro. Why don't you believe me?"

He made a few notes. "Marie, I only know what you tell me."

"Well, here's what I'm telling you. I went with my friend Lena and Rebecca to visit Barry Claridge at Kerrville State Hospital. When Lena and Rebecca went down the hall, Barry suddenly came out of his supposed catatonic state. He said he was faking insanity to cover for Rebecca's actions. Said his mother killed Luca because he threatened to expose her for blackmailing him."

"You know that Mrs. Claridge is one of my clients. Although this is secondhand information, I must report it."

I freaked out. "What I say to you is confidential. You promised. And I promised Barry. He said that Rebecca is dying. You probably know this. Barry said he would reveal everything after she dies. Once the truth is out, you will be relieved of any ethical requirement."

"I'll have to consult my lawyer on this. In the meantime, I urge you to tell the authorities. Your lawyer is an officer of the court and will know what to do."

"Maybe that is the excuse to call Ryan?"

"Marie, this situation is too serious to treat it like an advice column in *Seventeen* magazine."

I got his point. "In other words, grow up. I'll call him."

"I will keep your confidence only if you tell your attorney. I cannot risk violating my professional ethics."

We were quiet for a bit and then he referred to his notes. "Any progress on your feelings about your father? Any inexplicable nightmares or instances of recurring dreams?"

"Sometimes before sleep, I see a shadow move toward me, but I can't identify anyone."

"Do this for me. Before you go to sleep, relax and invite the shadow into your aura."

"My aura?"

"That is the arc of energy that emanates from you."

"You want me to see my father abusing me, don't you?"

"Only if he is the shadow. Don't you want to know the truth?"

"What does it matter? I have found a life. I'm not just an arts supporter, I am an artist. My sons have jobs. I'm out of debt. Free. I feel so contented. Even if things don't work out with Ryan, I want for nothing, and I will be fine."

"I think it would be good for you to resolve your feelings about your father's emotional abuse."

I took a moment to decide just what my feelings were. I didn't like my father. But he was my father and I loved him, in spite of his failings. His anger. His alcoholism. His terrible mistakes. "Dr. Lockett, I may be my father's daughter, but I am not his rage."

He wrote something in his notepad, then peered at me over his readers. "Mrs. Donovan, I'll give you an A+ for that one."

I thanked him, then plunged ahead with a request that I quickly realized I should not have brought up. "I know you see Avery and Shawn in the evenings now. But when you meet them next, could you speak to them about being honest, trustworthy, and reliable? Ryan already gave them a fatherly speech. I hoped you could too."

Dr. Lockett looked exasperated. "Marie, I thought we straightened this out during our first visit. My role is to guide clients' self-discovery, not give fatherly advice."

"I just thought, as long as they were seeing you…"

"Marie, here's some advice, but it's not for your sons. You've spent most of your adult life hoping someone else would parent your twins. During the football years, you left the chore to babysitters while you partied, fooled around, and toyed with the cello. After football you abdicated the parenting of your adolescent sons to Cole. He turned out to be a ringleader, not a father. Now, they are adults. But they are still impressionable. It's never too late to talk to them about honesty and reliability."

"I don't think they will listen to me."

"They may not appear to listen, but they will hear your words. And those words will matter, maybe not at that moment, but as time goes on. Let me know how things go."

"Oh, dear. One of your assignments?"

"By next session. And remember, tell your lawyer about this Barry Claridge murder evidence. I will not let you slide by. Ethically, I'm walking a thin line, especially since your remarks pertain to another of my clients, who is going to answer some hard questions from me."

Chapter Forty-Four

TIME TO PARENT

I was a wreck by the time Shawn arrived home for dinner. Earlier that morning, my sons had accepted my invitation to talk with negative curiosity in their replies, as if to say, "What does Mom want now?" But neither of them would turn down a home-cooked meal, now that I have stopped helping them financially, except for housing.

Cutting them off was a Dr. Lockett assignment to both the boys and me, and I know it got their goat. They gamely asked me to give them six months to save for a deposit and moving expenses. I said yes. At least we have a deadline. Six months from now, they will be in their own apartment.

Still in his business suit from work, Shawn arrived first. "Avery stayed late. Said he'll grab a ride."

"Did he remember we are supposed to talk tonight?"

"He says you and Dr. Lockett are trying to take over our lives."

"I'm trying to provide resources. Guidance."

Shawn poured himself a Sky vodka and ginger ale, with teaspoon of sugar and a squirt of lemon juice. "Moscow Mule. But we need some copper mugs to do it right."

I sipped on my Bloody Mary while we waited for Avery. After

a half hour, I was about to give up. "I had hoped to speak to both of you, but I guess one is better than two."

"I can tell Avery what you said, Mom. We probably know what it is, anyway."

"What's that?"

Shawn's almond-shaped eyes searched the ceiling, delaying. "Your boyfriend is moving in, so you want us to move out."

I was stunned. "I would never do that to you. Ryan has his own apartment in Uptown. And I'm not sure he's my boyfriend. We're kind of taking a break."

Shawn looked relieved. "Good. That guy is too serious, anyway."

"At times, being serious is important."

"All right, Mom. What's this dinner talk about?"

"Let's wait until Avery gets here. I wanted to tell you…"

Just then, I heard a door close, and there came Avery, spitting image of Cole in a charcoal window-pane suit. In fact, it was one of Cole's suits. A tailor had worked magic for my sons with Cole's extensive wardrobe.

Avery pointed to Shawn's Moscow Mule. "That for me?"

"I'll make you one. We were worried you might not show."

"I figured if you had to endure Mom's speech alone, you'd give me a lot of shit and Dr. Lockett would give me that *look* of his, so I decided to reward you with my presence." Avery grinned that charming smile Cole employed when he got away with murder. "Still love me, Mom?"

"Both of you. Just as much as the other." My patented phrase.

"Shawn figures we gotta move because of this Ryan dude."

"No, Ryan has his own apartment. My home is yours until your six months are up. Time for you boys…time for you men to live on your own."

"Okay, so what's this about?"

"Well, it's about me. And about you. As you know, I'm seeing Dr. Lockett too. During my sessions, I discovered something. Actually, even before Dr. Lockett, I realized I have not been an ideal mother. Oh, I've done the cooking, cleaning, and laundry, but I have not done much disciplining or guidance. I thought I didn't know how to raise males, so I left that to your Dad. But he was a good-time guy. Cowboys' games, golf, drinks. I don't know if he ever taught you how to be men. Honest. Trustworthy. Reliable."

Avery did an embarrassed guffaw. "Mom, we know that stuff."

"What stuff?"

"We know you gotta be honest."

"But your father was anything but honest. I'm sorry to say that, because I know you loved him."

Shawn looked at me, and his eyes filled with tears. "Hell, Dad even cheated at 'Go Fish.' That used to make me so mad."

"Mom was the only one we could beat at cards," Avery laughed.

"But I never taught you anything. We never had serious talks."

"You made things go right for us," Shawn said.

Avery took another swig. "Still, it's hard when people give us shit about Dad. They think we are like him, or will be."

"Your lives are your own, not your Dad's failings with Odyssey, or the successes of those Super Bowl rings you wear with so much pride." I watched as the twins looked at their huge rings and thought over my comment. "Did you learn anything from your visit with Ryan Ingles?"

Shawn rolled his eyes. "He's like a really big school principal."

I chuckled, then asked louder. "But did you *learn* anything?"

Avery looked at me directly, something he rarely did. His twinkling eyes ignited my heart, as if Cole were there again.

"Like Shawn said, we know this stuff. Coach Drew gave us holy shit in high school when we did anything wrong. And we heard this stuff at church. You and Dad dragged us every Sunday, remember? Hey, Shawn, do you remember that Sunday school teacher who wore those thigh-high purple boots?"

"You could see up her skirt, and she didn't wear any panties!"

The boys laughed like the kids they sometimes still were.

I laughed too, but felt my effort to have "the talk" was going nowhere. I tapped the table to get their attention. "This is the same kind of deflection your father used to pull. Laugh everything off with your irrepressible charm. Slide by on your good looks and natural talent without so much as a commitment. But I won't have it from you. Give me your word that you will be honest, trustworthy, and reliable men. In all dealings, all aspects of your lives, personal, financial, legal. I want promises. And I want them now."

The twins glanced at each other as if to say, "We gotta say this now? Out loud?"

"Shawn? Avery? Your word?"

"Gosh, Mom. You're shouting."

"Yes, I am. Now, do I have your word?"

Both issued exasperated sighs and stared at the table or floor.

Then Shawn began, "I promise to…how did this go, Mom?"

"Raise your right hands. I promise to lead a life…"

They raised their hands and repeated.

"…that is honest, trustworthy and reliable…in all my personal, financial, and legal dealings."

Avery added "Amen" with a smirk.

Then I reached across, held their hands and gave them my most earnest look. "Your word is your bond. If you have any moral questions, please ask me for advice. I have not walked a perfect path, but I've learned from my mistakes and would be happy to help."

They mumbled, "Yes, ma'am."

It was done. My assignment.

After that, our dinner conversation was a bit muted, mostly related to work goings on. Over dessert, they complained about some of their difficult clients and asked me how I handled people like that at the funeral home.

"I do my best to keep a smile on my lips. It's something I learned long ago, and it works. Even when I'm talking on the phone, if I smile when I'm speaking, my tone lightens, and I can feel the other person relax on the other end of the line."

"I might look stupid talking on the phone with a big grin," Avery said.

"I'll do anything to get these assholes to chill out," Shawn said.

Hopefully, the impact of my little speech opened a door. My sons asked me for advice. Perhaps, down the line, more of my words would guide them to make the right decisions. And they would be less their father's sons than mine.

❧

RYAN AND I HAVE NOT SPOKEN SINCE OUR INTERRUPTED DATE two weeks ago. I am dying to tell him about the Barry situation—in fact, I must, so after my talk with the twins, I had enough confidence to call Ryan. Might as well handle all assignments in one night.

He gave me a very tentative "Hello..."

I forged ahead. "We've both been busy. Can we catch up? I need a date for my cello debut and hoped that would be you."

He was quiet for a moment. "I thought you gave up on me for being a jealous jerk."

He thought I had broken things off? "I am nowhere near through with you. In fact, I even need a lawyer. Can we meet before opening night? I have to tell you something, but not by phone."

Chapter Forty-Five
INCOMPETENT

A fter orchestra rehearsal downtown, I met Ryan for a late dinner at a Japanese restaurant on Cedar Springs Road. I always hate driving on that street because Cole died there, so when I approached the spot where he was hit by the limo, I turned up a block, went through an alley, then turned back onto Cedar Springs and valeted my car.

When I spotted Ryan at a corner table, he was wearing his reading glasses as he studied the menu. With his specs on, I recognized the "Diver" I had known in college but, now that we were older, I found this Diver far more attractive. Like a cozy sweat suit in the winter. Could I see this man in my family room each night, peering at a magazine or a book?

My silent answer was yes. Oh, my, that sent adrenalin rushing, but I dared not tell Ryan.

Sakes arrived, then seaweed salads, chef's selection of sashimi, and my rainbow rolls. We chatted about rehearsals and his heavy caseload. Then he asked me about my legal issue.

I had not wanted to press, preferring to have dinner with Ryan the man, before I dealt with Ryan the attorney. But we were alone in our little corner, so I told him about my visit to see Barry.

"Do you think this might be the proof to clear my name?"

"Proof? Unfortunately, the law would see your testimony as hearsay, unless Barry would admit everything. If he's sane, he won't. He's already proved that. Tells you one thing, then tells police another."

"Even so, shouldn't we tell the police?"

"Barry is in the 'Never Land' of Texas law, bound over for trial but declared incompetent. Right now, he floats in the system as innocent until proven guilty. Anything he says, until he has been declared mentally competent, will not be admissible."

"But he told me, clear as day. Rebecca did it."

"His attorney will say he is delusional. Schizophrenics have this mentality, 'the devil made me do it.' For Barry, the devil may be his mother. She made him do it. Or you made him do it. As your attorney, I don't want to stir Barry's pot."

"Ryan, I am not a psychiatrist, but Barry was as sane as you or me when he spoke. He flipped into his crazy act the moment Lena and Rebecca came back into the room."

"Schizophrenics can flip in or out, depending on their degree of paranoia and delusions. Right now, you're in the clear. I know you want a firm, clear resolution, but let's not do anything to muddy the waters."

That decision did not sit well, but I did my best not to pout. I wanted to enjoy our evening and not let "too many people in the room." Still, I had hoped Barry's admission was my ticket to an unclouded reputation. As I ate plum ice cream, I did my best to be a cheery companion. Sometimes you have to stifle your wants so you don't mess things up.

Afterward we went to Ryan's apartment and made love. Each of us seemed a bit tentative, unlike the amazed and passionate lovers we were in the Seychelles.

Even as he gently thrust inside me, my mind kept churning about Barry's revelations. In spite of Ryan's counsel, I wanted a resolution. All shadows gone.

Chapter Forty-Six

OPENING NIGHT

I had waited twenty-five years for this moment, and I was not going to blow it by throwing up on my new black lace and satin gown. Two thousand dollars at Neiman's, but Lena said it was a tax write-off.

"Just be sure to wear it only for orchestra performances. Believe me, I write off every single black suit I own."

The stage director had assigned me a dressing room, a courtesy Rebecca had orchestrated for my debut. She was either sucking up or being genuine. One never knows about Rebecca.

"She's gone to see Barry, but she'll attend next Thursday's performance. She said, 'Break a leg,'" the stage director said.

Actually, I was relieved Rebecca would not be there.

Nervous as a bat, Lena hovered. Offered to tease my hair, put on more lipstick, file my nails even shorter, something a cellist has to do to keep from twanging the strings or ticking the fingerboard.

"Lena, stop fussing! You are making me tense."

Just then a knock, which Lena answered. Owen peeked in with Shawn, Avery, and my father. Yes, Dad and Owen had flown in for my debut.

To keep from messing my mascara with surprised tears, I gaped my eyes wide and blinked at the walls. "I'm sorry. I'm just so happy. I only wish Mother…" And then the tears and shudders came heavily.

Lena gave me tissues while Owen patted me, as did Shawn.

Avery did the macho thing, "Mom, you're a mess."

"She's got a right to be emotional. I for one am very proud of my sister." Owen held my gaze, and I knew he felt the same bond I had been pleased to discover about him. We were family.

Dad reached to hug me, but I shied away. From the disappointment on his face, I wondered if I should have let go. As I had discovered in my session, Dad was a guy who drank too much and raged at his daughter and wife—my mother whom I loved dearly. I wasn't sure I could forgive Dad for all that.

He held up his hands in surrender. His eyes were teary. "Marie, I'm twenty-five years sober. I just wanted to wish you good luck."

I stated as matter-of-factly as I could. "You know why I don't want to hug you, don't you, Dad?" More a challenge than a question.

His eyes filled with tears. "If it helps you, I didn't mean those things. No excuse. But I am sorry for my behavior, and I hope you will forgive me. Step Nine." Then he turned toward the door.

Owen tried to calm things down. "Marie is under a lot of stress. Let's give her some breathing room. Lena, I trust you can undo the immense mascara damage that our surprise visit has caused."

"Count on me, Brother. I've brought back the dead."

The lights flashed backstage. "Lena, you've got ten minutes."

After everybody left, she wipes, smeared, painted, blushed. When she finished, I looked better than I did before and probably would again. "I want to hire you. Available?"

"You are on, Sister."

Someone knocked. "Mrs. Donovan, orchestra to the pit."

I faked the Norma Desmond scene from *Sunset Boulevard*. "All right, Mr. DeMille, I'm ready for my close-up."

Lena laughed. Hearing that familiar sound eased my nerves. I was not alone in this. I had friends, family, and love.

As I joined my fellow musicians, any sad memories about Mother's death or Dad's raging shadows vanished. I was finally in my element, a member of an orchestra. A cellist. First-chair at that. Maestro Ron had chosen me after yet another blind audition.

As he mounted the podium of Claridge Hall and took his bow to wild applause, the tension grew. He turned to the orchestra, looking natty in his black tailcoat and white tie. The tuxedoed and gowned audience rustled in their seats, then hushed expectantly when Ron raised his baton.

I watched for his first downstroke to the overture, called "Over Hill and Dale." From that point, my training, my passion for my instrument, all the things Eric had taught me, and all the things Maestro Ron has taught me took over. My fingers were merely the conduits for Britten's score.

After the overture, my parts came in sporadic, energetic seesawing moments. As a cellist, you have to be precise but move rapidly, like a fairy. You cannot dwell or drag. At times, my cello played as an answer to the horns. Other times my cello asked questions of them. By the time our orchestra was in full motion, I was relishing the power of the musicians in concert. I hoped the audience felt our ardor, our collective spirit.

On the podium, Maestro Ron whirled, bounced, spat, and sweated. On stage above our heads, the performers soared through their dark comedic roles. We could see them on monitors in the pit, and it was fun to know the insider details about the missteps in rehearsals, the pratfalls, the arguments, the tantrums.

Oh, yes, the tantrums. Divas are so named because they are. And maestros are so named because they are. We musicians merely support the production, although there would be no opera without us.

And this opening night audience knew it. The applause afterward was deafening. The musicians blushed and peered at one another, until Maestro Ron gave us the signal to stand for a bow. Then the applause and cheers deepened. What a reward. To have an audience hear the sounds I loved to play. Hear my cello and me, making music together.

When we took another bow, I peered above the rail but did not see anyone I recognized, until one broad, brown-haired head peeked over. A handsomely tuxedoed Ryan had come forward from the right wing.

I grinned. He smiled back, and I could see his eyes streaming. He patted his heart and blew me a kiss. From my vantage, all I could give him was my warmest smile and grateful nod.

After I packed my cello away, I saw Ryan again in the Green Room. Maestro Ron had invited me. A perk for my debut.

Doreen was there with a date, an odd looking bald guy who introduced himself as Eugene. He owns a Cadillac dealership in Plano, he said. Poor Eugene didn't know he wasn't supposed to talk to me until Doreen retrieved him. She gave me the most awful glare before she yanked Eugene away.

Tina LeBlanc flitted over. "Why Marie, who knew such talent lurked under your dear little cherry blossoms."

"My dear Tina, thank you for your support," I murmured, but my tone was the snidest I could muster but still remain somewhat civil.

As usual, Tina simply bubbled a foolish giggle and scampered to join her neurosurgeon husband Georges, a balding Austrian who usually got stinking drunk at every opera event.

My family eventually lumbered in. The boys gave me high fives. "Great job, Mom. You wowed 'em."

Owen, too. "Congratulations, Sis. You've waited a long time for your star to shine."

Dad extended a hand but avoided my eyes. "Well done, Marie. Your Mother would be proud."

That's all he said. That's all he could say. After all, I had accosted him in my dressing room, perhaps unfairly, since my Dad has a genetic condition. Yes, he had been wrong. Yes, he did damage. But he apologized. And I had to put that behind me. Otherwise the shadow would linger.

So, I did what I felt like doing. I reached for my father.

"Thank you for coming tonight. And I'm proud of you for your long sobriety." Then I hugged him like a daughter would hug her father, and I kissed him on the cheek like a daughter would kiss her father, because after all, he was.

His eyes misted. "I'll bring my wife next time. She would love all this. Would love to see you play."

"Good, Dad. I'd like that." That was somewhat of a lie, but Dad had tried and I had tried. Sometimes best you can do.

After Dad, the twins and Owen went to hit the buffet, I fielded questions from patrons and congratulated the cast. I also kept an eye out for Ryan, who was working the Green Room like the potential chairman of the Opera board that he was.

Lena waved at me from across the Green Room as D'Posse hovered around Terrance to get their names in his morning column. The hack did not congratulate me, and I dreaded what he might write.

I wasn't about to seek his praise. Here I used to be a wealthy patron who applauded the performers. Now I was one. I was proud to swim in this sea of talented artists.

As the party dwindled, my mind drifted to Cole. To a wish that he could see me now. I hoped he would have been proud. There were so many sides to Cole. The younger, passionate man, sometimes tender, sometimes childish, often so very charming. The brutal Cole, angry, and abusive. The narcissistic Cole, so focused on himself, his work, his addictions, his dealings.

Cole was far different from the maturity and consistency I've experienced from Ryan, who suddenly was at my arm. "Had enough of this self-puffery? Let's go back to my place. I'll scramble some eggs, we'll sit by my fake fireplace, and pretend we are somewhere cold enough to snuggle."

I looked at him with gratitude. "You're on."

As we strolled out, an inebriated Doreen grabbed my arm. I tried to pull away, but her eyes blazed in that dithering way when her obsessive nature kicked in, and all hell would come at anyone who attempted to disrupt her babble.

"I've got Maestro Ron in my corner, and you'll be out of that first chair before you know what hit you."

With the speed of a young linebacker, Ryan pried loose Doreen's grip. "You have no power. You simply have a big mouth. For the sake of your alimony checks and your future with opera society, you will do nothing to injure Marie's career. Otherwise, I will sue you for libel. And because of your physical assault of her tonight, which I and others around have witnessed, I can strap a restraining order on you. That would mean you could never attend an opera again. Think about it, Doreen. Just think before you speak. And while you're at it, do us all a favor and just...shut the fuck up."

Doreen's face fell to her sagging décolleté. But she was silent.

Ryan gleamed all the way to the car. "For decades, I have wanted to say that to her. Isn't that a wonderful way to tell someone off? Who was the first person ever to say, 'Shut the fuck up?' We should Google that."

In Ryan's car, he kept hollering, "Shut the fuck up!" at every stoplight, laughing gleefully as we made our way to his apartment, where those eggs, the toast, the fake fireplace, his loving touch, and our resurgent passions were the perfect ending to my debut.

If only life were love and nothing more.

Chapter Forty-Seven

OUT AND IN

with Terrance Nichols

"All Good Things..."

I f you've grown weary of operatic divas throwing themselves off cliffs, overcome by guilt, joy, or love, you would be delighted by last night's performance of Benjamin Britten's "A Good Summer's Night's Dream."

Go. See. Do. An absolute romp.

The orchestra was buoyant. The cast vibrant. Metroplex Opera's new Maestro Ronald Garrison was dashing, yet firmly in control. The collective triumph was as if all things required to elevate an opera company drove up in a van last night and got out.

Dare we hope Metroplex Opera has at last arrived? The sets, rented from San Francisco, were inventive. The costumes, on loan from Chicago, were a vision. The stage direction was superb, and the cast, appearing in companies worldwide, were spot on in their roles.

Compared to the somber pit dwellers of the last two seasons, the orchestra was reenergized. Having Maestro Ron as resident creative director, rather than endless rounds of guest conductors, certainly played a part. And perhaps our talented musicians have moved beyond the sordid murder of former Maestro Luca

Scarlatti, who was killed in a bloodbath almost two years ago. The case remains unresolved, but I won't go into that now.

I must not forget the always-stunning Marie Donovan, a past president of the Opera League, who debuted eloquently at first-chair cello. From my box above the pit, I could hear her instrument's lush tones. I don't know its provenance, but aficionados can look forward to hearing more from this recently discovered artist.

Many opera musicians do double duty with the Dallas Symphony Orchestra. Perhaps a cello concerto will appear on Mrs. Donovan's performance calendar?

On a final note, this column is one I thought I would never write. Instead, I imagined I either would have been fired by now, destitute from libel lawsuits, or dead at my keyboard, latté in hand.

But as they say, all good things must come to an end.

Twenty-five years ago, I landed a job as copy editor with the *Dallas Daily Herald*. I was ill-equipped for the post, which required an obsessive eye for detail and the patience to endure unrelenting tedium. Somehow, I survived to write obituaries, then lifestyle pieces, until I attended my first operas, symphonies, and ballets.

Eureka! I found my voice among the artisans and local elite.

Since that time, the Dallas arts scene and the people who support it have been my focus and my passion. I have been called a gossip, a wag, and a hack, but my readership has kept me employed doing the job I love.

However, this is my final "Out and In" column. You might say I got a better offer. After living on a columnist's salary far too long, I must go for the big bucks.

To my readers, associates and friends, I extend an affectionate *adieu*. I have enjoyed meeting so many intriguing people. And I have relished the opportunity to tell my side of the story.

Chapter Forty-Eight

THE LEAP

My mobile phone rang as soon as I drove to my day job at the funeral home. Ryan was eager to find out if I had read Terrance Nichols' praise.

"He surprised me. I figured I'd be slammed."

"He wouldn't dare. You were wonderful. Everybody said so, except, well, my beloved Doreen."

"Shut the fuck up," I mimicked with a whisper.

He laughed, then paused. "Do you think you'll try out for the symphony orchestra too?"

"That would mean a lot more rehearsals and practice. I'd have to quite my day job and spend nights at rehearsals."

"I'd be jealous again."

"You can come along."

"That would get old for both of us."

"Probably."

He wanted to chat more, but he got another call. But our conversation made me wonder if I should quit my day job and focus solely on my cello. I didn't want to let Lena down. Surely she was wondering if I'd stay on, since her beau Terrance had hinted that I should try for the Dallas Symphony. But that orchestra has more than 30 concerts each year. I would need time off for rehearsals and events. I decided to talk this over with Lena. Besides, we were overdue for one of our therapeutic lunches.

When I walked in the funeral home, I shrieked in amazement. The Embalming BoyZ had decorated my desk with a spray of pink roses, adorned by hundreds of tiny black plastic cellos. I imagine they got the wee instruments from one of the many catalogs kept on hand to provide clients with their choice of decorative junk for floral arrangements.

I noticed one of the BoyZ peeking out from the back. I called out, "How very Elvis of you."

The most feminine one, Ray Diamond, bounced out giddily. He had sprayed his hair pink with black stripes for the occasion. "We must celebrate your success. A happy hour at the Round Up?"

I grimaced. "Do we always have to go to a gay bar?"

"Oh, Marie. Be enlightened. Although you've already landed a man, we're still on the prowl."

Luckily my desk phone interrupted. A client calling for Lena. She wasn't in yet, so I took the message.

By noon, Lena still hadn't showed, but that was not unusual. Now and then, Lena takes her time coming in. Still, I worried a bit and called her cell phone. There was no answer. No answer at her house, either. I left messages on both lines about drinks after work.

Over the course of the morning, three sets of clients arrived for appointments. I did my best to explain our services, show caskets, and so forth. The BoyZ came out to help. They kept suit jackets and ties in the embalming room, just in case, so, all morning and through the afternoon we ran Verano Highland Park Funeral Home.

We set up three memorials and two "Life Celebration" events, one with dinner catered by the deceased's favorite barbecue joint, and the other with a motorcycle ride for the dearly departed's Harley buddies. Along the way, I touted the BoyZ abilities to make bodies more lifelike.

One man desperately wanted his sister to be frozen, so I told him we could do that through a cryonics facility in San Antonio. He left happy.

Now I understood Lena's job. Clients were in sorrow, confused, or frustrated. I wanted to comfort them, but I also had to convince them to buy expensive caskets and embalming services, even if the body was going to be cremated. Technically, legally, I was not supposed to handle all that, since I was not a licensed funeral director, but Ray Diamond was licensed, and he signed all the papers.

When we were able to lock up for the day, we five went to the Round Up. I insisted on a side table instead of the bar, as I wanted to avoid hearing someone ask, "Aren't you Marie Donovan?".

The BoyZ and I chatted for a while, but I drank quickly and used motherhood as my excuse. "Guys, I loved the roses and cellos, but I'm beat. Gotta head home. Dinner still to cook."

Ray tisk-tisked, "Marie, get in touch with your rowdy side."

The other BoyZ nodded, apparently disappointed in me, but after I slid out of the booth and walked toward the front, I glanced back. All four had moved to the bar to flirt, clearly not missing me.

As I headed out, I was surprised to catch a glimpse of Terrance Nichols seated at a corner table. I thought about going over. Maybe he was waiting for Lena, but then I worried about approaching him, for fear I might discover he was meeting a male partner. What would I do? Tell Lena? Break her heart again? I for one wouldn't want a bisexual fiancé hanging out at the Round Up, even if he was there for a post-retirement drink with pals.

Outside, I looked for Lena's car but didn't see it.

Ryan had texted that he had to work late, and that was fine. With no rehearsals for two weeks, I was ready for a quiet night. I brought home pizza and salad, then waited for Shawn and Avery. Over slices and beers, they complained about their black day on the stock market, while I complained about having to run the funeral home without Lena's leadership.

"She was gone the entire day but never called. I'm starting to worry."

After dinner, we three exhausted American workers watched the news, then gave in to hot baths and beds. Tuesday would be another day that arrived too early.

Tuesday was also the first day Terrance's "Out and In" column did not appear in the *Daily Herald*, which I usually read at work between phone calls. I have to say, I missed his sardonic humor and salacious innuendos. He was frequently vindictive, but always intriguing, that is, when he wasn't pointing accusations at me.

Tuesday was also another day that Lena did not appear, and this time, the BoyZ and I shared worrisome concerns. I asked Ray to watch the desk while I went to Lena's house.

On the drive over, I wondered if Terrance and Lena had met at the Round Up. Maybe they were planning an elopement?

As I pulled in the drive of her Preston Road stone mansion, I parked near the garage and peeked in a side window, where I could see Lena's car. There was no answer to my repeated knocks and doorbell rings. That scared me. What if she had fallen? Or maybe she was ill?

I called the Highland Park Police. Wouldn't you know, but the officer who sauntered up the driveway was the same guy who tried to charge me with petty larceny.

At first, he didn't recognize me. "You a family member?"

"No. But we are like sisters."

"She may be out of town."

"She would have told me. She's my best friend. I work for her too. She owns Verano Highland Park Funeral Home."

"Oh, I've seen her ads on TV."

"Yes. She didn't come to the office yesterday or today, or answer calls. And her car is here. What if something's wrong? She might be ill. Can you break the lock?"

"First, you gotta file a missing person's report. Do that, and they'll send someone out." He got a glint in his eye. "Oh, I remember you. You're that Donovan woman."

"Yes. And I remember you. You gave me a ticket for petty larceny. My lawyer got that ticket dismissed, and we filed a complaint on your record."

"Piece of paper nobody will ever see."

"You received payback for your Odyssey investment, right?"

"I did. Surprised the hell out of me."

"You can thank me for that."

"You also got off for that murder."

"That's because I did not commit the murder."

"They'll get you for something," he said as he turned his back.

"I'll get you fired for something, you arrogant jerk."

That comment at least paused his strut before he got in his car.

After he drove off, I went to Highland Park Police Station and filed a missing person's report. I also mentioned that rude officer. The officer on duty assured me someone would follow up on my complaints. And he assured me that Lena's information would be entered into the Texas Department of Public Safety Missing Persons Clearinghouse.

"I'll send a different officer out to check the home."

I wasn't sure what he meant. "Someone will go inside?"

"If the officer thinks it's warranted."

"I say it's warranted. She didn't come to work yesterday or today, but her car is in her garage. For all I know, she may be ill, or might have fallen. We need to get inside."

"An officer will meet you in an hour, ma'am. We have to get a locksmith. This situation happens a lot and, I'm telling you, the so-called missing person gets madder than hell when we've broken in. We'll have to get a locksmith. And you've got to pay for that."

"I'll do it. Just send someone out. Please."

As a ponytailed locksmith in a "Hard Rock Cafe" t-shirt picked the side door to Lena's home, a police officer told me to remain outside. The alarm went off, and the officer answered the call from the security company. I heard him give them his officer's badge ID and some secret code the police have. The alarm stopped.

Then the officer called out, "Highland Park Police, Mrs. Verano. Are you home? I am inside to see if you are all right."

From outside, I heard him march through the downstairs, calling out Lena's name, and then into the garage. He opened and slammed Lena's car doors. Popped the trunk. Then I heard him shuffle back inside, then thump upstairs, where his voice called, "Mrs. Verano? Police officer."

Again, there was no reply. Minutes later, he came out and told the locksmith. "Lock it up."

"But this is crazy. Lena would never leave like this, without letting the funeral home know."

"Even workaholics take a break. Give her time. She'll get in touch. There's no sign of struggle. Nothing out of place. I checked all closets."

"Were any suitcases missing?"

"I wouldn't know ma'am. Would you be able to tell?"

"I don't know."

"I'll take you upstairs if that will ease your mind."

While the locksmith nodded to music on his headphones, the policeman and I went upstairs to Lena's bedroom, then into her closet, a huge room unto itself, with shelves and drawers for everything, and a sliding ladder to retrieve her many pairs of shoes. On one side was Lena's wardrobe of black suits, black pumps, and white and ivory blouses. On the end, I saw a row of suitcases and reached to touch them. There were no spaces to indicate where a missing suitcase might have been.

The officer gave me a sanctimonious smile. "Satisfied?"

"No. My friend has vanished. And Terrance Nichols retired two days ago. They are engaged."

"Well, that's it, ma'am. They probably eloped."

"That's what I'm afraid of."

"Mrs. Donovan, until we know more, we need to lock up and get security turned back on. Homeowners really get teed off when we meddle in their personal lives."

"Darn that Terrance Nichols."

"Since he is her fiancé, add his name as a 'person of interest' to that missing persons report. Whenever either name pops up, that will raise a red flag. Until that time, we can't do more."

With that, he as much dismissed me.

I called Ryan. He was as puzzled as I was. Asked the same questions the officer did. "Sounds like they eloped. But if she doesn't show or call after a while, I can put Billy Bob on it."

"Oh, gads. More fees."

"Before long, you'll own half this firm, anyway. So this investigation would be on me."

That took me aback. "Half this firm." Did Ryan just hint at marriage? Not a proposal, but a test? Should I ignore it? Dodge it? Say something off-putting like, "I'm not ready to jump into another fire."

Or should I take the leap my heart truly felt?

Chapter Forty-Nine

RITZ CARLETON, DUBAI

FAX TO: B.B. Hughes Investigations, Dallas, Texas
SUBJECT: Transcription of security video
FROM: Forensic Transcription Services, Dubai, UAE

Not responsible for errors. Transcription is best possible, considering audio/video quality.

Location: Ritz Carlton Hotel Dubai, pool spa
Subjects identified as:
Terrance Harold Nichols, U.S. Citizen, Passport #8361048274
Lena Levin Verano, U.S. Citizen, Passport #2840174829

NICHOLS: Do you think they've noticed we're gone?

VERANO: You are supposed to be gone. You announced your retirement.

NICHOLS: Maybe you should have done that. Sold the biz. Had a retirement party before you vanished. They'll be looking for you.

VERANO: Having second thoughts?

NICHOLS (laughs): Every fucking day since I met you.

VERANO: Great. Already the end of a beautiful friendship.

NICHOLS: Miss your pals at the funeral home?

VERANO: Not really.

NICHOLS: I thought you and Marie were BFFs.

VERANO: I kept her close. She had so much guilt over Cole's schemes, I think she would have paid back the millions he stole from me after her house sold.

NICHOLS: But you got paid back.

VERANO: Lucky turn of events. Who knew? Marie Donovan, international sleuth.

NICHOLS: I think Ingles' pal Billy Bob Hughes did the heavy lifting. He pointed the finger at Barry Claridge.

VERANO: I still can't believe that idiot Barry confessed to *our* crime. How dare he? "Oh, I'm having a nervous breakdown. Mommy. Mommy."

NICHOLS: Stupid detectives never wondered how an opera tenor or a housewife could do all that.

VERANO: We couldn't have done it, either, without your idea with the Tabun. I'm glad you knew where to get it. Saved me the trouble of zapping Luca with my ancient defibrillator. It might have killed us all.

NICHOLS: Well, it didn't. Amazingly enough, here we are.

(glasses clink) To our future. I didn't promise to support you, did I?

VERANO (laughs): Not on your savings. I don't think the Arabs would appreciate another "Out and In" column.

NICHOLS: Shhhhh. I think they stone fags here.

VERANO (laughs): Speaking of, I loved watching you toy with Luca. By the time I injected the Tabun joy juice, Luca's erection was so enormous, I wanted to jump on it.

NICHOLS: That might have been fun to watch.

VERANO: The bastard deserved what he got. Screwed that pathetic Barry. I had to listen to their desperate fucking. That ended things with me and Luca.

NICHOLS: Luca screwed me too, remember.

VERANO: I forgive you. I fell for him too.

NICHOLS: Marie suspected everybody but you.

VERANO: I don't understand why she didn't remember that I'd sat right beside her during the League meeting. When I asked for a tissue, she handed me her fucking purse. Took me three tries to get her keys back in the purse after she came back from the bathroom. (laughs)

NICHOLS: Tinkle. Tinkle. Marie and her cherry blossoms.

VERANO: Oh, she wasn't all that bad. I did like Marie. We had fun talking about men and our troubles. Problem was, she was a professional victim. Perpetually abused by the great Cole Donovan.

NICHOLS: The Adonis.

VERANO: I took care of that problem too.

NICHOLS: What do you mean?

VERANO: I didn't intend to. Poor impulse control.

NICHOLS: You killed Cole Donovan? But how could you get a hunk like him over the rail?

VERANO: I threw him.

NICHOLS: Holy shit, Lena, you that strong?

VERANO: Jujitsu is all about surprise. I used an *uchi mata* throw. And the very next day, your "Goodbye to an Adonis" column asserted to the entire city that Cole had jumped.

NICHOLS: So, I became your accomplice, long before I became your accomplice.

VERANO: Something like that.

NICHOLS: What now, my evil pet? Do we stay in Dubai forever?

VERANO: There's no extradition treaty with the United States.

NICHOLS: But the Feds can request extradition.

VERANO: A request that United Arab Emirates will ignore.

NICHOLS: As far as we know, there isn't any evidence to convict us, anyway.

VERANO: There's Luca's dick.

NICHOLS: Jesus, Lena. You kept it?

VERANO: It's hidden in a freezer at the funeral home. Looks like a lonely Italian sausage.

NICHOLS: God, I hope nobody finds that. DNA will prove it's Luca's.

VERANO: Who cares? We've left the building.

NICHOLS: I guarantee someone has filed a missing persons report. Those go into an international system.

VERANO: Cooperative nations only. If we want to travel, we can take a private charter. Or buy a camel. (gets out of spa) Let's order dinner in the room.

NICHOLS: After dessert, you can teach me more. I'm getting better these days, don't you think?

VERANO: Just don't let up after we get married and have kids.

NICHOLS: Marriage? Kids? Oh, well. You're the one who's buying.

VERANO (laughs): Just remember, buyer's remorse can set in any day. It has before, and not just with Luca and Cole.

Chapter Fifty

"WE" BUSINESS

W hen Billy Bob e-mailed me that transcript, I read it, but I wouldn't believe it. Not Lena. Not my so-called "Sistah." My God, the woman must be a heartless psychopath.

All the way to Ryan's office downtown, my heart pounded with shock, anger, and pain. What kind of woman would lie like that, and for so long? Connive to murder my husband, not to free me, but to get revenge for her losses. And murder Luca so brutally and then frame me.

She was the one. Why didn't I notice? *She* sat beside me at the League meeting. *She* got my keys when I went to the bathroom. Now I remember, *she* asked me if I had a tissue. I even handed her my purse.

When I got to Ryan's office, we met in the conference room. Billy Bob gave me a hug, as did Ryan.

"More than likely, Lena made impressions of your keys and had copies made," Billy Bob said.

"Why didn't I put this together? She made excuses to leave the meeting early. She knew my home security code. Makes you wonder if you can trust anybody anymore."

Natalie walked in the conference room about then. "I'm sorry that my data sleuthing resulted in unpleasant news for you this time around."

"Not to mention the discovery of a sausage-like tidbit in a freezer at Verano Highland Park Funeral Home," Billy Bob snickered.

"At least Marie is truly in the clear," Colleen said.

"No need to apologize, Natalie. When Marie told me Lena was missing, I mentioned it to Billy Bob and then Natalie got a hunch. She found data tracks from a charter jet out of Dallas and followed it to Dubai immigration. It's like they were daring us to find them. The idiots didn't even bother to fake passports. "

"They didn't have to. There's no extradition treaty. They'll simply stay in Dubai," Natalie said.

I sniffled through angry tears. "I hope they rot, after what they put me through."

Billy Bob's big, bald head nodded. "The FBI has ways. Tit for tat, if you get my drift."

"What do you mean?"

"Our government might wind up with two Arab criminals that the UAE wants extradited to their country."

"Prisoner swap?" Ryan asked.

"Might be a long wait. America only does that to get back hostages or downed pilots," Natalie said.

"Marie, what would you do if you saw Lena again?" Colleen asked softly.

"I don't know. She killed my sons' father. Broke their hearts. Broke my heart too. I thought I had a sister. But Lena was so cavalier on this transcript. And the brutality of killing Luca..."

Ryan shrugged. "Better Lena stays in Dubai. I don't think I could control myself if I ever saw that psychopath again."

"Boss, I have no intention of defending you in a murder trial. I'd rather stick to taxes," Colleen said.

I nodded to Colleen in agreement. "I've had enough murder trials and psycho murderers. How about we focus on tax evasion and cyber investigations? We could hire Billy Bob and Natalie full time."

"What's this 'we' business?" Billy Bob snickered as he glinted at Ryan, and then back to me. "Something I should know about a merger?"

ABOUT THE AUTHOR

Pat Dunlap Evans was born in Michigan but her family moved to Texas, where they lived in San Antonio for a few years, and later Dallas. She was Lieutenant in the Golden Debs at South Oak Cliff High School and an honors scholarship recipient at Southern Methodist University. An early marriage and the birth of three children plunged Pat into the world of motherhood until the kids were old enough for Pat to go back to school herself. She completed her bachelor's and master's degrees in English at University of Missouri, Kansas City. That degree offered an emphasis in creative writing, putting Pat on a path to fiction writing.

Pat's first husband was a quarterback with the Kansas City

Chiefs. She used her experiences as an NFL wife as background for the novel *Out and In: a mystery-thriller*, and also a bit in *Backstory: behind the scenes of a famous film-thriller*. After a long marriage, Pat stressed her way as a single mom through a career in advertising and marketing, with posts in Dallas and Austin. A second marriage to Dr. Bill Evans enabled Pat to focus on her true love of writing. Pat has published three novels, *To Leave a Memory: a warm coming together*, *Out and In: a mystery-thriller*, and *Backstory: behind the scenes of a famous film-thriller*.

To fulfill a bucket-list dream, Pat and Bill moved to the Big Island of Hawaii in 2020. The pair enjoy golf, sunsets, snorkeling, exploring, and visits from family and mainland friends.

Thank you for reading this work. If you enjoyed it, please add your "stars" to Amazon and Goodreads. Your support is greatly appreciated. And follow this author on Amazon to receive news and updates.

For information about speaking engagements, book signings, or screen rights, please contact AustinWriterGirl@Yahoo.com.

A CONVERSATION WITH THE AUTHOR

1. Where did you get the idea for this novel?

After writing the very emotional *To Leave a Memory*, I wanted to try my hand at a page-turner mystery with a female protagonist. I also wanted to use my long-ago experiences as an NFL wife as a backdrop for a novel. But let's be clear. Cole Donovan is not my ex-husband, and I am not at all Marie Donovan. However, many NFL wives I knew during our long-ago era had similar experiences. We felt as though we didn't count. Didn't exist. We were insecure and lacked any identify beyond our husband's fame. That's where Marie's somewhat desperate "neediness" comes from. The rest is fictionalized to be a heartfelt but fun read.

2. Did you always want to become an author?

Not really, although they say you should do the first thing you try to do as a child. For me, that was writing a neighborhood newsletter. Other than that, I had few aspirations. Mother simply told me, "Get a teaching degree just in case." Later on, I thought I might like to be a hair stylist. I was known for cutting a great bob in Virginia Hall at Southern Methodist University. But I always excelled in English classes. Writing came easily. I used to bang out college papers right before class and made good grades.

3. Did you major in creative writing?

My first interests at S.M.U. were Spanish and math. Years later, I majored in P.E. at University of Missouri, Kansas City. I thought I might coach high school swimming, but I kept taking English classes. One of my freshman comp teachers took me aside and convinced me to look at an English major, so I signed up for American Literature and Creative Writing. That's where I met Professor James C. McKinley. He was bright, articulate, and funny as hell. I was enthralled. I followed him like some sort of academic groupie from class to class, fixated on his intellectual magnetism. The classes I took with Jim and the friends I made in the English department became my mainline escape from the win or lose world of football. I changed my major.

4. Was *To Leave a Memory* your first novel?

No. After I got my bachelor's and master's degrees I tried to publish a novel during the late 1980s, but it was an amateurish work based on my fifteen years as wife of an NFL quarterback. Probably due to the commercial aspect, it was almost published. "Almost" was the key word. After a divorce, I had three children to support and suddenly needed to make a living. I went into public relations and advertising for almost thirty years and sidelined the fiction writing until I had time to write.

5. What is *To Leave a Memory* about?

My debut novel is a poignant tale about a family struggling to move beyond grief. That sounds terribly sad, but there are many funny and joyous moments. In fact, there is more humor in *To Leave a Memory* than in *Out and In*. Young children added a lot of humor, and the main characters are intellectuals, so wit was easier to incorporate. It's difficult to have a lot of humor in a mystery, although I always try to give readers a smile now and then.

ACKNOWLEDGMENTS

For the support and encouragement of my husband William M. Evans, M.D., I am grateful. Thank you for giving me time the write, as well as brainstorming plots on our back patio.

Many thanks also to Jean Jenkins, developmental editor, MSRewrite.com, for her guidance. And my Dallas design buddy Pam Boyd Roberts and I sweated through the book cover designs via many e-mails and phone calls.

For the encouragement from family and friends, I am humbled. My children, Reed Livingston Bates, Stacy Livingston VanBecelaere, and Kelly Livingston, have tolerated and encouraged my writing most of their lives. Reed even helps with proofreading.

I've also dedicated this novel to my wondrous grandchildren Matthew Kenneth Wabindato, Hannah Drew Bell, Ava Christine Bell, Annie Grace Bell, Emma VanBecelaere, as well as my great-grandson William Dayton Wabindato and his sister Hailey Dean Wabindato. Go forth and multiply. May a far better writer than I blossom from your gene pools.

ALSO BY THIS AUTHOR

TO LEAVE A MEMORY

If you enjoy films like "On Golden Pond," you'll love *To Leave a Memory*—a heartwarming, funny novel about a Georgia family that learns to forgive and rediscovers how to love.

> "*To Leave a Memory* is a warm portrait of a family coming together to forgive... The colorful dialogue keeps the story moving... There's a pleasing amount of healthy talk about sex... Forgiveness comes in moments sentimental but tender, and even Andrew's post-stroke syntax has a chance to shine."— **Kirkus Reviews**

BACKSTORY

Backstory: Behind the Scenes of a Famous Film-Thriller is an edgy, funny, scary portrait of a Texas single mom's quest to find new love and fame as a Hollywood screenwriter, unaware that a murderer is stalking her and her daughter. Told as "the true story" behind a 1990s award-winning film, the novel weaves a colorful patchwork of emotions, quirky characters, laugh-out-loud scenes, touching relationships, and a shocker ending for readers to unravel with a wry smile.

See the bonus chapters on the next page!

BONUS CHAPTER: BACKSTORY
FORWARD: A Note To the Reader

Throughout the life of famed screenwriter Meredith Mayfield, one saying proved true. Life imitates art. Several decades after Ms. Mayfield's film thriller *Those Who Try* was nominated for best original dramatic screenplay at the 1992 Academy Awards, this collection of her writings reveals the backstory of her first successful work.

Readers will encounter varied formats, including personal letters, screenplay scenes, this *Foreword*, and an *Afterword* by the editors. Dated from 1988 to 1990, Ms. Mayfield's letters speak candidly to Roland Holmes, her film professor at Columbia University, where she earned an MFA. The screenplay excerpts are from *Those Who Try*. For screenplay terms, we provide a brief glossary:

ALL CAPS — Indicate scenes, signs, first appearance of a character, sounds, or items of interest.

INT. / EXT. — Interior or exterior shots, location, and time.

INSERT — A camera shot of an object or text.

INTERCUT — Camera shots between characters or scenes.

O.S. — The voice heard is off screen.

M.O.S. — Without sound.

SUPER — Superimpose, usually text.

V.O. — An unseen narrator.

❦

Never fear, there isn't a test at the end. However, each section appears in a different format for a reason.

RH and JH,
Editors

INT. AUSTIN POLICE STATION — NIGHT — 1990

SIGN: "City of Austin Police Facility"

In a dingy interview room, a hotshot young
DETECTIVE paces in front of a distraught MERRY
MAYFIELD, 38, still pretty with black bobbed
hair. She sobs into her quivering hands.

                    DETECTIVE

   Ms. Mayfield...I realize this is a trying
   situation, but I need you to calm down.

Merry valiantly tries to stop crying.

Detective hands her a box of tissues.

She blows her nose, then inhales in a deep
shudder.

MERRY

A nightmare of nights...I'd give anything
for you to go away.

DETECTIVE

You mean me, or what happened tonight?

MERRY

Too many nights. But especially tonight.
Oh, my baby...

LETTER ONE

August 3, 1988

Dear Roland,

Well, I made it through my first week in Austin, Texas. There's much I've wanted to tell you, but I delayed writing so I could get a grip.

I can just hear you shouting, "Don't just put words on paper. That's typing. Ask yourself what you feel about what you think. Art is emotion!"

I do try, Professor Brilliance.

༄

My father died three days before I moved. Our dear friend Sigrid likely told you about that, but you didn't care enough to express your sympathy. You with those liquid-blue eyes that ignited my spirit with the revelations I craved, you could not call to say, "I am sorry about your father."

No.

The cause of death was *esophageal varices*, cirrhosis of the liver, and acute emphysema—a horrifying list of conditions meaning that the blood vessels in Dad's throat had burst because he drank a gallon of vodka each day, and his lungs had so many holes from chain smoking that he gasped, gasped, and gasped.

From this rather biting description, you can tell I didn't adore my dad. I've always envied women who had a classic "first love" relationship with their father. But my dad was an oddball, darkly handsome and brilliant, but an alcoholic, a booming-voiced loner obsessed with his own maleness. He could lecture me for hours about testosterone and estrogen, and why men were strong, and women were weak. This trait was fueled in part by the booze, one drink every hour, or so he bragged to us at one of the many family intervention sessions I attended when my brother Brandon or Mom tried to get Dad to stop drinking.

That's why Dad's death added an even greater jumble of emotions to our moving day that included a cacophony of eureka moments, oh-no's, and angst. But since truth is stranger than fiction, Dad's death and our wild journey have produced several new scenes for me to include in my comedy-drama screenplay— yes, still working-titled, "Those Who Try."

As for the lead actress, imagine the adorable Demi Moore as me.

The story begins with my optimistic plan: Drive from Greenwich, Connecticut, to my dad's house on Cedar Creek Lake in two and a half days. We'd stop first in Knoxville, Tennessee, then mush on to Dad's lake house for the night before heading to Austin and the funeral Brandon insisted on having.

The travel time was totally possible. Eleven hours to Knoxville. Twelve more to the lake house, which is about an hour and a half southeast of Dallas. The kids would take turns driving. My oldest daughter Nora wasn't bad behind the wheel, and my fourteen-year-old, Claire, had her learner's permit. Once at the lake, we would gather the things we wanted from Dad's house, load them into a U-Haul truck, then drive this now-three-vehicle caravan to Austin in time for Dad's memorial service, to be held at the Eternal Spirit Center the following day.

A carefully crafted plan, but overzealous because life got in the way.

When we finally drove away from the Greenwich house, there was stuff crammed window to window inside both cars. I was driving a metallic-brown 1976 Very Used Olds Cutlass Supreme with a light-tan vinyl top. It's not a bad looking car, but I'm sure you'll remember when I drove only new Mercedes. (I had to sell mine so we could eat.) Trailing behind the Cutlass was our twenty-six-foot ski boat on a double-axle trailer—a ridiculous contraption to haul, but more about that later.

My angry seventeen-year-old, Nora, who is blond and blue-eyed like her father, was driving her blue-and-white 1978 Volkswagen van with our two huge red setters, Edith and Louis, on the third back seat. The veterinarian had given us pet tranquilizers to keep the dogs calm. Perched in that seat, the two looked like a pair of redheaded hippies wigged out on some *primo* stuff.

Of course, the weather gods decided to storm on us the first day of our trip. From dawn to sunset, dark clouds, lightning bolts, and thunder rumbled across the sky, while rain pummeled both cars. This delayed us terribly. Also, of course, the boat trailer broke down at precisely midnight, fifty miles east of Knoxville. In the rain, rain, rain, storm, storm, storm.

A kindly trucker stopped to help. "Bad wheel bearings in that right front wheel, little lady. Good thaaang you got a double-axle trailer, or you'da lost the whole rig."

There was no way to fix the wheel bearings that night, so the kids watched from the van as I stooped in my blue rain hoodie and held the trucker's yellow flashlight in the rain, rain, rain, while he hunched in his yellow slicker, jacked up the trailer, and took off the right front tire. He put that tire under the boat cover, and then he chained the front axle to the trailer frame and jacked it high enough so the right wheel rim wouldn't hit the pavement. That meant the left-front wheel couldn't touch the ground. Lastly, he added air to the trailer's back two tires so as to carry the additional load.

"You can head on down the highway now, little lady. Those back tires'll hold 'er."

Where is it written that kindly truckers actually know what they are talking about? After I pulled out on the highway with the kids following in the van, the over-pumped back tires on the trailer swelled from the added pressure and started scraping and screeching against the trailer body. That spewed a rocket trail of steam and smoke from singed rubber—so much so, I could barely see Nora's VW behind me, that is, until she started beeping madly and flashing her lights.

I pulled over. Of course, it was still raining. Black as death. 1:00 a.m.

Scottie, my twelve-year-old son, kept hollering, "This is the most horrible thing that has ever happened to me, and I have my own mother to thank for it."

I parked the Very Used Cutlass and the boat trailer on the highway shoulder, turned on the flashers, then ran back to the van, where I squeezed between the slobbering dogs and tried not to cry. Nora drove us into Knoxville, where we checked into a Quality Inn. So exhausted I couldn't sleep, I sat in a desk chair and nursed a paper cup of gin, listening to Edith and Louis pant and the children breathe.

All night long, I tried to figure out how to get to Dad's funeral on time. I'd have to find a mechanic to fix the boat trailer, then put Edith and Louis in a kennel (they'd probably have nervous breakdowns), drive the van to the airport, take a plane with the kids to Austin, endure Dad's funeral service, fly back to Knoxville, retrieve the van, rescue Edith and Louis, hope the boat trailer was fixed by then, and drive the rest of the way to Dad's house. This was my determined plan.

My brother Brandon was not going to have this to hang over my head for the next half-century. He is the hero child that families of alcoholics often have. A control freak, intent on making things happen the way he demands they should, instead of the way they will happen because life has its own way.

Then it hit me. Dad would have been furious that he was having any funeral, especially one officiated by Brandon's evangelical-minister wife, Deanna, at her Eternal Spirit Center. Although our dear mother had reared us kids as Catholics, Dad was an agnostic—if not a downright atheist—who always refused to say whatever step Alcoholics Anonymous requires drunks to spout about there being a higher power. In spite of this, Brandon had pronounced that Dad's funeral would be an Eternal Spirit ceremony, because that was the kind of service Brandon would have if he died right then.

So, as the sunrise peeked under the Quality Inn vinyl drapes, my determination to get to Dad's funeral diffused into reality. Call it Godot, call it common sense, call it Dad's spirit. But as I listened to three adolescents and old two dogs sleeping deeply, I had my eureka moment.

"I am risking my children's lives and my sanity to get to a ritual that Dad wouldn't stand for if he were alive."

I called Dear Pluppy Brandon. I could just see him on the other end of the line—his dark-mustached mouth huffing and puffing, his mud-brown eyes a frenzy of neurotic overcompensation, and his still-tenor voice annoyingly abuzz with plans.

"Merry, you're exhausted, confused, and under stress. You shouldn't make decisions now that you'll regret for the rest of your life. I will fly to Knoxville and help you get the trailer fixed. You'll never forgive yourself if you don't come to Dad's service."

That's Brandon—ready to tell me what I need to feel and do.

"I've been having some nice talks with Dad. He knows why I can't be at his funeral."

Brandon didn't laugh. "Merry, let me speak to Nora."

"She's asleep."

"Merry, I insist."

I shouldn't have let him.

As Nora told me later, "Uncle Brandon thinks you're going nuts. He said, 'If your mother continues to hear voices or if she starts acting weird, call me or a doctor.'"

Damn Brandon! He is forever laying out neurotic paths for me to follow. But I said no to Brandon's nervous breakdown. I did not go to my father's funeral. Instead, I spent that next day locating a mechanic to fix the boat trailer, but he couldn't do it until the following day. So the kids and I drove Nora's van back to the Cutlass and boat trailer. I got in and slowly drove on the highway shoulder until we got to the exit for the Quality Inn. The kids drove behind me in the van, flashing security lights. Going that slow, we made it to Knoxville without singed rubber and smoke.

The next morning, the mechanic arrived in a beat-up yellow pickup with his wife and baby. When he got out, I realized he had only one arm and a patch over an eye. Goodness, how could this one-armed, one-eyed man fix my trailer?

Turns out, his wife was his missing body parts. She held their baby on one hip and hoisted a wrench or jack with the free hand. Neither of them said much—just nodded toward this or that tool until the job was done.

After I paid them the three hundred dollars I couldn't afford, the kids and I, Cutlass, boat trailer, and Nora's van with the dogs headed back on the highway. The sky was still cloudy, but at least the highway was dry. From then on, we seemed to float mile after mile, until about the time of Dad's funeral service, when the sun broke through and basked us in the golden light of a most beautiful summer day. We even got to see a glorious, huge red Texas sunset before nightfall, when we arrived at Dad and Mom's house about 10:00 p.m.

It was spookier than hell pulling into that driveway, now that nobody lived in my parents' home. As I walked in the front door, I had a tremendous case of *déjà vu*, since I had experienced a similar life event only six months before—the death of my mother—which Sigrid probably told you about too, but I won't bore you with the details now. Maybe later, if I can dredge up the feelings.

You'll notice how I'm avoiding pain in this bit of caustic prose. And yet, as I turned on the lights, I felt the joy and comfort of being at home, this time without the annoyances of the unhappy people who had lived there—the loud, alcoholic father; the martyred mother; the overbearing brother. And I, who was so exasperated by them all.

The house was lakefront, so after I fixed a martini and made a late-night snack of chicken soup and peanut-butter crackers for the kids, we went down to the dock and took a moonlight swim in the warm summer waters. Gliding along in the midnight waves, I felt a glorious sense of victory, as though we were the lone survivors of a hundred-year war we had won.

"This trip has been the most horrible thing that ever happened to me, and I have my own mother to thank for it," my son pronounced again.

Shades of his Uncle Brandon's mantra, repainting gloom.

"My dear Scottie, be glad if this remains the most horrible thing. And count your blessings that you are safe. In some species, mothers have been known to eat their offspring."

"Gross, Mom," all three said simultaneously, followed by huge sighs.

For revenge, I made them take showers at 1:00 a.m. Then we played rock, paper, scissors to choose beds. Needless to say, none would pick my father's bed.

"His ghost will probably wander around that room," my fourteen-year-old Claire hollered.

So, I did it. Donning my nightgown, I went into my parents' bedroom, sensing the aromas of an old man's mustiness and my mother's tears. Then, so tired I could barely see, I crawled in my dead father's bed and whispered," Good night, Dad. I hope you are now at peace."

As I pulled up the covers, I felt his spirit envelop me. I slept soundly, flat on my back, spread-eagled like I'd seen my father sleep. I awoke the next morning in the very same position.

After breakfast, the kids and I rented a U-Haul truck to hold some of the furniture I wanted from my parents' house. We loaded the truck until noon, then locked up the house and headed south again.

Roland, you would have been astonished at this incredible caravan. I drove the white-and-orange U-Haul, Nora drove the Cutlass hauling the boat trailer, and Claire drove the van on her learner's permit—heaven help her—learning how to drive a stick shift the hard way.

Turns out, my U-Haul didn't have first or second gears, so I had to start off in third, and the fucker kept dying. The air conditioner on the VW van ceased to exhale cold air somewhere south of Corsicana, so the kids transferred Edith and Louis to the back seat of the Very Used Cutlass. Then the AC on the Cutlass quit near Waco. Apparently, we had burned up the transmission by hauling a boat trailer such a long way.

But what the hell. We made it to Austin. Samuel Beckett would have been proud of us. As would the ever-bizarre Jean Genet.

My only regret in missing my father's funeral was that I did not see the ethereal Deanna in action as minister or preacher—whatever she calls herself. Dear Pluppy Brandon videotaped the event and has delivered a black-plastic VHS cassette, which stares at me with its white-reel eyes. I have not played it. Maybe never will.

Regardless, we're moved in. Not unpacked. But in. It's lonelier than hell. I so miss the times spent with you, my dear pal Sigrid, and others I refuse to name.

More later in the delightful comedy drama, *Those Who Try*.

Love,
Merry

See your favorite online retailer for a copy of
Backstory: Behind the Scenes of a Famous Film-Thriller

Made in the USA
Monee, IL
21 November 2023

47006573R00185